PRAISE FOR

THE GRAY GHOST

"A fast-paced tale that reaches back to the early days of automotive glory. . . . A complicated and clever plot . . . The Fargos are great series characters, whip-smart and altruistic. . . . Thriller fans will delight in this latest escapade. Cussler and coauthor Burcell have delivered a winner." —*Kirkus Reviews* (starred review)

"Refreshing . . . [The plot's] imaginative mix pumps new energy into [the] series." —*Publishers Weekly*

"The Fargo novels . . . deliver the goods for readers seeking action, adventure, and larger-than-life characters."

—*Booklist*

"Cussler and Burcell knocked this one out of the park. *The Gray Ghost* is a thrilling adventure novel with tons of action and a deep, vibrant cast of characters. The pacing is quick and their writing is sharp, rarely giving readers a moment to stop and catch their breath."

—*The Real Book Spy*

TITLES BY CLIVE CUSSLER

DIRK PITT® ADVENTURES

Celtic Empire (with Dirk Cussler)
Odessa Sea (with Dirk Cussler)
Havana Storm (with Dirk Cussler)
Poseidon's Arrow (with Dirk Cussler)
Crescent Dawn (with Dirk Cussler)
Arctic Drift (with Dirk Cussler)
Treasure of Khan (with Dirk Cussler)
Black Wind (with Dirk Cussler)
Trojan Odyssey
Valhalla Rising
Atlantis Found
Flood Tide
Shock Wave
Inca Gold
Sahara
Dragon
Treasure
Cyclops
Deep Six
Pacific Vortex!
Night Probe!
Vixen 03
Raise the Titanic!
Iceberg
The Mediterranean Caper

SAM AND REMI FARGO ADVENTURES

The Gray Ghost (with Robin Burcell)
The Romanov Ransom (with Robin Burcell)
Pirate (with Robin Burcell)
The Solomon Curse (with Russell Blake)
The Eye of Heaven (with Russell Blake)
The Mayan Secrets (with Thomas Perry)
The Tombs (with Thomas Perry)
The Kingdom (with Grant Blackwood)
Lost Empire (with Grant Blackwood)
Spartan Gold (with Grant Blackwood)

ISAAC BELL ADVENTURES

The Cutthroat (with Justin Scott)
The Gangster (with Justin Scott)
The Assassin (with Justin Scott)
The Bootlegger (with Justin Scott)
The Striker (with Justin Scott)
The Thief (with Justin Scott)
The Race (with Justin Scott)
The Spy (with Justin Scott)
The Wrecker (with Justin Scott)
The Chase

KURT AUSTIN ADVENTURES
Novels from the NUMA® Files

Sea of Greed (with Graham Brown)
The Rising Sea (with Graham Brown)
Nighthawk (with Graham Brown)
The Pharaoh's Secret (with Graham Brown)
Ghost Ship (with Graham Brown)
Zero Hour (with Graham Brown)
The Storm (with Graham Brown)
Devil's Gate (with Graham Brown)
Medusa (with Paul Kemprecos)
The Navigator (with Paul Kemprecos)
Polar Shift (with Paul Kemprecos)
Lost City (with Paul Kemprecos)
White Death (with Paul Kemprecos)
Fire Ice (with Paul Kemprecos)
Blue Gold (with Paul Kemprecos)
Serpent (with Paul Kemprecos)

***OREGON* FILES**

Shadow Tyrants (with Boyd Morrison)
Typhoon Fury (with Boyd Morrison)
The Emperor's Revenge (with Boyd Morrison)
Piranha (with Boyd Morrison)
Mirage (with Jack Du Brul)
The Jungle (with Jack Du Brul)
The Silent Sea (with Jack Du Brul)
Corsair (with Jack Du Brul)
Plague Ship (with Jack Du Brul)
Skeleton Coast (with Jack Du Brul)
Dark Watch (with Jack Du Brul)
Sacred Stone (with Craig Dirgo)
Golden Buddha (with Craig Dirgo)

NONFICTION

Built for Adventure: The Classic Automobiles of Clive Cussler and Dirk Pitt
Built to Thrill: More Classic Automobiles from Clive Cussler and Dirk Pitt
The Sea Hunters (with Craig Dirgo)
The Sea Hunters II (with Craig Dirgo)
Clive Cussler and Dirk Pitt Revealed (with Craig Dirgo)

CHILDREN'S BOOKS

The Adventures of Vin Fiz
The Adventures of Hotsy Totsy

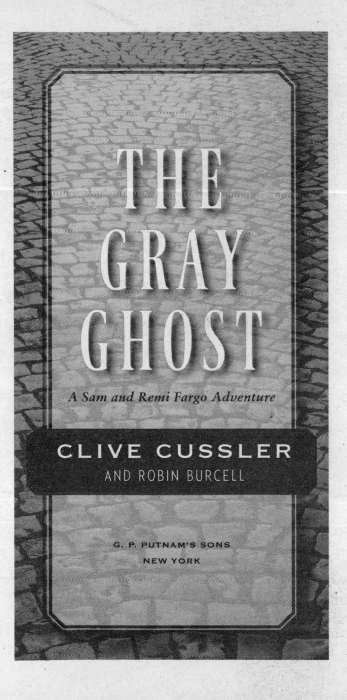

THE GRAY GHOST

A Sam and Remi Fargo Adventure

CLIVE CUSSLER

AND ROBIN BURCELL

G. P. PUTNAM'S SONS

NEW YORK

PUTNAM
— EST. 1838 —
G. P. PUTNAM'S SONS
Publishers Since 1838
An imprint of Penguin Random House LLC
penguinrandomhouse.com

The Library of Congress has catalogued the G. P. Putnam's Sons hardcover edition as follows:

Names: Cussler, Clive, author. | Burcell, Robin, author.
Title: The gray ghost / Clive Cussler, Robin Burcell.
Description: New York : G. P. Putnam's Sons, 2018. |
Series: A Sam and Remi Fargo adventure ; 10
Identifiers: LCCN 2018012901 | ISBN 9780735218734 (hardcover) |
ISBN 9780735218741 (epub)
Subjects: | BISAC: FICTION / Action & Adventure. | FICTION / Suspense. |
FICTION / Thrillers. | GSAFD: Adventure fiction. | Suspense fiction.
Classification: LCC PS3553.U75 G73 2018 | DDC 813/.54—dc23
LC record available at https://lccn.loc.gov/2018012901

First G. P. Putnam's Sons hardcover edition / May 2018
First G. P. Putnam's Sons international edition / May 2018
First G. P. Putnam's Sons mass-market international edition / May 2019
First G. P. Putnam's Sons premium edition / May 2019
G. P. Putnam's Sons premium edition ISBN: 9780735218987

Printed in the United States of America
1 3 5 7 9 10 8 6 4 2

CAST OF CHARACTERS

Reginald "Reggie" Oren—a cousin of Jonathon Payton

Charles Rolls and Henry Royce—owners, Rolls-Royce Limited

Jonathon Payton, 5th Viscount Wellswick

Elizabeth Oren—Reginald's wife

THE PAYTON HOME FOR ORPHANS

Toby Edwards—an orphan

Chip Edwards—an orphan

Will Sutton—a private detective from Manchester hired by Rolls-Royce Limited

Isaac Bell—an American private detective, the Van Dorn Detective Agency

Miss Lydia Atwater—a schoolteacher at the Payton Home for Orphans

Byron, Lord Ryderton—Jonathon Payton's friend

Mac—a car thief

Eddie—a car thief

Finlay—a car thief

Barclay Keene—owner, Barclay Keene Electric Motor Works

THE PRESENT DAY

Sam Fargo

Remi Fargo

Eunice "Libby" Fargo—Sam's mother

Albert Payton, 7th Viscount Wellswick

Oliver Payton—Albert's nephew

Kimberley—concierge, the Inn at Spanish Bay

Selma Wondrash—the Fargos' head researcher

Zoltán—the Fargos' German shepherd

Professor Lazlo Kemp—a Fargo researcher and cryptologist

Pete Jeffcoat and Wendy Corden—Selma's assistants

Geoffrey Russell—the Fargos' personal banker

IN MANCHESTER

Arthur Oren—a very distant cousin of the Paytons

Colton Devereux—ex–Special Forces, works for Oren

Frank—works for Oren

Bruno—works for Oren

Mrs. Beckett—housekeeper, Payton Manor

Allegra Payton Northcott—Oliver's sister

Trevor Payton Northcott—Allegra's son

Dex Northcott—Allegra's ex-husband

David Cooke—Albert Payton's solicitor

Bill Snyder—a private detective working for Cooke

Chad Williams—mechanic, the Gray Ghost

IN ITALY

John and Georgia Bockoven—photographers for *Sports Car Market*, owners of a vineyard and B and B

Paolo Magnanimi—owner, Hostaria Antica Roma

Luca—an acquaintance of Lorenzo Rossi

Lorenzo Rossi—a broker of stolen goods

Marco Verzino—the owner of the Trevi Fountain apartment

IN FRANCE

Monsieur Marchand—the manager of Lorenzo Rossi's Paris office

Suzette—Marchand's secretary

THE GRAY GHOST

PROLOGUE

MANCHESTER, ENGLAND

March 1906

Late for work, Reginald Oren raced across the street, the cobblestones slick from the night's rain. Dodging a horse and carriage, he jumped over a puddle, then ran toward a brick building that took up half a city block. He shrugged out of his overcoat, hung it on a hook just inside the door, and quietly entered a large workroom filled with a half dozen young men sitting at their desks, their attention focused on the office on the far side of the room. No one noticed that Reginald was late, and he took his seat, glancing toward the office's open door, where Charles Rolls and Henry Royce, both dressed in dark suits, were talking to a policeman.

"That looks ominous," Reginald said, glancing over at his cousin, Jonathon Payton, who sat at the desk next to his. "What did I miss?"

"It's gone."

"What's gone?"

"The forty-fifty prototype."

"When?"

"Last night. They went there this morning to finish up the coachwork, and it was gone."

Reginald leaned back in his chair as he looked around the room, then focused on the men in the office, imagining what this would do to the company. Rolls-Royce Limited had put all their money, and that of their investors, into this improved six-cylinder engine. Every last penny had gone into the design of that, as well as a chassis meant to withstand the harsh country roads. When the world seemed to laugh at them, saying it couldn't be done, they'd persevered. And now, when they were on the verge of accomplishing the impossible . . .

Jonathon leaned toward him, lowering his voice. "Was Elizabeth pleased?"

"Pleased?" he said, unable to draw his gaze from the office. Reginald's wife, Elizabeth, had taken their newborn son to visit her mother, but, for the life of him, he couldn't figure out why Jonathon would bring her up at a time like this. "About what?"

"About the pianoforte."

A shame he couldn't hear what they were discussing in there, and he finally turned toward his cousin, belatedly recalling last night's conversation, when he'd solicited Jonathon's assistance. "Undoubtedly, she will be. Meant to thank you for helping my friends and me move it, but you'd disappeared. One minute you were next to me, the next you were gone."

"I guess I had a bit much. Not sure what happened." He was quiet a moment, then whispered, "You won't mention that to my father, will you?"

"Of course not." Jonathon's father, Viscount Wellswick, had raised both boys after Reginald's parents died, though Reginald always suspected he'd have ended up in an orphanage if not for the intervention of Jonathon's mother. Ironic, considering that she was the reason their fathers had been the bitterest of enemies. Reginald's father had been in love with her, but her fortune was needed to restore the viscountcy, so she was wedded to Jonathon's father instead. He often wondered if she regretted the marriage. Her husband, the Viscount, was frugal beyond belief, as well as a strict disciplinarian. He certainly wouldn't have approved of either of them spending a night at one of the local taverns, drinking ale with the neighborhood residents. The Viscount was all about propriety. How it would look to his friends if his son and nephew stepped out of line. Appearances were everything, which was why Reginald and Jonathon were expected to oversee the running of the orphanage that bore the Viscount's name. Jonathon, in line to be the next viscount and heir to the Payton estate, was expected to be there six days a week, usually stopping in after work. In Reginald's mind, that was the one advantage of being the poor relation living under his uncle's roof. He was only expected to volunteer his time at the orphanage twice a week. Of course, that was in addition to the six days a week both men spent working for Rolls-Royce.

There were no free rides in the Payton home, the old man thinking that working at a job each day built character. Had the Viscount discovered Reginald had led Payton astray, he'd likely toss Reginald, his wife, and their son out on the street. "Not to worry," Reginald said, turning his attention back to the office. "Your secret of drunken debauchery is safe with me."

Reginald watched the men talking in the office, the faces of the two owners, Rolls and Royce, looking drawn, the loss weighing on them. The stolen car, named the Gray Ghost for the color of the body and the quietness of the forty-fifty engine, had been kept a secret from all but their investors for fear that someone might try to steal their ideas. Apparently, it had never occurred to them that someone might steal the entire car. Payton's father, the Viscount, had offered the family warehouse to store the car while they were fitting it with its custom coachwork, hoping to enter it into the Olympia Motor Show in just a few months. Reginald and Jonathon had discussed the idea that the vehicle would be more secure there, less likely to fall prey to anyone skulking around the factory, stealing plans. Jonathon, however, was the one who'd presented it. "Tough break, this happening on your watch, don't you think?" Reginald said.

"Quite. I expect they'll sack me for it."

"Have they said anything to you?"

"No," Payton whispered, his face paling as Mr. Rolls shook the officer's hand, then escorted him out the door.

Mr. Royce stepped out after them, looked right at Jonathon. "Do you have a moment?"

"Right away, sir." Jonathon Payton rose, not looking at his cousin as he walked toward the office.

"Close the door."

"Yes, sir." He shut the door behind him.

Reginald, eyeing the journals on top of a cabinet against the office's wall, casually walked over, picked up the topmost one, and pretended to read it. The wall was thin enough to hear what was being said.

"You've no doubt heard what happened?" Mr. Royce asked Jonathon.

"I have."

"You realize what dire straits we're in?"

Reginald leaned in closer. In charge of the books, he knew every penny the company spent and what would happen to their investors if they didn't recover that car and start turning a profit. They'd go bankrupt, his uncle, the Viscount—who'd invested everything—right along with them. Jonathon's response, though, was covered by the return of Mr. Rolls, who nearly ran into Reginald as he came back from seeing the officer out.

"Pardon," Mr. Rolls said, stepping past him. He started to open the door, paused, looking over at Reginald, and at the other young men, sitting at their desks, their attention focused on what was happening in the office. "I daresay, we're all frightfully worried over this setback. But we'll get past it. In the meantime, let's all get back to our tasks, shall we?"

The young men nodded, as did Reginald, and their employer gave a worried smile, then entered the office. "This is disastrous," he said, pushing the door closed. It didn't latch tight. "We have to find that engine."

"Why would anyone bother?" Mr. Royce asked. "The blasted coachwork wasn't even finished."

"Why do you think?" Rolls replied. "Sending spies

sniffing around, trying to best us. Whoever it was, they stole it because they couldn't build anything close to what we have."

"Problem is, it's still in the prototype stage. If they get it out there before we do, we lose it all. Every investor we have will pull out."

"Good point. What if we lose the patent?" Rolls said. "We have to get that car back before the Olympia Motor Show."

"The policeman suggested we hire a detective."

Mr. Rolls made a scoffing noise. "Not sure we want that to get out to our investors. Can't even keep track of our own products before they find their way into the hands of our competitors."

Jonathon Payton started to speak, his voice cracking. He cleared his throat and started again, saying, "What about those parts we sent out to be machined? If we could get them back in time, we might have a chance to finish that other forty-fifty."

"Brilliant idea," Royce said. "They've got to be ready by now. Give them a ring, Payton. If they're ready, see if they can't get them on the next train. We might just save this company after all."

One week later . . .

Just before sunrise, ten-year-old Toby Edwards and his nine-year-old brother, Chip, picked their way down the street, avoiding the low spots where the rain flowed down from the previous day's storm. They stopped at the entrance to the alley. "Wait here," Toby said, moving his brother into the shadows. "I'll be back soon."

"Why can't I go? I'll be quiet as a mouse."

"Just wait. If anything happens, run back."

The boy nodded, and Toby moved off. The last time he'd stolen something from the bakery, he'd nearly gotten caught after stepping in a deep puddle. The water had soaked through the worn soles of his boots, squeaking with every step he took. A customer was the one who'd heard, calling out to the baker that a thief had broken in, then chasing after him.

He wasn't about to make that mistake again.

Worried the baker might catch him again, he'd stayed away for several days, until hunger drove him out once more. This time when he reached the back of the shop, he wiggled his toes, grateful that they were dry. He glanced back, could just make out his brother in the dark. Satisfied he was waiting as he should, Toby moved in.

The waiting was the hardest part. He breathed in the scent of fresh-baked bread drifting into the alley. Every morning, the baker opened the back door a crack, just enough to let his gray tabby in and out. The door was locked tight, and Toby wondered, after nearly getting caught, if the man had realized it left him ripe for theft. Every minute that slipped by, Toby despaired. About to turn away, he heard the door open. The cat slipped out, its tiny paws silent on the wet cobblestones as it walked toward him, then rubbed its whiskered face against Toby's patched trousers.

When the cat meowed loudly, Toby crouched beside it, petting the feline's head, feeling it purr against his fingertips. "Hush, you," he whispered, watching the door.

Finally, he heard the faint tinkle from the bell that hung on the shop's front door, followed by the baker's deep voice greeting whoever it was that had walked in. Usually it was the servants from the big manor houses that ventured out this early, those who didn't bake their own bread.

Toby edged over, listening, before slipping through the door. He was immediately enveloped in heat, wishing he could find a spot under the table to spend the night where he wouldn't be seen. To be that warm while he slept . . .

Right now, food was more important. Suddenly he stopped, his heart sinking. The basket the baker had always left on the table with the burned and broken loaves wasn't there.

The table was empty.

His eyes flew to the door that led to the front of the shop, just able to make out the perfect loaves stacked in baskets on the counter.

For a moment, he wondered how hard it would be to race out there, grab one, and keep running.

He could never do that. It was one thing to take what was going to be tossed out, quite another to brazenly steal something the baker made a living from.

Stomach rumbling, he backed from the room, his foot hitting a wooden crate near the door. He froze, grateful when no one came racing into the kitchen. When he turned to leave, he saw what was in the crate. Nearly a dozen rolls, the tops a bit too brown, the bottoms black as coal.

Unable to believe his luck, he stuffed several rolls into his pockets, resisting the temptation to take every last one of them.

Slipping out the door, he raced down the alley, pausing to grab his brother's arm. The two boys darted around the puddles, then out to the street, where massive brick warehouses lined the railroad tracks. Toby and Chip lived in the orphanage on the other side. After a quick look behind them to make sure no one was following, Toby guided his brother that direction. When they reached the corner, he saw a man astride a black mare champing at the bit. The horseman, struggling to keep his mount under control, looked their direction.

Toby grasped Chip's hand, holding tight. Instinct told him to continue on past, as though that had been their intention the entire time.

As soon as they were out of sight, they broke into a run. Up ahead, Toby saw an alcove and pulled Chip into it, hiding his brother behind him.

A few seconds later, he heard the staccato clip of the horse's hooves on the cobblestones. Toby peered out, caught a glimpse of the man, and pressed back against the wall, praying the shadows would hide them.

"Who's that?" Chip asked.

"Quiet."

"I'm hungry," Chip whispered. "And cold."

There was a familiarity about the man when he'd looked over at Toby.

As though he'd seen him before.

And this was what bothered Toby. Something told him that if he didn't find out who the man was, his brother and sisters wouldn't be safe.

After their father, a coal miner, died of black lung disease, their mother had moved them all to Manchester, working in one of the textile mills. But then she'd taken ill, too, and could no longer care for them. They'd lived the last year at the Payton Home for Orphans. Had it not been for Toby's trips to the bakery, he and his siblings would have starved.

He had to get back to his sisters, but the only way to the orphanage was across the railroad tracks. Seconds ticked by, and the low rumble of an approaching train grew louder. Suddenly the horseman turned and galloped back toward the tracks.

"Wait here," Toby said, tucking his brother safely in the shadows.

THREE DAYS AGO, if someone had told Toby that he'd be brave enough to follow a horseman in the dark to see what the man was about, he might have laughed. He was the least brave person he knew. But his mother had made him promise to look after his sisters and brother, and that's exactly what he intended to do.

He'd gone no more than a few feet when Chip appeared at his side. Toby backtracked, taking his brother's hand. "I told you to wait."

"I don't want to stay by myself."

Toby considered taking him, until he remembered that feeling of terror when he'd almost been caught stealing from the bakery. "Hold these for me," he said, pulling three of the four rolls from his pocket and helping his brother put them in his. When he pulled out the fourth roll, he held it up. "If you stay here until I come back for you, I'll let you have the extra one."

Chip's eyes went wide as he stared at the burnt bread. But then he shook his head. "If I have that, what'll you have?"

"Ate one in the kitchen before I got out," he said, hoping the rumble of his stomach wouldn't give him away. "So hungry, I couldn't wait. But you want that extra one, you have to stay here."

"Why?"

"You don't want Lizzie or Abigail to see you eating it. You think you can do that?"

"Yes."

When Toby gave him the last roll, he gripped it in both hands, holding it up to his nose.

"Don't leave here until I come get you," Toby said, gently guiding his brother back to the alcove. As soon as Chip was safely tucked away, Toby started the other direction, keeping to the shadows.

As he neared the tracks, he saw a wagon stopped just on the other side, a stack of lumber strewn across the rails. Stars faded from the predawn sky, still too early for anyone to be out to help the driver who'd spilled the load. The man seemed unconcerned about moving the wood, instead just sitting there, holding the reins of his team, as the train approached.

Why would someone be moving lumber at this hour . . . ?

His eyes flew back to the horseman in time to see him lifting a mask over his face. In the distance, on the other side of the tracks, he saw two other horsemen, both masked.

"Blimey . . ."

The train squealed to a stop, sparks flying up from the rails. He looked at the men, saw the pistols they held. Fear coursed through his veins. He pivoted, about to run off, when someone grabbed him from behind, clamped a hand over his mouth, and dragged him beneath the wooden staircase near the corner building.

Toby clawed at the hands, trying to squirm free.

"Quiet!" The man pulled Toby back, his hand so tight Toby could barely breathe. "You want them to hear you?"

Several terror-filled seconds passed before he realized the man wasn't there to hurt him. He whispered in Toby's ear again. "I'm going to let go. Not a word, lad. Understand?"

Heart thudding, Toby nodded. The man lowered his hand, and Toby sucked in air, stealing a glance at his captor. He was tall, in his late twenties, and dressed all in black, a bowler covering his brown hair. "Who are you?"

"Will Sutton," he said. "Been following this gang since last week. Thought they were just after engine parts.

Turns out, they had something bigger in mind." His blue eyes were focused on the horsemen racing toward the stopped train.

Toby peered between the splintered stairs as the engineer stepped out from the locomotive, the first horseman pointing a gun at him. The engineer lifted his hands, backing up. The brakeman appeared behind him, his hands going up as well. The other two horsemen rode past, stopping three cars down, boarding. They climbed to the top of the car, opened a trapdoor, and disappeared below.

"Interesting," Will said. "I'd think it would've been locked."

Toby had no idea what he was talking about. His attention was on the first horseman. "I know him."

"What?"

"That man with the gun. Seen him in the orphanage, I have."

"You're sure?"

Toby nodded. "That's why I followed him."

Will kneeled in front of Toby, holding him by the shoulders, his eyes boring into him. "Did he see you? Out there in the street?"

"I— Maybe." He thought about it. Surely the man had been too far away? "I don't think so."

"If he comes back to the orphanage, make sure he doesn't see you."

"Why?"

The rattle of wagon wheels caught their attention. The driver shook the reins, the team of horses pulling the wagon around to the freight car, next to the two waiting horses. The freight door opened, and the two men started tossing heavy wooden crates into the wagon bed, each landing with a thud. They followed with large canvas bags, which landed with a metallic ring.

When they'd emptied the car, the two men jumped down and mounted their horses. The wagon driver cracked his whip. The team of horses took off down the street, followed by the two horsemen.

The third horseman, the one Toby recognized, watched his men, then turned back to the engineer and brakeman. "On the ground. Now!"

They kneeled, both lying facedown near the tracks. The horseman circled the two men, his gun pointed toward their heads. He fired twice. The gunshots cracked, the sharp report echoing off the bricks of the warehouse.

Unable to look away, Toby's knees buckled and he sank to the ground. A soft whimper grew louder.

"Quiet, lad," Will cautioned.

But Toby wasn't the one whimpering.

His brother, the half-eaten burnt roll in hand, stood in the middle of the street, crying. "T— Toby . . . ?"

The horseman pulled at the reins, whirled his steed about, his eyes landing on the boy. He lifted his gun, aiming.

Will swore, darted out. The first shot missed. He grabbed Chip, swinging him around, practically throwing him at Toby, as another shot rang out. He stumbled forward, falling to his knees, just a few feet from Toby, as the horseman fired again. When he fell forward, he looked right at Toby, mouthing something he couldn't hear.

Trapped beneath the staircase, tears welled in Toby's eyes as he gripped his brother's hand, unable to move, transfixed by the dark stain growing on Will's back, only vaguely aware of the horseman breaking open the pistol, reloading.

"Boy . . ." Will said, his voice a soft rasp.

Holding tight to his brother, Toby took a step forward, not sure what to do.

"Run!"

PEBBLE BEACH, CALIFORNIA
CONCOURS D'ELEGANCE

The present day, August

A salt-tinged breeze swept in from the water, rippling the white canvas tents where spectators stood, drinking champagne. Beyond the tents, sunlight glinted off the hoods of the classic cars parked on the newly mowed emerald green grass. Two young children ran between a blue and white 1932 Auburn V-12 Boattail and a white 1936 Auburn Speedster, laughing as their parents raced after them, catching their hands, then drawing them back away from the cars.

Sam Fargo guided his wife, Remi, out of the parents' and children's path, her attention fixed on the auction book she held. "Anything of interest?" he asked.

"Besides very rare cars?" Remi cleared her throat. "It says there's a 1929 Bentley, owned by Lord Albert Payton, Viscount Wellswick. Please tell me your mother's *not* expecting us to bid on that?"

"Of course not."

She looked over at him, her green eyes hidden behind dark sunglasses, her auburn hair tucked beneath a wide-brimmed straw hat. "You have *no* idea why we're here to talk to him, do you?"

"I know it has something to do with cars."

"That narrows it down," she said, focusing on the program, turning the page. "Viscount Wellswick has three cars listed for auction. Why on earth would he bring them all the way over here when he lives in Great Britain?"

"The cars aren't here, he is."

She closed the book, taking a look around. "I'm beginning to think he's very rare. Your mother did say he was meeting us at ten?"

Sam checked his watch. It was nearly eleven. "Maybe I got the time wrong." He slipped his phone from his pocket, calling his mother. "Hi, Mom—"

"Did you talk to Albert?" she asked, before he had a chance to comment.

"That's why I'm calling. We were wondering if you'd heard from him."

"No, but I'm sure he'll be there. I'm at the dock or otherwise I'd get you the name and number of the motel he's staying at." He heard the sound of a boat engine in the background. His mother, Eunice "Libby" Fargo, ran a charter boat in Key West for snorkelers and deep-sea fishing. What had been a hobby for her when his father had been alive was now her passion. It wasn't all that long ago that she'd spent more days on land than on sea. Now in her seventies, the reverse was true, and she wasn't willing to drop anchor anytime soon. "It's possible I got the time mixed up," she said.

"Any chance you know more about what he's looking for?"

"Just what I told you the other night— Have to go. Taking a group out now. Call me back if you don't hear from him soon."

She disconnected.

"Well?" Remi asked.

"Still a mystery."

The only thing he really knew was that according to his mother, Albert Payton, the 7th Viscount Wellswick, was a distant relative of his. "He's family, and he's in financial trouble" was what she'd told him when she'd called a couple of nights ago, asking if he and Remi could meet with him when they were in Pebble Beach for the Concours d'Elegance.

Sam wasn't the type to walk into anything unprepared, but when he'd tried asking her what sort of trouble, she said it had something to do with a car and finances.

It was the reference to finances that had bothered him, not that he was about to mention this to his mother. He and Remi were self-made multimillionaires, partly due to Sam's inventions, including an argon laser scanner, a device that could detect and identify mixed metals and alloys at a distance. These days, he and Remi tended to focus most of their energy working for the charitable foundation they'd set up. Amazing, though, how every time an article that mentioned their fortune appeared in some magazine or on the internet, there was no shortage of friends and relatives who suddenly remembered vague connections to Sam and Remi, looking for funds to invest or hoping for a handout.

As much as Sam wanted to believe that someone wouldn't try to get to him through his mother, he knew better. Up until two days ago when his mother had called, he'd never even heard of Viscount Wellswick. "Probably not even a real viscount," Sam said, dropping his phone into his pocket. "What sort of British royalty stays at a motel?"

Remi held up the program. "The sort that's forced to sell off cars at auction."

"Since he's not here now, it's a moot point. Let's just enjoy the day."

They strolled across the grass, taking their time to appreciate the vehicles on display. Remi stopped to admire a row of classic sports cars, in every hue of the rainbow. "It just goes to show that museums aren't the only places that house fine art."

"These just happen to be on wheels," Sam said. "Look at that motor. Now that's a work of art . . . 630-liter engine—"

"Designed by Dr. Ferdinand Porsche," Remi continued.

"Stop stealing my thunder."

Sam was stepping aside for a photographer, who was trying to set up a shot of the vehicle with the Pacific Ocean in the background, when Remi tapped him on the shoulder. "Isn't that Clive Cussler's car? The one he finished restoring in 2010?"

"Sure looks like it." They walked over to the sea foam green car, and Sam read the placard aloud. "1948 Delahaye Type 135 Cabriolet . . . I definitely like the color change. And the saddle brown leather interior works perfectly. The details . . ." He circled the car. "The Art Deco detail. That is Art Deco detail, isn't it?"

"Okay, Sam, you can stop salivating. You're like a kid in a candy shop."

"Who wouldn't be? Every year we come, there's always something new."

"I have to admit, it wouldn't be August without a trip to Pebble Beach."

Sam looked at his wife, about to comment on how fortunate they were that Clive always had guest passes waiting for them, when someone near the champagne and refreshment tent caught his eye. A dark-haired man about Sam's age, mid-thirties—far too young to be the missing Viscount—watching every move the two of them made.

Considering how many people were around, Sam found the man's interest odd. "How about a quick glass of champagne?" he asked.

"Before lunch? A bit of an early start to our day."

"Yes, well, in this case," he said, taking her arm in his, "we'll need a prop to find out why we seem to be so interesting."

"Intrigue. How fun. Who're we interested in?"

"There's a man wearing a yellow shirt with a green sweater tied around his shoulders at the far left corner of the champagne tent."

"Yellow? Green?" She gave a casual glance in that direction. "Really. If you're going to spy, why would anyone want to wear a color combination like that?"

Sam pretended interest in the 1937 Delahaye on their left as they strolled toward the tent. "Maybe he's trying not to look the part of a spy. Or," he said, leaning down close to her, "he's simply entranced by your beauty and can't take his eyes off you."

"Hmm. Highly unlikely. The latter, in case you're wondering. Too many far more striking women around here for me to be the center of attention, don't you think?"

"Not in the least," he said, glancing over at his wife. Remi had chosen a Dolce & Gabbana late-summer afternoon dress, in navy blue with white polka dots, with an off-the-shoulder neckline, and gathered sleeves that dropped to her elbows. The three-tiered gathered skirt was mid-calf, and the slightest breeze moved the delicate cotton voile. Perfectly polished red toenails peeked from her white Valentino sandals. Her straw hat matched a shoulder bag just big enough to hold the essentials: lipstick, comb, driver's license, credit card, cell phone, a 9mm Sig Sauer micro-compact handgun, and a concealed-carry permit. "You're a knockout, Remi. Always were, always will be."

"Very wise answer, Fargo." She gave him a dazzling smile, then turned her attention to the champagne tent. "We know he can't be a *spy* spy."

"A what?"

"Government intrigue and world conspiracy. More international jewel thief, dressed like that, wouldn't you say?"

No doubt she was thinking about their last escapade, which sent them to South America searching for the lost Romanov jewels. "Unless he's interested in your wedding ring, he's going to be sadly disappointed."

The way the man was watching them from behind one of the corners of the tent told Sam that he was definitely interested in something about them. He and Remi approached the table where a young woman in a crisp white shirt and black vest was pouring champagne into flutes. Sam picked up two, handing one to Remi. "You take the left, I'll take the right."

She lifted her glass and took a sip. "See you on the other side."

Sam watched as his wife expertly weaved her way through the guests, waiting until she was halfway across the tent before making his way in the opposite direction, toward the man, who suddenly found his attention divided between them. When Remi raised her glass in a toast, Sam did the same, and the two closed in.

Their target, apparently, hadn't realized they were zeroing in on him until they were just a few feet away. Sam walked up, clapped him on the back. "Wow. Didn't expect to see you here. Did you, Remi?"

"Not in the least. The people we run into at Pebble Beach, it just amazes me at times."

The man's blue eyes widened as he looked from Sam to Remi in disbelief. "It's you!"

Considering that Sam expected him to deny, to at least pretend, he hadn't been watching them, his statement came as a surprise. "How do you know us?"

"Of course, I don't know you," he said, with a strong British accent. "Not personally. You really do look just like your photographs. What luck to run into you straight-away."

"Lucky, indeed," Sam said, wondering what sort of game this guy was playing. "Didn't quite catch your name."

"Forgive me. I'm Oliver Payton. But you'll be wanting to talk to my uncle, Albert. Please wait while I fetch him?"

"Right here," Sam said.

He and Remi watched the man walk off, Remi saying, "Our missing Viscount's nephew?"

"Apparently. Assuming the man really is a viscount."

"Your mother seems to think so."

"She's not nearly as jaded as I am. Besides, how is it I've never heard about him until now?"

Remi gave him a sidelong glance. "Lack of interest in your extended family tree?"

"Only because the branches seem to multiply every time we turn around."

"Do I detect the slightest bit of cynicism? Don't answer that." She nodded to Sam's left, where Oliver was helping a white-haired man down the slope of rough grass onto a cart path. "Our Viscount and his nephew are back."

When they reached the champagne tent, the Viscount brushed Oliver's hand from his arm. "I'm old, not an invalid."

Oliver gave a hesitant smile, clearing his throat. "My uncle, Albert Payton, Viscount Wellswick. This is Sam Fargo and his wife, Remi. They're here about the car."

The old man grumbled something under his breath about the car being his, turning an accusing glare in Sam's direction. Suddenly his expression softened. "You look just like Eunice."

The last person Sam had ever heard calling his mother by that name was a clerk at the DMV when she'd let her driver's license expire. She'd always hated the name, instead going by Libby, a diminutive of Elizabeth, her middle name. "She mentioned you were here about a car?"

Albert nodded. "I— Yes. That you might be interested in the prototype of the Rolls-Royce Silver Ghost. I— I don't have a lot of money. I'm not sure the show's the best place for it. But I have a few good ideas on where someone might hide a classic car. I know they're far-fetched, but if you'd only hear me out . . ."

Sam and Remi exchanged glances. No doubt a swindle about to happen, and not a very good one. When it came to cons, Sam liked to let them think they had the upper hand—the better to keep them off guard. "You have a card? I'll look into the matter and get back to you."

The man's face fell as he patted his pockets. Either he was an extremely good actor or he'd pinned a lot of hope on that odd speech he'd just given. "No."

"I have a mobile," Oliver said. "Will that do?"

"Of course. Remi?"

She handed Sam her flute, then took her cell phone out, entering the number that Oliver recited to her.

"We'll be in touch," Sam said, placing both glasses on a nearby table.

He and Remi walked off, Remi asking, "What do you suppose his game was?"

"I'm not sure that he even knows." Sam checked the program Remi still held, something about it spurring his memory. "Didn't we read a recent article in *Sports Car Market* about a viscount selling off a number of classic cars?"

"The same man: Albert Payton," Remi said. While Sam's memory was sharp, his wife had near-photographic memory for anything she read. It amazed him how she was able to recall the tiniest details. "Downsizing in an attempt to save the family estate. But I don't recall reading that they were selling a prototype Rolls-Royce Silver Ghost. You don't think he was talking about the one that was stolen back in 1906? Of the first ever forty-fifty?"

They both stopped in their tracks.

Sam looked at Remi. "We need to find that man."

But when they turned back toward the champagne tent, he and his nephew were gone.

It took Sam and Remi a few minutes to find the Viscount and his nephew in the crowd. They'd moved to the other side of the champagne tent, both men looking out toward the ocean.

"I don't think they're interested," the younger man, Oliver, said.

"They just want to think about it. They . . ." His shoulders fell. "All those families. What do I tell them?"

Oliver put his arm around his uncle. "We'll think of something. I promise."

Remi elbowed Sam.

He cleared his throat, giving both men time to compose themselves. "Mr. Payton?"

The two men turned, Oliver looking surprised, his uncle looking confused.

"A few more questions." Sam was about to ask why they'd contacted his mother, of all people, when that feeling of being watched hit him a second time. He scanned the crowd, catching sight of a broad-shouldered man with a military buzz cut. The man's gaze slid past

Sam as though searching for someone else, waving as he walked in that direction. When Sam turned to see who he was waving to and found no one, he looked back, discovering the man had disappeared into the crowd.

While it was highly possible the matter was all very innocent, something told Sam that Oliver and his uncle had been the focus of attention. Clearly, they needed to learn more from them, but not out here in the open. "Let's find somewhere quiet, where we can talk."

"Lunch," Remi said. "I'm starved. Assuming we can get in anywhere."

"I'll call the hotel," Sam said. Getting into any of the restaurants on the Peninsula was almost impossible during the Concours d'Elegance. As always, Sam and Remi were staying at the Inn at Spanish Bay, and that certainly helped when last-minute reservations were needed. He called the concierge desk, glad when Kimberley answered the phone. "Sam Fargo," he said, having to move aside when a man who was intently reading his program almost bumped into him. "Any chance you can find us a table for lunch? Party of four?"

"Shouldn't be a problem, Mr. Fargo. I'll just confirm with the restaurant. Please hold."

Sam's eye caught the man who'd nearly run into him as he walked quickly away, suddenly with purpose. The moment he met up with Mr. Buzz Cut, the same person who'd been watching them earlier, Sam realized it'd been no accident. They or the Paytons were being followed. "Why don't we start wandering toward the shuttle," Sam said to Remi, eager to lose their tail, wondering if there were any more out there.

They didn't have to walk far. Kimberley got back to him, said she'd secured a table at the Taproom, one of the restaurants at the Lodge.

Drinks ordered, Sam eyed their two guests. "My mother was a bit vague about why you needed to meet with us. If you wouldn't mind filling us in . . . ?"

The old man leaned toward his nephew. "Were we looking for him?"

"Yes," Oliver said. "The car, remember?"

"Quite right." Albert nodded, his attention on Sam. "We thought you'd be the perfect benefactor for my car."

Perfect benefactor, Sam decided, was an odd choice of words. "This Silver Ghost prototype that you mentioned?"

"The same."

"Exactly how are you and my mother related?"

"Do I know your mother?"

Oliver smiled at his uncle. "Second cousins, isn't it?"

"Ah, Cousin Eunice."

Interesting, since Sam's mother had never mentioned this side of her family to him until this requested meeting suddenly came up. "She told me something about a loan," Sam said, trying to get them back on track. "What is it you need the money for?"

"The short version is," Oliver said, "that we've lost everything and we're looking for a loan before they repossess our land and home. We've tried to sell off what we can to get by, but so many make their living off the land they rent from us, entire families—generations, even—we're hesitant to make a deal that might displace them."

While Oliver spoke, Sam's attention shifted to the door, wondering if the prototype of the Silver Ghost had anything to do with the men he'd seen following them. At the moment, it appeared they'd made it to the restaurant without being tailed. Still, he wasn't about to take chances and he kept watch while they ate.

Remi did an admirable job keeping the conversation focused during the meal, the better to evaluate Albert Payton and his nephew. "They couldn't rent from the new owners?" Remi asked, as the waiter arrived to clear the table.

Oliver gave a tight smile, avoiding any look from his uncle. "The one and only offer on the land that we've seen, well, they've refused to guarantee that they wouldn't evict."

Albert gave a firm nod. "We are not selling."

"The thing is," Oliver said, "I don't know how we got to this point. One day we were fine, the next everything was lost. I—" He looked at his uncle, then back at Sam. "I blame myself. I should've taken over the books sooner. I'm still trying to make sense of it all."

"Framed," his uncle said, nodding. "They're trying to take everything from me. Everything."

"You don't know that," Oliver said.

"Don't I?" He looked at Sam, his eyes lucid, sharp. "I'll tell you exactly who it is. And why."

The waiter placed a leather folder with the check in it next to Sam.

Albert watched as the waiter retreated, then looked at Sam. "I— What was I saying?"

"Someone framed you."

He nodded. Whatever thought he'd been about to utter, though, was lost. The older man's memory problems seemed real. That didn't eliminate the possibility, however, that the younger man, no matter how sincere he appeared, was taking advantage of his uncle or attempting to take advantage of them. Sam directed his attention to Oliver. "What is it that you're hoping we can do? Or what is it that my mother suggested we do?"

"She said you might be interested in using the car for collateral. For a loan."

"My mother said that?"

Oliver shifted in his seat, looking suddenly uncomfortable. "Just enough to help me get his estate back in the black and keep our tenants from being evicted. I'm sure that if I can figure out what went wrong, whatever it was that started this tailspin, we can recover."

"Quite my fault," Albert said, looking at his nephew for confirmation.

Oliver reached out and clasped his uncle's hand. "He's been a good landlord. I don't think these families could make it if we sold and they had to pay rent at full value. I—" He looked at his uncle, then back at Sam. "As I said, I blame myself."

"Framed," his uncle said again. But any revelations about who was behind it, if anyone, weren't forthcoming.

Sam tucked his credit card into the leather folder, handing it to the waiter as he approached. "It sounds complicated."

"I quite understand if you don't believe us," Oliver said. "Sometimes I'm not even sure what's going on. I know Uncle Albert believes someone else is responsible. And I believe him. I've burned through my sabbatical time and the last of my savings. And since I'm out of funds, I have to go back to work. I— I don't know how else to help him or learn what really happened."

Remi reached over, laying her hand on Oliver's arm. "If what he's saying is true, that someone else is behind this, you should call the police."

"My wife is right," Sam said. "It's really not something we do."

"You hunt treasure, don't you?"

"That's different."

"How? The actual Silver Ghost is worth fifty million,

if not more. Surely the Gray Ghost has to have a similar value."

"That certainly is the question," Sam said. "Where's it been all this time?"

"During World War Two, it was stored away due to the bombing. There it sat, until we were forced to start liquidating. But no one really knew its worth. We'd sold off at least a dozen classic cars by the time we came across the Gray Ghost under its dustcover in the barn. When we realized what we had, we contacted Rolls-Royce, hoping to get an idea of the vehicle's worth."

"Did they give an approximate value?" Sam asked.

"That's just it. They said they couldn't place a value, since it was only the prototype."

"Only?" Remi said, her brows rising.

"My thoughts exactly. But, then, they offered to buy it, saying they'd send someone out to take a look and give an estimate."

"Thieves," Albert said. "Not going to sell it."

Oliver smiled patiently, saying, "That was his feeling at the time as well. But they never came out to look."

The waiter brought Sam the receipt. He added a tip, signed it. "So no offer?"

"They never got that far in the conversation. Some other people came out and talked Uncle Albert into entering it into the London Concours, saying it would generate interest and increase the value."

"Not sure it should be in a London show," Albert said. "Changed my mind."

"A bit late, sorry to say," Oliver said. "It's entered."

Loud cheering erupted from a group of men at a nearby table watching golf on the TV mounted on the wall, one of the players having birdied. When the room quieted once more, Oliver said, "Come take a look, see if you think it's worth the collateral of a loan. We can offer a drafty manor house with comfortable beds and free tickets to the car show next week, where the Ghost will be on display. Other than that . . ."

Sam glanced at the door, but, so far, no familiar faces. "Unfortunately, we have a charity event we're sponsoring in a few weeks. I'm not sure we can fit it into our schedule."

Remi kicked him under the table as she smiled at Oliver. "Would you excuse us for a moment. My husband and I need to check our calendar." When she turned toward Sam, her smile was still in place, but he recognized that look. Remi had made up her mind.

"Keeper of the calendar," Sam said, nodding at his wife.

He and Remi moved off a few feet toward the maître d's podium, where two couples dressed for golf were waiting to be seated at a table. Remi stepped past them into the hallway, Sam right beside her, as she asked, "Is there some reason we aren't jumping on this?"

"Four reasons, in fact. First, he wants a loan. We have no idea what the real value is. You realize we could be spending a lot of money for very little return?"

Remi scoffed. "There are more important things in life besides money, which we have plenty of." She made a slight nod toward Oliver but kept her eyes on Sam. "The guy's down on his luck. Selling off family heirlooms to make ends meet. Flying all the way out here just to talk to us? If we were ever that desperate, I'd like to think someone would step in to help us. I say we accept. Your mother, apparently, thinks the same or she wouldn't have sent them to meet us."

"They probably conned her as well. How is it I've never heard of these relatives before?"

Remi crossed her arms. "That's only two reasons."

Sam looked over at the door as it opened, a cool breeze sweeping across the restaurant. "Reasons three and four just walked in."

Remi looked over at the two men Sam said had been following them. "Which furthers my argument that we need to help them."

"You're right," Sam said, watching the men from the corner of his eye. "So what's our plan to get them out of here without being followed?"

"You take Oliver and his uncle in the hallway, then downstairs. I'll waylay the Buzz Cuts and lose them in the hotel lobby. We'll meet outside by the service entrance. I doubt they'll follow any of you while I'm standing so close. And if they do . . ."

"Don't make too much of a mess, Remi. I like coming here."

"Funny, Fargo. You're like a bull in a china shop. And that's exactly why I'm leading them on a wild-goose chase. So much more subtle than you taking them on, don't you think?"

While Remi went to engage the Buzz Cuts, Sam returned to the table. "Why don't we wait for Remi in the lobby of the hotel. She wants to say hello to some old friends."

Oliver and his uncle looked puzzled but followed Sam out. When he looked back, he saw the men start toward them, then stop when Remi blocked their way, engaging them as only a woman can. Once out of view, Sam led the Payton men down the staircase.

"Isn't the lobby on the upper level?" Oliver asked, as they trailed him out the door to the parking lot.

"Yes, but we've had a change of plans. We can wait for Remi out here." Sam found a spot near the garbage cans' enclosure behind the restaurant. Remi appeared about five minutes later. "Everything okay?" Sam asked.

"Better than okay." She tossed a key fob in her hand as she led them toward the upper parking lot to a row of Lexus vehicles. And they weren't being followed. "We have a car waiting for us."

All the Pebble Beach hotels had loaner cars for guest use, but it usually took prior arrangements to reserve one, especially during a busy event like the Concours. "How'd you arrange it?"

"A woman's wiles. And some help from Kimberley, who made sure the keys were waiting at the front desk of the Lodge." She took a good look around before heading to the white sedan in the middle of the lot. After using the remote to unlock it, Remi tossed the key fob to Sam. "I thought we could take this back instead of the shuttle, head to the airport in the morning."

"Nicely done, Mrs. Fargo." He kept an eye on the

parking lot as the others slid into their seats. Once everyone was buckled in, and they were safely on the road, he looked at the Paytons in the rearview mirror. "You realize two men have been following you since you've been here?"

"What?" Oliver asked. "Why would anyone want to follow us?"

"Hard to say, but between this possible fraud you mentioned and the value of that car your uncle owns, I'd guess it has something to do with one or the other."

"Or both," Remi said.

"That's what we hope to find out."

"So you'll help?" Oliver asked.

Sam looked over at Remi, then back in the mirror at Oliver. "No promises yet. Let's wait until I check into things and get a feel for what's going on."

The next morning, after seeing Oliver and his uncle to the airport, Sam and Remi flew home to La Jolla in their jet. Selma Wondrash, their Hungarian-born researcher, met them at the door. As usual, their German shepherd Zoltán, also Hungarian-born, was beside Selma, his tail wagging in excitement. The dog rushed toward Remi, shoving his nose against her knees as she reached down to scratch him behind the ears. "I missed you, too," she cooed.

"How was the flight, Mrs. Fargo?"

It didn't matter how many times Remi or Sam tried to get her to use their first names, insisting that she was more family than employee, she'd always reverted back to "Mr." and "Mrs." In the end, it made her happy, which made them happy. "Smooth as ever," Remi said. "Anything exciting on the research front?"

"A few promising leads, but it'll take more time to dig deeper," she said, looking past Remi to see Sam unloading the bags from the car. "I'll get those, Mr. Fargo."

"After sitting on the plane for a couple of hours, a little exercise will do me good," Sam said, as he set the suitcases near the stairs. "Let's go have a look at what you dug up for us."

They followed Selma to her office, where the overhead fluorescent lights accentuated the subtle pink and purple streaks in her short hair. Selma had always been a bit quirky, wearing tie-dyed shirts that seemed at odds with the rather conservative dark-framed glasses that usually hung from a gold chain around her neck. The hair, though, was a newer style, one that Remi and Sam noticed Selma had adopted after Professor Lazlo Kemp began working for them, and she and Lazlo started spending more time together. Sam and Remi had never commented on the matter; they figured Selma would let them know when she was ready—assuming there really was something to the relationship.

Her office, where most of the research and assistance happened in the Fargo household, was a large room with state-of-the-art computers. Normally, she worked with two part-time assistants, Pete Jeffcoat and Wendy Corden, who were currently in Africa overseeing a Fargo Foundation project, the building of a self-sustainable school for children that used solar and wind to power the lights and to run the pump for the well. Lazlo was there, however, his chair scooted up next to Selma's desk. His specialty was cryptography, but these days he was a jack-of-all-trades.

"Quite the find here," he said, his English accent still strong even though he hadn't lived in Great Britain for years. He was looking at computer screenshots of an old car.

"Is that the Gray Ghost?" Remi asked.

"The Silver Ghost," he replied. "Doing a comparison. Aside from the names there are some very subtle differences."

Remi leaned in for a better view. "Such as?"

"The most obvious being the color," he said, pointing to the screen. "The Gray Ghost being gray." He brought the cursor to the frame of the other photo, bringing it to the foreground, moving it so it was side by side with the Silver Ghost. "The interior coachwork is different. The Silver Ghost has green leather, the Gray Ghost blue. Whether the same or different companies, hard to say until we research further. Back then, it was all bespoke. You picked the company and what features you wanted. No two cars were alike."

"So, the car's legit?" Sam asked.

"Without seeing it in person, it appears so."

Selma handed Sam several sheets of paper. "These are what I found on the theft in 1906. Not much on the car after that. Information's a bit sparse."

Sam looked through the papers as Selma took a seat at her desk next to Lazlo, pulling out even more papers from a file folder. "These," she said, handing them to Sam, "are what I thought you'd want to see."

"What are they?" he asked, handing Remi the first stack before taking the second.

"What I think is the real reason behind the theft of the Gray Ghost. It might change your mind about making this trip. At the same time the car was stolen in '06," Selma told Sam, "an American agent from the Van Dorn Detective Agency, by the name of Isaac Bell, was in England following a group of criminals responsible for a number of train robberies in America. Apparently, two of the gang members fled to England and joined up with a bunch of thieves and robbed another train, which was carrying a treasure worth about a million dollars."

"And you think it has something to do with the car?" Remi asked.

"It's the only explanation. Isaac Bell recovered some of the stolen treasure as well as this Rolls-Royce they call the Gray Ghost. One of the car thieves was a man named Reginald Oren. But here's where it gets a little muddied."

Sam looked up from the papers. "What I'm reading here makes it seem like an early case of corporate espionage."

"That was my take on it as well," Selma continued. "Reginald Oren was employed by Rolls-Royce. But he had connections with the gang responsible for the theft of the treasure. And it's not really clear if the treasure and the car were found together."

"So, maybe someone thinks that missing part of the treasure is hidden in the Gray Ghost?" Remi said. "Or maybe a hidden map? It might explain why the Paytons are being followed."

"Makes sense," Sam said. "Any idea what part of this treasure is still missing?"

"Lazlo reached out to acquaintances of his familiar with the local history in England and Manchester just after the turn of the century. They believe it's around half."

"Five hundred thousand dollars?" Remi said. "The Gray Ghost has to be worth more than that."

"Don't forget inflation," Selma said. "Five hundred thousand gold sovereigns from 1906 are worth close to three hundred times that much just for the gold. Close to one hundred and fifty million."

Remi whistled.

"That car's worth a pretty penny," Sam said.

"And about to go on public display," Selma reminded him.

"I'm still not convinced that we should involve ourselves," Sam said. "Who's to say the Paytons are on the up-and-up?"

Remi eyed the screenshot of the Gray Ghost, then picked up the phone on Selma's desk, holding it toward Sam. "Can't wait to hear this call to your mother, you telling her you think her relatives are conning her."

Sam took the phone from Remi, dropped it back in the cradle. "Now that I think about it, a quick trip to Great Britain seems perfectly reasonable."

Arthur Oren opened the folder, revealing a color print, an artist's rendering of a coat of arms he'd recently had commissioned. Oren's family name should have read "Oren-Payton." A few generations ago, the Oren-Payton brothers fought over their inheritance, the older brother taking the Payton name when he became Viscount Wellswick, the younger brother adopting the Oren name when he was forced to leave everything behind to make his own fortune. The two never spoke again.

What his distant relative had failed to do when he'd walked away all those years ago was create a new family crest.

Arthur Oren had finally rectified that detail, using the original version and adapting parts of it for his own. The artist had done a fine job, and Arthur imagined what it would look like, full-sized, hanging in the Great Hall, once he recovered the manor from those Payton thieves. With the endgame so close, he'd taken the liberty of having this new design drawn up, one that more closely resembled the original family crest.

After the Paytons had usurped the ancestral home, they'd removed the raven from the shield and chosen a dragon on a red background, meant to signify their role as guardian of the treasure and service to their country. The artist's new design had rectified that substitution by changing the red background to maroon, meant to signify victory in battle. But second, and most importantly, he'd removed the dragon and replaced it with more than the original single raven, this time including one for each generation that had suffered at the hands of the Paytons.

This last alteration made Arthur smile, and he ran his finger across the ravens, relishing their symbolism: divine providence, endurance, and, most significant, as the bringers of death.

A fitting end to the descendants of those who'd usurped the Oren lands—and any who got in the way of his recovery of it all, he thought. His brown-haired secretary, Jane, knocked on the door. "Sir? Colton Devereux is here to see you."

"Send him in."

"Right away."

She returned to her office. A moment later, Colton entered, taking a seat in the chair opposite his desk without being asked. Deciding to ignore such presumptuousness, Oren closed the folder containing his sketch. "What've you found so far?"

"The old man decided to show the car after all."

"How'd you manage that?"

"By convincing the family that it would raise the value of the car should he ever decide to sell."

And sell he would. Albert Payton was broke, thanks to Colton. One more reason that Oren was dependent on his skills. Colton and the team of men he had working for him were the best money could buy. A mix of Special Forces and computer hackers—black hatters, Colton called them. They were a near-unstoppable force, loyal to Colton and therefore loyal to the person paying his exorbitant fee. It was Colton who'd come up with the idea of hacking and depleting the Payton accounts, forcing the sale of their assets, allowing Oren to buy them for a tenth of the value while hiding behind the shell companies Colton had set up. "You're sure he's entering the car into the show?"

"Absolutely," Colton said, lighting up a cigarette, again without asking.

The man smoked nonstop, a fact Oren found surprising, given his muscular appearance as well as his background in the Special Forces. Then again, he usually stood back and let his men do the heavy lifting.

Colton exhaled a stream of smoke, pocketed his lighter. "I told him that the organizers were so excited about putting the car on display, they were willing to waive the entry fee. Once he heard that, he was all for it. I've added the entry fee to your tab."

"Noted," he said. "What about the rest of it?"

"Most everything's going according to plan."

"Most?"

"The nephew, unfortunately."

"Him again." Somehow they'd miscalculated Oliver

Payton having such a sentimental attachment to the farmers who'd lose their lands if the Payton estates were sold. With every step forward Colton's men had made, Oliver had somehow found a way to save everything. Still, the one thing that had started this, the Gray Ghost and its secret, was very close to being Oren's. Assuming they could keep Oliver from getting in the way. "What's he done this time?"

"Took his uncle to California, no doubt looking for a buyer for the Gray Ghost. The good news is, while they were gone, we were able to take care of a few matters."

"Did he find a buyer?"

"We're not sure. Beyond the initial phone call to someone named Libby in Key West, nothing was done electronically."

The news startled him. "He's not aware we're tracking his movements?"

"Oliver? I seriously doubt it. I'm sure he's certain it's just a spate of bad luck involving his uncle. Memory issues, I should imagine."

"How'd he manage to get two tickets to California? I thought the money was gone."

"Reward points from an account we weren't aware of. Trust me, we won't make that mistake again," he said, reaching over to pick up Oren's empty coffee cup and saucer. "You done with this?"

"Quite," he said, hiding his annoyance as Colton removed the cup, took the saucer, and rested his burning cigarette on it.

Smoke swirling up, he pulled his cell phone from his

pocket and read some text he'd received. "It seems we have the names of those he spoke with in Pebble Beach . . . Sam and Remi Fargo."

"And who are they?"

"Not sure yet." Colton scanned the text. "It's possible they realized they were being followed. Oliver running into the Fargos was a complication we didn't expect . . ." He read for a bit longer, shrugged. "Very minor."

Something in Colton's tone told him that he was downplaying the information. "Forward everything you have on these Fargos to me."

He nodded, pressed a button on his phone, returned the device to his pocket, and stood. "They're searching the names now. I'll send a full report to you as soon as we have it."

About thirty minutes after Colton left, Oren's computer dinged with an incoming email. He opened it, read the dossier on Sam and Remi Fargo. Sam Fargo graduated summa cum laude with an engineering degree from Caltech, was trained in weapons and hand-to-hand combat while employed at the Defense Advanced Research Projects Agency. After leaving DARPA, he met and married his wife, Remi Longstreet. She, apparently, hailed from the East Coast, a graduate of Boston College, with a master's in anthropology and history, with a focus on ancient trade routes. The two started the Fargo Group, which they eventually sold for millions, now devoting their time to running the Fargo Foundation, which, apparently, was all about charity work. By the time he finished reading the entire dossier, including the fact that both held valid concealed-carry permits, he wasn't so sure that either Sam or Remi Fargo were as minor a problem as Colton had suggested.

Not that he was worried. He read the last line in Colton's email: *The timing of the Payton visit to the Fargos is suspicious. If they interfere, we'll take care of it.*

Oren opened his file folder and took another look at the black ravens. So fitting, he thought.

The bringers of death.

Sam drove the rental car while Remi navigated the country roads outside of Manchester, using the map on her phone, finally seeing the manor house in the distance, thinking it looked very regal.

"Must have been something in its heyday," Sam said, as they cruised up the cobblestone drive. "A place as old as this must cost a fortune in upkeep."

"Imagine what it must be like to lose everything." Remi took it all in, sighing. "How does anyone survive that? I'm not sure I could."

"As resourceful as you are? You'd find a way," he said, parking the car.

A frail woman in her late sixties, her gray hair pulled into a bun on top of her head, stood at the open door, waiting for them, as they walked up. "Mr. and Mrs. Fargo, I hope your trip was pleasant."

"Very," Sam said. "You must be Mrs. Beckett."

She gave a slight nod. "Mr. Payton was called out on an emergency or he would've been here himself to greet you. But he's asked that you make yourself at home." She waved for them to follow her in. "I'll see you to your rooms. You'll be in the North Wing on the first floor. Would you like me to carry your bags?"

"We can manage," Sam said.

She led them up the stairs, then down the hall, where Remi found it hard to ignore the obvious squares and rectangles on the white walls where paintings used to hang.

Mrs. Beckett stopped to open a door, stepping back to let them enter. "His Lordship prefers to stay in the Dowager Cottage, where he takes supper. At six. We find the routine—and less stairs—is easier for him. If you'd rather rest after your long trip, I'd be glad to send a tray up."

Remi glanced at Sam, who gave the slightest shake of his head. Tired as they were, this might be the only opportunity to talk to Albert Payton without his nephew around.

An opportunity they weren't about to pass up.

"That's very kind of you," Remi said. "But we'd be honored to join His Lordship."

"Very good. I'll come around for you just before six. A bit of a maze, this house. Especially to get to the South Wing." Mrs. Beckett gave a stiff smile, then backed out of the room, closing the door behind her.

As promised, she returned before six to take them to dinner, leading them through a maze of hallways allowing them a glimpse into numerous rooms, walls bare, furniture gone. She stopped at a closed door, looked back at them, her dour expression softening. "Try not to think ill of us, keeping His Lordship out of this part of the house, under lock and key. A bit of a wanderer, of late. And seeing the empty rooms confuses him. He likes to pop over from the cottage in the morning to take breakfast in the Conservatory before he starts his day. He likes to tend the roses. Rather than disrupt his routine, we simply lock the rest of the house, which helps keep him on task. The Conservatory and the Dowager Cottage still have their original furnishings, which helps to keep him grounded."

She paused in the doorway, looking back at them. "A few weeks ago, someone left the garden gate ajar, and off he went. Found the keys to his nephew's car, no one the wiser, until a constable brought him 'round after he wrecked it. We're grateful he wasn't killed, that we are." Surprisingly, after they stepped through, she locked the door behind her and handed the key to Sam. "It's a master. You'll need this to get back to your room."

Sam took the key, slipping it into his pocket. "We'll be careful."

"The Breakfast Room and Conservatory," she said, opening yet another door.

Remi saw at once why he preferred eating there. Two of the room's walls were floor-to-ceiling windows, the third had French doors that opened to a square of lawn surrounded by a high brick wall covered with jasmine. To the left was the garden gate, the one Mrs. Beckett said had been left open. To the right was the rose garden. They stepped out onto a flagstone patio, Mrs. Beckett leading them down a graveled path that crossed the vast lawn to a quaint cottage that looked like a dollhouse version of Payton Manor.

They passed through the arched doorway into a small parlor, where a gray Persian cat jumped up onto the pianoforte for a better view of the people who'd invaded his space. Mrs. Beckett shooed him off as she passed, then led them through another archway to where Albert was seated at a round table set for three.

He stood as they entered. "Well done, Mrs. Beckett. I quite forgot we were having guests or I would have met them myself."

"Sam and Remi Fargo," she announced.

Albert nodded in greeting. "I daresay, your names sound familiar. I hope you'll forgive me, but I don't recall how we met."

"At the car show in Pebble Beach," Sam said.

"Yes, of course," he said, as he shook hands with Sam. "The oddest thing . . . You remind me of someone. Sit. Sit. I'll think of it in a minute. About to have dinner. You will stay?"

"We'd be glad to," Sam said, as he and Remi each took a seat.

Albert nodded, looked at the housekeeper. "Two more for dinner, Mrs. Beckett."

"Very good, sir." She removed the lids of the serving dishes, steam rising from the pork medallions in one and the mixed vegetables in the other.

"Wish my nephew was here. Off doing something or other." He stopped, his eyes narrowing as he studied Sam. "I know exactly who you remind me of: Cousin Eunice."

Remi looked at Sam, whose expression remained neutral on hearing his mother's given name. He still wasn't convinced that the Paytons hadn't played up this relationship to get closer to them. Curious, Remi smiled at Albert. "You have a cousin named Eunice?"

"Haven't seen her in years." He pushed his chair back. "Have a picture of her somewhere . . ."

Mrs. Beckett set her hand on his arm, preventing him from standing. "Perhaps, M'lord, you'll allow me to fetch your album. You have guests, after all."

"What's this 'M'lord' rubbish? Family doesn't 'M'lord.'"

She smiled patiently, as she handed him a serving spoon, then turned to leave. "No, sir."

"Or 'sir,' either," he called out as she left the room. "Woman's lived in this house almost as long as I have. I daresay, she's earned the right to call me by my first name."

"Selma," Sam and Remi said at the same time, laughing.

"Selma?" Albert echoed.

"A woman who works for us," Remi explained. "No matter how many times we ask her to use our first names, she insists on being formal. We've learned to live with it."

His expression turned cloudy, as though he'd already forgotten what they were talking about. By the time they were nearly finished with their meal, Remi was convinced the man wasn't acting. When Mrs. Beckett returned, he looked up at her and smiled. "A shame Oliver couldn't be here. Guests for dinner."

"He'll be 'round for breakfast." She handed him a thin brown leather photo album about the size of a paperback novel.

"What's this?" he asked.

"You asked me to bring it."

"Did I? Whatever for?" He opened it, turning through the handful of pages until he reached the last photo. "Don't remember putting these in here."

"Oliver went through your pictures," she said, clearing their dishes. "Put it together for you for the visit."

He stared at the last photo, then looked at Sam. "I remember. Your mother used to bring you here when you were just a lad. You and Oliver used to love banging on that old piano," he said, nodding toward the parlor. "Horrible racket, that."

"Do you play?" Remi asked.

"No. Not sure why we still have it. Belonged to . . . Well, I don't recall who."

"May I?" Sam asked.

He handed the album, still turned to the last page, to Sam.

Remi leaned over to see a photo of Sam, just a toddler, sitting on the piano bench with another boy about the same age, each wearing a suit and tie. "Oliver?" Remi asked.

Albert's smile was bittersweet. "At my son's funeral. He was just a few years older than the two of you."

Sam peered at the photo. "I don't recall any of this."

"Neither do I, most days."

Sam turned the pages, working toward the front of the book, stopping at a photo of his mother, in her late teens or early twenties, blond and dark-eyed like Sam, standing next to a dark-haired man about the same age. Judging from the hairstyle of Sam's mother, Remi guessed the photo was taken in the late 1960s or early ’70s. “Is that you?” Remi asked Albert.

He looked at the photo and smiled. “My brother, Oliver’s father,” he said, reaching out, turning to the front of the book. “This one is my favorite. Thick as thieves, those two. Always going on about that car. Something they wanted . . . For the life of me, I can’t remember.”

Sam and Remi stared. The photo was of his mother and Albert’s brother—both sitting in the front seat of what was most definitely the Gray Ghost.

You still doubt him?" Remi asked, once they were alone in their room.

"No one's that good of an actor." Albert had let Sam borrow the photo album and he was studying the photo of his mom and Oliver's father in the car. "How is it she never told me about this side of our family?"

"Maybe she didn't want the fact you're connected to royalty to go to your head?" She sat next to him on the bed, taking his phone from the nightstand and scrolling down to his mother's number. "I'm sure there's a good reason. Call."

He pressed the number.

His mother answered on the second ring. "Everything okay?" she asked. "How's Albert?"

"Fine, for the most part. Is there some reason you kept this branch of the family secret?"

She laughed. "What secret? We used to visit all the time when you were little."

"When?"

"Are you telling me you don't remember those summers in Manchester? You and Oliver used to play together."

"Other than the picture I just saw, can't say it's ringing a bell. Why'd we stop?"

"Life, your father's job. And after the terrible accident—the fire—"

"What fire?"

"At Payton Manor. If I recall, it had something to do with the old gas lighting, which hadn't been converted to electricity yet. There was an explosion, and the entire east wing went up in flames. Albert managed to get the children out, but his own son died from smoke inhalation. I'm afraid his wife never forgave him, as if it had been his fault. She divorced him not long after that. And Oliver's parents were killed just a few years later. The family's just had a string of bad luck." She gave a deep sigh. "Time and distance . . . you know how it is. We lost touch."

"I saw a photo of you and Albert's brother sitting in the Gray Ghost."

"Is that the old Rolls-Royce? I loved that car!"

"The same. I don't suppose you know anything about it?"

"Any memories I have are from decades-old photos stuffed in some box somewhere."

Sam eyed the photo in the album. "Albert told me that you and his brother were always searching for something in that car."

She laughed. "Heavens, but I'd forgotten all about that. Albert's dad was so mad when he'd discovered us in the barn. And when he learned we'd found the car, I thought he was going to die of a heart attack. He said the car was cursed and ordered us not to tell anyone about it. We were kids, playing treasure hunters. No doubt where you got your fascination for treasure hunting from."

Remi made no effort to refrain from laughing.

"Back to this curse. Did he say why?"

Libby laughed again. "To keep us out of the barn. If I'm not mistaken, they hid it there during the war. You are helping them, I hope?"

"I'm reserving judgment," he said.

"All they're asking for is a loan, Sam."

"The loan, I have no problem with."

"Then what?"

He thought about the men who'd followed them in Pebble Beach—not that he was about to worry his mother with that sort of detail. "We have a few things we need to iron out first. I'll let you know when it's all taken care of."

"At least you know they're not trying to pull one over on us," Remi said, once he disconnected.

"The only thing I know for sure is that they want money, and someone wants something they have."

"Obviously, the car."

"But why follow them all the way out to Pebble Beach when the car is here?"

They were no closer to answers the next morning when they met Oliver and his uncle for breakfast. Oliver dismissed the matter when Sam brought it up. "Why would it have anything to do with the car? Way out there?"

In a rare moment of lucidity, his uncle said, "They

want the Gray Ghost. That car's cursed. Nothing but trouble ever since."

"That's what my mother remembered," Sam said. "A curse. Any idea what sort?"

"Haven't the foggiest," Albert replied.

Oliver cleared his throat. "You should have sold it years ago." Deciding to change the subject, he smiled at Sam and Remi. "Sorry I wasn't here for dinner. A bit of an issue on one of the farms. I trust your evening was pleasant?"

"Very nice," Remi said. "Your uncle was showing us the photos you'd put together. Mrs. Beckett brought them down."

He looked at his uncle, then Sam. "His memory of those days is better than mine. Apparently, you and I were mates. Don't remember a thing about that."

"Don't feel bad," Sam said. "Neither do I."

Oliver looked over, noticed his uncle hadn't touched the food on his plate. "Eat up, Uncle Albert. We have a ten o'clock train to catch."

THE TRAIN actually passed through the southernmost tip of the Payton estate on its way to London, and Oliver pointed out a few of the farms visible in the distance. "The tenants have lived on this land for generations," he said, his voice laced with pride. The four were seated at a table, facing each other. "And I hope they continue to do so. Unfortunately, their farms aren't the most profitable."

"How long has the land been in your family?" Remi asked.

"Since the recovery of the Gray Ghost. Prior to that, it belonged to the Payton-Orens."

His uncle made a scoffing noise. "Cutthroats and thieves, those Orens."

"One Oren," Oliver said, leaning back in his seat. "Reginald Oren was responsible for the theft of the Gray Ghost and the robbery of the King's Treasury back in 1906."

"Definitely a colorful past," Remi said.

"Cursed," his uncle said again. "Reginald Oren made sure of that. Nothing but trouble ever since. That's what killed your father."

Oliver shot an exasperated look toward his uncle before looking out the window at the passing scenery. "I suppose if you can blame a farming accident on a car that had been hidden away by that time, then yes. Now, shall we find something more pleasant to chat about?"

While Oliver discussed the workings of one of their farmer tenants, Sam's gaze swept over the other passengers, noting one in particular, on the opposite side of the aisle, who was reading the newspaper. The cut of his hair reminded Sam of the man who'd followed them in Pebble Beach. Definitely not the same person; still, something about him bothered Sam.

"I could use a cup of coffee," Sam said, standing. "Would anyone else like something?"

"Nothing for me, thank you," Oliver said. "Uncle Albert?"

A soft snore escaped Albert's lips as his head fell forward.

"Guess not," Sam said. He looked at Remi, who started

to rise. "Don't get up. I know how much you enjoy the scenery. Watch it for me, would you?"

His back to the man, he gave a slight nod to his right.

Remi settled into her seat. "Don't take too long. I can use the caffeine."

Sam turned, pulling out his cell phone, his attention on the screen as he strolled past, filming everything in front of him. He left that car, walked through the next two cars, then retraced his steps. When he reached Remi's side, he held up his phone, saying, "Got so absorbed in the email, didn't realize I was going the wrong direction."

Remi smiled and pointed toward the opposite door. "Food car is that way."

"Now you tell me."

He repeated the process on his way to get the coffee. As he waited for his order, he watched the video, then sent it to Remi.

There were three men on that train watching them. The two from Pebble Beach, one in each car adjoining theirs, probably keeping their distance in case they were recognized, and the third man pretending to read the paper a few seats down.

If nothing else, it was going to make their time at the car show a lot more interesting.

LONDON

Sam warned Oliver about the men watching them on the train, telling him to keep an eye on his uncle. "Stay close," he said, noting the number of security guards in front of the convention center. "I doubt they'll approach either of you in such a public place, but it's best not to take chances."

Remi took the program from the man who collected their tickets, opening it up to the map. "Looks like the Gray Ghost is all the way in the back."

"Let's have a look," Sam said, scanning the crowd. So far, he hadn't seen their friends from the train, or anyone else who looked as though they were following them. Then again, in this venue, it wouldn't be easy to spot a tail because of the numerous vendor booths preventing a clear line of sight. Still, he was glad to see the guards manning every entrance and exit, and a number of others roamed the floor.

The four walked between rows of booths, the vendors selling everything from books about cars to the latest, greatest concoction ever formulated to restore paint luster. The scent of grilled meat drifted toward them from a stage where a cooking demonstration was taking place using a suitcase-sized barbecue meant to be transported in the trunk of a car.

"Worried about flare-ups?" the demonstrator asked the audience, then used a spray bottle to mist the cooking surface on his left with some sort of oil. Flames shot through the grill, and the audience gasped, leaning back as though they could actually feel the heat. "As you see on this off-brand barbie, your meat ends up burnt. But on our no-char surface"—he sprayed the second grill with the same mixture, nothing happened—"no flames."

"That," Remi said, nodding at the barbecue, "would have come in handy on a few of our jungle expeditions."

"If you have a car to haul it in."

"You're not willing to carry it?"

"Not even for you, Remi." They continued past the cooking show, stopping behind a gathering centered at the back of the building. The crowd parted slightly, giving them their first view of the fabled Gray Ghost. "That, however, I'd consider hauling around."

"And I'd let you . . ."

Sam, seeing that Oliver was guiding his uncle toward the car, nodded to Remi, who quickly moved to one side of the two men while Sam moved to the other, and they weaved their way through the onlookers, finally stopping at the velvet rope surrounding the Gray Ghost. The car sat on a circular platform, the overhead lights reflecting on its smooth gray paint. All the brightwork was nickel-plated, polished to a mirror finish. The blue leather interior looked smooth and supple, not a crack to be seen anywhere on its surface.

Oliver's brows went up. "Well done, don't you think, Uncle Albert?"

"I won't let them have it."

"No one's taking it anywhere."

"Eh," the old man said, his expression turning to a scowl. "Bunch of cutthroats. Only reason they haven't stolen it is because it doesn't run."

"Of course it runs," Oliver said. "Chad fixed it."

"Chad? I don't know any Chad."

"The mechanic I found." He turned toward Sam and Remi, saying, "He did a brilliant job. Even more impressive firsthand. Once they close for the day, we'll take a proper look after everyone leaves."

"I bet—" Albert stopped as alarms blared, and lights over each exit flashed on and off. Everyone in the room started looking around as though trying to decide if the alarm was legitimate. In less than a minute, security guards and uniformed personnel began herding the crowd toward the doors, while ushers went down each row of stalls, announcing that the building needed to be cleared. A few vendors balked at being forced from their booths but reluctantly left when it was apparent the alarm wasn't ending anytime soon.

Speakers crackled above them as a voice cut in: "Please walk to the nearest exit. This is not a drill. Please walk to the nearest exit. Thank you."

"Wonder what it is?" Oliver asked, taking his uncle by the arm again.

"Cooking demonstration gone bad?" Remi suggested, nodding that direction, where thick black smoke was streaming up.

"Cross that grill off our list," Sam said, drawing Remi, Oliver, and Albert toward the exit. Someone screamed when flames reached the top of the cubicle. The crowd surged forward, separating the four of them. "Uncle Albert!" Oliver turned about, trying to find his uncle.

Sam scanned the faces, looking for Albert. "You don't think he's gone back to the Ghost, do you?"

"Undoubtedly," Oliver said. "I'll check."

"We'll take a look around the booths and meet you out front. It's possible he was swept out with the crowd."

Sam and Remi split up, meeting near the entrance.

"Nothing," Remi said.

"Check outside. If you find either of them, stay close to the doors in case our friends from the train are anywhere nearby. I'm going to make another pass."

Sam worked his way around a second time, no sign of either Oliver or his uncle. The place nearly emptied, he returned to the entrance, hearing the faint sirens of the responding fire trucks. He stepped out, finding Remi waiting nearby. "Nothing."

"There's Oliver!" Remi pointed down the left side of the building.

He and Remi hurried toward Oliver as he tried to get into the building through one of the side doors.

A security guard stopped him. "Sorry, sir, no one can go back inside."

"My uncle! I can't find him anywhere."

"Fire's already out. Just a lot of smoke. You have to move away from the door."

"Let's wait up front," Sam said, drawing Oliver toward a row of benches near the entrance. "Remi and I will keep searching. You wait here in case he comes out."

"Thank you," Oliver said, surveying the faces of the people milling about. "I don't think he'll go far. He's obsessed with the Ghost."

The sirens grew louder, and within a few minutes several fire trucks sped into the drive, one parking in front, the two others driving on either side of the building.

Thirty minutes later, they still hadn't found Albert.

Unfortunately, security wouldn't let them back in the building. Oliver, pacing near the entrance, stopped and pointed to a man speaking with one of the firefighters who'd just left the building. "The event manager. He should be able to help us."

The three approached, and the man turned toward them, a neutral smile on his face. "I daresay, quite the bit of excitement, that."

"We need to get back in the building. I think my uncle's still in there. Probably worried about his car."

"Nothing to worry about. The fire's out and all the cars are safe."

"Can we go in?" Oliver asked.

"They'll be letting everyone in in just a few minutes. We've shut the cooking demonstration down. Can't imagine what anyone was thinking, bringing that sort of thing here. Not even sure how they got in the door."

As promised, security opened up the entrance, allowing those who still waited back into the building. Sam, Remi, and Oliver filed in behind the dozens of other car enthusiasts who refused to let a little smoke stop their visit. The three wasted no time, walking straight to the back, murmuring from the crowd growing in intensity.

Oliver stopped in his tracks, looking at the empty stage. "The Gray Ghost! It's gone!"

Not only was the car gone but so was Oliver's uncle.

The officer taking the missing person's report seemed very interested that Albert had disappeared just prior to the theft. "Any chance he might have taken it? Driven off, as it were?"

Oliver's face paled. "I'd say no, but he did drive off in my car a few weeks ago, wrecking it. At the time, he'd told me he was looking for the Gray Ghost. We'd just sent it to the garage for repairs."

"Would he have been able to start it?" the officer asked.

"I don't really know," Oliver replied.

"How?" Remi said. "The car was on a platform. At least a foot off the ground. Even if he could start it, how would he get it off?"

"Ramps?" the officer suggested.

Remi checked the platform, didn't see any. "Where would he have gotten them from?"

"There is one other possibility," Sam said, taking out his phone. "These three men were following us. Two of them," he said, showing the video he'd taken on the train, "were tailing us in California. The third, I've never seen before."

"Well done," the officer said. "We'll need a copy of that for the investigation." The officer gave him an email address, then looked at Oliver, asking, "You might ring up your insurance company. Let them know."

"The car's the least of my worries."

"I'm sure we'll find your uncle. If he did take it, he's bound to attract attention." He handed Oliver his card. "Give a ring if you think of anything else. Or if your uncle shows. Try not to worry. We have a crack team of investigators on it." The officer closed his notebook and tucked his pen in his pocket. "In the meantime, we'll have a look at the video surveillance. Perhaps we'll get answers there."

Remi and Sam moved off a few feet, as Oliver and the officer spoke. "You don't think he really drove off in that car?" she asked Sam.

"Unless he dragged those ramps over himself, drove the car off and hid the ramps right after, no. Hate to say it, but either Albert Payton wandered off or someone kidnapped him."

"Which makes you wonder how they got it and him out of here," Remi said.

"Smoke and mirrors?"

Oliver returned, staring at the officer's card. "I should never have agreed to let him bring that car here. He's right. It's cursed. I'm almost afraid to ring the insurance company. This has to look dodgy to them. What if they accuse us of setting up the theft for insurance fraud?"

"Why would they think that?" Sam asked.

"Because of the fraud my uncle's already being accused of. Every one of our accounts has been depleted."

Remi gave him a reassuring smile. "I'm sure it'll be fine."

"Let's hope so," he said, still searching the faces around him again. "I can't imagine where he's gone off to."

Nor could Remi, not that she was about to say it. "It's possible that he's just wandering around somewhere, unable to remember where he is."

"Absolutely," Sam said. "Why don't you wait here in case he returns. Remi and I will take a walk around, see if we can't find him."

Oliver nodded, looking eminently relieved.

Remi glanced back, making sure they were out of earshot. "What're the chances he wandered off?"

"After everything that's happened? Pretty slim. Unless that car was spirited away on a fire truck or tucked in with the barbecues, it had to have gotten out of here somehow. There's no way he drove off in it. Someone would've seen him."

"One good thing about that car," Remi said. "It's certainly going to stand out. Lead the way, Fargo."

While Oliver waited for his uncle at the entrance, Sam led Remi around the building. "It'd be nice to know which of these bay doors was used to get the Gray Ghost and the other cars in and out." The first set they passed seemed too close to the front, which would've drawn too much attention. They continued on, stopping in front of a roll-up metal door that could easily allow the cars to be moved for the show.

The wind gusted, and Remi brushed her hair from her face as she took a look around. “It seems to be out of view of the main entrance.”

“Has to be the one,” Sam said. “It’d be nice to get in there. If we can figure out how they got the Ghost out, we’ll have a better chance of finding Albert.”

“Hey! What’re you two doing back here?”

They turned to see a gray-haired security guard, probably late fifties, walking quickly toward them. When the guy lifted his radio as though to call for backup, Sam gave Remi a nudge with his elbow. “Time for a little charm.”

This area's off-limits to the public," the security guard said to Sam and Remi. "You both have to leave."

Sam stepped back, letting Remi take the lead. She smiled sweetly, waiting until the security guard was nearly on them. "Our cousin's uncle is missing and we're trying to find him. I don't suppose you've heard anything?"

"Sorry, ma'am. You'll have to check with the police. I'm just event security."

"Oh. I'm sorry. We're not from here. I saw the uniform and thought—"

"Americans?"

She nodded. "My husband and I just flew in to visit my husband's cousin. And now this. We're not even sure where to turn."

"My cousin," Sam said, following Remi's clueless American lead, "made a missing person's report. We were hoping to have a quick look around. In case he wandered away."

"Alzheimer's," Remi added. "When the fire alarm went off, we got separated. The last we saw of him, he ran toward the Gray Ghost."

The guard eyed Sam. "Your cousin owns that car?"

"His uncle, actually. The one who's lost. We think he was worried the car would be damaged in the fire."

"We were hoping," Remi said, nodding toward the door, "that he's somewhere inside the building. He gets so turned around."

The guard stared at the two of them a moment, before saying, "Don't mean any offense by it, but I heard one of the police officers asking if the old man could've driven off in the car."

"Wouldn't someone have seen him?" Sam asked.

"Good question," he replied. "You'd hope a bloke driving an antique car like that would be noticed."

"You'd think," Sam said, though he seriously doubted Albert was involved. With his diminished mental capacity, no way could he have orchestrated such a feat, never mind be an active participant.

"Could the car still be inside?" Remi asked.

"No," the guard said, shaking his head. "Not a chance."

"More important," Sam said, "could my uncle still be in there?"

"Far more chance of that," the guard said. "Plenty of places a bloke could hide."

Remi, her eyes pleading, reached out, touched his arm. "I know you're busy, but is there any way we could have a peek inside the building? What if he's in there and needs our help?"

The guard seemed to think about it, then pulled out his keys. "Couldn't hurt to take a pop in, have a quick look. Hate to think something happened on my watch."

He unlocked the side door, peering inside first before opening it wider. "Shall we?"

They followed him in, Sam asking, "How do you think they got it out? Without anyone seeing, that is."

"Hard to say," the guard said. "Bit of a dodgy neighborhood, 'round these parts."

Remi gave the motorized overhead door a pointed look. "How do you think they got it past here without anyone seeing?"

"Had to have been a truck parked outside this very door," the guard said. "All the confusion with those fire trucks up front, maybe no one noticed. Not that I saw a truck. Then again, I got called in for the fire, so if a truck managed to make it back here before the fire trucks—"

"Aren't there cameras?" Sam asked, having seen them mounted high above, encompassing both directions of the road that circled the building.

"I expect the police are on top of that."

Remi looked around, wide-eyed. "How on earth did they get the car from the auditorium to here and out the door?"

"Portable walls," the guard said, nodding toward the gray wall separating the back bay and storage area from the central part of the convention floor. "They slide open. Whoever was behind that theft had to have a crew ready to open up these walls, move the car from the floor to here, close the walls, then get the car out through the bay door and up onto the back of a truck." He opened a few doors that led to smaller storage rooms and what looked like a receiving office, with clipboards on the wall and stacks of paperwork on the desk. Albert Payton was not in any of them.

"How long would that take?" Sam asked.

"If they knew what they were doing, less than five minutes. Who'd notice in all that confusion?"

Good point. "Working here, you must have your suspicions . . . ?"

The guard gave a noncommittal shrug. "Wasn't back here, I was out front."

"No trucks drove out?"

"Didn't see even one. Not sure how they'd drive past the fire engines out front."

"So who's good for it?" Sam asked.

He looked over at Sam, his expression saying that the answer was obvious. "Don't take this the wrong way, but everyone was talking about it when we learned the Gray Ghost was entered into the car show. Car like that'd be worth millions. The first thing we all said when it ended up missing, well . . ."

"Insurance?" Remi said.

"Not saying that's what it was," he replied. "Just what I heard."

While Remi and the guard talked, Sam quickly looked around, taking everything in. If nothing else, it confirmed in his mind that this was not an operation that an old man with memory problems could handle on his own. Three men following him, however . . . "You seem to have a good grasp on everything around here. If it was an inside job, how do you think they set it up?"

"Couldn't say for sure. Interesting thing is, we had a

couple of alarms go off more than once the nights leading up to the theft, including last night. If they stole the car that quick, why not take it last night when no one was here?"

"Convenient," Sam said. "You think they were setting things up?"

"Figured that at first, but what went off was a pressure alarm beneath the car. The car wasn't moved."

"Maybe figuring out how to move it?"

"Possibly. The first night that alarm went off, they came in through the north door, on the other side of the building, then back out the same way. Whatever those blokes were doing around that car, it had nothing to do with timing the theft from here."

"Maybe because they already knew how long it'd take?"

"About as long as it took to bring it in. Roll these walls back, roll the car out, open the bay door. Not a lot to think about there."

His cell beeped and he pulled it out, reading a text message. "Sorry, but I've got to cut the tour short. Duty calls." He walked them back to the side door, opening it for them. "I'm sorry about your cousin's uncle. I'll keep an eye out. Still, I'm going to have to ask you to head up front. The back here is closed to the public."

"We appreciate your help," Sam said, leading Remi that way. The moment the guard disappeared inside, he and Remi made a beeline for the back.

As they left the convention center, Sam said, "It's highly possible that Albert was kidnapped, because he went back to the car as it was being stolen."

"Possibly," Remi said. "Or maybe he saw it and tried to follow."

"If we can figure out how they got it from the premises without being seen, maybe we can find him. If we're lucky, they took him with the car, let him out somewhere nearby."

Sam stepped away from the building for a better view of the surrounding area. The fire trucks were long gone, and the crowd milling near the building had thinned considerably. He and Remi walked toward the far side of the arena, where a truck was backing into one of the loading docks, the sign on the side reading *Charles F. Goodland Trucking*. A moment later, they saw the same security guard coming out the door, holding a clipboard, his attention on the driver, not them. The service road that circled the convention center widened near the loading dock, allowing the trucks to back in and out. A high razor-wire-topped fence separated the property from the outside neighborhood. There were also four similarly topped gates leading to streets in the neighborhood, the chain links woven with slats to block the view. If he had to guess, they were strictly for emergency access and kept locked at all times. He and Remi walked to the closest gate and he peered through its slats, seeing rows of garbage cans lined up against it. On the other side, a thick rusty chain with a padlock hanging from it secured the gate. Although both lock and chain looked intact, the space was too narrow for them to reach through and make sure it hadn't been tampered with.

"If they got out," Sam said, "it was through one of these gates."

They turned back, walking toward the convention center's entrance, still crowded with people waiting to get into the car show. When they reached the entrance, Remi nodded toward the road on the left. "I know we discounted this road earlier because the fire trucks were blocking it, but Albert could've walked in that direction on his own."

"Good idea." Judging from the direction of the rooftops, the road appeared to go in the general direction of the convention center's service area. "Maybe we'll figure out which gate that truck used and which direction it took off in."

They followed the stretch of road, the buildings on either side mostly industrial, the doors shuttered, and no cars anywhere. From the looks of it, this area closed up tight on the weekends, and for a while the only thing they heard was their own footsteps. After several minutes, though, they picked up on an odd echo, and Sam unzipped his jacket for easy access to his gun.

Remi looked back, seeing nothing but the empty street. "Sounds like we have company."

"Since we turned the corner."

She linked her arm through Sam's, glancing behind her once more, before casually leaning her head on his shoulder. "Lovely."

"Whoever it is, they're not worried about anyone hearing them."

"Good news or bad?" she asked, as they walked faster.

"Considering that they seem to have picked up the pace? I expect we'll soon find out."

The road forked in front of them.

Sam scanned the street on both sides, searching for a position of defense. A catwalk between two buildings on their left caught his eye, and he took Remi's hand, leading her that direction.

As he and Remi neared the alley, he looked back, seeing one of the men from the train following. They emerged into the alley behind the buildings. On their left was the high razor-topped gate leading to the back of the convention center, the rusty chain cut, merely hanging there, but the fence appearing secured. On their right, two more men from the train walked quickly toward them. The good news: they now knew how that truck got off the grounds without being seen. The bad news: they were trapped.

They'd been set up. Herded down the catwalk into a trap.

Sam, gun drawn, moved Remi toward the garbage cans lining the gate. The man from the catwalk jumped him, knocking Sam's gun from his hand. Remi went after the weapon as the second man launched himself at Sam. Sam threw a right hook and staggered backward, hitting one of the garbage pails, then sinking to his knees.

Remi had edged her way near Sam's gun when the third man's shadow suddenly appeared on the ground in front of her, the gun he held evident. "Don't even try it," he said.

She lifted both hands, backing away.

Sam looked over at her.

"Fargo!" she warned, as the second man moved in. Too late, he kicked Sam in the side. Sam doubled over. He caught himself on a garbage can, struggling to stand upright.

"Get him, boys," the gunman said, his expression victorious.

One of the men reached for him, but Sam dropped his shoulder, swinging the garbage can. It struck the first attacker, knocking him against the second. As Sam pushed them into the gunman, Remi knocked over a full can, rolled it across the cobblestones, garbage spilling out. One of the men stepped in the trash, lost his footing, bringing the other man down with him. Remi dove for Sam's revolver and fired, nicking the gunman's arm. He fell back against the garbage can, landing in a heap atop the other two men.

"Police!" someone shouted, as the gate rattled behind them.

Remi turned to see the security guard standing on the other side of the slatted fence and she ran over, pulled the chain, allowing him to open the gate. The three men scrambled to their feet, the garbage can rattling as they kicked it away, then raced down the alley.

"Are you okay?" the guard asked.

Remi nodded, as Sam moved next to her, she casually taking his gun and tucking it away so it wouldn't be seen. Neither of them were allowed to carry in this country and having to explain why they were in possession of a firearm would tie them up for hours. "How'd you know we were in trouble?"

"Heard the commotion from the loading dock. Followed by the gunshot . . ." He gave them both a good once-over. "No one hurt?"

They shook their heads, Sam saying, "They missed us. Are the police on the way?"

The guard nodded. "Do me a favor. Don't mention I said I was the police. We're not supposed to do that. Just thought it might speed things along."

"It worked," Remi said, as Sam examined the chain-link gate closer.

"Fire access," the guard said. "Fire Department keeps a key."

Sam pulled the chain from the fence. "I guess we know why no one saw the truck."

The security guard took the chain and lock from Sam, examining the freshly cut link. "You'd think they might've noticed this."

"Not at first glance," Sam said. He nodded at one of the still-standing garbage cans. "The car thieves cut the lock, moved the cans, replacing everything once the truck drove out."

"You think that's why those men attacked you? Seems strange they'd be watching for that long."

"Who knows?" Sam said, though Remi was sure he had a fair idea. Considering that someone had been following Oliver and his uncle since Pebble Beach, and on the train here, it stood to reason they were waiting to see what Oliver might do once the car was stolen. "I'm sure they'll appreciate you letting them know how the car was stolen. And we'd appreciate being left out of the matter. Any chance we can leave this in your hands?"

The guard eyed the lock, the dented cans. "Seeing as how no one was hurt, don't see why not."

The gunman certainly wasn't going to report his injury. Sam left his business card with the guard. "In case there're any problems. But if you can do this without our involvement, we'd appreciate it."

Sam took one last look down the alley, then he and Remi left through the open gate, back toward the convention center. "We better look for Oliver and make sure he's okay. The last thing we need is to have him turn up missing, too."

Arthur Oren paced his office, waiting for word that the car was safely on its way. Finally, the phone on his desk rang, and he picked it up when he saw Colton's number on the caller ID. "You have news?"

"Everything went as planned. The car is safely on its way back to Manchester."

"Good, good. How long until you start the next phase?"

"Depends on the old man. We're keeping him engaged until needed. There is one problem, though."

The elation Oren felt after hearing about the car suddenly faded at the tone of Colton's voice. "What problem?"

"The people from California that I told you about? Sam and Remi Fargo? They were at the car show with the Paytons when the theft went down. The two decided to investigate the area, and we thought to follow them, take them out right there. Unfortunately, the Fargo woman got ahold of her husband's gun. Frank was lucky she's not a good shot. Barely a graze. Still, the Fargos got away."

"You said they were a minor problem."

"More resourceful than we expected. Don't worry, we'll be better prepared next time."

"Let's hope so. And the next phase? You're sure there'll be no issues?"

"As I said, everything's ready. Once we get the old man back to Manchester, we'll implement it."

"What about the Fargos? If they were brash enough to investigate at the convention center, they might try to intervene in Manchester."

"We'll make sure it's not an issue."

Oren looked at the closed file folder containing his new family coat of arms. "Make sure it's not. Next time, bring bigger guns. I'm counting on you."

After several hours, with no word on Albert's whereabouts, or the location of the Gray Ghost, Sam, Remi, and Oliver took the train back to Manchester, Oliver constantly checking his phone for missed calls or messages.

"They'll find him," Remi said. "I'm sure he's fine."

Oliver nodded. "I hope so. I'll never forgive myself if anything happens to him. Allegra was against showing the car. I should have listened."

"Allegra?" Sam asked.

"My younger sister. I should call her." He stared at his phone a few seconds, as though composing himself. "I'm not even sure what to tell her."

Sam stood. "Remi and I will give you some privacy."

He smiled, gave a slight nod, then pressed her number, put the phone to his ear.

Sam and Remi stood at the opposite end of the car while he talked. Unlike their train trip to London, this time they weren't being followed. Not that he expected to see anyone now that the Ghost had been stolen.

They waited until he finished speaking before returning.

"Did you get in touch with her?" Remi asked, sitting across from him.

He stared out the window, his expression vacant. "She blames me. Saying it's my fault for losing him at the show."

Remi reached over, clasping her hand around his. "We'll find him."

"I CAN'T IMAGINE how he must feel," Remi said, as she and Sam readied for bed that night. "Having his uncle go missing on top of all this?"

"At least the police are working on it." Sam walked over to the window, looking out at the full moon. He pulled the curtains closed before getting into bed. "Hopefully, we'll learn more in the morning."

Remi climbed in next to him, fluffing the down pillow behind her head. "I hope so."

She snuggled up next to him and he put his arm around her, smiling as he recalled the way she'd flung that trash onto the ground, tripping up those three thugs, then recovered his gun. The next thing he knew, he was waking to the sound of a rooster crowing, the sun up, Remi already in the shower.

The scent of cooked bacon greeted them as they joined Oliver at the breakfast table in the Conservatory. "No word on my uncle, unfortunately. But Mrs. Beckett insists that we eat. I hope you slept well?" he asked, his smile looking strained. "Sometimes the farm noises can be distracting."

Remi smiled. “I loved hearing the sheep at sunrise.”

“Probably not the rooster?” Oliver asked.

“That,” Sam said, “we could’ve done without.”

“Life in the country. You get used to it, eventually. I know I should have noticed, but do you take coffee or tea in the morning?”

“Coffee,” they both said in unison.

He handed Remi the silver pot, looked down at his plate of food, eyeing his scrambled eggs with distaste. “I was quite hoping to hear something by now.”

“I’m sure it won’t be long,” Sam said, trying to put on a positive face. “The police in London are very competent. No doubt they’re making headway, even now.”

The housekeeper appeared, waiting quietly in the door until Oliver looked her way. “Yes, Mrs. Beckett?”

“Your sister rang. She’s at the police station. They’ve found your uncle.”

He pushed his chair back, standing. “Why wouldn’t they have called here? He’s not hurt, is he? Did Allegra say anything?”

“She didn’t, sir. Just that you should get there straightaway.”

“Thank you, Mrs. Beckett.” He looked at Sam and Remi. “Please, finish your breakfast.”

“Actually,” Sam said, “we’ll be glad to drive you. After everything that’s happened, it might be a good idea to have extra sets of eyes and ears.”

“Right you are.”

The three met out front, where Sam’s rental car was waiting, the keys in the ignition. A gray-haired man walking with a pronounced limp approached from a door in the side of the garage, nodding at them as Oliver made the introduction. "Thank you, Jones."

"Sir."

Oliver gave an embarrassed smile as he watched the elder man walk off. "It's all very formal around here. 'Sir' this, 'M'lord' that. Something I'm no longer used to. Uncle Albert hates it. Every one of these people here are like family to him and he can't figure out why they insist on all the formalities."

Sam slipped in behind the wheel, Remi taking the backseat, leaving the front for Oliver. "He mentioned that at dinner our first night."

"In truth, we really can't afford the handful of staff remaining, but my uncle couldn't bear to let them go. They have nowhere else. Allegra's son even lived here for a few years when she was going through her divorce. Nasty business, that."

"How many staff are left?" Remi asked from the backseat.

"Three families here in the manor cottages, not including the four farmers."

The drive into Manchester took about twenty-five minutes, during which Sam was glad to see they hadn't been followed. At the station, Oliver nodded toward a woman standing out front, her light brown hair pulled back in a ponytail. "My sister, Allegra," he said.

The moment she saw him, she walked over, her blue paisley dress fluttering in the wind. "Where've you been?" she asked. "I rang at least an hour ago."

"I came as soon as I heard."

"Well, not soon enough. Uncle Albert's been arrested."

"What? When? Whatever for?"

"Sometime early this morning. They're accusing him of insurance fraud for stealing the Gray Ghost."

"Preposterous. There is no insurance."

Allegra looked at Oliver as though he had lost his mind. "You didn't have the car insured?"

"Apparently, something happened, because their records show that we canceled the appointment for them to come out and look at the car. They never drew up a policy. The last time it was insured was before World War Two."

"That's not the worst of it," she said, drawing him toward the station. "They're charging him with murder."

Oliver stared at his sister for several long seconds before turning to Sam and Remi. "If you'll please excuse me, I need to find out what's going on."

"Like I said, maybe we should go with you," Sam said. "Just in case."

"I'm sorry, who are you?" Allegra asked.

"My friends," Oliver said. "Sam and Remi Fargo. They're guests at Payton Manor."

Her brows went up a fraction. "Not exactly the place to drag guests, Oliver. Is there even any furniture left?" She smiled at them. "Pleased, I'm sure. But if you'll excuse us, this is a family matter, and we need to arrange for a solicitor."

"Actually," Sam said, "we are family."

"His mother and Uncle Albert are cousins," Oliver said. "He's Cousin Eunice's son."

"It's possible we can help," Sam added, "if you can tell us what happened."

She crossed her arms, her expression turning dark.

"He's in jail. Arrested early this morning for murder. I'm not sure what else to tell you."

Oliver's face turned pale.

"Did the police say who he was suspected of killing?" Sam asked. "Or where it happened?"

"It was a warehouse fire, and the man who died was a security guard."

"A security guard? Murdered?" Remi asked.

She nodded. "The firefighters found the body after they put out the blaze. They say he was one of the security guards from the London Motor Show."

Sam looked at Remi, who was doing an admirable job of appearing very neutral. Probably she was thinking the same thing he was, that the man killed was someone involved in helping to get the car out of the showroom during the false fire alarm. "And your uncle?" Sam asked. "Where was he when all this happened?"

"That's just it, I don't know. He says he has no memory of anything but driving off in the Gray Ghost."

Oliver stared in shock. Finally, he shook himself, saying, "Uncle Albert can't remember what he had for breakfast on a good day. How would he remember that?"

"I have no idea. The police are preparing search warrants for his properties now."

"That doesn't make any sense," Oliver said. "Why on earth would he be murdering a security guard? Especially for a car he already owns."

"They're saying he did it for insurance," Allegra said.

"For the last time, the blasted car has no insurance."

"He didn't know that, did he?"

"I have no idea. Even so, that's a far cry from murder."

"Where was this warehouse?" Sam asked. "London?"

"No. Here in Manchester. On Alberg Street."

Oliver suddenly looked sick. "Our warehouse?"

"Uncle Albert's warehouse, yes. They're saying that he killed the security guard and set the fire as a distraction to steal the car."

"I still don't believe it. He could barely drive my car when he took it two weeks ago. I can't picture him trying to drive the Ghost. And, definitely, not murder anyone."

It was clear Oliver believed his uncle was innocent. But history was filled with stories of relatives being surprised how many proverbial skeletons were actually stuffed in the closets of their loved ones. And most police weren't likely to arrest without strong evidence. "What proof do they have?" Sam asked Allegra.

It was several seconds before she answered. "Video of Uncle Albert driving the Gray Ghost from the warehouse right before the fire. There was a camera mounted on the building across from it. I've asked to see the video, but they won't let me. They'll only show it to his lawyer and he doesn't have one, yet."

"Then we need to get him one right away," Oliver said.

"I'm working on it," Allegra said. "But in order to hire him, we need money, which is why I need you. You have guardianship over Uncle Albert. With no money to speak of, the solicitor is asking for Payton Manor as collateral." She pulled some papers and a pen from her purse.

"Where do I sign?"

"Oliver," Sam said. "Before you sign anything, let us at least get an attorney—if nothing else, to look over those papers."

"I couldn't ask—"

"We insist," Remi said. "This is stressful enough without worrying about losing your home."

He nodded. "Thank you. You're probably right."

"Let's go in and see what the police have to say," Sam suggested.

They learned little more than what Allegra told them. Since Oliver had power of attorney for his uncle, he at least was allowed a short visit, while the others waited in the lobby. When he walked out several minutes later, he looked as bewildered as he had when he'd first learned the news.

Allegra, who'd been pacing the entire time, stopped, looked at her brother. "Well?" she asked.

"Just as you said. The detective told me there's video of Uncle Albert climbing in the window of the warehouse just before the fire started in the office. A few minutes later, he's opening the garage doors and driving off in the Gray Ghost."

"See? Can we just sign the papers now and get him a solicitor?"

"The thing is," Oliver said, almost as if he didn't hear her, "how could he remember the location of a warehouse he hasn't been to in years when he couldn't even find his way home that afternoon he wrecked my car?"

"He wrecked your car?" Allegra asked. "Why am I only just learning about this?"

"The point is, he couldn't find his way home from downtown Manchester to Payton Manor, so how would he find his way to that warehouse from London? That's over four hours. Longer, even, when you consider the speed limitations of the Gray Ghost."

"Clearly he didn't drive it. It had to have been in a truck."

"But who drove the truck?" Oliver asked. "The dead security guard? Uncle Albert only remembers waking up in the car. As expected, he can't recall where it is."

Sam and Remi exchanged glances, Sam thinking that video evidence was pretty strong. Remi's expression was one of surprise mixed with disappointment, undoubtedly hoping for proof of the man's innocence, not his guilt. Remi tended to root for the underdog, and up until this moment, that had clearly been the case.

Apparently, she wasn't ready to give up, asking Oliver, "After talking to him, what do you think?"

"Only that he would never murder anyone."

Allegra crossed her arms, her expression stern. "Maybe not on purpose. But you have to admit, the insurance fraud . . . He still has moments when he's all there."

"Fewer and farther between. There is nothing you can say that'll let me believe he's guilty of any of this."

"The video," she said.

Oliver's face fell, and he sank into a chair. "Uncle Albert isn't a thief or a murderer. That's not how he taught me to live. And in those moments of lucidity, would a man intent on selling off the last of the family possessions to save his tenants resort to something like this?"

Remi nodded. “He has a point.”

“The problem is,” Sam said, “the police believe otherwise or they wouldn’t have arrested him. The investigators are looking for something more concrete than your belief that he’s a man of character and worth, which gets you nowhere in court when faced with this sort of evidence.”

“The most obvious?” Oliver said. “He couldn’t possibly climb in that window on his own. And no way could he drive that car at night without his glasses. Probably not even with them. You heard what happened when he took my car.”

The mystery deepened, and Sam looked at Remi, noticing her brows go up almost imperceptibly. She was as intrigued as he. “The way I see it,” Remi said, “it can’t hurt to take a quick visit to that warehouse and have a look around.”

Allegra looked aghast at Remi's announcement. "The warehouse? You think that's wise? In the midst of the police investigation?"

"We're only going to look. Should be safe enough if the police are there."

"You can't be serious, Oliver," Allegra said. "Think about it."

"I trust Sam and Remi."

"Well, I'll have no part of it." She stuffed her papers back in her purse. "If you're going to go off on this wild-goose chase, someone needs to stay by the phone in case of emergency." She stalked off, clearly perturbed by their intentions.

"She'll be fine," Oliver said. "A bit bossy, ever since her divorce, and stressed from raising her son on her own." He stood. "Shall we?"

THE WAREHOUSE was located on the south side of town, surrounded by a sea of old brick warehouses constructed around the turn of the twentieth century. The police had come and gone, as evident by the yellow crime scene tape pulled away and stuffed in a garbage can, its long ends fluttering in the breeze.

Facing the street was the main entrance, a double door constructed of heavy corrugated iron. It was a massive affair barely wide enough to allow a modern truck through. The doors were secured shut with a chain and massive padlock that looked strong enough to stop a locomotive. All the windows of the warehouse had been boarded up with plywood.

"We should walk around the perimeter of the building," said Sam.

Quietly, almost afraid of making a sound, they walked through a century of trash and foliage, pausing to listen but hearing nothing except an occasional chirping from a male bird trying to seduce a female.

As they rounded the last corner, Sam thought he heard a scraping noise behind him. He drew his gun, motioning the others to be silent. But it was nothing, just a brief puff of wind blowing a branch of a tree against the building.

Oliver eyed his weapon, looking mortified. "Is that really necessary?"

"I wish it wasn't," Sam said. Given their experience in London, he wasn't about to take any chances. He kept his gun down by his side.

"What, exactly, are you looking for?" Oliver asked.

"Not sure yet. Something out of place. Hoping I'll recognize it when I see it."

He paused in front of the building across the street,

noticing a camera mounted near the roofline and pointed toward the Payton warehouse. "Who owns that place?"

Oliver looked in the direction of the camera. "I haven't the faintest."

"Might be worth it to find out."

"He had to have climbed in one of these," Remi said, pointing to one of several boarded-up windows along the front. "The others around back are too high."

In fact, the lower part of the window frame was a little over waist-high. "He doesn't really have the upper body strength to pull himself up," Oliver said.

Remi checked out the camera on the other building. "Seems like an odd choice of entry for someone committing a crime."

Sam walked over to the recessed door leading to the office. He motioned Oliver and Remi into the protected area.

He looked at Oliver. "What did your uncle keep in this warehouse?"

Oliver shrugged. "A few old cars and farm equipment he sold off when he needed the money."

"Any chance we can get inside?"

"Of course." As Oliver pulled out his keys, a gunshot cracked, bits of brick hitting them.

Sam stepped in front of Remi as she pulled Oliver next to her in the doorway. The gunman was somewhere to their left.

Two more shots hit the wall beside them from the right. "Remi?" he called out, unable to spot the second shooter.

"We're fine. I came prepared." She already had her Sig Sauer drawn.

He gripped his Smith & Wesson, scanning the street. "Not trying to pressure you, Oliver. But we need in. Now."

"One of these keys," Oliver said.

Sam kept his focus outward, gun aimed, as Oliver, hand shaking, worked at the lock on the warehouse door, unable to find the right key.

They needed to move.

Oliver dropped the keys as several shots hit the building.

"Remi?"

"Got you covered, Sam."

She fired once in each direction as Sam gave the door a hard kick, but it didn't budge.

Abruptly, Oliver pushed Sam aside, threw his shoulder against the door, and watched as the Fargos stared, dumbstruck, at seeing it swing open and crash against its hinge stops.

"Where did you learn how to open doors like that?" asked Remi, highly impressed.

"From three years on the Manchester Unified Soccer Team—"

Oliver was interrupted by a spray of shotgun pellets that ricocheted off the bricks beside Sam. Remi wasted no time raising her Sig Sauer, and she fired around the doorway but was unable to spot the gunman. Sam laid down a short barrage of fire at two targets he spotted on the roof of the building next door.

Oliver threw his arms over his head at the crack of the gunshot, as shreds of brick cut tiny furrows in his forehead. Sam shielded Remi when she rammed against Oliver, propelling him through the open doorway. He emptied the Smith & Wesson at the gunmen on the roof. One clutched his shoulder as he fell over the edge of the parapet. He was quickly dragged away by his companions.

The office was black with soot, the floor still wet, everything reeking of charred wood. There was a second door leading into the warehouse that was also locked. Oliver threw his shoulder into it. The moment they were through, Sam slammed the door closed, Oliver pushing a heavy workbench against it. All were breathing heavily when Remi checked the men. The only injuries she found were the lacerations on Oliver's head.

"We need something heavier to block the door," Sam said, scanning the concrete floor. He spotted a rusty engine block hanging from a red hoist's chain and pulleys less than fifty feet away. Sam and Oliver, shoulder to shoulder, rolled the engine block on the hoist's overhead rail unit until it was hanging over the workbench. Oliver lowered the hoist's iron hook until the hunk of iron it was supporting thumped on the bench's surface, securely blocking the doorway. And none too soon.

They heard footsteps in the office, then someone shouting, "Get that door open."

Sam spoke to Remi in a low vice. "How many shots do you have left?"

"Three. How about you?"

"Just reloaded," Sam whispered.

"Come closer to the door," came a gruff voice. "We can't hear you."

Sam silently motioned everyone back. Just as they moved farther away, hugging the concrete floor that reeked with rancid diesel oil, a deafening blast of automatic gunfire filled the warehouse.

"Down!" Sam shouted, shielding Remi beneath him. Oliver froze, and Sam reached up and pulled him to the floor as another barrage of bullets ricocheted off the engine block. Lying on his stomach safely below the spread of bullets, Sam looked around the warehouse and took stock. It was empty except for two classic vehicles, a dark green 1929 4½-liter Blower Bentley and a classic 1917 Ahrens-Fox fire engine, against the rear wall. Frozen in time, neither looked like their tires had rolled over a street in a century. They were parked side by side next to a metal tool cabinet and under three skylights coated with layers of soot and dust that only allowed a dim blanket of daylight to leak through to the interior of the warehouse.

To their left, at the far end of the ancient building, stood the impassible corrugated iron doors, unfortunately secured on the outside with the huge chain and padlock. They saw no sign of another exit. Or useable phone.

He checked Remi, who seemed well composed, using her cell phone to call for help. Not so for Oliver, his skin tone ashen, a sheen of perspiration glistening on his forehead. Sam noticed he was cradling his right elbow, blood seeping through his fingers. Sam quickly pulled off Oliver's coat and saw a deep gash and led him to a seat behind one of the two desks pushed together as a workbench. “Remi,” he shouted, seeing a stack of clean orange rags folded on the counter near a pegboard. “Toss me a couple.”

Remi grabbed several, bringing them to him. He folded one as a compress, pressing it against Oliver’s arm, knotting two others together to hold it in place. At least it wasn’t arterial. He’d survive—assuming they could escape.

Whoever was out there wasn’t worried about stealth, their heavy boots shuffling across the floor with whatever they were doing. A few seconds later, complete silence, and Sam hoped the men had given up. But then the strong scent of diesel reached them, the oil flowing under the door, pooling beneath the engine they’d used to block it.

Suddenly they heard a new rippling sound, followed by a loud woosh, as a growing holocaust raced across the warehouse floor.

Oliver reared back, fear bordering on panic. “Fire! There’s no escape!”

Remi ignored Oliver and calmly informed emergency services that the Payton warehouse was on fire. “Please hurry. Mr. Payton is trapped inside. Please hurry,” she repeated in her best uptight tone.

Sam grabbed the fire hose from the wall, hoping it was still connected to the outside water hydrant. He aimed at the blazing fire, opened the valve, and was rewarded with a lame spurt.

Remi had pocketed her phone and grabbed an extinguisher from the rack on the wall. One twist with both hands and it broke off in a cloud of dust, along with an avalanche of mummified rat bones. Undeterred, she aimed at the fire. Nothing happened.

"Now what do we do?" Oliver muttered, shrinking into the corner.

Sam and Remi's eyes locked on each other for a moment, well aware they might never see tomorrow. In unison, they turned and stared at the old Ahrens-Fox pumper fire engine.

Sam possessed a flair for creating a plan of action during the worst of times, and it took him no more than ten seconds to calculate the odds. He held his focus. His eyes still locked on the big red fire engine—not just any engine, it was an Ahrens-Fox, the Rolls-Royce of firefighters.

His childhood passion came flooding back as he remembered riding his bicycle to a fire station with his pals, helping the firemen polish their equipment in exchange for a free ride, with siren shrieking, bell ringing.

The firemen didn't call it a fire truck, but a pumper. The engine was a massive four cylinders behind the radiator, and a maze of valves and faucets mounted beneath a big nickel-plated ball that increased pressure enough that it could throw water onto the roof of a forty-story building.

On occasion, the firemen would show the boys how to open certain valves so they could shoot water over a cornfield behind the station.

As Sam recalled the events of twenty-five years ago, when he felt he had to work a complicated crossword puzzle in just minutes, he judged the distance from the pumper to the iron door. Eighty feet for acceleration, then add the momentum and the weight of impact and deduct the drag of the flat tires.

At best, it was a toss-up.

Remi had found a piece of wire and was using it to tie her hair up in a ponytail. "Couldn't be worse," she said, with a grim smile thrown toward Sam.

Black smoke was rising and flowing through the shattered skylights and becoming a cloud that soon spread and stained the sky outside. Burning debris from the rafters fell on everything, starting small fires. The heat was already unbearable, and their breathing was starting to come in painful gasps.

"Oliver. Oliver!" Sam shouted. "Oliver!"

But Oliver was lost in fear. He sat like a statue, his face ice white, eyes glazed, blankly staring at the blazing rafters ready to fall. Remi clapped her hands right in front of his eyes, trying to get his attention.

Sam shook the man's shoulder. "Oliver! The fire engine, does it run?"

"I don't know," he murmured. "It should." He seemed to stare right through Sam as he answered. "Got the Bentley running, so we could sell it."

"Why is it still hidden away in a warehouse?"

"Collectors claimed it had a replica body and too many flaws. They all refused to pay me, so I hid it away."

"And the fire pumper?"

"My grandfather kept it in a building on the farm as a safety vehicle in case of fire in the buildings or the fields."

Sam looked at Remi with a look that belonged in a pickle jar. "If we get out of here, we'll rewrite the book."

Sam walked over to the grease pit that was sunk into a trench below the concrete floor. The flaming diesel was throwing up a torrid wall of fire like lava bursting from a volcanic eruption on the Big Island of Hawaii.

Sam had no more patience.

"What about the pumper? It's bigger and heavier, to ram the doors?"

Oliver continued to stare right through Sam. "The Bentley is . . . faster. Couldn't sell it. The deal fell through. Must have some gas in its tank."

Sam ignored Oliver's mumbled reply, rushed over to the pumper, and raised the hood. The gas valve was in plain sight. He checked to see if it was in the closed position as a safety measure in case the Ahrens-Fox had sat for any length of time. He switched the lever to the on position and then checked to see if the battery showed any signs of life. There was a weak display of sparks when he tapped the two terminals together, but not nearly enough juice to turn the big four cylinders fast enough to cause combustion.

"Is that it?" Remi asked, her voice slightly above a murmur through the clean shop rags she'd wrapped as a mask around her face to prevent her inhaling the acrid fumes. "How do you plan to start this thing?"

At that moment, Sam felt the floor vibrate under his

feet seconds before the far section of the warehouse roof crashed to the concrete floor in an explosive typhoon that seemed like it was controlled by a madman.

Faint sirens began to be heard over the deadly intensity. But by the time the firemen arrived, it would be too late.

With every minute, death crept closer. The only bit of fortune that came their way was that the Ahrens-Fox had been parked directly in front of the huge door, their only hope of escape.

Remi was standing close to Sam but spoke no more. She kept staring at those damned doors as if she could part them with her mind.

Sam looked at Remi. "Better you hop in the driver's seat than me."

Remi stared back at Sam as if he was a tree stump.

"What makes you think I can drive this old thing?"

"I have to start her from the outside. If I'm successful, I can get seated and launch the pumper in time to strike the door."

Remi shook her head. "There must be another way."

"If you don't listen to my instructions," he said hoarsely, "we all die."

She had never heard Sam speak to her with his voice so cold. A scowl crossed her face, but she said nothing. She knew this was no time to waste arguing with him when his mind was set. Every moment, fiery debris from above fell in a storm that came closer and closer to the ancient fire engine.

Sam's eyes were set, sweat was pouring down his face,

yet there was no expression of fear. He looked into the eyes of his sweetheart and said, "Time to go. Take the seat behind the steering wheel. Oliver, get onto the fire truck."

Oliver blindly tried to climb into the truck on his own. Sam gave him a boost, and he slid into the section behind Remi.

"The lever on the left side of the steering wheel controls the ignition," Sam explained. "Pull it down to its stop when the engine begins to turn over and fire. The right lever is the throttle. The top stop is the idle position. When it begins to start, jiggle it a few inches up and down to build up the revolutions per minute until the engine smooths out. Use it as you would a gas pedal on a car." Next, he gave her a quick instruction on shifting the gears of the transmission.

"How can I start it," asked Remi, "with a battery that's almost dead?"

Sam held up a hand and produced a silver-plated crank. "This is how I have to start the engine. I'll take over when the engine fires up."

"You'd better hurry it." Remi barely got the words out before the blaze surrounding the pumper began assaulting the tires that started hissing.

Sam ran to the front of the truck and yelled back to Remi, "Ignition on."

"On!" Remi repeated in a choked voice.

Sam remembered how to crank an ancient engine. He and his buddies used to drive the school majorettes onto the field before the football game in an old Model T

Ford with no self-starter that had to be cranked by hand until the engine turned over and began running.

He grabbed the crank by the handle, braced his arm, and heaved.

The crank barely moved a quarter of a circle.

Again. This time he managed to make a full swing, as the oil began circulating inside the engine. The third pull came a little easier, but there still was no indication the engine was going to start.

Sam looked up and saw flames dancing along the rafters and support beams overhead. Then as he tightened his hand on the crank, he peered through the maze of pipes, pumps, and valves over the front of the radiator to see if Remi was still conscious and able to grip the steering wheel with one hand with the other hand on the gearshift.

Grim determination was etched on her lovely face.

Sam lost track of the time as he turned the crank but still no burst of exhaust. His arms were so numb he felt as if they had abandoned his body. He began to gasp more from the physical effort than from the fumes of the fire. After a few more spins of the crank Sam was physically finished. Curiously, he was not conscious of the blisters rising on his hands. He sank to one knee, heart pounding, lungs heaving, vision fading, certain he could make only one more twist of the crank.

He would crawl up to the seats and embrace Remi for one last time.

Despite the turbulence, his body reeling, he heard her calling him.

At first, his foggy mind dismissed it. Then he saw her waving at him over the windshield. He shouted that he was done in, but she shook her head and yelled back, "The engine turned over on the last crank. I'm not sure, I think I heard it pop from the muffler."

Sam struggled to his feet and grabbed the crank handle. His final effort, urged on by his beloved soul mate. This time he swung the crank using both hands with the little strength he had left. There was a muffled pop out the exhaust pipe. Sam felt as if he entered another dimension. With renewed effort, he swung the crank again.

This time the popping sound became a low growl as Remi pumped the gas pedal to raise the rpm's. The old engine coughed a few times and began to growl, then turned over smoothly without losing a beat.

"I'll take it from here!" Sam yelled to Remi above the crackling flames now in tune with the crumbling walls of the warehouse. "Take the passenger seat and hunch down."

The huge tires hissed as they rolled over the spreading pools of burning oil. No time to be clever, Sam aimed the big silver-plated globe in front on a straight course toward the huge iron barrier, put the truck into first gear, and mashed the gas pedal to the floor.

The Ahrens-Fox approached the iron barrier at a speed Sam didn't think possible. He gripped the steering wheel with one hand and threw an arm around Remi when the pumper was less than five feet from the massive doors.

At almost the same instant of the collision, the entire roof and the two remaining walls collapsed in a black glow of whirling smoke. The pumper plunged into the great door with a horrendous crash that sounded like the burst of an explosive.

The massive door refused to fall after the old vehicle came to an abrupt stop. Sam was surprised to see so much damage to the fire engine. Amazingly, it was still running, but the valves and pumps on the front end were a mangled mess.

“Hit it again!” Remi shouted like a cheerleader at a college football game.

Sam made no reply except to grind the transmission gear into reverse, backing up fifty feet, before shifting into first gear.

Crouched behind Sam, Oliver looked as if he was lost in a tunnel.

Sam ignored the growing agony in his hands and tightened his grip on the steering wheel as he rammed the gas pedal into the floorboard. The engine rattled like it was about to blow apart, but it responded by leaping forward and smashing into the door. Agonizing seconds that seemed like a full minute passed but nothing happened. Then slowly, incredibly slowly, the hinges began tearing away from the doorframe where they had been welded. Shattered, they ripped away, the massive door seeming to hesitate, frozen in time, before falling forward and crashing flat onto the cobblestone street with a great roar. Sam steered through the burning debris until they were in the clear and stopped under gushes of water from the firemen Remi had called.

Taking deep breaths to clear their lungs, they climbed down to the street.

"Now, that was a close call, Fargo," Remi said.

"You doubted us?"

"Never us. The fire truck."

"An Ahrens-Fox? How could you?" Sam took Remi in his arms, brushed the hair from her face, kissed her sooty forehead, backed away, holding out a little something he found. "I believe this is yours. A souvenir to remember an exciting day."

Remi's eyes widened as she reached behind her head, groping in her mussed hair for the little wire she had used to tie her ponytail. Sam passed it to her. "I found it on the floorboard below the brake pedal."

Remi put her arms around his neck and pulled him down to kiss him.

"I remember now why I married you. You're hopelessly sentimental."

Once the fire department had cleared what was left of the building, and the police report made—without mentioning that Sam or Remi had shot back at the gunmen—Sam watched as the investigator took photos of the door they'd escaped through.

"You're lucky you got out," the officer said.

To be sure, Sam eyed what was left of the building. Had it not been for the antique fire engine, they would never have escaped.

He looked over at the building where the camera was mounted, asking the investigator, "Any chance we can get a copy of that video?"

"I'll check into it for you."

Turned out that the camera was non-operational.

A little too convenient, in Sam's mind, especially considering the camera was working when it showed Oliver's uncle stealing the car.

THE NEXT MORNING, at Payton Manor, as the three sat around the breakfast table, Sam wondered why they'd been specifically targeted. "Either someone was watching the place or someone told them we were on our way there."

"Nobody here would do that," Oliver said. "I trust my uncle's staff implicitly." He was looking a lot better than he had last night after they'd taken him to the hospital. The wound on his arm was deep and required a few stitches. Mostly, he was suffering from shock, but after a good night's rest he'd recovered sufficiently. "They'd never do anything to hurt him."

"Well, someone knew we were there." The real question was, for how long? Whoever it was, they had the inside knowledge of Oliver's movements ever since Pebble Beach, possibly even before. "I think we're going to have to back up a few steps. We need to talk to that attorney Selma hired for your grandfather. If anyone can tell us what's going on with this case, he can."

Sam called the number Selma had given to him, on speakerphone.

"David Cooke's office," a woman answered.

"Sam Fargo, here, with Oliver Payton. Is Mr. Cooke available?"

"One moment, please."

Cooke answered a minute later. "Glad you called," he said. "I've hired a top investigator for the case. Just heard back from him about that video the police have. According to his report, a couple of things of note. First, the white-haired man climbing in that window looks a bit too fit to be a seventy-something-year-old with memory problems. More importantly, the video's grainy enough to be useless for a positive identification."

"Which, apparently, didn't stop the police from arresting him," Sam said.

"Because of all the other circumstantial evidence, including that the Viscount owns the warehouse where the murder took place. Whoever set him up put a lot of thought into it. Which brings me to my next point. The car show in London. The cameras worked up until the fire alarm sounded as the distraction to empty the convention hall. A little too convenient that suddenly there was a malfunction, and no video exists of the theft. Also, the video from the days leading up to it were deleted."

Sam and Remi exchanged glances. "Agreed," Sam said. "Too convenient."

"It gets even more interesting. The security guard who had access to the cameras? He's the chap found dead at the Manchester warehouse fire. Autopsy still pending."

"Anything on him?"

"Not yet. Scotland Yard's working on restoring the digital images leading up to the fire alarm. Unfortunately, that's all my investigator has so far."

"That's a good start," Sam said.

"Quite. I can tell you this much, though. It doesn't seem to be a crime of opportunity. My investigator informs me it seems to be a rather sophisticated operation. A lot went into the planning, even killing one of the men involved. In other words, Mr. Payton needs to be careful, as does anyone around him."

"We'll all be careful," Sam told him. "Thanks for the update."

"That," Remi said, as Sam disconnected the call, "certainly is troubling."

Oliver's brow furrowed as he looked at Sam. "I have to wonder about the dead security guard. Why go to all the trouble to kill him? Just so Uncle Albert would be arrested?"

"If I had to guess," Sam replied, "it was to make sure nothing led back to whoever's really behind this. You and I both know your uncle couldn't have done this on his own, which means that security guard was a loose end. Your uncle was a convenient target to throw suspicion."

Oliver folded his napkin, set it on the table, pushed his plate away. "Who would do this to him? He must be worried sick."

"At least the solicitor Selma hired has a decent investigator to help look into things," Remi said. "We don't have to wait for the police to release the details."

Sam checked his phone. "Speaking of . . . Text from Selma." He opened it, read it aloud: "Rolls-Royce commissioned two demonstrator cars to be shown at the 1906 Olympia show. When the Gray Ghost was damaged, they replaced it with the unfinished Silver Ghost, which made its official debut in March of '07."

"Nothing else about the Gray Ghost?" Remi asked.

"Looks like the Silver Ghost got all the attention after that."

"Prettier paint job?" Remi said.

"That, and more press," Oliver added. "The Gray Ghost was the one that suffered the hard knocks before they put the Silver Ghost through the trials."

"This is interesting," Sam said, scrolling through the text. "There's no official record of the Gray Ghost. Selma says the chassis number you gave us, 60543, isn't registered. Every source she found shows that they skipped that number—which would have been on the fourth chassis." Sam looked up from his phone, eyeing Oliver. "Know anything about that?"

"As a matter of fact, yes. A rather unusual story, in fact."

Maybe more tragic than funny," Oliver began. "Back in 1906, when the Gray Ghost was stolen, the current viscount, being friends with Rolls and Royce, invested everything in their company. More specifically, in the development of the forty-fifty. He was counting on the return on his investment to pull him out of the debt incurred by his nephew's gambling. Very much like my uncle's situation, he was worried about his tenants. And there was an orphanage he supported. And, well, the point is, he was counting on that car making the Olympia show to make him money.

"It's been a while since I read the history, and some of the details are fuzzy. Something to do with an American detective, Isaac Bell, from the Van Dorn Detective Agency, on the hunt for two men wanted in New York for bank robbery and murder. Thanks to Isaac Bell, the man and his gang were caught, and Bell was rewarded by the Crown for the recovery of the treasure—well, part of it at least."

"Exactly what did that have to do with the Gray Ghost?" Sam asked.

"As I said, a bit of a tragic story. Especially considering how it was this detective crossed paths with the Payton-Orens and the train robbers."

"Payton-Orens?" Remi said.

"The former family name before the Fourth Viscount had a falling-out with his younger brother, the older taking the name Payton, the younger Oren, the two never talking again."

"Must've been some argument," Sam said.

"Over a woman, I believe. Though, not as bad as what came later. At least no one lost their life over it. In truth, it might be easier if you read about it yourselves rather than trying to glean anything from my faulty memory. The early viscounts all kept a family journal."

"You think there's one from the time period when the Gray Ghost was stolen?"

"Absolutely. I was duty-bound as the heir to learn family history. Some of the journals were rather dry. That one, however . . ." Oliver stood. "Let's have a look, shall we?" He led them down the hall into the library, pausing in the doorway. "I'll get the curtains. It's a bit dark in here." He crossed the room and pulled open the drapes, light spilling across a bare parquet floor into a room devoid of all furniture. Floor-to-ceiling shelves filled with books lined all four walls, however. "My uncle couldn't bear to part with the books . . . Some have been in the family for centuries."

"Impressive collection," Remi said, examining a few.

He smiled to himself as though remembering happier times, then walked up to one of the shelves, his fingers skimming over the spines of thin leather-bound volumes. "Should be here somewhere . . . Odd," he said, looking on the shelf above it and the shelf below. "I don't see it."

Sam joined him, searching through the volumes. "Maybe out of order?"

"They're numbered," he said. "Volume five is missing."

"Or misfiled," Remi said.

They started searching the shelves, though Sam doubted they'd find it. With everything that had happened to Oliver and his uncle so far, no doubt someone had taken that volume. "Any idea what was in it?" Sam asked.

"Read it a few times, as a lad. Quite the writer, my ancestor. I daresay, a few of his stories were worthy of being published. Less a journal, more like a novel. The story of that detective and how he rescued the Gray Ghost was as exciting to me as any modern-day superhero. But that was many years ago. Some of the finer details escape me." He stood there, staring at the shelves, then pulled a slim volume out, handing it to Sam. "This might be a good one to start with. It's the journal right before the theft of the Gray Ghost." He opened it, quickly turning through the pages until he was close to the end. "This is the next-to-last entry in this volume. And where I think it all started."

JOURNAL OF JONATHON PAYTON, 5TH VISCOUNT WELLSWICK

1906

Nearly a week after the Ghost was stolen, Mr. Royce called me into his office and handed me an envelope, asking me to take it to the address given, then wait for an answer.

My being sent on an errand wasn't unusual, and so no one seemed to notice when I took my overcoat and left. I looked at the envelope, saw it was addressed to a Mr. Isaac Bell at the palatial Midland Hotel, the same establishment where Mr. Rolls and Mr. Royce first met when they decided to form Rolls-Royce Limited. When I arrived, I was met by a tall blond-haired mustachioed man dressed all in white who'd, apparently, been watching for me.

I handed him the envelope.

He opened it and read the missive, his eyes moving from the letter to me on occasion. When he finished reading, he tucked the letter and envelope into his breast pocket, telling me that his answer was yes, that he accepted the offer of my assistance . . .

I STARED AT THE MAN, who'd introduced himself as Isaac Bell. "Forgive me," I said. "I'm not sure I understand."

"Your employer didn't mention that I'm a private detective?"

"No, sir."

"With the Van Dorn Agency. I'm here about the train robbery."

The crime had occurred several days after the Grey Ghost was stolen. Three men had been killed, shot by the robbers. A king's ransom stolen, and, along with it, the machined engine parts that Rolls-Royce hoped to use to put together a working forty-fifty engine in time for the Olympia Motor Show.

It suddenly occurred to me that one of the dead men had also been a private detective hired by Rolls-Royce to find their stolen car. "I'm so sorry. This man was a friend of yours?"

"I didn't know him, but he was an associate, and I have an allegiance to find out who killed him. I've been hired to find out who killed the three men and who robbed the train."

"Forgive my impertinence, but why am I here?"

"Your employer has offered your services to assist me in my investigation."

"But why?" I asked, certain there must be some mistake.

"I need someone who knows the area. As such, it's important that you tell no one that we're working together. Three men have already been killed. I'd rather not add another to that count."

I wasn't sure what frightened me more: that this Mr. Bell expected me to agree to this working arrangement or that when he talked about death the warmth in his eyes turned to steel. "Why me?" was all I could manage.

"I asked for someone trustworthy, but also someone whom no one would suspect would have the nerve to work with a detective."

I couldn't help a twinge of embarrassment over that description. Shadows made me jump. No one would suspect me of having the nerve to do anything remotely brave. "Perhaps you misunderstood. I'm certain you'd rather have my cousin, Reggie. He's the brave one in the family."

"You care about Rolls-Royce?"

"Of course," I said, not fully realizing that Bell had drawn me outside and into a waiting carriage.

"Then you'll do." Before I knew it, we were halfway down the street, when Bell asked, "What do you know about the train robbery?"

"The engineers were killed. And a private detective."

"He was hired by Rolls-Royce. There were engine parts on that train."

A feeling of guilt hit me. "I ordered those parts."

"Don't you find it the least bit odd?"

"Surely it was a coincidence."

"Interesting you'd say that," Bell replied, "because that's precisely what I was wondering."

Several minutes later, the carriage stopped, the driver letting us out on a street corner next to a brick building about four stories high.

Bell pointed toward the railroad tracks. "That's where it happened."

I looked in that direction, feeling slightly nauseated at the thought.

"If I'm not mistaken," Bell continued, "it was just before dawn. The night watchman found a load of lumber spilled at the crossing."

"A setup to stop the train?" I asked.

Bell glanced at me. "You're a quick study. You'll do just fine." We walked closer to the railroad tracks. "The detective who'd been following one of the robbers was killed right here. In the street. Shot in the back." Isaac stared at the ground for several seconds, then to his right, where wooden stairs led up to a second-story entrance. "Which doesn't make sense. By all accounts, he was very experienced. Why?"

"Running for his life?"

Isaac pulled out a gold pocket watch. "What time was the robbery?"

"Just before dawn."

"I'll see you then."

"I beg your pardon?"

"Here. Tomorrow. Before dawn." He started to turn away, then stopped. "If Mr. Royce didn't inform you, you're not to tell anyone that we're working together."

"WHAT ARE WE LOOKING FOR?" *I asked at dawn the next morning. We were standing at the tracks where the robbery had taken place.*

"Wondering who's out at this hour. Besides us, of course."

No one that I could see. The brick-fronted factories were dark. We turned right, the streets empty, no sound but our own footsteps.

Suddenly Isaac stopped. "Did you hear that?"

"Hear what?"

"A tinkling bell," he said. "This way."

We crossed the street, turned the corner, and discovered a bakery open for business. A bell rang as he opened the door, the scent of fresh bread greeting us as we entered.

A gray-haired shopkeeper was handing change to a young woman, who had several loaves in the basket on her arm. Isaac held the door for her as she left, then introduced himself to the baker, asking if any of his customers had mentioned seeing anything out of the ordinary the morning of the train robbery.

"Naught but servants out that early," the shopkeeper said. "None mentioned anything to me." We thanked him, and started to leave, when he added, "Of course, there's the boy."

"What boy?" Isaac asked.

"Caught him digging through the rubbish one morning a few weeks back, so I started leaving the burnt loaves by the door. Make it easier for him, poor lad. A few loaves were missing the day of the robbery. None the next few days. Hasn't been back since."

"Any idea where he lives?" Isaac asked.

"I'd guess, the streets. Skin and bones, that one. Sometimes a younger lad comes with him."

The baker showed us the back door that was cracked open wide enough to let out his tabby cat and, next to the door, a wooden crate filled with the burnt bread.

I stared at the unappetizing rolls with their blackened bottoms, at once saddened and horrified to think anyone could be so hungry as to dig through rubbish or steal into a shop to take the cast-offs. What I wasn't prepared for was Isaac's suggestion that we come out each morning to wait for the lad.

"How will that help?" I asked.

"The fact he stopped coming after the robbery is telling," Isaac said. "Perhaps he saw something."

We returned the next morning, watching as the baker let out his cat, then he disappeared to the front of the shop as the little bell rang, announcing the first of an early string of customers. At least we were able to sit in the kitchen near the warmth of the ovens instead of the cold alley out back. On the third morning, after the baker opened the door for his cat, Isaac and I again waited. Just as I'd convinced myself this was a waste of time, a soft scrape outside the door caught our attention. In the shop, behind us, the little bell tinkled over the front door, making me wonder if the sound might scare off whoever was out there. I started to move toward the back to peer out, but Isaac lifted his finger, urging me to remain where I was. After several seconds, certain that the arriving customer had scared off our would-be burglar, I saw a small hand reach in, grasping one of the rolls, noting the child's fingernails curiously clean for so young a thief.

Oliver cleared his throat as he looked up from the journal. "Perhaps this one starts a little too early. In case you haven't guessed, Reginald Oren had it in for his uncle and was skimming from the orphanage and sabotaging Rolls-Royce by stealing the Gray Ghost. The next journal goes into more detail on how the Ghost came into my family's possession. Given to us in thanks."

"That's quite a thank-you gift," Remi said.

"Small, when you think about who Reginald was planning to sell the Ghost to. A competing motorcar company wanted the forty-fifty plans. They were trying to put Rolls-Royce out of business."

"So the Gray Ghost never made the show?" Sam said.

"No. They put the Silver Ghost in instead, even though the coachwork hadn't been completed. And the rest, as they say, is history."

"Imagine," Remi said. "Sitting on a car that valuable all these years and not even knowing it."

"Considering the car's missing and Uncle Albert's accused of murder," Oliver replied, "it doesn't really matter at this point, does it?"

"We're going to find it, and whoever's behind setting up your uncle."

Oliver gave a nod. "Let's hope so."

"You were saying something about a reward," Sam said. "For the recovery of the treasure. Was it significant?"

"Truthfully, I have no idea. Why?"

"Right before we flew out, Selma found some reference to the robbery of the King's Treasury. Something about not all of it being recovered."

"What rubbish," Oliver said. "Someone thinks that treasure's sitting in the boot of the car?"

"That, or the reward you were talking about."

Oliver shook his head. "As much as I'd love that to be the reason, I was there when we pulled that car from the barn. The only thing we found was decades of dust."

"The possibility exists that someone thinks the treasure's connected to the Gray Ghost."

"I suppose it's worth exploring," Oliver said. "But the Gray Ghost wasn't the only forty-fifty that Rolls-Royce gave out as part of the reward. There were two other forty-fifties included," he said, searching a different shelf for the missing book.

"Three?" Sam said, looking over at him. "You mean there's more than one forty-fifty from that time out there?"

"What? Well, yes. The Gray Ghost, of course, and two others, one to the American detective and one to the Viscount's friend who helped the night they recovered it."

Sam looked over at Remi. “We should have Selma look into those other two cars. Maybe there’s some connection.”

Remi made the call. When Selma answered, she put her on speaker, and Remi caught her up on what they knew so far.

Selma was intrigued. “Two other forty-fifties? During the same time?”

“Any chance you know what the value might be?” Sam asked.

“Not an exact price. More like hot gossip from the London Motor Show. Thirty to thirty-five million was the average value being tossed around. Lazlo said he heard that if it went up for auction, it might sell for as high as forty million.”

Sam whistled. “Quite a haul. Especially if there are two others out there.”

Oliver, who was still searching the shelves for the missing journal, nodded. “In fact, they were all outfitted by Barker and Company.”

Sam moved to Remi’s side, telling Selma, “Might be a good idea to see what you can find on those two cars. Never know what might turn up.”

“I’ll get on it,” Selma said. “Who were the original owners?”

“A detective who helped with the arrest in ’06,” Sam said. “The other person.”

Oliver’s nose was buried in one of the diaries. “I’m just looking it up now. This is the volume after the missing one. Rather boring in comparison, but it does mention something about the cars . . ." He turned a few pages, scanned, turned a few more. "The writing's difficult to decipher at times. Some of the ink seems to have faded over the years."

Sam looked over Oliver's shoulder, trying to read it himself. "If it's okay with you, we could overnight this to Selma, let her and her assistants take a look. They do a pretty good job when it comes to restoring documents."

"I don't see why not. As long as we get it back."

"We'll take good care of it," Selma said. "How many volumes are there?"

"About twenty," Oliver said.

"And one's missing?"

"The one detailing the theft of the Gray Ghost."

"Any other volumes mention the car?" Selma asked.

"A couple of them do," Oliver said, apparently well versed on what they contained. "One's from World War Two. It details when Uncle Albert's father hid the car in the barn we found it in."

"What about local experts?" Selma asked. "Anyone else who knows the history of your car? Might be worth talking to."

"Actually, there is," Oliver said. "The mechanic who worked on the Gray Ghost. We picked him because of his expertise in Rolls-Royce restoration."

"Exactly how much work did he do on the car?" Sam asked.

"Had the car for a good fortnight before we got it back. Surely he would have mentioned something if he'd found anything important, wouldn't he?" Oliver glared at the diary, then at them. "Blast it all, I'm being naive about that, aren't I?"

Sam glanced at Remi. "Guess we know where we're off to next."

The moment Arthur Oren stepped out of his town house, down the steps, to the front walk, Colton's black Mercedes rolled up—one of the things he liked about the man: his extreme punctuality. If he said he was going to be somewhere at a certain time, he made it happen.

"I trust things are going according to plan?" Oren asked, as he slid into the passenger seat.

Colton checked the side mirror, then pulled away from the curb. "As expected. As long as everyone keeps their end of the bargain, we should be fine."

Arthur looked at him, but the man's gaze was fixed out the window, presumably on the traffic. "What do you mean by that?"

"Exactly what it sounds like. Everyone knows their part, the payments are made, I expect all to continue without issues."

To Arthur, it sounded almost like a veiled threat, but he chose to let it go. For now. He didn't want anything to ruin this moment. They were finally on their way to see the Gray Ghost, find the secrets it held, and take the next step in securing his fortune and his hold on the Payton estates. All the planning, all the dreams, were finally coming to fruition, and he settled back in his seat, forcing himself to relax during the drive.

Colton, however, broke the silence with the worst sort of news. "The old man has a solicitor. My understanding is, he's very reputable."

Reputable meant competent, something they'd hoped to avoid. "He was supposed to be destitute," Oren said. "How can a man who hasn't a cent to his name afford that?"

"Oliver, it seems, has convinced the Fargos that his uncle is worthy of their help. They hired the attorney."

"Out of the goodness of their hearts? I find that hard to believe. There has to be some sort of collateral. They barely know—" He stopped, looked over at Colton. "The only thing of value Oliver and his uncle have left besides Payton Manor is—was—the Gray Ghost."

"Maybe that's it," Colton said, signaling for a right turn, never once looking at Oren. "It'd make sense. Not that it'll do them much good. They're hoping to recover the Ghost, no doubt, and we both know that won't happen."

Oren drummed his fingers on the center console, his well-manicured nails clicking on the burled wood. They could hope all they wanted. The Paytons were never getting their hands on that car again. Even so, he wouldn't relax until he'd completed the rest of his plan. They needed to keep the Paytons' finances on the brink. One step away from disaster, all so Oren could deliver the final blow and see them ruined forever. That would be his vindication, he thought, suddenly noticing that Colton had slowed down considerably. The road leading to the warehouse was a straight shot, the better to see anyone approaching. "Is something wrong?"

Colton eyed the buildings, checked his rearview mirror. "It never hurts to take precautions. I don't like surprises."

"Neither do I. Now, back to the Fargos. What do you intend to do about them?"

"That depends on how involved they plan on getting. If they're merely offering up the services of this solicitor and his investigator, have at it, I say."

"What if they get the old man off?"

"They won't. The evidence is irrefutable. Otherwise, the police wouldn't have made an arrest. So far, all they've received is a copy of the police report and the video, neither of which will do them any good."

"You'd better be right," he said, as they cruised past the warehouse. Colton pulled around and parked in the back. "After all the problems Oliver has caused, the last thing we need is more distractions."

Colton looked at him, as he shut off the engine. "*Distractions* being the key word. It won't alter the endgame. As I said, everything's going as planned."

"Really?" Oren asked, as they got out and walked up to the warehouse door. "I thought you were planning on taking the Fargos out. What happened with that plan?"

"A slight setback, is all. They've turned out to be a bit more troublesome than anticipated."

"How hard is it to knock off two socialites?"

Colton gave him a sidelong glance, as he paused to light a cigarette. He blew out a long stream of smoke, then said, "Is that what you think they are? Or did you not read the dossier I sent?"

"I did. But I thought you were better than that."

"Because I am better than that, their social status is exactly why we can't kill them without careful planning. Especially after that fiasco at the Payton warehouse. Like it or not, they're connected to Oliver. If they go, it needs to appear unconnected to the Paytons or you'll risk scrutiny when you take over the estate."

Deep down, he knew Colton was right. It was, after all, why he hired the man. To make sure mistakes weren't made. "Maybe step up the planning."

Colton ignored him, as he unlocked the door and the two stepped inside. Cigarette hanging from his mouth, he keyed the code into the alarm pad, switched on the lights. The two men turned around, staring at the empty space.

Colton ripped the cigarette from his mouth, dropped it onto the ground. "I don't understand . . ." He pulled out his phone, called one of his men. "Where's the Gray Ghost?"

The volume was high enough for Oren to hear the silence at first before his man said, "What're you talking about? It was right there last night when I set the alarm."

"Well, it's gone."

It took a moment for Oren to register what he was seeing and hearing. When he finally came to his senses, he looked over at Colton. "Tell me again how everything's going according to plan?"

Allegra was ambitious. Which is why it troubled her to know that Oliver, someday to be the 8th Viscount Wellswick, cared less about the title and more about the farmers. She, on the other hand, had a son to think about, which was what made their family history so interesting. Chances were good that if Oliver continued down the path he was on, her son would inherit everything.

Whether there'd be anything left to inherit remained to be seen, she thought, looking over at her ex-husband, Dex Northcott, who sat at the dining table, reading, while he ate the leftovers she'd hoped to save for dinner. A slow reader, he turned a page, paused to look over at the television in the front room, where a football game was on. The player dribbled the ball past the defense, then kicked it. When the goalkeeper caught it, Dex turned back to the book, the fifth journal, which told the story of the Gray Ghost, stolen in 1906, and how an American detective named Isaac Bell had helped to find it, all while he was hunting down a group of notorious bank robbers.

She regretted the day she'd ever told him that story,

one she'd first read when she was about her son's age, her early teens, after Oliver had found and read it. Back then, she'd thought it was all made up. One of her ancestors having a bit of fun with their family history. It wasn't until her uncle had brought out the Gray Ghost, hidden in a barn on the property, that she'd even recalled the story. Apparently, she wasn't the only one.

"Mum . . ."

She nearly jumped. Her son, Trevor, was staring at her. "Did you want something?"

"I asked where the Nutella was."

"Same place as always. In the cupboard."

"We're out."

Dex gave them an annoyed look. "Do you mind? It's hard enough reading this ancient cursive without you two making all that noise." Loud cheering broke out on the television, and he looked that direction but was unable to see because Trevor was standing in the way. Swearing, he slammed the book onto the table, then stalked around the boy and into the front room.

"Let's have a look, shall we?" Allegra said, walking over to the cupboard and opening it. "Imagine, right where I told you it was," she said, pulling out the Nutella jar. When she turned around to hand it to him, he'd picked up the journal from the table and was reading through the pages.

"Why's Dad reading this? Looks pretty old."

"It's nothing," she said. "Belongs to the manor."

He turned away when she tried to take it from him. "Is it Uncle Albert's?"

"Sort of." One thing Trevor had developed over the

years he'd lived with her uncle was a deep and abiding love for the man. Which meant she had to be careful if she didn't want him to develop an inordinate interest in the book. All it would take was a few computer clicks, and he was bound to start linking some of the more unusual goings-on with what was in that journal. Since that was the last thing she needed, she gave a casual shrug. "His great-great-great-grandfather, or some such. Known for his tall tales, according to Uncle Albert."

"Really?" He turned another page and walked out of the room, forgetting about his sudden need for food.

She would have gone after him if her cell phone hadn't buzzed and she had to backtrack to the front room to find it, where she'd left it on the coffee table. Annoyed and disturbed when she saw the caller ID, she answered. "I told you not to call me here," she said, lowering her voice.

"The Gray Ghost is missing."

Before she even had a chance to process his words, her ex-husband moved in behind her, grabbing her phone so that he could hear the call as well. Her heart started thumping. "Missing?" was all she could manage. "How?" she finally added.

"We're still trying to figure that out."

"Did you have a chance to search it?"

"Not yet. Who's good for it?"

"Good for what?" she asked.

"Who do you think has the car? Who stole it?"

With no idea what to say, she closed her eyes, feeling Dex's hot breath on her fingers as he gripped them and the phone, listening in on the call. "Chad," he whispered in her ear.

She pulled away, looking at him, confused.

He pointed to the phone, mouthing the name again.

"Chad . . . ?" she said aloud. Dex nodded.

"Who's Chad?" the caller asked.

"The mechanic he hired. Supposed to be one of the foremost experts on those antique clunkers. The only one who knew he had the car to begin with. Oliver is on his way to see him tomorrow." She heard the faint squeaking of the chair in the office. "I have to go. My son's home."

"I'll call tomorrow." The phone beeped when the call ended.

"Nicely done," Dex said.

"What are you talking about? Who else would take the car?"

He turned toward the dining table, grabbed her arm, holding it tight. "Where's the journal?"

Her heart skipped a beat at the anger in his eyes. "Trevor has it."

"How'd that happen?"

Because you're an idiot, she wanted to say. "It was sitting on the table. He saw it and picked it up."

"And you didn't think to take it from him?"

"I didn't want to draw attention to it. I know my son," she said, a subtle dig that Dex had never been there for them. "It's bad enough that he's questioning your presence here. He'll grow tired of reading it and get back to his computer. We just have to wait."

He squeezed harder, his fingers digging painfully into her flesh.

"Are you quite finished?" she asked, refusing to cry out.

"For now."

He pushed her arm away in disgust, stormed over to the armchair, sitting down with enough force to move the heavy piece of furniture back a few inches.

Long ago, she'd learned that it was better to remain on an even keel when dealing with him. Now that he was back, it was even more important. For Trevor's sake.

She walked to the office, peeking in the door, her son barely noticing her, absorbed in reading the diary. Trevor had taken over the room after her divorce, somehow putting together a computer from the boxes of electrical equipment that her ex had left behind, then working a part-time job and buying a newer desktop. These days, he was perfectly happy staying in that room, glued to the monitor, doing, well, whatever it was he did on the computer. The only time he came out was when he had to go to school or to eat. In the past, his isolation worried her. Now, however, she was grateful.

It kept him out of Dex's affairs.

She looked back toward her ex, his focus on the telly. Perfect. Quietly, she stepped into the office. According to Trevor's teachers, his comprehension of the written word—unlike his father's—was more than brilliant. He retained nearly everything he read. Moving closer, she peered over his shoulder to see what he was reading.

25

JOURNAL OF JONATHON PAYTON, 5TH VISCOUNT WELLSWICK

1906

T was my fault. I tried to grab the boy's wrist, but he saw us, taking off down the alley as fast as a cellar rat chased by a cat. Isaac Bell and I raced after him. When we emerged from the alley to the street beyond, there was no sign of the child.

Isaac, certain he couldn't have gone far in that time, drew me back into the alley, insisting we wait, in his words, "for however long it takes."

We hunkered down near a refuse pile, the smell of soured trash almost overpowering at first, then fading as our senses dulled. Isaac and I both wore heavy overcoats and gloves, protecting us from the cold. The child had neither, and the quick glimpse of his arm I'd seen at the shop told me that the patched sleeve of his threadbare coat was far too thin to offer much warmth.

As the cold permeated through my heavy layers, I felt certain the child must have escaped or was freezing to death somewhere because of our presence. About to suggest that we split up and begin a search, Isaac pointed to our left. The child emerged from an alcove across the street, where stairs led down to a basement door of the mercantile building. He hovered at the top of the stairs, edged his way out, raced 'round the corner. Isaac and I followed as the boy ran toward the railroad tracks . . .

"WE HAVE HIM," Isaac said, bolting down the street.

I could scarce keep up with the detective as he raced after the child, cornering him beneath the stairs of a factory about midway down the block.

By the time that I caught up with them, I was completely out of breath. "We mean no harm," I said, my chest heaving.

The boy cowered against the wall, his eyes wide with fright, as he regarded us. He lingered on me, as he slowly stood, edging away from Isaac. Suddenly he darted past me.

Isaac was faster. He grabbed the boy, lifting him in the air and holding him out, as the urchin squirmed and kicked.

"I'm sorry, I'm sorry!" the boy cried. "You can have the bread. I won't do it again. I won't!"

"Hush," Isaac said. "We don't care about the bread."

"Let me go!"

"Information. We're willing to pay." Isaac looked over at me. "Show him the money."

It took a moment for his words to sink in. I quickly

reached for my coin purse, holding out two shillings for the boy to see. "Yours," I said, "if you'll talk to us."

He eyed the money, his demeanor changing from scared to suspicious. But then he looked at my face, his eyes going wide. Suddenly he struggled harder, shouting, "I won't tell. I won't. I promise! I promise! Please let me go."

Isaac nearly lost his grip on the boy. "Won't tell what?"

The boy refused to look up again, this time angling his eyes downward. Which was when I recognized him. My father had insisted I attend a meeting at the orphanage to learn why there was a shortage of money. It had been that day. "I saw you at the children's home."

Tears sprang to the lad's eyes, and he seemed to crumple in Isaac's arms, the fierce wildcat turning into a trembling mess. "Please don't hurt me. I didn't see anything."

I was about to reassure him when Isaac asked, "What didn't you see?"

"That man what killed them blokes. I didn't see. I didn't." He buried his face into Isaac's chest, struggling to breathe as loud sobs wracked his chest.

Isaac held him tight, as he looked at me over the top of the boy's head. "I believe we have found our witness."

WE TOOK THE BOY to Isaac's suite of rooms at the Midland Hotel, where we discovered that food was a far better motivator than any amount of money. Isaac questioned him as he ate, and, with each answer, I felt my world crashing in.

"He's mistaken!" I said, unable to believe the child's words. "There's no other explanation."

"That remains to be seen," Isaac said, sitting at a table in the parlor in front of an arched window that overlooked the street below, the clip-clop of horses' hooves and the squeak of carriage wheels drifting up. Isaac looked at the open door to the next room, where the child had fallen asleep on the bed. "You believe the lad saw you and your cousin at the orphanage a few days before the robbery?"

"That had to have been it. My father asked me to have a look at the ledgers, due to a sudden shortage in funds. As patrons of the charity for the orphanage, he feels it's our responsibility to ensure that nothing was amiss."

"And what were the findings?"

"My cousin assured me the books held only one or two errors. Nothing that would suggest a mismanagement of the funds."

"Your cousin assured you? This wasn't your assessment?"

I felt a twinge of worry. "He offered to look at the books. He's much better at figures."

"Was there anyone else with you besides your cousin that afternoon?"

"Our driver."

"Did he ever leave the carriage?"

"No."

"Only you and your cousin?"

"He's not a thief."

"Quite possibly he's a murderer. Which is far worse."

"Impossible. He and his wife have a newborn son. He'd never—"

"By any chance does your cousin gamble?"

"Occasionally. I know he's had a few losses. But nothing

terribly serious." A feeling of dread came over me as I reflected on the various times Reginald had borrowed money after a night at the gambling halls. But he wasn't so heartless as to steal funds meant to feed the poor and destitute . . .

Or was he? If he could do that, was it a far cry to think he could arrange a train robbery and murder any witnesses? "Surely, you don't think . . . ?"

Isaac leveled his gaze on me. "We need to have a look at those ledgers."

Remi waited next to their rental car while Sam put their suitcases in the trunk.

Oliver reluctantly handed over his own suitcase. "Do you really think this is necessary?" he asked, as Sam put it in next to the other two, then closed the lid. "Staying somewhere else?"

"Definitely."

"Because," Remi said, seeing how worried the man lookcd, "if Sclma finds out whcrc thcsc two othcr cars are located, we'll be ready to go."

When Sam looked over at her, as he walked around to the driver's door, she raised her brows, tilting her head toward Oliver. The man had enough to worry about without the added burden of what might happen if they stayed at Payton Manor. "Right," Sam said. "Save us a trip back here. The sooner we get all this information together, the better for your uncle."

"Didn't think of that," Oliver replied, taking the backseat, behind Remi, as Sam slid into the driver's seat.

Remi smiled at Oliver, glad to see he appeared relaxed.

The real reason they had him pack a bag was that they didn't trust that they'd be safe at the manor. That morning, just before dawn, Sam had awoken to a dog barking. When he got up and looked out the window, he'd seen someone in the distance, watching the house. The moment the sun came up, the man drove off in a dark sedan.

Not that he or Remi had been surprised, especially after everything that had happened these past few days. It did, however, give them reason to suspect that Oliver might not be safe if left on his own—something he'd actually considered, pointing out that a few days' rest would help his injured arm heal faster.

The events concerning his uncle and the estate were beginning to wear on him, and the effects were obvious. He jumped at the slightest sound, and the circles under his eyes grew darker each day. About ten minutes down the road, Remi looked back and saw that he'd fallen fast asleep. When he started snoring, Sam checked the rear-view mirror, then Remi. "Didn't want to say anything, but we've been followed since we left the estate."

Remi looked in the side mirror, seeing a dark-colored vehicle in the distance. Oliver lived far enough out in the country that traffic on these roads was infrequent. They still had miles to go before they hit the motorway, where they could easily lose the car in traffic. "Watchful eye?" she said, keeping her voice low.

"For now." He patted his Smith & Wesson in the holster hidden in his jacket. "If they get any closer, take a tire out."

She slipped her 9mm Sig Sauer from the glove box,

placing it along her right thigh, in case it was needed. The car, however, kept a safe distance, the driver, apparently, content to simply follow—for now.

When they finally neared the motorway, Remi pulled out her phone and accessed the map app, the address of the mechanic already entered. Chad Williams lived in a small village north of London, which meant they still had several hours of driving. And several hours of being tailed. She glanced in the side mirror, noting the car was still behind them. "What're the chances it's just someone heading to London like we are?"

"I'd believe it, if I hadn't seen them watching the house this morning. Same car. The good news is, it's only one car."

When Sam hit the motorway, he headed north instead of south. The car followed, matching their speed. After ten or fifteen minutes, Sam pulled alongside a bank of cargo trucks, coasting next to them. "Keep an eye on our tail," he told Remi, his eyes locked on the rearview mirror. A moment later, he braked sharply, veering the car between two of the trucks.

Unable to squeeze in behind them, the sedan drove alongside their car, the driver glancing over. Remi took a picture with her cell phone. "Looks familiar," she said, as Sam coasted along between the two trucks, watching for the next exit. When they reached it, Sam suddenly turned off. Their tail, however, was unable to make the lane change in time and continued on down the motorway.

Oliver stirred as Sam braked to a stop. "Something wrong?"

"Took a wrong turn," Sam said, driving beneath the overpass to get on the motorway going in the opposite direction.

Oliver nodded, sat back, and within a few minutes was asleep again.

"Why that exit?" Remi asked. "Not that I was worried, but there were four other exits before that could have gotten you back on the motorway as quickly."

"Because his next exit is eight miles from here. Depending on how fast he drives, or if he wants to risk backing up with all that traffic hurtling toward him, that should buy us at least ten or fifteen minutes."

"Clever, Fargo." She watched the exit in her mirror, saw nobody else taking it. "Looks like we're in the clear."

"For now."

She enlarged the picture she'd taken, for a better view. "One of our two friends from Pebble Beach."

"Followed us all the way out here?"

"As entertaining as we are? People just gravitate toward us."

Sam laughed. "Have you ever considered that we should tone it down a bit? Explore a more sedentary life?"

Remi looked over at him. "Right. You let me know when you're ready and I'll start researching our options. What were you thinking of? Gardening? Needlepoint?"

"Worthy hobbies."

"For someone who enjoys that sort of thing. You? Not in your DNA."

"Skydiving or spelunking, maybe?"

"Hmm . . ."

He looked over at her as she typed something into her phone. "What're you doing?"

"Sending that photo to Selma, to go with that video you took on the train. Maybe we can get an ID . . . Done," she said, pressing the send button. "Now, about your new hobbies . . ."

They passed several small villages, on through rolling green hills dotted with cottages, farmhouses, and scattered sheep. Once they left the motorway, Oliver awoke, surprised to find how far they'd driven. He pointed toward a church spire in the distance. "That's Chad's village. First right after the church."

Sam turned onto a cobblestone street, following Oliver's directions until they'd reached Chad's shop.

Oliver directed him around the corner. "Easier to park over here. His aunt lives just down the street. He uses her carriage house to work on one of his classic cars."

Sam turned, parking about midway between Chad's shop and his aunt's carriage house. When the three of them walked up to the shop, they discovered the garage doors locked tight and a *Closed* sign hanging in the window.

Oliver nodded in the other direction. "Let's try the office," he said. "Maybe he's taking a break." He led them down a graveled path that led along the side of Chad's shop. "Ah, yes. See? The door's open."

He started forward, but Sam blocked him with his arm. "Wait here," he said, drawing his gun. Which was when Remi noticed the splintered doorjamb.

27

Sam aimed his gun toward the office door, signaling for Remi to cover his back and Oliver to remain behind while he checked the shop. Standing to one side of the threshold, he listened a moment, not hearing a sound.

Two steps in he saw the shop's office had been ransacked. A desk chair was turned over, the drawers opened, and file cabinets emptied. Another door led to the garage, where a late-model blue BMW was parked, driver's door ajar. Other than that, the car looked relatively untouched. Not so the rolling tool chest, with all its drawers opened; same with the doors of the metal cabinets along one wall.

The place, however, was empty, and he returned outside. "Someone was looking for something," he said, stepping aside so they could see.

"Oh no . . ." Oliver stood in the doorway, shaking his head. "He's not—"

"Here," Sam finished for him.

"Thank goodness," he replied.

"You don't happen to know what car he drives?"

It took a moment for Oliver to draw his attention from the ransacked office. "Sorry?"

"Car?"

"Oh, right. When he drove out to Payton Manor, he was in a yellow Renault. But he also drives a lorry for the cars."

Sam walked up to Remi, saying quietly, "Call the police. I'm going to take a look and see if the car is parked anywhere nearby."

He walked around to the front, then back through the alley. The flatbed tow truck was there, but the car wasn't. "What about this carriage house you said he uses?"

Oliver's expression brightened. "Of course he'd be there. Why didn't I think of that?"

He led them down the street, stopping in front of a driveway that led to a garage behind a two-story house, both half-timbered, with high-peaked thatched roofs. "Chad's aunt lives here," he said. "She doesn't drive, so lets him use the carriage house."

"The police are on their way," Remi said, joining them.

Sam tugged on the lock hanging from the hasp on the garage doors. "Oliver, maybe you should wait by the shop. Let me know when the police arrive."

Remi eyed the lock, turned to Oliver, smiled. "I'll meet you there in just a minute." She waited until he was gone, then stood guard while Sam picked the lock and slid open the door. He did a double take when he turned on the light switch, saw the antique gray Rolls-Royce parked inside.

Remi stepped in after him. "Is it . . . ?"

When his eyes adjusted to the interior light and he saw the weld marks and color differences of the body, he shook his head. "Too short. Maybe an early twenty–twenty-five."

Remi found a clipboard filled with papers on the workbench. She lifted a page, followed by several more, saying, "Franken-Rolls. Pieced together, apparently. The rebuilt engine's from one car, the body another, and the chassis . . . Well, if I'm reading this receipt correctly, it's a replica."

"I guess we know his specialty," he said, looking around at all the various body parts stacked in the corners and hanging on the walls, along with engine parts. "Could probably cannibalize everything in here and put together a fairly decent car."

He returned his attention to the rebuilt car. Not exactly a prime specimen. There was some rust on the body, and the seats were clearly in need of reupholstering. The body was similar to that of the Gray Ghost, even down to the color of the torn leather upholstery, and he wondered if it had also been built by Barker Coachworks.

Remi lowered the clipboard and looked around. "You get the feeling that whoever was here meant to come back?"

"Definitely," he said. The vehicle's engine was exposed, the tool chest rolled up right next to it. And sitting on top of the chest was a full mug of coffee and an ashtray, where a cigarette had burned into one long ash. He walked Remi out. "Do me a favor. Stay with Oliver until the police arrive. Make sure he's on the same page as us. I'd rather keep our involvement low-key."

"Easy enough. What're you planning on doing?"

"Have a better look around. Whatever happened, the guy left in a hurry. It'd be nice to know why."

He looked at the house, saw a white-haired woman peering out the window at them. The curtain dropped, and, a moment later, she opened the back door, waved. "Over here!" she said. The woman's smile faded as Sam and Remi approached. "Oh, you're not the plumber . . . ?"

"Actually," Remi said, "my husband is very handy with a wrench, just show him what you need done." She looked over at Sam, her green eyes twinkling. "I'll go check on Oliver."

With no other choice, he smiled at the woman. "What is it you need help with?"

"A clogged garbage disposal. I was rather hoping you were the plumber. Chad said he'd call one for me."

"How long ago was that?" Sam asked.

"Well, this morning, of course. He was helping me, but something happened, and he had to leave. He did say he'd call someone. But then, that was five hours ago."

"How often do you see him?"

"Every morning, working on that car out there before he starts work at his shop. Heaven knows what he finds so fascinating about that rusty old thing."

Sam followed her into the kitchen, eyeing the half-filled bucket sitting beneath the open drain trap. "What happened?"

"Potato peels. My garbage disposal didn't like it much better than the celery that got stuck last week."

He picked up the pipe wrench from the floor in front of the cupboard. "They don't like carrot peels, either."

She sighed. "I'm not sure my disposal likes anything. Chad keeps telling me I should replace it."

"Any idea where he went off to?" Sam asked, climbing beneath the sink to empty the peels that were stuck in the trap.

"I have no idea. He'd just loosened the pipe when he got a phone call. Talked for a couple of minutes, then left."

"That right?" Sam asked, clearing the pipe, fitting it back into place. "Wonder where he took off to?"

"Wherever it was, he was in a hurry."

He gave one last twist with the wrench. "If you have a towel, I'll wipe this down for you."

"Thank you. That's very kind of you," she said, picking up one from the counter. "Hard for me to get down there, these days."

Sam mopped up the water that had spilled, got up, held the towel over the sink, wringing it out. "Don't suppose you heard what they were talking about?"

"You can hear for yourself. He left a message on my machine. Something about a ghost."

28

"A ghost?" Sam said, as the woman handed him a clean dish towel to dry his hands.

"That's what I heard. I wasn't trying to eavesdrop. It's just that he had the call on speaker while he was working under the sink. It was all very odd. Something about how they knew he'd taken their ghost and to bring it back. He said he didn't know what they were talking about. All he had was a phantom. Honestly, I have no idea what it was about. Something he didn't want to talk about in front of me, because when he saw me walk in, he picked up the phone and turned off the speaker." She offered an apologetic smile. "I would have left to give him privacy, but, before I knew it, he was racing out the door."

"Did he say where he was going?"

"No. But later he said he'd call a plumber for me. I don't think he did, though, or someone would have come by now, don't you think?"

"Probably." Sam ran the faucet, turned on the disposal. "Good as new," he said, as he shut them off.

"I can't thank you enough. How much do I owe you for this?"

"Glad to help." He nodded at the telephone on the wall. "You were saying something about Chad leaving a message?"

"Yes. I was outside, and the recording came on before I could get to the phone." She pressed a button on the answering machine, stood back so he could hear.

It's me. Oliver is on his way there and he's not answering his phone. I need you to get a message to him. They're—

The sound of the phone picking up, then, *Chad? Is that you? Why are you talking so soft?*

Just get this message to Oliver. He's on his way.

What about my sink? You said you'd fix it.

I'll call for a plumber later. Can you get the message to Oliver?

Of course.

Tell him to bring the Ghost or— I have to go.

Chad?

The line went dead.

The woman smiled at Sam. "That's it. All very strange. I have no idea what he's mixed up in—something to do with those cars, probably."

As much as Sam didn't want to alarm the woman, clearly the man sounded stressed. "I'd be glad to pass on the message to Oliver. Would you mind if I recorded it on my phone? Then he can hear it for himself."

"Is he here?"

"Just down the street, at Chad's shop."

"Oh. Did he bring his uncle? I should go say hello."

She made a beeline for the front door, opened it, stopped at the sight of a police car. Her expression was one of mild curiosity, not something Sam expected to see. "The police are still here?" she asked. "I thought they'd left already."

"You know what happened?"

"Someone broke into Chad's shop last night. He was here at the time, thank goodness. I told him it wasn't a good idea to live there after the last break-in." Shaking her head, she watched as Remi and Oliver walked the constable back to his car, waved as he drove off. "This used to be such a quiet village—"

"There was another break-in?" Sam asked.

"A couple of weeks ago. Probably just some vandals, since nothing was taken. Still . . ." She gave a tired sigh. "I don't think I'll mention this to my sister. She keeps telling me I need to sell this place, but I won't. I like it here." Giving a determined nod, she looked at Sam. "I'm sure you have better things to do than listen to an old woman . . . And I have a sink full of dirty dishes that need washing."

"APPARENTLY, the burglary was already reported," Remi told Sam when he returned.

"So I heard," he said. He played the recording of the phone call for Oliver. "Any idea why he thinks you have the Ghost?"

"None," Oliver said. "Can you play it again?" He listened, shook his head. "Why would he accuse me of having it? He knows it was stolen from the show."

"Maybe," Remi said, "he thinks your uncle took it, and now you have it. After all, it's still missing."

"I don't know why . . ." He sat in a chair, looking perplexed. "This is getting more complicated by the second. I'm beginning to regret talking my uncle out of taking that offer for Payton Manor and the car. It wasn't near enough to settle his debts, but it might have kept him out of jail." He sighed, then stared out the window, looking lost.

Sam was about to give a few words of encouragement when he thought about what Oliver just said. "Can you give me the details on this offer you were talking about?"

"Surely I mentioned that?"

"Of course he did," Remi said. "They didn't want to sell because of the tenants."

"I realize that. I'm more interested in if they specifically mentioned the Gray Ghost when they made the offer for Payton Manor?"

Oliver drew away from the window. "Well, yes. Which is what made it so attractive. Just . . . What Remi said. He refused to guarantee that our tenants could remain on the property."

Sam and Remi exchanged glances, Remi's brows going up in question. "Who?" they both asked at the same time.

Oliver didn't seem to hear them, and Sam crouched down in front of him so that he had no choice but to hear. "Who made the offer, Oliver?"

"Some distant relative, from what I understand."

"Do you recall the name?"

"Heavens no. I didn't handle it. Allegra did. Why?"

Sam stood, looking over at Remi, who was already typing *distant relative* into her phone, probably texting Selma. "Maybe it's related to all this."

"Related? How?"

"The sudden interest in the car, his offer, and the fact it was stolen."

"But . . . this?" he nodded to the mess inside Chad's shop. "Part of it?"

"No doubt. Try calling again."

Oliver called the number, his eyes widening when someone answered. "Chad? We've been trying to reach you. Where . . . ?" He listened a moment, then said, "Yes. Okay." Disconnecting, he stared at the phone's screen for several seconds.

"What's going on?" Sam asked.

"I'm not sure. But he says he'll tell us when he gets here. He's just a few minutes away."

29

Taking no chances, Sam gripped the butt of his gun while he kept a close eye on the street, waiting for Chad's arrival. When his yellow Renault finally pulled up, Sam made sure Chad was the only one in it and not being followed. "Looks like he's alone."

Oliver met him at the door. "Whatever's going on? Your aunt said something about the Ghost?"

"They think I have it," Chad said.

"Why?" Sam asked.

"I have no idea," he replied, just seeming to notice Sam and Remi for the first time. "Who are you?"

"My friends," Oliver said. "I told you about them when I called last night. Sam and Remi Fargo."

"I didn't know you were bringing them here."

"Why wouldn't I? They're helping me and my uncle."

"I—" He looked at the mess around him. "Second time, you know."

"This happened before?" Sam asked.

He nodded. "A few weeks ago, right after Oliver and his uncle had the Ghost brought here."

"Any idea what they were looking for?" Sam asked.

"Then or now?"

"Either."

"I— They had to be looking for the Ghost."

"It wasn't here at the time?" Sam said.

He shook his head. "I kept it in my aunt's carriage house. No way was I keeping that car here. Her entire house has alarms and cameras. Same with the carriage house."

"This place doesn't?"

"It does. Either I didn't set it or they got past it somehow."

Probably the latter, Sam realized.

Chad started to pick up some of the papers on the floor that had been pulled from the desk drawers, pausing as he looked around. "Why— Why would they think I even have it? That first time, I thought it was kids—until today."

He looked at the papers he'd gathered from the floor, his expression lost.

"Here," Remi said, taking the items from him. "You should sit. Can I get you some water?"

He nodded, as he sank into the desk chair, looking around the room. "None of this makes any sense. Why trash my office? Clearly the car's not here."

"Maybe looking for an address," Sam said. "Somewhere you might hide it."

"Except I don't have it. Nor do I know where it is."

"Your aunt mentioned something about a phone call," Sam said, "when you were over there this morning."

"Oh no." He started to rise. "I told her I'd call a plumber."

Remi returned with a bottle of water from the compact refrigerator beneath the counter. "Sam took care of it for you."

Chad looked at Sam. "I— Thank you."

"She was a little surprised when you went tearing out of there," Sam said. "What was that about?"

"This bloke just started accusing me of stealing the Ghost. It didn't matter what I told him, he said if I didn't deliver it, I'd be sorry." His hand shook so hard as he twisted off the bottle cap, he spilled the water in his lap.

"Are you okay?" Remi asked, taking the bottle from him.

"No." Suddenly he dropped his head into his hands and started sobbing.

"Sam . . ."

Sam placed his hand on the man's shoulder. "What's going on?"

It was several seconds before he looked up, trying to catch his breath. "When I got the call from that man, I—" He sucked in a breath of air, looking dazed. "I could hear her cuckoo clock. He was calling from my mother's house."

"You're sure?"

Chad nodded. This time when Remi handed him the bottle, he drank several sips, then wiped his mouth and eyes with the back of his hand. "I drove out there to see for myself. Once I saw the car out front, I knew."

"Knew what?" Sam asked.

"The bloke who called. He was there. I couldn't even

go in. Just peeked through the window from the side yard like the coward I am." He looked at Remi, his eyes pleading. "What am I going to do? She's not involved in any of this." His head went down again as another sob escaped his throat. "This is all my fault."

Definitely something more going on here than any of them realized. Sam stood, angling his head at Remi to take over since she was far better at getting information from someone who was emotionally upset.

She moved in, taking Sam's place. "Why would you think it's your fault?"

This time he looked directly at Oliver. "I'm not the expert you thought I was. I made it all up for the money. I can work on cars, yes. But everything I know comes from the internet."

"But—" Oliver stared for a moment, his stricken look turning to one of anger. "You assured me you were the best. I saw your website. All those photos. Those awards . . ."

"My uncle's."

"Why?"

Chad shrugged. "Would you have brought that car to me if you knew the only Rolls-Royce I'd ever worked on without my uncle was the one in my aunt's garage?"

"Of course not."

"See?"

Oliver started to say something, but Remi cut in. "You must know something about these cars. After all, you got the Ghost up and running."

"When my uncle was alive, collectors would bring their cars to his shop for repair. He taught me everything he knew. After he died, no one was willing to take a chance on me. So, when I read that article about the Paytons finding the Gray Ghost, I made up a website and called them. And, well, you know the rest."

Sam moved next to Remi, hoping to get the conversation back on track. "About your mother. Was someone threatening her?"

"No. But I'm sure whoever it is means to."

"Why do you think that?"

"Even after I told him I didn't have the Gray Ghost, he said he wasn't interested in my excuses. Deliver the car or face the consequences. The thing is, I don't have it. The last I saw of it was here at my shop, when we were putting it on that lorry for delivery to the London Motor Show. That's it. I swear."

"Well, someone seems to think you have it," Sam said.

"Yes. And whoever this man is, he's sitting there drinking tea with my mother as though they were the best of friends."

"At least she doesn't know what's going on."

"Not helping, Sam," Remi said under her breath. Louder, she asked, "How do we get her out of there?"

"Call the police," Oliver said.

Something that Sam had already considered and dismissed. The last thing they wanted was a hostage situation. Or anyone getting shot. "One thing we're sure of," Sam said, "is that these guys have no problem pulling guns. I'm not sure I want to pit them against unarmed village constables."

"What other choice do we have?" Chad asked.

"Storm the castle and get her out."

The first thing they did was bring up a satellite map image of the village where Chad's mother lived, about fifteen minutes to the north. Sam and Remi studied the map while Chad described the neighborhood, pointing to the middle of an S-shaped street. "The main problem," Chad said, "is that her house is right at the center of the S. No matter which direction you approach from, her parlor window and front door have a view of the street. If this guy's looking out the window to the right, he'll see you coming before you see him. The only place that might work is on the west end of the street. My mum's hedge runs the length of her driveway, and you have to move out past the hedge to the street to actually see the corner here at the top of the hill."

"How'd you get a look without being seen?" Sam asked.

"Through the park behind her house." He ran his finger along an expanse of green that paralleled the next street over. "There's a gate that leads from the park to her backyard. It's overgrown with ivy, so I went in through that, up the side yard, then looked in through the kitchen window. He was sitting in the front parlor, watching the street. There's no way he even knows the gate's there."

"And there was only one man?"

"Just the one."

Sam studied the map a bit longer. "It could work. Remi, you could hole up at the top of the hill. I come in through the back gate. Oliver, you're at the park, with the car running. Chad makes the call, draws him out. Remi signals me that he's past the hedge, I go in, get your mom, and we're good to go."

"What if he takes her out with him?" Chad asked. "Like a hostage?"

"The fact your mother doesn't know she's a hostage makes it clear he's trying to keep it low-key. Last thing he's going to want to do is draw attention to his presence."

What he didn't mention was that Remi's presence at the top of the hill with her gun was in case of that very scenario. No sense in alarming either Chad or Oliver. For this to work, he needed them calm. "You good with that, Remi?"

"Definitely," she said, giving a slight pat to the small of her back where her Sig was holstered.

"How are we going to draw him out?" Chad asked.

"All you need to do is tell him you're parked at the top of the street. He has to walk out past the hedge. Get him out that far, we're good. It's all about the setup. We need him to believe you have the car."

"How?"

"First thing," Sam said, "we call your mother and get a handle on what it is we're dealing with. Be reluctant. If you're too eager to give details, you might spook the guy." After Sam went over a few pointers and details, Chad turned on the speaker of his cell phone and redialed the number. "What is it you want from me?" he asked the man who answered.

"The Gray Ghost."

"What makes you think I have it?"

"A reliable source," the man said. "And your dear, sweet mum informs us that you've been working on it at your shop."

"Clearly you've been here."

"Yes. And clearly it's not there. Where is it?"

Chad looked at Sam, who nodded, encouraging him to stick with their script. "Somewhere safe. I want assurances that my mother's not hurt."

"I'll let you talk to her yourself."

There was a muffled noise, then his mother's voice saying, "Chad? Is that you?"

"It's me, Mum. Are you okay?"

"What a silly question. Of course I'm okay. I'm having such a lovely time with two of your mates. I was showing them your website and telling them all about the car you're working on. That gray one. You're coming by with it, aren't you?"

Sam and Remi glanced at each other, Remi reaching for the pen.

"Mum—"

"As you can see, she's fine. Waiting for you. And the Gray Ghost."

"Yes," they heard his mother saying in the background. "One of those ghost names."

Remi wrote *time* and *stall*, pointed at the paper.

Chad nodded, saying, "It's going to take a few hours. I don't have it here with me."

"So you've finally come to your senses," the man on the other end said. "You have three hours to deliver the car to us. Or else."

"I need more—"

The line went dead.

"So much for storming the castle," Remi said.

"Remi's right," Sam replied.

"Why?" Chad asked. "You said this would work."

Oliver eyed the both of them, looking aghast. "I know I was against this, but you can't mean to just leave her there."

"We're not," Sam said. "But that plan's out. You heard your mother. She said two of your friends. As in more than one. That changes the odds significantly."

"But you both have guns," Oliver said. "You can't leave her there."

"That's the last thing we intend to do," Sam said. "It's just that after hearing their conversation, the plan we came up with won't work."

"No," Remi said. "But I have the perfect Plan B."

That's insane," Oliver said when Remi finished outlining her plan to the three of them. "You're asking us to make something out of nothing. It'll never work."

"It's brilliant," Sam said. "It could totally work."

Remi turned to Chad. "She's your mother. You're the one who has to make the final decision. And you're the only one who knows if we have half a chance of pulling this off."

Chad stared at the same spot on the floor for several seconds, clearly wrestling with the decision. Finally, he looked up at her, and then Sam, his dark eyes troubled. "I'm not saying yes. I need to know how do we keep my mother from getting hurt?"

"That part's easy," Sam said. "Kind of like the old plan. They're more interested in the car than her."

"Except in this case," Remi said, "we intend to deliver."

Chad gave a deep sigh, stood. "Let's go take a look."

The four of them walked down to the carriage house where the Rolls was stored.

Chad looked in the window, saw his aunt, gave a cheery smile, and waved, his face sobering as he turned back to them. "I'd appreciate it if you didn't mention any of this to my aunt. I'd rather not have her worried."

"Not a word," Sam said.

Chad opened the door and turned on the lights. "Anyone who's the least bit familiar with these cars will be able to tell straightaway this isn't the Gray Ghost the moment they get a good look at it."

Of that, Sam had no doubt. The fact that Remi's idea was so preposterous was what made it so appealing. Who would suspect them of trying to pass off a counterfeit car as the real thing?

"Silk purse, sow's ear," Oliver muttered.

"Maybe so," Sam said. "But if we work this right, they'll never get close enough to tell."

"They won't have to," Chad replied. "The silhouette's off. The body's too short. Those fenders aren't right. Straighter than the Ghost. Unless . . ." He looked around the shop, his attention lingering on some black fenders stacked against the wall. "We could switch them out for those. A little spray paint . . . Still, this Rolls doesn't have the style of the Barker Coachworks. They'll notice that right off. Look at how level those seat backs are."

"Any way we can fake it?" Remi asked.

He circled the vehicle, eyeing it as he walked. After a while he stopped, opened the front passenger door, climbed in, and kneeled on the seat. Suddenly he started pulling up on the leather upholstery, loosening it from the back. "I think I can work with this."

"Even if it means lessening the value of your car?"

"It's not like we're ripping up the Gray Ghost, trying to make it look like the lesser twenty–twenty-five that it is." He patted the back of the seat he'd just pulled up. "Great for tinkering with, and learning to rebuild an engine. Other than that, it's probably worth more as a source for spare parts."

"How long do you need?" Sam asked.

"I daresay, at least a couple of hours."

Oliver looked less than pleased, conflicted over the issue of Chad's pretense to gain access to the Ghost. It didn't help that his uncle was sitting in a jail cell, either.

Sam drew him to one side. "He may have misled you in the beginning, but it's clear he knows his stuff."

"Except that he lied."

"Water under the bridge."

Remi, overhearing them, realized that Sam's practical approach might not be the best way to convince Oliver of anything right now. The poor man looked as though he'd aged ten years in the last few days, stress etched in every line on his face. After his uncle's arrest and his near escape from the warehouse, he needed a softer touch. At the very least some assurance that he wasn't going to be in the line of fire. She reached over, put her hand on his arm, smiling softly. "And he is sorry. But when it comes right down to it, he was able to get the Gray Ghost up and running to your expectations. No one complained when he helped turn it into the showpiece it is, wouldn't you agree?"

"Yes."

"Isn't that what counts in the end?"

"If he lied about that, how do I know he's not involved in its theft?"

Sam, taking Remi's cue, said, "You really think he'd risk his mother's life?" He glanced toward Chad, who was pulling the fenders from the wall in order to disguise the Franken-Rolls. "I don't know him personally, but my gut instinct is that he's the kind of person who takes pride in his work and wants to do the right thing. Getting over this latest hurdle will bring us that much closer to whoever's really behind the theft of the Ghost."

"Exactly," Remi said. "When we figure that out, we're that much closer to clearing your uncle."

"You really think so?"

"I do."

"Not to mention," Sam added, "Chad will be an asset. Regardless of his fake pedigree, he knows what he's talking about. Still, if you want to back out, we won't stand in your way . . ."

Remi could see Oliver starting to waver. "The choice is yours, but we need him in our court."

"Your uncle needs him in our court," Sam said.

Oliver took a deep breath, then nodded, his gaze fixed on Chad and the car. "I trust your judgment. Let's do this."

32

The shop smelled of spray paint. Remi was putting the finishing touches on one of the fenders, which made Sam glad they were handling the drop-off out in the open where the smell wouldn't be an issue. Still, the most important aspect was the silhouette, and, two hours later, he squinted his eyes, trying to imagine what it might be like if the sun was shining on them, pleased to see that the car's silhouette somewhat resembled the Gray Ghost.

Close up was a completely different story. The spot welds on the new fenders were obvious, even with the gray spray paint covering them. The chrome work had been buffed to a shine, the rust dabbed with paint. And the seat backs, both front and rear, now formed an arch similar to the Gray Ghost. Surprisingly, the leather and stuffing attached to the support with duct tape blended perfectly with the old upholstery.

Unable to find a perfect color match, Remi had spray-painted the cracked leather, and the duct tape holding it together, a slightly darker blue. "One good thing," she said, tossing the empty spray can into the trash, "it doesn't look quite so worn now."

Oliver looked up from the headlamp he'd been buffing. "Let's hope they don't notice the color difference."

"If Remi's plan works," Sam told them, "it won't matter. They won't get that close . . . How much longer?"

Chad held up the blowtorch. "One last weld on the left front fender. But we need time to let the paint dry. If they touch the seats, we're done for."

"Like I said, we don't plan on letting them get that close."

"How're you going to keep them from seeing the car?"

"We time it right," Remi said, "the sun will be angled directly behind it, blinding them."

While Chad finished the welding, Remi went over what he needed each of them to do. Afterward, he looked at his watch. "Wrap it up. We need to get it loaded on the flatbed and put a tarp over it."

Since their plan had changed, eliminating the need for a sharpshooter at the top of the hill, Sam and Remi flipped a coin to see who was going in the back way to get Chad's mom out. Remi lost the toss. "Is it wrong that I want to see their faces when they realize the car isn't the Ghost?"

"Hate to spoil your fun," Sam said, "but I'm hoping we're long gone before that happens."

He rode with Chad, who drove the flatbed trailer, while Remi drove Oliver in their rental car, the four meeting up on the street near the park, where a few teenage boys were kicking a rugby ball around on the grass. Sam and Remi put in their Bluetooth earpieces, and he called her phone. "Ready?"

She patted the gun holstered beneath her shirt, then eyed the ivy-covered wall. "Where exactly is this gate?" she asked Chad.

"See where the boy in the yellow shirt's standing? Right behind him."

"Got it. Can they see it from the inside?"

"Only if they go digging through the ivy."

"Oliver," Sam said. "You stay with the car. As soon as Remi comes out with Chad's mother, be ready."

"I will be."

Sam and Chad walked back to the truck, Sam going over what he wanted Chad to say when he called the house. "Remi and I will be in touch by phone the entire time. We need to get those two men out of that house and up the hill before that sun goes down."

"You think it'll work?"

There were so many variables why it wouldn't, but Sam wasn't about to mention any of them. The last thing he needed was to have Chad thinking about the possibility of failure. "No doubt."

They drove around the corner, Sam directing him to park, just out of sight. They waited a few minutes until the sun was slightly above and behind the truck before driving past the corner house, stopping so that the flatbed and covered Faux Ghost cast a long shadow onto the paved street. If everything worked as planned, anyone looking at them from the front of Chad's house would have a hard time seeing much else but the silhouette.

"Loosen up the tarp on your side and make the call. Whatever you do, we need to get both men out of the house so Remi can get to your mother."

"What do I do if they see you?"

"Their attention's going to be on the car. I'll be inside the cab with the window open, watching over your shoulder. Don't forget, the sun'll be in their eyes."

Chad got out, unclipped the tarp, pulled it off, stood in front of the driver's door, turned the speaker on his phone to low so that Sam could hear the call. "The Gray Ghost is here," he said when they answered.

"Where? The only cars I see in front of your mother's house are ours."

"Look up the hill."

A moment later, a man walked out to the street, holding a cell phone to his ear with one hand, the other hand in his right jacket pocket, probably gripping a gun. He looked up the hill, squinting in the sunlight, then turned back toward the house. "Frank! Get out here!" A second man walked out, Chad's mother at his side. He looked their direction, shielding his eyes with his left hand, saying something to the man on the phone, who said, "Bring the lorry closer."

Sam tapped Chad on the shoulder as a reminder. "No," Chad ordered. "Not until you send my mother into the house. After that, walk up the hill. The car's yours."

The man hesitated, before saying, "You better not be trying something funny."

"I just want my mum safe."

The man said something to his partner, who, in turn, said something to Chad's mother. At first, she seemed reluctant to leave, but eventually she returned inside the house.

"Remi," Sam said softly. "She's on her way."

"I'm waiting for her."

When the woman closed the front door, the second man dropped his phone into his pocket and continued down the steps and into the street. They were about halfway up the hill when Remi said, "Slight problem. She thinks Chad's on his way here. She won't leave without him."

Great. Sam eyed the two men. In less than a minute they'd be close enough to see they'd been duped. Worse yet, there were several children walking on the street. "We don't have a Plan C," he told her. "Get her out of there before they're close enough to see the car."

"I'll try."

"What do I do?" Chad asked Sam under his breath.

"Hand them the keys to the truck, if you have to. We just need to buy Remi some time."

Sam watched as Chad, both hands held out, dangled the keys to the truck so they were visible. The two men stopped, one of them reaching for his gun. "Who are you talking to?"

"I just want to get my mum," he called out. "The car's yours." He tossed the keys at them.

"Get the keys, Bruno," the other said. "I'll call Colton and tell him we have the Ghost."

Sam slipped out the door on the other side, working his way to the back of the truck.

"Sam?" Remi's quiet voice sounded in his earpiece.

"So far, so good. Do whatever it takes to get his mother out of there."

"We've got her. We're on our way."

He peered beneath the Faux Ghost, watching as the two men strode up the hill. The man on the left, Bruno, stopped, his eyes fixed on the car. "What the . . ."

"What's wrong?" Frank said.

"That's not the Gray Ghost." Bruno drew his gun, about to turn back toward the house.

Sam gripped his Smith & Wesson, running around the truck to Chad's side, aiming at the two men. No way was he going to let them anywhere near his wife. Finger on the trigger, he was starting to squeeze when he saw two girls at the bottom of the hill, playing hopscotch on the sidewalk.

Directly in the line of fire.

"You ever play rugby, Chad?" Sam asked, holstering his gun.

"Yeah."

"Get ready . . ." He hopped up onto the flatbed trailer, picking up the tarp. "Hey, Bruno!" he shouted. "You forgot something."

The two gunmen turned and looked up at him. Sam heaved the tarp at Bruno, jumped, using the larger man's body to break his own fall.

At the same time, Chad charged at the second man, lowering his shoulder, ramming him in the chest.

They all hit the ground. The fall stunned Bruno. Sam grabbed him by his shoulders, pulled him up, slammed him back into the pavement, knocking the gun from his grasp. It fell to the blacktop a few inches away. Beside him, he saw Chad and the second man struggling, only then realizing they were fighting for control of the other gun. Chad had the weapon by the barrel, trying to push it away. He was losing.

Bruno glanced over, saw what was happening, his eyes finding the fallen gun a mere foot away. No way could Sam get to it or his own holstered gun without letting him go. Bruno gave him a sneering smile. "Say good-bye to your friend."

"Not likely," Sam said, driving his elbow into Bruno's face. He dove for the gun, fired at Chad's attacker, the ringing in his ears almost drowning out the other man's scream and the screech of tires of the flatbed truck that followed. Sam saw the flash of a knife blade from the corner of his eye.

As Bruno rolled to his knees, lunging at him with the dagger, Remi jumped out of the car, gripping her Sig with both hands. "Drop it," she ordered.

Bruno, his knife only six inches from Sam's throat, eyed the almost thirty-foot distance between them. "I've seen you shoot. You really think you can hit me from that far?"

She fired. The knife flew from his hand, clattering down the street. "Guess not," she said, moving closer.

Bruno raised both hands, a look of respect and fear on his face. A few feet away, his partner writhed on the ground, gripping his arm, moaning. Chad had wrested the gun from him, his hand shaking as he backed away.

"Are the police on their way?" Sam asked Remi.

"Any second now." She kept her focus on Bruno and his partner. "Imagine running into our friends from Pebble Beach all the way out here."

"Apparently, they didn't get the word," Sam said, taking the other gun from Chad. "We don't have the Gray Ghost."

He aimed the weapon at Bruno, about to ask who they were working for, when Chad's mother rushed out of the car, slapping at her son's hands as he tried to stop her. "Let go of me, Chad. What on earth has gotten into you?"

"Mum—"

She stopped short at the sight of Sam and Remi standing over the two men. "Why are these two pointing guns at your mates?"

"They're not my mates, Mum. They're criminals."

"Rubbish!" She stepped between Remi and the two thugs. "We had tea together. Put that thing down, young lady."

"Mum!" Chad rushed forward, pulling his mother back. The gunmen, seeing a break, scrambled to their feet, racing down the hill.

Remi aimed, following their path with her sight. "It'd be an easy hit."

"Let them go," Sam said, seeing the two little girls who had been playing hopscotch at the bottom of the street now standing there, staring at them, wondering what was going on. "I have a feeling we'll get another chance."

Remi lowered her gun but didn't holster it until both men had jumped into their cars, tires screeching as they drove off in the opposite direction. Once they were gone, she walked over, picked up the knife, turning it about in her hands.

"Do you have to tease the bad guys?" Sam asked, as she returned to the car. He had Oliver pop open the trunk so he could empty the recovered guns and store them.

"It's fun."

"For you, maybe. That knife was a lot closer to my head than yours."

"Oh, buck up, Fargo," she said, holstering her gun. "You'd have done the same. So why didn't you?"

He nodded toward the end of the street where the two little girls had come out of their state of shock, apparently, and were now racing back to their house.

Even Remi, an expert marksman, wouldn't have taken that shot. The only thing behind her target was Chad's empty house. She tossed the knife into the trunk, slammed the lid closed. "Now that the fun's over, I suppose we should get out of here before someone really does call the police."

"You call that fun?" Oliver asked.

Chad's mother planted her hands on her hips. "Will someone please tell me what is going on?"

Mum. Are you and Dad trying to steal from Uncle Albert?"

Allegra's heart clenched as she saw Trevor standing there, holding the journal. She'd always known he was bright. She'd just hoped that he wouldn't figure out things so quickly. To make matters worse, Dex walked in, looking at the two of them, his gaze landing on what was in Trevor's hands.

She tried to step between the two, but her ex snatched the journal and slammed it in the boy's face. "You want to accuse me of something? Then come talk to me instead of sniveling to your mother." Dex swung the book back as if to strike him again.

"Stop it!" Allegra said, grabbing the journal from Dex.

"I'm okay, Mum." Trevor wouldn't even look at her. He reached up, touched his red cheek. "It's fine."

"See," Dex said, taking the book from her and tucking it beneath his arm. He pulled a bottle of ale from the refrigerator. "You coddle him too much."

"You promised you wouldn't hurt him," she said.

Dex glared at her. "Yeah, and you promised you'd keep him out of my business. That didn't happen, now did it?"

How had this all gone so wrong? Obviously, she should never have answered the door when Dex suddenly appeared on her porch a few months ago, telling her he was a changed man. She'd foolishly believed his lies about wanting to build a relationship with their son. And she'd brushed off his absurd reasons why he was interested in the Gray Ghost and the Payton family history. It wasn't until Dex came up with the story about being threatened by this Arthur Oren—insisting that if she called the police, the man would kill him—that she began to question his motives. By the time she'd realized what was going on, why he'd spent the next few weeks pretending to be the perfect father to Trevor, it was too late.

When she'd tried to put a stop to everything, Dex pointed out how happy Trevor was with him there. Wasn't she interested in securing the boy's future? All she needed to do was make sure that her uncle placed the Gray Ghost in that car show, to help raise its value. Where was the harm in that? After all, her uncle needed to sell the car in order to save Payton Manor.

Foolishly, she'd believed him.

Even after the car was stolen, and her uncle arrested for murder, she hadn't quite realized the depth of Dex's involvement. After all, he was the one who brought her the papers to have Oliver sign over Payton Manor so that they could hire the best solicitor. He'd been so helpful, so caring. Had it not been for the Fargos' timely arrival, Oliver would have gladly signed it.

It wasn't until after the Fargos hired another solicitor that she took the time to actually read the document that Dex had given her. Her bruises were still healing from when she'd confronted him with her suspicions about who was behind the theft of the Ghost.

That she could handle.

It just never occurred to her that Dex would threaten to kill Trevor if she didn't continue to cooperate.

That was all it took, and suddenly she was a blithering mess, getting in deeper and deeper, as Dex ran his scam. Naively, she'd thought that if her son never knew what was going on, Dex would get what he came after, then leave.

Just keep Trevor safe.

She looked over at her son, who had opened the refrigerator, his back to them, taking an abnormally long time to search through the three items within. Somehow, she'd fix this. All she needed to do was get him out of the house. "Trevor," she said, "I need you to leave. Go stay with one of your friends."

"The boy stays here," Dex said.

"Now," she ordered, in the voice she reserved for *Do it or else*. "You can come home when your father leaves. I'll be okay."

Trevor closed the fridge, turning toward her, the mark on his face still red. She saw the fright in his eyes and knew he didn't believe her. He'd seen some of her bruises.

She didn't care. "Go."

Trevor started to edge away, and was nearly out of the kitchen, when Dex set his ale on the counter, pulled a gun, pointed it at her. "Maybe I wasn't clear enough. The boy stays."

Trevor froze, his face paling.

She couldn't have moved if she'd wanted to. Pulse pounding in her ears, she stared down the barrel of Dex's gun. He'd kept it hidden until now.

Seconds ticked by, as she frantically tried to think of what to do.

"Mum?"

The look in Trevor's eye, him realizing what sort of monster his father was, broke her heart. Her mind raced. The only reason she and Trevor were in this mess was because she'd wanted to keep him safe. She had to concentrate on that. Thinking about anything else was not an option.

"It's okay," she said, as calmly as she could manage. "Your father's not going to hurt anyone. Are you?" she said, trying her best to focus on Dex, not the weapon he held.

He studied her for a moment, his eyes devoid of any emotion.

That, more than anything, frightened her.

"Let me tell you how this is going to work," Dex said. "We're going to spend the next week cozy on the couch." He used his gun to motion them toward the front room. When they both sat, he took the armchair. "One of you will always be with me. If either of you tries anything, leaves, doesn't come back, I'll kill the one left." He gave a shrug, took a long sip of his ale. "Not like I haven't done it before."

Don't show fear, she told herself, willing Trevor to follow her lead. He was a smart boy, always had been. He'd learned long ago that the best way to keep his father calm was to not cry, not show fear, and not raise his voice. To do otherwise resulted in a beating.

As promised, Dex refused to let either of them out of his sight at the same time. If she left the room, he held the gun on Trevor. And, likewise, if Trevor left the room, the gun was turned on her. That night, the three of them slept in the same room, she and Trevor on the floor, Dex pulling the mattress up to the door so that neither of them could escape.

The thing that frightened her the most was Dex's promise that if anyone attempted a rescue, he'd kill Trevor first and then himself, leaving her alive to suffer. There was no question in her mind that he meant every word and so she dutifully did his bidding, knowing that her best hope was to cooperate and wait.

She'd lost count of the time as the three sat in the front room, she and Trevor on the sofa, pretending to watch the game, Dex in the armchair, drinking a bottle of ale, still trying to read the journal.

A knock at the door startled her and she almost spilled her glass of water. She reached over, grasping Trevor's hand in hers, willing him to be silent.

35

Dex set the journal on the table, drew his gun, walked to the door, looked out the peephole. He looked back at her, putting his finger to his lips.

A second knock, this time a man calling out, "Allegra? I can hear the telly. I know you're in there. I'm not leaving until we talk."

Dex, using his gun, motioned her over.

She lowered her glass to the table, walked to the door.

"Find out what he wants," Dex whispered, "and get rid of him."

"Who is it?" she called through the door.

"Bill Snyder. I'm the private detective. I work for your uncle's solicitor. I have a couple of questions. About your uncle's case."

"Would you mind coming back? I'm not feeling well."

"It'll only take a few minutes. If you can open the door."

Allegra looked at Dex.

It was several seconds before he responded, leaning in

close, whispering, "Try anything funny, Trevor's the first to go."

She nodded, and he backed up, motioned for Trevor to precede him from the room down the hall into the office, closed the door behind them.

Taking a deep breath, Allegra told herself it was completely reasonable that a private detective would come talk to her. Her uncle was in custody for murder, after all. When she opened the door, she remembered to smile. "Mr. Snyder. How can I help?"

As much as she tried to block his view, he stood about a head taller than her. "May I come in?"

"I'd prefer you didn't."

He looked past her into the front room. "I take it your uncle's housekeeper rang?"

"Mrs. Beckett? Perhaps when I wasn't home. Has something happened?"

"She mentioned that the last time you popped in, you took a book from the library. She thought it might be the missing journal that your brother was looking for. We think it might help with your uncle's case."

It took her a moment to process the man's words. The only thought going through her head was that Dex was in the office, holding a gun to her son.

Focus. Breathe. Appear concerned.

"The journal? What does that book have to do with my uncle?"

"We're not sure, of course, but your brother seemed to think there were some entries in that particular volume that related to the stolen car."

"What's in there was written over a hundred years ago. Why would it be important?"

"That's what we hope to find out. And why Mrs. Beckett said she'd call ahead." He stepped to the side, looking at something behind her. "Naturally, that's why I assume you have the journal there on the table. You knew I was coming by for it."

She realized that if she objected, it would bring even more attention to her possession of the book—still, she needed to try. "I— I was hoping to keep it for a few days. I brought it home for my son to read. Ever since he went to live with my uncle, he's been fascinated with the viscountcy."

"I didn't realize anyone else lived at Payton Manor but your uncle and Oliver."

"This was a few years ago. Back when my husband and I were getting our divorce. I— I just felt it was best."

"I'm sure your son must have enjoyed his time there. It's a beautiful estate."

"Trevor loved it there," she said, wishing she'd let him stay, as he'd wanted, instead of forcing him to come home because of her misguided maternal notion to be near her son. What she needed now, though, was to get this man away from her house—the sooner, the better. "You said you had a couple of questions. What are they?"

"The journal, of course. We'll need that for the investigation."

Dex would object, but there was little she could do. It was clear the man wasn't going to leave without it. "Is there anything else?" she asked, retrieving the journal and handing it to him.

He slipped the small volume into the breast pocket of his suit. "Actually, yes. Your brother mentioned that there had been an offer on the estate. He thought you'd know who it was."

"The name escapes me."

"He thought it was some distant relative."

"Something makes me think it was some cousin to one of the viscounts generations ago." Trying to hurry him along, she said, "If you have a card, I'll give you a ring if I remember it. Right now, I'm too tired to think."

"Of course," he said, reaching into his suit pocket. He pulled out a small gold case, slipping a card from it. "Do you recall anyone ever coming around and asking questions about your uncle or the Gray Ghost before the car show? Or remember anyone at his house when you were there? Someone who didn't belong?"

In fact, she did, not that she was about to tell him. "People asking about the car? Honestly, I paid little attention. Oliver handled all that."

"What about here?"

"At my house? No. Just me and my son."

"You're the only two that live here?"

"Yes."

"He's how old?" the PI asked, finally handing her his business card.

"Sixteen."

"Is he home?"

"No. I'm here by myself. Why?"

"Just curious. I see the Toffees still have the game tied." He nodded at the television when it was clear she had no idea what he was talking about.

"Oh. Right. I have it on more for background noise."

He gave a benign smile, thanked her for her help, then left.

The moment she closed the door and turned the lock, Dex stepped out of the office, shoving Trevor in front of him, forcing the boy to the couch. Dex looked at the table, gave her an accusing glare, as she took a seat next to her son. "You gave him the book?"

"What was I supposed to do? He came here precisely because Mrs. Beckett saw me take it."

"You were supposed to get rid of him."

"I did. If you'd let me answer the house phone once in a while, I might have taken her call and been forewarned that she was sending him here. How was I supposed to know that's what he was after?"

"Not that we need it," he said, looking at Trevor. "You seemed to figure things out. Tell me what's in that journal?"

When Trevor didn't answer, Dex pointed his gun at him.

Slowly, she reached over, placing her hand on Trevor's, feeling his fingers trembling beneath hers. "Trev," she said, giving his hand a reassuring squeeze as she took a steadying breath. "Tell him what he wants to know."

"They— They found a boy who they thought might have seen the train robbery."

"Keep talking," Dex said. "What else did you read?"

36

JOURNAL OF JONATHON PAYTON, 5TH VISCOUNT WELLSWICK

1906

I refused to think that my Cousin Reginald was part of the train robbery, certain that the boy was mistaken, and that Isaac Bell's detective skills were lacking. And yet, there we were in his hotel with a child who insisted that my cousin was the very man who had killed the detective and the two train engineers. As much as I wanted to leave those premises, the only way to prove my cousin's innocence was to assist Mr. Bell in his investigation. Clinging to my certain belief, I was relieved when Bell suggested he must find a way to view the ledgers at the orphanage without drawing attention . . .

"We need to create a distraction," Isaac said. "Get the headmaster's attention so that I can go in and examine the books."

"I can help," came a small voice from the next room.

Isaac and I looked over at the boy, Toby, who was now sitting up in the bed. He seemed to have a bit more color about his cheeks, I hoped from eating a good meal and not from any illness.

"How?" Isaac asked.

"I can show you how to get in." When Isaac turned his full attention to the boy, he added, "I've run away before, trying to find my mum. You can say you found me and were bringing me back."

That's exactly what we did, but not before Isaac instructed Toby and me on what to say and do at our arrival, warning us that we had no way of knowing if the headmaster was involved. If he was part of the plot, we couldn't walk in and simply ask to see the books without arousing his suspicion.

At the orphanage, we left Isaac to find the way in through the back while I took the boy through the front door, asking to see the headmaster. The gray-haired man didn't question Toby's running away. Merely tousled the boy's head. "Off with you. To your lessons." His smile seemed forced. "Very kind of you to go out of your way to bring young—" He looked over at Toby, as though suddenly forgetting his name—assuming he ever knew it. He cleared his throat and smiled. "Yes, well, we were quite worried when we discovered him gone."

A loud thump came from the floor above us. The headmaster's eyes narrowed as he looked up at the ceiling. "If you'll excuse me."

"I'd like to see the classroom," I said quickly.

"Another time, perhaps." A second thump above us was

even louder than the first. "I have work to do. And, apparently, rats to ferret out."

I froze. The truth was, I'd never stood up to anyone. Not my father, not Reginald, not anyone. But I pictured Isaac in the midst of burgling the office, his warning about the headmaster echoing in my head. When the man started to move past me, I stepped in front of him. "I— I did not give you leave."

Surprise, then suspicion, clouded his eyes. "I doubt your father would approve of this intrusion."

It was a tactic Reginald had often used, invoking my father's name. Even now, my instinct was to back down, apologize, just as I'd always done—lest word get back. "Intrusion?" I said, trying to sound offended. And though I knew I'd never be able to withstand the challenge, should he decide to call my bluff, I added, "Shall we go fetch my father to ask?"

The man's brows went up. Surprisingly, though, he turned and led me down the hall, opening the door to the classroom himself.

There were at least fifteen boys sitting at tables, listening to a woman, who stood at the front of the room, reciting the alphabet as she wrote each letter on the chalkboard. Her brown hair, tied back with a black ribbon, fell to below her shoulders. When she turned to address the classroom and noticed us in the doorway, I was struck by her beauty. Her blue eyes met mine, and it was several seconds before I was able to move.

I'd wished everyone else in the room gone so that I could talk with this vision uninterrupted, but any courage I'd mustered with the headmaster's help fled as I looked upon her.

I forced my eyes away, spying young Toby sitting at the back of the room, his attention on his writing slate. His presence reminded me of our mission: creating a distraction so that Isaac could gain access to the ledgers. I looked around the classroom, searching for something I could use as an excuse to capture the headmaster's attention, keeping him from his office. And then it struck me. "Madam, why are there no young ladies in this class?"

The woman glanced at the headmaster, who suddenly remembered his place and made the introduction. "Forgive me. Mr. Payton, may I present Miss Lydia Atwater."

She curtsied, and I gave a nod. "Miss Atwater, why are there no girls present?" I repeated.

"A question I have asked since me first day here."

I looked at the headmaster, waiting for an answer.

"We find," he said, "that training the young girls to work in the kitchen and the scullery better prepares them for life outside the orphanage."

Miss Atwater's chest rose, her cheeks turned a becoming shade of pink, but she said nothing. She didn't need to. I saw it in her eyes.

Emboldened by her presence, I said, "The young ladies living here are not servants. They're children. I expect their presence in the classroom at once. And bring these children something to eat. How can they possibly learn if they're hungry?"

He stared at me, aghast.

"Perhaps you failed to hear my directive?"

"At once, sir." He hurried out the door.

I was vaguely aware of the boys looking at me with a new admiration. But I only had eyes for Miss Atwater. I wanted to approach, to hold a simple conversation, but all the insecurities of my childhood, and my father's domineering rule, rushed back. "You'll forgive me for the interruption, Miss Atwater."

She smiled. "You've done us a great service."

I wanted to stand there forever. I wanted to ask her to walk with me, to accompany me somewhere, anywhere, even though I knew my father would disapprove of such a match. A viscount's son and a governess? He wouldn't stand for it.

And I had never gone against his wishes.

Aware that there were fifteen pairs of eyes watching me, I bowed. "Miss Atwater."

She gave a slight curtsy. "Sir."

I wondered if I'd ever have the nerve to talk with her again.

Tempted to turn back, I forced myself out the classroom door, stopping short when I saw my cousin striding down the hall toward me.

His steps faltered when he saw me, a look of surprise on his face. "Payton, old boy. What are you doing here?"

Unable to think of a thing, I blocked his view into the classroom where young Toby sat, telling myself that I'd grown up with Reginald. My cousin was not a murderer.

He couldn't be.

When I looked back, I saw Miss Atwater continuing her lesson on the alphabet.

Reginald followed the direction of my gaze, laughed.

"I'd quite like to see your father's face when he discovers his dutiful son and heir has fallen for a common governess. You're likely to send him to an early grave."

It occurred to me that I'd been given the perfect excuse for being there. I drew my cousin from the door. "You won't tell Father, will you?"

"Your secret's safe with me."

"I say, why are you here?"

"I left my gloves when we came by a few days ago, to look over the ledgers. I thought I'd dash in and get them." He started past me.

Worried that he'd discover Isaac's presence, then realize we suspected him of embezzlement, I blocked his way.

A look of suspicion crossed Reginald's face, and I knew I needed to think of something fast.

On Sam and Remi's advice, Chad, still looking a bit shell-shocked after the rescue of his mother, convinced her and his aunt to visit the coast for several days. In the meantime, Chad's aunt invited them to stay at her home while she was gone. "I know your friend fixed my clogged drainpipe," she said to Chad, as he carried her suitcase down the stairs for her. "But I really would like a plumber to have a proper look." She smiled at Sam, who stood at the bottom of the stairs. "No offense, young man."

"None taken."

She gave a firm nod, turning her attention back to her nephew. "Please don't forget to water the garden. I don't want to lose my vegetables while I'm gone." She reached over, tugging at the hem of his shirt. "And tuck this in. How do you expect to find a young woman if you look like that? Did my sister not teach you how to dress?"

Chad looked slightly embarrassed, as he guided her out the front door, where his mother sat in the waiting taxi. Once the women were safely off, he returned to the house. "You're sure they'll be safer?" he asked, watching out the window as the taxi departed.

"Definitely," Sam said, as Oliver's cell phone rang. "The farther away from us, the better. At least until we figure out who's behind this."

Oliver, who was seated at the kitchen table, answered, waved Sam over to him. "I'm not quite sure when we'll be returning to Manchester . . ." He pressed a button, set the phone on the table. "It's Bill Snyder, the private detective recommended by David Cooke," he said.

"Who's David Cooke?" Chad asked.

"His uncle's solicitor," Remi replied quietly.

"You're on speaker, Mr. Snyder," Oliver said. "The Fargos are here with me."

"I'll try to keep this brief," Bill said. "I had a chat with your sister yesterday. She had the journal after all. A bit reluctant to turn it over, but, in the end, she gave it to me."

"The missing journal?" Oliver said.

"Quite. I took the liberty of reading a bit to be sure. Young boy who witnessed a murder, American detective Isaac Bell assisting the Viscount . . . ?"

"Good show, then."

Sam and Remi took the seat next to Oliver, asking, "Was there anything else you saw that would explain the sudden interest in the Gray Ghost?"

"Nothing that stands out in the few pages I read," Bill said. "Unfortunately, time was an issue if I wanted to make the cutoff for shipping. I was under the impression that you wanted it sent to your researcher. She should get it tomorrow."

"A shame," Oliver said. "Thought we might have a go at it, ourselves. See what turns up."

"You're in luck," Bill said. "My secretary scanned it. I'll have her send a digital copy to you first opportunity."

"If you could send a copy to Remi as well," Sam said, "I'd appreciate it."

"Mr. Payton?" Bill asked. "I'll need your permission for that."

"Absolutely. In fact, if you can copy the Fargos on all the correspondence, I'd be most grateful."

"Very good. Something else you should be aware of, Mr. Payton," Bill added. "A bit of a feeling that your sister was hiding something."

"She can be a bit strange. I wouldn't worry too much."

"Maybe so, but the reason she gave me for having the journal in her possession seemed . . . odd. It's possible the timing was mere coincidence. She mentioned taking it so that her son could read it."

Oliver leaned back in his chair, his expression softening. "Good lad, Trevor. Lived with us for a bit during her divorce. Stands to reason she'd think this. Can't tell you how many times I've told Allegra that the boy should read them. After all, unless I meet someone and start a family, which doesn't seem likely in my current state, he is the next in line for the viscountcy."

Sam and Remi exchanged glances, Remi sharing a similar thought: the timing of Allegra taking that journal—in the midst of the investigation of her uncle's arrest for murder—was highly suspicious. "It could be coincidence," Sam said, more for Oliver's sake than any real belief that the detective's instincts were faulty.

"Perhaps," Bill said. "That, however, is only part of the picture. I was there midafternoon. One of those bright sunny days, and her curtains were closed tight, and she was reluctant to let me in. Mind you, this last could be because she was by herself, and there was a strange man at her door. But it was precisely because she said she was by herself that I found her behavior unusual."

"For what reason?" Remi asked. In her mind, someone with the years of investigative experience that Bill Snyder had was generally well qualified to make such an opinion.

"The television was on. Football. I made a comment about the score, and it was clear she had no idea what I was talking about."

Oliver laughed. "That part would be true. Allegra's never followed sports."

"There was also an open bottle of ale on the table."

Oliver's smile faded as he stared at the cell phone.

"What is it?" Sam asked him.

"I'm beginning to wonder if any of this has anything to do with my grandfather at all. Her reprehensible ex-husband, Dex, suddenly appeared back in the picture a few months ago, trying to charm her. He's the sort that only comes around when he needs money. In fact, he's the reason Trevor came to live with us when they were divorcing."

"Define *reprehensible*," the detective said.

"Allegra never came out and said anything to me, and Trevor certainly never mentioned it, but we always suspected the man was physically abusive to her. If he's there, I'm not at all surprised that she'd try to hide it from you. She knows quite well what I think of her ex and she'd worry that you'd tell me."

"That might explain it," Bill said.

Sam wasn't ready to write off any possibility that someone else close to the family was involved. "What's your gut instinct?"

"Given that I'm reporting directly to her brother," Bill said, "a past abusive relationship would certainly explain her behavior. Especially if she doesn't want Oliver to know they're back together. Sad to say, this wouldn't be the first time I've seen this happen."

When Remi reached over, casually placing her hand on top of Sam's, he knew immediately what she wanted. The concern etched on Oliver's face seemed to magnify in the few short minutes they'd been on the phone. As if the man needed more to worry about, on top of his uncle's arrest. "I know you have your hands full with this investigation," Sam said, "but is there any chance we could impose on you to keep an eye on Allegra and Trevor?"

"I wouldn't want to overstep my bounds, Mr. Fargo," Bill replied. "So long as you're aware it may not have anything to do with Albert Payton's case . . ."

"We're willing to pay the extra cost," Sam said. "I think we'll all rest easier, knowing she and Trevor are safe."

"I'll see to it, Mr. Fargo. If there's nothing else, I'll get back to work."

Oliver looked relieved once the call ended. "I don't know how we're ever going to pay you back for all you've done."

"No need," Remi said. "You're family. You'd do the same, I'm sure of it."

"Remi's right," Sam said, as his cell phone buzzed on the tabletop. "Having your sister and Trevor looked after means we can concentrate on how best to help your uncle." He looked at the caller ID, surprised and a bit alarmed to see Selma making a video call, since, according to California time, it was just after two in the morning.

Nothing good ever happened at that hour.

Is everything okay?" Sam asked calmly, not wanting to alarm Remi. It wasn't all that long ago that someone had tried attacking them in their home at Gold Fish Point, nearly destroying it in the process. Even though they'd recovered and rebuilt, turning their home into a near-impregnable fortress, he still worried, and knew Remi did, too. He could see it in her eyes as she waited for Selma to answer.

"Fine, Mr. Fargo," Selma said, her face filling the screen, as she peered at him over the tops of her dark-framed glasses. Lazlo was hovering in the background. "Just another all-nighter. We were looking into the possibility that Isaac Bell was given a forty-fifty. If so, there's no record that he shipped the car to America. If he sold it in England, we haven't found anything."

"It's also possible," Lazlo added, leaning into view of the screen, "that he gave it away. Apparently, he was extremely wealthy."

"Of course," Selma said, "we're assuming the car he received from Rolls-Royce for his part in the recovery of the Gray Ghost is a forty-fifty. Is there a possibility it was a different model?"

Oliver couldn't say for sure. "Does it make a differ ence what car he was given?"

"It could," Selma said.

"In retrospect," Oliver said, "I assumed it was a forty-fifty, because that was the car gifted to my family. It's highly possible that Rolls-Royce gave him a different car. Maybe a thirty hp. Especially when you consider the forty-fifties were still in the prototype stage then."

"If we're lucky, it's in the journal," Sam said. "You should be getting it tomorrow."

"They found it?"

"At Allegra's."

Selma's brows went up, but she kept her comments about that revelation to herself, merely saying, "We'll have a look when it gets here . . . Not the reason for our call, however."

"You have our full attention," Remi said.

"During our research, we found a Rolls-Royce forum that mentioned an early-model Silver Ghost about to be auctioned somewhere in Italy. The timing of when this rumor appeared fits in with the theft of the Gray Ghost."

"I'm hoping you've narrowed that down a bit," Sam said. "That's a lot of country to cover."

"Unfortunately, no. Like I said, it's a rumor only, but enough of one that several people are talking about it. We thought it worth investigating. I sent an email to your friend Georgia Bockoven in case she's heard anything."

"Good thinking," Remi said. At one time, Georgia

and her husband, John, traveled the globe photographing cars and writing articles for *Sports Car Market*. They'd long since retired to Italy, buying a villa and small winery in the hills near Chianti, which they turned into a bed and breakfast destination. Even so, they were still involved in the car world. "Have you heard back from her?"

"Just got the email," Selma said, "which prompted my call. Mind you, according to Georgia, this is a friend of a friend of a friend—in other words, the reliability of the information is questionable."

"Noted," Sam said. "What was the info?"

"He, apparently, knows of a dealer in Italy who sells high-end jewelry and art. Usually recognizable names. Fabergé, Rembrandt, Bierstadt. But he's also brokered the occasional classic car."

"Fine art on wheels," Remi said, repeating what Sam had told her in Pebble Beach.

"An apt description," Lazlo replied.

"The rumor that comes in to play," Selma continued, "is the dealer's occasional foray into rare stolen art. Georgia's working on it from her end, and we're working on it from ours."

"We're sure about this auction?" Sam asked.

"If the rumor's true, it's this weekend. One of the many things we don't know is, exactly which car."

Sam thought about how long the Ghost was missing. Long enough, perhaps, to make it to some secret auction to be sold?

"Can they really turn over a stolen car that fast?" Remi asked.

"It's possible," Sam said.

"It's also possible," Selma added, "that whoever stole it did so for that very purpose. To sell it."

"Quite right," Lazlo said. "Done all the time in the underworld. Someone with enough money puts in an order, and the broker facilitates the theft. The money paid is astronomical, and the piece sold is usually never seen again."

"The point being," Selma continued, "that the timing of this secret auction this weekend, and the rumor of an early-model forty-fifty coming on the market is worth looking into. If you do, Georgia wanted me to let you know that you're welcome to stay with her at the villa."

"Thanks for looking into that," Sam said. "Anything else?"

"Just wondering how your Faux Ghost trade for Chad's mother worked out?"

"It was one of Remi's finest ideas. However, let's just say it wasn't our finest moment," Sam replied.

Remi laughed. "We almost needed rescuing from the woman we rescued."

"One good thing came out of it," Sam said. "Now that she and her sister are safely off, there's nothing holding us back from doing a full-out search for the missing Ghost. Dig up what you can on this broker. I think a trip to Italy's in order. I'd like to take a closer look at him." He looked over at Oliver and Chad. "We can certainly use your help if you'd like to come with us."

Oliver's eyes widened at the suggestion. "You can't seriously think that someone who's dealing in stolen goods is going to let you just walk in and demand to see the car, do you?"

"Maybe not. But if someone there knows where the Ghost is, we're certainly not going to wait for an invitation."

39

Remi, absorbed in reading the journal entry on her tablet, barely noticed the two-and-a-half-hour flight until they started their descent into Ciampino Airport. Outside, the blacktop of the tarmac rippled with heat waves, the summer sun beating down as the Fargos' jet landed, taxied toward the hangar they'd rented for their stay. By the time Sam, Remi, Oliver, and Chad cleared customs and immigration, then picked up the rental car, the four were grateful for the air-conditioning in the car during the two hours it took to drive to the villa.

Remi eyed the acres of vineyards and the long, winding drive shaded on both sides by tall sycamore trees. At the top of the hill, a wide wrought iron gate blocking their passage now swung open. Georgia, a tall woman with short dark hair, wearing a flowing white linen dress, stepped out onto the terra-cotta-tiled porch as they got out of the car.

"Remi, darling! So good to see you!" She gave Remi a kiss on each cheek, and turned to Sam. "Handsome as ever."

"Georgia," Sam said. "As beautiful as the day we first met. I swear, you don't age."

"You're such a wonderful liar." She smiled as Sam introduced her to Chad and Oliver. "The Viscount's nephew," she said, shaking Oliver's hand. "Did I understand that you and Sam are actually related?"

"Cousins," Oliver replied.

Georgia turned, with amused expression, in Sam's direction. "Had I only known, I'd have thrown a very large party."

"Cousins," Sam said, "several times removed."

"Don't let him fool you, Georgia," Remi said. "Sam's only five hundredth or so in line to the throne."

Georgia laughed, as she beckoned them inside. "No living with you now, is there, Sam?"

"Trying not to let it go to my head." He looked past her into the house. "Where's John?"

"Winemaking. Never-ending job. He should be up in a little while."

They stepped into the cool interior, the same terracotta tiles from the porch on the floor inside. Georgia showed them to their rooms, pausing as she was about to leave. "Had I known earlier you were coming, I'd have canceled the group renting the villa this weekend, and you wouldn't have to rush out."

"We'll be fine," Remi said.

Georgia smiled. "I'm not sure I will. College students on summer break. One of my friends rented to them last year, but he was booked up. Apparently, they're loud but very respectful. The one advantage is, they all sleep in late. The mornings are quiet." She led them upstairs. "If you need help finding a place after this weekend, I have other friends who've joined the bed and breakfast club. I can find you a lovely place to stay."

"If we're lucky, we'll find what we need in a day or two."

Georgia's face clouded with anxiety. "I don't suppose there's any way I can convince the four of you to give up this search? I've heard this dealer can be dangerous. There are rumors that he's connected to the Mafia."

"We at least have to look into it," Sam said.

Her smile was grim. "I do hope you'll change your mind. Even so, I'm glad we'll have a chance to catch up. You haven't made dinner plans, have you?"

"None."

"Then I'll see you after you have a chance to freshen up. We'll dine on the veranda around eight. I'm looking forward to having you try our Chianti with dinner."

Remi joined Georgia before the men returned from their tour of the wine cellars beneath the house, hoping for a chance to catch up with her friend. The veranda overlooked the vineyards they'd seen on the drive up, the evening sun painting the rolling hills with a golden glow. A light breeze rippled through the vines, rustling the broad leaves.

Remi sighed. "It must be wonderful looking out at this each night. I'm a bit envious."

"Don't be. We're actually considering selling."

"Why? I thought you loved it here."

"What's not to love? Unfortunately, while it was one

of those ideas that look good on paper, the reality is that running a boutique winery isn't nearly as profitable as we'd hoped. Hence, the bed and breakfast angle."

Remi looked over at Georgia, noting the worried look in her eyes. "If you need help with anything, you'll let us know."

Georgia gave a slight shrug, smiled. "There're worse things than being poor. Like not seeing a good friend in years and years. Come, sit." She led Remi to a glass-topped table, with several wicker chairs set around it. She opened a bottle of prosecco that had been chilling in an ice bucket, poured two glasses. "Now, tell me all about this car you're hunting for. How very exciting it all sounds."

"Frustrating, is more like it," Remi said. "That car was practically stolen from right beneath our noses."

"Selma mentioned that. And no idea who took it?"

"Not yet. I don't suppose you've heard back from this mysterious friend about the secret auction?"

"Another auction actually came up, this one in Milan, though I'm not sure it's at all the one you're looking for. Someone had the bright idea of combining cars with fashion and selling high-priced tickets. What makes this a possibility is that a late entry is creating a lot of buzz. A Rolls not previously seen on the market. But it's specified as an 'early model,' not an '06 or '07. I have two press passes that will get you in the door for an up close look at the cars."

"When is it?"

"This weekend," Georgia said. "I still haven't heard back on the other one. It's by invitation only. Very private, no tickets, no press. Also a Rolls—near Rome, though."

"No year?"

"Early forty-fifty, is what I heard." She leaned back against the flowered cushions, the wicker squeaking beneath her weight. "As I mentioned to Selma, the person I'm waiting to hear from is a friend of a friend of a friend. Maybe not even that close. I'm talking to someone who is intermediating, I suppose you could say. All very hush-hush, which means they won't even know that I'm the one making inquiries. It took some convincing to assure him you want the car for a very private collection. The undeclared sort." She looked at Remi and smiled. "I hope you don't mind that I painted you and Sam as less than savory investors?"

"If it gets us in the door, I'm sure we'll weather the stain on our reputations."

"That's what I thought. So, what else is new? I see you and Sam are still out traveling the world. You're not feeling the urge to stay home and start a family?"

Remi laughed as she tried to picture her and Sam settling down with a baby. "Let's just say nothing in the immediate future. Plenty of time to think about that later."

"I'm serious. I worry about you, Remi. Part of me hopes this person doesn't call back. What if something happens to you out there? That old saying, life turns on a dime? There's a reason for it."

Remi reached over and touched her friend's arm. "We're careful. And you know Sam. He's not going to let anything happen to me."

Georgia looked up as John climbed the steps from the garden, followed by Oliver, Chad, and Sam, who was carrying two bottles of Chianti. "Speaking of, here's your fearless husband now."

Sam placed the bottles on the table, then brushed his hand on Remi's shoulder as he took the chair next to hers. "What are you two talking about? Or do I want to know?"

Georgia's phone rang. She leaned forward, nearly spilling her drink as she scooped it up to check the caller ID. "It's him."

"Who?" Sam asked, as Oliver and Chad took a seat in the remaining chairs, while John opened a bottle of wine.

"Her contact," Remi whispered. "About the cars."

Georgia signaled for them to stay quiet while she answered, her Italian so rapid-fire, Remi had a hard time keeping up, until she switched to English, saying, "They're here with me now. I'll check." Georgia pressed the mute button on her phone. "If you can make it to Rome, he says his friend is willing to meet somewhere public, but no large crowds."

"Remi?" Sam asked.

She knew the perfect restaurant. "Ask him if he's familiar with Hostaria Antica Roma on the Appian Way."

Georgia repeated the location. ". . . Very good. *Ciao.*" She hung up, telling them, "He'll meet you there tomorrow at noon."

"Tomorrow?" Remi said. "That makes it difficult to get to the other auction."

"What auction?" Sam asked.

"Milan," Georgia said, telling him about the event.

"Sorry to say," Sam said, "we can't be in two places at one time."

"Oliver and I can go to the Milan event," Chad said. "If it turns out to be nothing, no time wasted."

Remi checked Oliver, noting his hands clasped tightly on the arms of the chair. The poor man looked ready to bolt, and she could hardly blame him. "Are you okay with that?" she asked.

He took a deep breath, squared his shoulders, and said, "If it helps with my uncle's case, then yes."

"Looks like we have our itinerary for tomorrow," Sam said.

The early-morning sun poured through the window as Arthur Oren watched his son, not quite two, crawling beneath the table to retrieve a plastic block that had landed there. Arthur Junior would inherit everything one day, including all that Oren had added to the family fortune—and all that he'd soon acquire from the Payton side of the family.

The boy picked up the bright red block, looked over at his father wide-eyed, placed the corner of the block in his mouth, babbling something unintelligible. His ever-present nanny bent down and pulled the toy out. "No, AJ."

"A little dirt won't hurt," Oren said, reciting what his mother had always told him.

"Yes, sir," she said, then distracted AJ with a stuffed bear.

The boy crawled over, reaching for it, saying, "Ba-ba."

"Bear," she corrected.

"Ba-ba," the child demanded, as the phone rang.

Bruno's number showed on the screen.

Oren waved at nanny to take the child from the room. The moment the door closed, he picked up the receiver. "Did you get it?"

"It wasn't the Ghost."

"What do you mean, it wasn't the Ghost? Did no one look?"

"They used smoke and mirrors. Had us fooled."

He sat there, seconds ticking on a wall clock behind him, hoping he'd misunderstood. But the long stretch of silence on the other end told him otherwise. "What happened?" He listened as Bruno went over the details. The moment Oren heard the Fargos mentioned, he bristled with anger. "How is it those two keep finding their way into the middle of my business?"

"You don't think they stole the Ghost, do you?"

He considered the possibility. "I doubt they'd go to the trouble of concocting a fake car, if that were the case."

"Why not? They're all about money. Fool us, keep the car, and who's the wiser?"

Except that Oren had read enough about the Fargos to know otherwise. "They're too altruistic. They wouldn't risk someone's life over material possessions. At least we can cross them off the list."

"You don't think Colton has it?"

"Of course not." He swiveled around in his desk chair, glancing at the clock on the wall. Colton was due any moment now. "Take another look around Payton Manor. There's a lot of barns that aren't being used anymore. After all, they found the car in one of them. Maybe he has it there."

"Won't be able to get out there until tomorrow," Bruno said. "Had to take Frank to get his arm stitched. Someplace where they wouldn't ask questions about gunshots."

"Just do it," he said, hearing footsteps outside the door, then a soft knock. "I have to go."

He dropped the phone in its cradle just as Colton walked in, making a wide berth around the red and blue plastic blocks on the floor.

"No smoking," Oren said, as the man started to pull out a cigarette. "Not with my son in the house."

"Doesn't your ex normally keep the boy?" he asked, returning the cigarette to the pack.

"She's on a trip."

Colton pulled out a chair in front of the desk, using his foot to clear the blocks from the floor in front of him before sitting. "I take it your attempt to recover the car wasn't successful?"

"Unfortunately, no," he said, thinking about Bruno's suggestion that Colton was behind the theft of the Ghost. The very idea that the person he'd paid to steal it in the first place was perhaps responsible for stealing it a second time on the sly . . . It seemed absurd. "Turns out the car was a fake."

"You think this mechanic took it?"

"I'd say it's highly unlikely. The Fargos were involved, and I don't see them risking anyone's life for a car, no matter how valuable."

Colton, who'd been eyeing the toys scattered about the room with an expression bordering on distaste, suddenly looked up at him. "What do you mean, the Fargos were involved?"

"My men planted themselves in the mechanic's house with his mother. Leverage."

"Are you insane?"

"It worked."

"How? You still don't have the car. You're lucky the police weren't called." Colton reached out, kicking one of the blocks at his feet. The red plastic square rattled across the floor, landing in front of Oren's chair. "Another fool move like that, your kid'll be visiting you in prison. Assuming your ex lets him near you."

"Are you threatening me?"

"Far from it. Since you're the one paying my salary, it's in my best interest to make sure you stay out of jail."

"My men were acting on credible evidence that the mechanic had the car."

"Credible? Who was your source?"

"Allegra."

Colton's brows went up slightly. "Oliver's sister? Interesting. By any chance did she volunteer this information out of the blue?"

"Of course not. I called her and asked. Clearly she was wrong. But her guess seemed logical at the time. After all, this Chad fellow was the man who helped Albert and Oliver ready the car for the London show."

Colton absently reached for his cigarette pack, suddenly remembered, lowered his hand. "Did it ever occur to you that she was being a little too helpful?"

"I asked her who she thought was good for it."

"What about that ex of hers?"

"If not for him, we wouldn't have had the Ghost at all. Besides, he's nothing but a petty crook. I doubt he has the means to pull off such a thing."

"You're sure?"

At the moment, Oren wasn't sure of anything except the nagging thought that Colton had all the advantages in this venture. Despite Bruno's suggestion otherwise, it occurred to Oren that there was really no one he could trust but himself. "For one, Allegra doesn't drive. Two, unless she's suddenly flush with cash, she'd never be able to have the funds to hire someone to steal the Ghost. Three, do you really think she could somehow have gotten past your security? Strike that last question. Apparently, someone did."

"There was nothing wrong with my security."

"Except for that one glaring flaw. The Ghost was in your warehouse and it's now missing."

"We'll find whoever was behind the theft. That you can count on. In fact, I have a very good lead in Italy."

"What lead?"

"A Silver Ghost that suddenly just came on the market. An auction for very select clientele."

"You think it might be the Gray Ghost?"

"We can't be sure. But the timing is highly suspect. If there's any possibility that it is the Ghost, you'll need to get on it before Oliver or the Fargos hear about it. The last thing you want is to cross swords with them."

On this, they agreed. That Oliver had taken up with the Fargos to help save his uncle's home was beyond infuriating. For someone who'd never shown any interest in getting married and producing an heir, the man was a sentimental fool, protecting his uncle's estate even though he had no one to pass it on to except Allegra's son. "I wish we could put an end to his relationship with the Fargos. Their interference is costing me time and money."

"Do you think they know why you're after the Ghost?"

"Does it matter?"

"It might. Maybe if we found the Ghost and it was returned to Payton, they'd back off."

"Quite right," Oren said. "Let's give a car worth millions upon millions to the very man I've spent the last year trying to financially ruin. Brilliant idea. Do you have any more scintillating plans you haven't revealed?"

"No one said you had to give it to him in one piece."

"Have you taken leave of your senses?" Oren replied, wondering if he should rethink his dismissal of Colton as the mastermind behind the theft of the stolen Ghost. "Only an idiot would purposefully ruin a car worth tens of millions of dollars."

"It's not like you can sell it on the open market."

"Maybe not, but there are plenty of buyers who'd make a private sale for their own collection just to say they have it. Isn't that how you found the auction for this Ghost in Italy?"

Colton merely regarded him with those dead brown eyes of his.

The man was infuriating. "Returning the Gray Ghost is not an option. I intend to recover it. Period." Oren leaned back in his chair, taking the moment to calm himself. "Back to the Fargos. I'd prefer they were dead. How do you plan on taking care of it?"

"As I said before, killing them outright will only bring unwanted attention. There's a far better way to keep them out of your affairs, and later—when they end up dead—anyone who hears what happened will nod in understanding at how two, young, once-wealthy socialites took their own lives. In fact, I've already started implementing it."

"I'm listening . . ."

JOURNAL OF JONATHON PAYTON, 5TH VISCOUNT WELLSWICK

1906

I still held out hope that my cousin was innocent. Even so, I dared not let him get past. How would I explain Isaac Bell's presence in the headmaster's office? And what of the boy, Toby? I couldn't let Reginald see him.

I knew I must have seemed as though I'd suddenly lost my wits, standing there, my tongue cleaved to the top of my mouth. As a look of annoyance crossed Reggie's face, I was vaguely aware of Miss Atwater's melodic voice drifting out of the classroom as she taught the alphabet.

It was clear. I was smitten.

A year ago, my father had arranged for a proper introduction to an heiress of his approval, hoping our betrothal would soon follow. Suffice it to say that Reginald was now married to the young woman, my father pointing out that he'd only courted her because of my interest. The truth was that I was happy for him. She and I would not have made a good match.

Miss Atwater, however . . . she was different, and part of me was reluctant to use her as my excuse for being here. I wouldn't have, except that Reggie's mild annoyance started turning to suspicion.

"'TIS RASH," I said to Reginald, "I know. But I came back hoping to catch a glimpse of Miss Atwater, and now I feel the fool. She never even noticed me on our first visit." Perhaps because she'd never seen me. I tried drawing Reggie away. "Please don't look in there, lest she notices us. Accompany me outside."

"To what purpose?" Reginald asked, looking past me into the classroom.

I grasped his arm, guiding him down the hall, then out the door. "To work up the nerve to ask if she would consider allowing me to call on her."

I paced in front of the carriage, pretending—nay, there was no pretense whatsoever—I was so besotted that I needed help with what I should say to Miss Atwater.

Reginald was at once amused and annoyed. "She's a schoolteacher. And a bit long in the tooth. Do you sincerely think she wouldn't be flattered by your attention?"

I ignored his assessment of the woman, whom I found perfect. "And what if she says no?"

"Either declare your intentions and risk your father's wrath or go back to being the coward you are—and never knowing what may happen."

Reginald had always been braver, stronger, faster, smarter. As children, I had often been the one to hang back, let my cousin take charge. It was easy to fall into that role now because I needed to keep Reginald out here, away from the headmaster's office. But the truth of his words stung. I had always allowed my father to run roughshod over my interests. Reginald's, too. And so, when I asked for pointers on how to approach Miss Atwater, I was very serious. "How do I do it?"

Before Reginald had a chance to answer, Isaac Bell came striding around the corner. He didn't look at me or my cousin until he was nearly on us, and all he did was tip his hat and continue past as though he knew me not at all.

I was fortunate that, at that very moment, Miss Atwater appeared at the top of the stairs, drawing our attention away from Bell.

"Sir?" she said.

I was lost in her blue eyes, and it was a moment before I realized she was addressing me. "Pardon?"

"I wanted to thank you. For insisting the young ladies being brought into the classroom."

Reginald gave me a sly look.

"Happy to oblige," I said, thrilled that she'd seen fit to seek me out.

She gave the slightest of curtsies, about to leave.

"Miss Atwater?"

She turned back, looking at me with an expectation I wasn't prepared for. After a moment of awkward silence, she said, "I should get back to the children."

"Would you do me the honor of allowing me to call on you?" My words came out in a rush.

Even so, she smiled shyly, saying, "I would find that most agreeable."

MY DELIGHT over the prospect of calling on Miss Atwater was tempered by my reluctance to entertain the notion that my cousin was responsible for the theft of the Grey Ghost.

Isaac Bell still believed that Reginald had masterminded the theft while he and I were employed at Rolls-Royce Limited.

If so, was he also the masked man who'd held up the train and killed the engineer and brakeman? The embezzlement, I could almost believe—the work of a brash man who'd gotten in over his head with gambling debts—especially after Isaac had found proof that the books had been altered. Someone had stolen the money. But murder? All to facilitate the theft of engine parts that Mr. Rolls and Mr. Royce were counting on to finish the half-built Silver Ghost in order to enter it into the Olympia Motor Show instead of the stolen Grey Ghost?

As preposterous as it sounded, I dared not mention it to my father, his health being delicate. I tried to put it from my head that night as I called on Miss Atwater, ignoring the strange palpitations of my heart when I thought of her.

We ate dinner and took in an operetta, both enjoying ourselves enough that Miss Atwater agreed I could call on her again. She lived in the caretaker's cottage behind the orphanage with her brother and his wife. Neither of us wanted the night to end, so I dismissed my carriage, deciding to walk her home. As we strolled down the sidewalk, I sensed the presence of someone behind me. When I looked back, I saw nothing but shadows.

"Is something amiss?" she asked.

Emboldened by the possession of my father's brass-handled cane, and wanting no harm to come to Miss Atwater, I gathered my courage. "Wait here. I'll be but a moment."

I left her at the corner, certain that what I saw in her blue eyes was unwavering trust. Turning back, I gripped the heavy cane and retraced my steps, hoping to discover the source of my unease. Whatever had caught my attention was nowhere to be found, and I chided myself for being so jumpy, certain that my imagination had conjured sounds where there were none. "'Twas nothing," I said, turning back to her.

But the street was empty.

I ran to the corner, searching frantically, looking at the railroad tracks, wondering if she'd crossed over to the orphanage. "Miss Atwater?" I called out.

I heard a rustling and started to turn. And then I felt a sharp pain as someone hit me over the head.

The following morning, Chad and Oliver took a train north to Milan while Sam and Remi made the almost three-hour drive to Rome to meet with Georgia's contact. Sam turned onto Via Appia Antica, the car bouncing over the cobblestones as they headed up the hill. Neither of them had been to their friend's restaurant since it had moved from its original setting among the ancient columbaria crypts, and Remi was curious if the new location, on the same road, would have as much character.

About three miles in, the tomb of Caecilia Metella, built in the first century B.C., loomed up ahead, the tower overlooking the gardens of the new restaurant. Sam parked the car, and he and Remi walked up the graveled drive, stopping as a tall, dark-haired man carrying a bottle of sparkling wine in a bucket of ice burst out the kitchen door.

"Scusi," the man said, almost stepping past them until he made eye contact. "Remi! Sam! Wait here, I'll be right back," he added, his Italian accent thick. Paolo Magna-

nimi continued past them into the garden, where customers sat at white-cloth-covered tables, some set beneath large white umbrellas, others in the shade of the trees.

When he returned, he shook Sam's hand, gave him a big hug, then kissed Remi on both cheeks. "I was very happy to see your names on the reservation list."

"It's been too long," Remi said. "I've missed your tiramisu."

"But not me?" Paolo replied, with a laugh.

"That goes without saying."

"Come. I have your table ready." He led them across the lawn to a table set apart from the others. Pink roses grew at the base of the stone ruins that ran the length of the parklike grounds. Paolo pulled out a chair for Remi, while Sam took the chair next to hers, sitting so that his back was to the wall. After exchanging pleasantries, Paolo left to see to his other guests.

Forty-five minutes later, with no word from Georgia's contact, Sam and Remi decided to order without him. They'd just finished their meal when he finally arrived.

Luca, as he introduced himself, was dressed in a custom suit, the crisp white shirt open at the collar. He was in his late forties, his brown hair peppered with gray. "I had hoped to be here before now," he said, sitting in the chair next to Sam's, his dark eyes darting from side to side as he took in everyone seated around them. "I tried calling your mobile but couldn't get through. I was told you wouldn't leave without me, so I came as soon as I was able."

"Don't worry about it," Sam said. "You're here now. Have a bite to eat."

"I wish I could, but I really do need to get going."

"At least stay for the tiramisu," Remi said. "It's my favorite in all of Rome."

As if on cue, Paolo appeared with a third serving of the dessert, which he placed in front of Luca, before picking up Sam's credit card. Luca took a bite, his eyes widening. "Oh, that is good." He took another bite, finished it off, before sitting back, with a sigh, grateful for the espresso served along with it. "Makes me wish I'd been here for the entire meal."

Sam moved the conversation back on track. "Our friend was telling us that you have information on an upcoming auction of an early-model Rolls-Royce Silver Ghost?"

"Please don't take this the wrong way. I took the liberty of looking into your backgrounds on the internet. You seem like a nice couple, unlike the people who generally attend. They don't care much about where the car came from or returning lost property to its rightful owner. In fact, some of them are as likely to kill to get what they want as they are to pull out their checkbooks."

"We're extremely careful," Sam said. "Is documentation provided?"

"Not for this auction. The less documentation, the better. The success depends on the absolute anonymity of the buyers and the sellers. The broker who handles these transactions would never reveal the information. This is, how do you Americans say it? The big league."

"How do we get in touch with this broker?"

He studied Sam a moment as though weighing his

decision on what he should say. "It's ten thousand euros cash, in denominations of twenties, just to walk in the door—if you have an invitation. The latter I can get you for another ten thousand. I prefer mine in hundreds. Easier to carry."

"That's a pretty steep price," Sam said.

"Take it or leave it."

"We'll take it. Where do you want to meet?"

"If you have pen and paper . . ."

Remi handed both to him, as Paolo walked up, whispering something in Sam's ear. "I'll be right there," Sam said. Paolo smiled, stood back a few feet as Sam turned to Luca, saying, "What time?"

"Half past nine. The auction starts at ten."

"Until then."

"The address," Luca said, handing pen and paper back to her. "Thank you for the tiramisu. I'll see the both of you tonight. With the cash." He pushed his chair back, stood. "If I didn't mention, it's black-tie."

"Ten thousand euros?" Remi said, after he left.

"A small price if it gets us the information we need," Sam said, as Paolo again walked up, now holding a small machine. He showed Sam the receipt it had printed. "Declined?" Sam said. He handed Paolo a different card. That was also declined, as was Remi's.

Paolo gave them an apologetic smile. "Sometimes these machines are finicky."

"Don't worry about it. Maybe some computer glitch somewhere." Sam paid with cash instead.

"We better call Selma," Remi said, taking out her cell

phone. "If anyone can figure it out, she can." Her call wouldn't connect. "Luca did say he couldn't get through to us. Maybe we're too far out from the city center. You try, Sam."

He did. Same result. "Hate to bother you, Paolo. May I borrow your phone?"

"Of course. Right this way."

Sam and Remi followed him across the lawn. Remi waited outside, while Paolo showed Sam the phone, then left to attend to customers. Sam returned about five minutes later, his expression diplomatically neutral.

Paolo saw him, walking over. "Is everything okay?"

"Just a mix-up at the bank. Glad I had enough cash to cover lunch."

Remi gave Paolo a hug. "The meal, as always, was fabulous. And I absolutely love your new location." She waited until they were well out of earshot before asking, "Did you find out what was going on?"

"Not even close. I spent the last few minutes with one of the credit card companies, who informed me that I'd canceled that card about an hour ago. I assured her I hadn't."

"She didn't believe you?"

"Even worse, she didn't believe I was me."

"How is that possible?"

"Not sure. I couldn't reach Selma or Lazlo. Busy signal."

Remi held up her phone as they walked to the car, hoping to find some connection. "This doesn't make sense. They've worked here before." She looked over at

Sam. "What do you mean, a busy signal? We have call waiting . . ."

"Exactly."

"What's going on?"

"It's time we find out."

Sam unlocked the car doors, opening Remi's, before walking around to the driver's side. He started the engine, the air conditioner blasting, then took off down the road, going over all the possibilities of how and why their cards were declined.

Not quite the same, but what came to mind was that Oliver and his uncle had suddenly found themselves destitute, which was what led to them selling off their possessions and putting Payton Manor on the market. While Oliver had naturally assumed that his uncle was somehow responsible, Sam now believed otherwise. "I hate to say it, Remi. There's only one reason I can think of that all this is happening."

"That would be . . . ?" she asked, holding her cell phone at various angles, still trying to get a signal.

"Every account frozen, no access to money or credit. Sound familiar?"

She looked up in alarm. "You're saying someone hacked our accounts? How vulnerable are we?"

"Right now, our biggest problem is being stuck in a foreign country with no assets. If that's the case, it could take days or weeks to sort through it all."

Remi's moment of panic was over, her expression turning to one of determination. "If they're targeting us, we're on the right track."

"Or it could just be that we're helping the Paytons, and someone wants to stop us."

"Or both. We definitely need to talk to Selma."

"And if we can't get in touch with her? We need to get into that auction. We need cash."

"And the proper clothes to get into a black-tie affair."

"I'd say a quick trip to the airport. Get some money, our satellite phone, and clothes from the jet that'll get us into the auction. We'll figure out what's going on from there."

When they arrived at the airport, what they didn't expect was to find their jet locked in a hangar with no sign of their crew. When they tried to get access, a uniformed security guard was called, the young man standing quietly behind a dark-haired female clerk who was hesitant to tell them the jet was being held for non-payment and any access forbidden until the bill was paid.

"How?" Sam asked. "It was paid before we arrived."

"My apologies, Mr. Fargo, but the account has been frozen, and the credit card charges reversed. When we tried to contact you by mobile, you didn't answer. We had no choice. Unless, of course, you are here to make the payment?"

Something he couldn't do, since neither he nor Remi had a credit card that would work. "Any chance we can get on the jet?"

"Unfortunately, it's beyond my control."

"We'll get the money," Sam said. "Once I know the jet's safe. And my crew."

"They haven't been in touch? Your pilot assured us he'd be in touch with you to straighten this entire matter out."

Sam and Remi exchanged worried looks, Sam saying, "Can you at least show us the jet? How do I know it's still there?"

The young guard stepped forward. "I'm sorry, Mr. Fargo, but until payment is made, I'm going to have to ask you and your wife to leave the airport. We would appreciate if you did so quietly."

Sam didn't know Italian law. Whether the lockdown of their jet was standard procedure for unpaid bills or manipulation by whoever had hacked their accounts mattered little, their inability to access their aircraft was going to make life a lot harder—probably the very reason behind it.

Short of storming the hangar—not an option with the number of armed guards stationed at the airport—he thanked them for their time. As he and Remi started to turn away, she reached over, placing her hand on Sam's arm. "What about my medication?"

He looked over at his wife, her expression so open and vulnerable, he almost believed she was in dire medical need. Sam turned to the security guard, doing his best to appear worried about her health. "Can you at least escort my wife onto the plane to get her pills?"

The guard eyed Remi, then the woman behind the counter, who gave a slight nod. "Just make sure that's all she removes," the woman said.

"Let me get my cart," the guard said. "I'll drive you out there."

When he returned with the electric cart, Sam started to follow Remi, but the woman held up her hand. "Sir, you'll have to wait here. I'm bending the rules enough by allowing your wife onto the plane. Please don't make me lose my job."

He walked across the gray linoleum tiles to a row of hard plastic chairs to wait. Fifteen minutes later, the guard and Remi returned, Remi wearing what looked like a black silk scarf draped artfully around her neck.

"Grazie," Remi said to him. She took Sam's arm, and the two left.

Sam regarded the very long scarf around her shoulders, noting the Valentino label just visible in one of the folds. "No suit or black tie?"

"One slinky gown and the satphone was all I could manage without him noticing. The petty cash box was empty."

"Hopefully, the crew took it. We at least know they'll have enough to survive on for the next few days. Their credit cards are on the same business account as ours."

"Where do you suppose they are?"

"Sitting in some air-conditioned hotel, sipping prosecco,

attempting to contact Selma to get this straightened out. Which is what we need to do as soon as possible."

"Sipping prosecco?"

"As tempting as that part of the plan is, we might want to hold off until we figure out what's going on."

The two walked out, the heat hitting them full force when they left the cooled building, waiting for the shuttle that would transport them to the parking lot. "I don't get this," Remi said, once they were in their car. She untied the dress from around her neck, tossing it into the backseat. "How could it happen?"

"Does it matter?" He backed out of the parking space, the wheels squealing on the slick concrete as he turned. "We move on."

He paid the parking fee, waited for the cashier to wave him through, then pulled out into traffic, noticing a black Mercedes right behind him. He made a lane change. The Mercedes did the same. "Time to check that satphone."

She turned it on and tried to make a call. "Nothing."

No doubt about it. Whoever targeted them had covered all the bases. They were definitely pros, maybe someone with military or counterterrorism experience. Sam sped up to get around a van. The Mercedes did the same. He checked his rearview mirror, just able to make out the silhouette of the man driving it, recognizing the flattop haircut. "Unlock that glove box and get your gun. We're being followed."

Sam's attempt to lose the Mercedes failed when a second car, also a Mercedes, this one dark blue, pulled up behind them. The two cars kept a steady pace.

Remi placed her gun in the center console, shifted in her seat to see who was behind them. "That's the same man who followed us from Payton Manor to Chad's mother's house."

He let up on the gas, hoping for a better view. When he looked in the mirror, he recognized Bruno's ruddy face. Sam sped up. "You know what I find fascinating about this?"

"Fascinating? Not a word I'd associate with suddenly being destitute and being followed by whoever these people are."

"*Interesting*, then?"

"Much better word choice," she said, watching the side mirror.

"Someone hacks our account, we head to the airport, and they're there, waiting for us."

"I don't find that fascinating or interesting. I find it disturbing."

"They knew we'd be coming here. Our jet's here. All they had to do was wait in the parking lot, and there we were."

Remi looked over at him. "You are going somewhere with this? Or just pointing out that we're in trouble?"

"If they've hacked into our accounts, our phones, our credit cards, they have access to every charge we made. When we tried using the credit cards at Paolo's restaurant, they knew exactly where we were."

"Why didn't they just follow us from there?"

"That's what I was wondering. If I had to guess, the hack was very recent." He checked his mirrors. The two cars were keeping apace but maintaining their distance. "If that's the case, there wasn't enough time for them to get to the restaurant."

She looked over at him. "Logical guess is, we'd head to the jet for whatever we need?"

"Exactly."

"While I think your hypothesis is nearly flawless, how is that going to help us?"

"We need to regroup. Once we lose them, we have to figure out how to stay off the grid."

"We're broke, Sam. We're going to have to figure out how to survive."

He thought about what he had left in his wallet after paying for lunch that afternoon. "Two hundred euros isn't exactly broke."

"Unless, of course, you're trying to come up with

something to wear to an event where you have to look like you can afford to be there. The party and auction are black-tie. With one dress between us, we're going to have to draw straws to see who wears it."

"Not sure I can pull off black silk."

"Definitely not sleeveless black silk."

He switched lanes again. "The least of our problems right now. We don't even have the ten grand to get in, never mind the ten grand Luca wants for his invitation." He looked over at her, then back at the road, his eye on the two cars following them. "Don't you find it odd that they're just hanging back? Not even worried about staying on our tail? Or speeding up when we do?"

"I do find that odd. Especially considering the way you managed to elude them on our way out of Manchester. They have to be tracking us somehow."

"Possibly our cell phones."

Remi made sure both phones were turned off. The two cars were still following at a safe distance even with Sam doing his best to lose them.

"We can't go back to Georgia's," Remi said. "We'll lead them right to her."

She was right, of course. "We seem to be one step behind. Time to turn things around."

He hit the gas, pulled off the motorway, went back the other direction, took the next exit, headed down a long stretch of road, feeling as though he'd managed to lose the tail, until he noticed a car, so far back it was just a speck, but coming closer, until the blue Mercedes filled his rear-view mirror. No sign of Bruno's black Mercedes. Still,

Sam's evasive maneuvers should have worked to lose both cars, not just the one. "We know it's not the phones . . . Makes me wonder if they somehow put a tracking device on our car while we were at the airport."

Remi tapped her fingers on the slide of her weapon. "I could take out one of his tires."

"I'm not sure that'll help. Bruno's car is still out there. If they did put on a tracking device . . ."

"At least we can slow him down. One tail is better than two."

Sam eyed the narrow road winding through the low foothills, the rolling slopes covered with brown grass. This far out in the country, there wasn't a house in sight. In fact, they were the only two cars on the road. No innocent bystanders to get hurt, no witnesses—and no police. "If we're going to do this, now's the time."

Remi's green eyes sparkled with catlike anticipation as she finger-combed her red hair into a ponytail, rolled down her window, shifted in her seat to face the rear, gripping her Sig in her left hand. She braced it on the base of the frame of the open window. "Ready anytime, Fargo," she said over the wind.

Sam let his foot off the gas, slowing for a curve. The blue Mercedes gained on them. When it tried to pull alongside their car, Sam veered to the center, refusing to give it room, as he accelerated out of the curve. "Get ready," he said. "A straight stretch ahead." He sped up.

Remi leaned out the window, her hair whipping at her face as she took aim. He pressed the gas, trying to keep the distance steady, not seeing the pothole until it was too late. Remi fired just as he hit it.

"A little warning!" Remi called out, her shot missing.

"Sorry!" He gripped the wheel, steering into another curve, coming out of the turn, realizing too late the one disadvantage of being this far out in the country: poor road maintenance. Their wheels shuddered across the uneven pavement, jarring Sam and Remi with each bounce. They neared a narrow bridge up ahead, and, just beyond it, a sharp turn. "Maybe wait till we get out of this stretch," he shouted.

"Where's the challenge in that?" Remi's smile grew even more determined when Sam approached the bridge. She took aim as the Mercedes gained on them, its reflection filling her side mirror.

Crack! Crack!

The blue Mercedes veered suddenly from the road, spinning in a cloud of dust and debris, slamming into the bridge's parapet. It tilted up on two wheels, seemed to hover for a second, then bounced down the side of the hill.

"Nicely done, Mrs. Fargo."

"Thank you."

Sam pulled over to the side of the road. He and Remi looked out the window and down the hill at the crumpled car sitting at an odd angle at the bottom of the ravine.

"You think he survived?" Remi asked.

"If he was wearing his seat belt." Sure enough, they saw movement, as the driver tried opening the door.

She gave a tired sigh. "As many times as they tried to kill us? It's hardly fair I only got to take out his tire."

He pulled out, then continued down the road. "Dead bodies with bullets tend to bring the police out in droves. I'd rather not spend hours sitting in an interrogation room, having to explain why we're carrying guns in a country that doesn't allow it."

"Good point."

He checked the rearview mirror, catching the reflection of the sun on the roof of a sleek black car about a mile back. "Looks like Bruno finally found us. We better get out of here before he catches up."

45

Remi kept an eye on the rearview mirror, watching, as the black Mercedes followed at a safe distance. Sam had used every trick taught to him during his time at DARPA and still hadn't lost their tail, frustrating them both. At one point, Remi opened the sunroof to check the sky. "Okay, we know it's not a helicopter."

"Are you sure our phones are turned off?"

"Positive." Even so, she opened her purse to double-check the cells and the satellite phone. "They're sitting like bricks in my Hermès bag."

"You never know. Bricks might come in handy."

"Well, we know it's not the phones."

"Like I said, they had to have placed a tracking device on our car when we were at the airport."

Remi tapped her finger against the trigger guard of the semiauto resting on her thigh. "It worked once . . ."

"Let's not push our luck."

"You sure know how to ruin a girl's fun," she said, keeping her focus on the side mirror.

Sam checked the navigation screen on the car's dash.

"Right now, our best option is to find a place to park and buy enough time to find the device."

He drove to the city center, the roads turning more congested as they approached. Horns blared at the taxi drivers veering in and out of lanes, treating the rules of the road more like guidelines, in their hurry to get to their destinations so they could pick up their next fares. The rest of the cars moved at a snail's pace.

At least that gave Remi time to find a location she liked while keeping track of Bruno's Mercedes, stuck solidly three cars behind them.

"Find anything?" Sam asked, doing his best to put yet another car length between them.

Remi studied the navigation screen, using the toggle switch to zoom out, trying to find an area that might work. Her eyes landed on the Piazza del Popolo and the three streets that branched out from it like a trident. Just beyond it was the Piazza di Spagna, a location she knew quite well.

She pointed to the map. "You know that little street near the trident where we park when we come here to shop?"

"You mean when you come here to shop?" He glanced at the screen. "Sorry to say, it's not registering in my memory bank."

"Funny, Fargo. You've waited for me enough times. It's just down the street from the wineshop you like."

"That, I remember. What's your plan?"

"Find a place to park. I draw him out, have him chase me, you find the tracking device."

"I'd feel better if he was chasing me, not you."

"Except he's more likely to think I'm the easier prey. Once you find the tracking device, you come pick me up—hopefully, before he catches me."

He cocked a sandy brow at her. "Hopefully?"

"Just trying to be helpful, Fargo. After all, you didn't want me to kill him. Assuming you still want to avoid the police . . . ?"

"And where am I picking you up?"

"The top of the Spanish Steps."

Sam peered at the map on the screen, thought about it a moment, nodded.

When they were a couple of streets away from the Piazza di Spagna, Sam zipped down a narrow street, pulled over, and parked the car, angling it in a space barely big enough. Remi caught a glimpse of the black Mercedes parking at the end of the street, as she and Sam quickly walked the opposite direction, then ducked into the corner wineshop. The advantage—and disadvantage—of their location was that there were no doors, the interior of the shop wide open to both streets, allowing them to see anyone coming from either direction. Sam, his back to the entry, picked up a slim bottle filled with a pale yellow liquid, pretending to read the label. Remi kept watch, seeing Bruno jump out of his car and race down the street in their direction.

"He's on his way," she said, catching sight of the bottle of limoncello in Sam's hand. "Try not to forget, we're here for a purpose."

He grinned. "Me?"

Remi stepped out, taking a quick peek, surprised when she saw Bruno racing toward her one moment, then suddenly stop in the middle of the block, searching the crowded street for them. Unsure of which direction they'd gone, he returned to their rental car, intending to wait by it until their return.

She hefted her purse higher on her shoulder, feeling the weight of the three phones in it, wishing she'd had the foresight to leave them in the car. Too late for that, she watched as Bruno settled against the wall in front of their car, clearly in no hurry.

This was not going according to plan.

"Something wrong?" Sam asked, from his position inside the shop.

She gave an exasperated sigh. "Apparently, he's decided to wait for us."

Several seconds, then minutes, ticked by.

"He's just standing there," she said.

"He knows we need to get back to that car." Sam returned the bottle of limoncello to the shelf, moved to her side and peered over her shoulder. "You could always go out there and pretend to be lost."

"That should work. See you at the top of the stairs, Fargo." She leaned over, kissed him, and went out to the sidewalk, craned her head back, as though searching for a street placard high up on the side of the building. From the corner of her eye, she saw Bruno standing there, arms crossed, staring straight ahead. She stepped out farther, turning around as though lost, but the man remained planted like a Roman statue next to their car, never once turning her way.

Frustrated, she walked past the shop's entryway, ignoring Sam's grin, as he watched from inside. "Not helping, Fargo."

"Maybe less subtle . . . ?"

He was right. She did her best to look like a deer caught in the headlights as she stared at Bruno, shouting, "Sam! There he is! Run!"

Bruno looked up at the sound of her voice. The moment he saw her, he pushed off the wall, sprinting in her direction.

Remi waited a second or two longer than she should have, just to be sure Bruno saw her turn the corner. Keeping to the middle of the street, where she wouldn't be missed, she dashed past shoppers ogling the fashions displayed in the windows of the designer stores. Finally, she reached the piazza, turning left toward the Fontana della Barcaccia, only then realizing the bigger danger: disappearing into the midst of hundreds of tourists milling about the boat-shaped fountain and gravitating toward the very steps she needed to get to. If Bruno lost sight of her, he might end up turning back to the car—and Sam.

Somehow, she was going to have to keep him close enough for him not to lose sight of her. But as soon as she found a corridor between people to run through, the crowd swarmed in, closing the gap. Frustrated, Remi stopped at the railing of the fountain, leaning against it, pretending to be out of breath, waiting for him to catch up. The moment he saw her, she jumped back, trying to appear frightened, and darted into the piazza, running toward the Spanish Steps. The one hundred and thirty-five steep stairs, built in 1723, led up to the Trinità dei Monti Church, and the street that paralleled it, where she hoped Sam would be waiting with the car.

She burst out of the crowd and across the piazza, glancing back to make sure he'd seen her. This time there was no doubt. He followed, shouldering aside a camera-wielding woman who got in his way, ignoring her shouting as he raced past, trying to catch up to Remi, who'd already started up the right side of the stairs. About halfway up, she looked back and saw Bruno gaining on her. The purse, with the phones and her Sig Sauer, felt as heavy as a boat anchor. Hefting the bag onto her left shoulder to give the other shoulder a rest, she pushed on, feeling herself slowing from fatigue.

When she surveyed the stairs above, there was no one clear path up. The crowd shifted, people suddenly sitting in front of her, posing for photos, with the twin towers of the church at the top. They paid little attention to Remi as she tried to run past, suddenly having to change course because they changed positions for a better shot with their cell phones or cameras.

Her quads burned by the time she reached the top. A vendor selling cold water held a bottle dripping with condensation out toward her. Not even having enough breath to tell the man no, she looked back, saw Bruno about twenty steps below her, slowing down, but not nearly enough room for her comfort.

Traffic in front of the church was one-way, which meant Sam would have to come from her right on Via

Sistina and either continue straight past the church and the Spanish Steps to the left or make a sharp hairpin turn onto Via Gregoriana, which would bring him back the way he came. Certain he'd stay on Sistina, she immediately headed that direction. But as she searched the street, not seeing him or their car, the flaw in her plan became very apparent. Getting through Rome by vehicle could be a nightmare, especially around the more famous tourist destinations. There was no telling how long she'd have to wait.

What she needed was a place to hide. Out of breath, and with no energy to run farther, she ducked into an alcove of one of the shops, hoping Bruno might pass her by. Planting her back to the wall, she leaned over, her handbag slipping from her shoulder. Too tired to do much more than catch the straps, she let the weight of the purse rest on the ground, trying to fill her lungs with air, while she waited. It seemed forever before she noticed a shadow on the ground in front of her, then the sound of heavy breathing, which was almost lost in the heart-pounding pulse in her ears. Without moving, she looked up, saw Bruno blocking her way.

They stood there in a stalemate, Remi hoping Sam would pull up at any moment. But after what seemed an eternity, she realized she was on her own.

"Got you," Bruno managed as he sucked in air, his sweat-drenched expression one of triumph. He took a step toward her.

Remi swung her purse upward. The bag struck his

jaw, the phones and gun making a solid thwack. He staggered back, staring at her for one shock-filled second, when she brought her foot up into his groin. As he crumpled to the ground, crying out in pain, she stepped over him, saying, "But I got you better."

Sam pulled up as Remi stepped out from between two buildings. He gave a tap of the horn, leaned over and opened the passenger door for her. "How'd it go?" he asked.

She tossed her purse onto the floorboards as she slid in, wiping the perspiration from her brow. "There were a lot more steps going up than I remembered." She took a deep breath, then looked over at him. "Did you find it?"

He tapped the center console, where the small magnetic tracking device and its now-removed battery sat in the drink holder. "Tucked inside the bumper."

"I would've tossed it onto the back of a police car."

"Thought about it," he said, as Remi closed her eyes, her breathing fast and shallow. "But it might come in handy. If we need them to track us, we can always put the battery back in."

Sam saw the man at the top of the steps, selling water. Foot on the brake, he idled toward him, rolling down the window. "I'll take a bottle."

"One euro," the man said, holding up the dripping bottle.

"One euro!" Remi said. "I can wait."

Sam ignored her, digging the coin from his pocket. *"Grazie,"* Sam said, taking the ice-cold bottle and giving it to his wife. "I'm not the one who just did the three-hundred-step dash."

"Half that number—and we're broke, in case you forgot." She held the bottle up to her neck. "Even so, I love you for this."

He checked the mirrors, saw Bruno struggling to his feet. "Time to get out of here. Our friend's stirring," he said, watching the man lean over, hands on his knees, looking as though he might be sick.

Remi glanced back again. "Hmm. Guess I didn't hit him hard enough." She twisted off the bottle top, taking a long drink. "Any thoughts on how we're going to swing this auction without the buy-in fee?"

"I figured we'd just show up."

"And what good is that going to do? Even if we could convince Luca to let us in without the money, it's black-tie. Or need I remind you that your dress clothes are being held for ransom with our jet?"

"We are dressing in black, if that counts."

Remi's smile held a hint of devious mischief, as she settled back, buckling her seat belt. "That's what I love about you, Fargo. Even on a budget, you know how to show a girl a good time."

THEY ARRIVED just after nine at the broker's house at the top of a hill about an hour outside Rome. Luca wouldn't be expecting them for at least another half hour, with the beginnings of a plan in hand.

"No wonder he charges so much to get in," Remi said, as Sam drove up the winding road. The palatial-sized villa, taking up the entire hilltop, overlooked the lights of Rome in the distance. The sky glowed a muted gray-gold from the late-summer sun, dipping below the horizon. Judging from the number of cars parked in the graveled lot on the south side of the estate, most of the guests had already arrived. An electric shuttle was parked near the gate, two young men in dark suits leaning against the vehicle, one of them laughing at something the other said, until they noticed Sam and Remi's car.

The younger of the two walked over, leaned down, looking in the driver's window, moving from Sam to Remi, then down to their clothes. Before he had a chance to comment, Sam nodded his head toward Remi, saying, *"Ristoratori."*

The young man gave a knowing smile, pointing to the left, telling them to check in with the guard at the back gate.

"Grazie," Sam said.

"Caterers?" Remi asked, as Sam drove toward the rear of the house, pulling off to the side, once the shuttle drivers went back to their conversations.

At least fifty cars were parked in the lot, which was, thankfully, sloped away from the house and surrounded by oleanders. The thick bushes, some with white blooms, some with pink, grew high enough to offer cover. Sam grabbed his backpack, took out a pair of binoculars. He and Remi ducked behind one of the oleanders, Remi keeping watch out toward the parking lot, while Sam got a better look at the house.

The entire villa, set on the crest of the hill, was surrounded by a high wall topped with shards of glass. Guards manned the gates at the front, where the guests were shuttled to before they'd have to walk up two flights of stairs to get to the front door. He couldn't see the gate around back, but the shuttle driver had mentioned a guard there as well. Several hundred-year-old sycamores stood like sentries on this side of the wall, possibly offering a way over, but from here he had no idea what good that might do.

Remi glanced at him. "A helicopter would be nice right about now. Along with a small army."

"We have two guns," Sam said. "We're going to have to make do. You think you could bluff your way past those people?"

She studied the couple arriving at the door, the tuxedo-clad man handing his invitation to the guard. "That depends. Next step in the plan?"

"You get in, then find a way I can get in."

"Great plan, Fargo. I was hoping for something a little more specific."

He lowered the binoculars. "A place that size, we need a little recon inside so we know where to go once we're in there."

"You realize we're dressed like burglars."

"Isn't your dress still in the back of the car?"

"My dress, yes. But what about shoes?"

"Dazzle them with your beauty," Sam replied. "Who'll notice what you were wearing on your feet?"

"Except every woman in there?"

"Unless they're carrying guns, they're not the ones I'm worried about. Trust me, Remi. I've seen that gown on you. There's not a man in that house who'll be looking at your shoes."

"You're expecting me to walk in there without more of this plan in place?"

"I didn't marry you just for your looks. That was a happy bonus."

In the years that Selma Wondrash had worked for the Fargos, she'd gotten used to the sometimes odd requests they made, never mind the long stretches of working without a day or night off for weeks at a time, and the more often than not twenty-four-hour access the Fargos needed whether they were volunteering their time for a search and rescue operation or they were on the hunt for a lost treasure. That they paid her an exorbitant salary to compensate for this time made little difference in Selma's life except to say that she could retire today and not have to worry about how she'd survive. The truth was, even if they weren't paying her, she'd do it for free. They were more like family than employers, and she knew they felt the same about her. Which was why this sudden inability to get in touch with them troubled her. Perhaps it was because she was twenty years older than the Fargos, but she likened the experience to what parents must feel like when they can't reach their kids by phone and they don't know where they are.

The hardest part of waiting was the unbidden imagining of all the terrible things that might have befallen them—especially in the Fargos' world. Which was why she was staring at the phone on her desk, tapping her fingers.

Lazlo, sitting at his desk next to her, said, "They'll call. You know how they are when they're in the middle of something. Usually a jungle or some desert island."

"Except they're in Italy, where there's a surprising lack of jungles or desert islands. And they're on their way to a function probably filled with mafioso running a fencing operation for fine art."

"Right up their alley," he said. "You know as well as I that they're loving every second. Why, I have no idea, but they do."

"What if something happened and that's why they're not calling? We could start a used-car lot with the number of rental cars they've ruined. Those two are in enough near disasters that I've had to start coloring the gray in my hair."

He looked up at the short spikes on her head. "I quite like what you've done. Those bits of blue and pink . . ."

When she felt her face heat up, she turned away, pretending to concentrate on the missing journal that Albert's attorney had overnighted to her, as though she was suddenly worried about losing her place. It wasn't all that long ago that Lazlo had come to work for the Fargos full-time as a cryptographer and researcher. Looking back, she realized that she, a workaholic, and Lazlo, a recovering alcoholic, had done a fairly good job of tolerating each other's presence.

Somewhere along the way, she'd lightened up, and he'd sobered up.

Of course, it wasn't long after that they'd discovered they actually worked well together. She liked his dry sense of humor, and he liked her work ethic. More importantly, they both liked the Fargos. That, in her mind, made for a good professional relationship.

Lately, though, she was starting to discover that there was more to Lazlo than met the eye. He'd taken the time to learn about her late husband, an Air Force test pilot. He knew she liked Pink Lady apples over Fuji. And when the going got tough, and she was deep into research and tempted to raid the pantry upstairs for a quick snack instead of a meal, he took to the kitchen, his intent to make sure she ate right.

He wasn't the best chef in the world, but he'd bought a Hungarian cookbook, and his attempts to make goulash, stuffed cabbage rolls, and paprika chicken with dumplings were endearing, even if the dishes were a bit overcooked.

She stole a glance in his direction, grateful to see he wasn't looking at her, and hoping he didn't notice her embarrassment. He did, however, notice her sudden attention.

"You know you want to," he said, without looking up from the pages on his desk.

Shocked speechless, Selma wondered for a moment if he'd been reading her mind instead of his copy of the Viscount's journal. This time there was no hiding the color flooding to her cheeks. "I don't know what you're talking about," she said, trying to focus on the book.

"Ringing the Fargos," he replied, giving a pointed look at the phone. "While I'm quite sure they'll ring if they need something, you've been staring at the same page in that journal for the last several minutes. It's clear you won't be able to concentrate until you pick up the phone." He looked over at her, seemed to do a double take. "You're not coming down with a fever, are you?"

He reached over and touched her forehead, his skin cool against hers. "You do feel a bit warm."

"I'm fine," she said, scooting her chair back to put some much needed distance between them. Slipping a piece of paper into the journal to mark her place, she picked up the receiver, punching the speed dial for Sam's phone. Nothing. Not even a beep. She hit the hook flash, trying for a dial tone. "I don't think it's working."

Lazlo picked up the phone on his desk, got the same result. "I daresay, that explains why we haven't heard from them. I'll call the phone company and get a technician out here."

The relief she felt—knowing there was a reasonable explanation—disappeared when they discovered that their cell phones weren't working, either.

Lazlo was staring at his iPhone screen, waiting for it to reboot. "Quite coincidental, wouldn't you say?"

"Suspicious, is more like it," she said, turning to the computer and realizing the internet was down. "If it was just the landline and internet, I could almost believe it's bad phone lines. But cell phones, too?"

"You don't think someone hacked the Fargo accounts?"

"Let's hope not," she said. But after a quick trip to their closest neighbor to make a call, unsuccessfully, to the Fargos, then trying to get a technician out to fix the lines, there was no question about it. Someone had not only closed all the Fargo accounts, they were denying them access.

She called the bank next and discovered that those accounts had been frozen as well.

As much as Selma worried about the Fargos being out there without any money or way to contact them, she knew that her employers were resourceful. The Fargos would discover a way to get in touch. Of that, she had no doubt. And when they did, they'd be expecting answers to the history of the Gray Ghost. What she needed to do was finish her research, but when she sat down to read the stolen journal, she discovered her bookmark had slipped out. "What else can go wrong?" she said, turning the pages.

"Allow me," Lazlo said, taking the journal from her, quickly finding her place.

49

JOURNAL OF JONATHON PAYTON, 5TH VISCOUNT WELLSWICK

1906

I awoke to splitting pain in my head and the vague sensation that I was being watched. I cracked open one eye, moonlight surrounding me, as I tried to recall how it was I'd ended up on the ground behind some tavern next to a rubbish heap.

A voice from above startled me. I looked up, seeing nothing but the silhouette of something large and round. A cow with wings. No, a man with his hands on his hips.

In the dim light coming from an open door, I realized it was a barkeep, staring down at me, a stern expression on his face . . .

"I— I HAVE NO IDEA *how I got here," I said.*

"One too many pints, I'd say."

"That's just it. I don't remember drinking more than a glass of wine at dinner."

The bartender grunted in disbelief, as I sat up, trying to remember the circumstances that brought me here . . .

I'd had dinner with Miss Atwater.

When I tried to stand on my own, a wave of dizziness came over me.

"Can't hold your ale, eh?" the man said, catching me.

It was easier not to argue with him.

"Lucky I heard the ruckus out here," he continued, taking a step back once I was safely on my feet.

I looked around, trying to remember what happened. The sight of my father's brass-handled cane, shoved into the trash heap next to us, brought with it the vague memory of someone calling me "Lord High and Mighty" as they threw me on the ground. I turned to the barkeep. "I appreciate your help."

"Seems to me a gentleman such as yourself might offer a reward for saving your neck." He held out his hand, demanding payment. "Those blokes might've slit your throat, had I not walked back here when I did. At great risk to myself, I might add."

Grateful, I felt in my coin pocket, surprised to discover money still there. Relief turned to fear as I recalled Miss Atwater's sudden disappearance. "Did you see a lady with them? Was anyone talking about a woman?"

"Don't rightly know."

"You said you heard the ruckus. Think carefully, man. What did you hear?"

When a look of suspicion crossed his face, I pulled out several coins. "Tell me exactly what you heard."

He eyed the money, then me. "One bloke said he knew you'd follow the water. The other two laughed."

A fresh wave of nausea struck me as I thought of Miss Atwater, frightened and alone. "What else?"

"They dumped you here and said to meet in forty or fifty."

"Were they actually discussing time? Or could it have been something else?"

The man eyed me as though the question was absurd. "Don't rightly know. Just that when they saw me walking out here, the first man said to leave you where you were. That you wouldn't have the guts to go after them."

Had it simply been the Grey Ghost or the coveted forty-fifty engine, I would have been content to call a night watchman and be done with it. But the realization that they'd taken the innocent Miss Atwater spurred me to action. I knew, though, that I couldn't go after her on my own. "I need to get a message to someone."

The man grabbed the coins from my palm and turned back toward the tavern, giving the refuse heap a wide berth. "Funny how you toffs think I've got nothing but time. Got a business to run here."

"I'll pay double what I've given you."

He stopped at the door, looking back at me. "Triple, and I'll send a lad 'round."

"Triple, then. To Mr. Isaac Bell at the Midland Hotel. Tell him Miss Atwater's been kidnapped and to meet me—" Meet where? I realized the location was never mentioned. Still, if it really was Reggie behind all this, there was only one place he'd go. "Meet at my father's warehouse. The same message to Byron, Lord Ryderton." I gave him the address.

The barkeep muttered something about men who couldn't hold their drink, as he started to walk away.

Stomach roiling from the stench of the garbage and the blow to my head, I grabbed my father's cane from the refuse pile, breathing in the fresher air, trying to gain back my equilibrium. "Forty-fifty . . ."

Only one meaning behind that phrase, and not something that some cutthroat might have knowledge about.

I pictured my father's warehouse, wondering how I hadn't thought of it before. Perhaps my reluctance was because I'd refused to believe that Reginald was guilty of stealing the Grey Ghost. Now that I knew it was he, it really was the only place the car could be hidden.

The stolen car, however, was the last thing I worried about.

Miss Atwater . . .

During the fifteen minutes it took for me to clear my head, find the right direction, and walk to the warehouse, I prayed I wasn't too late.

50

Remi waited until darkness shrouded the Italian countryside before changing in the backseat of the car. She stepped out, smoothing the silk gown down her legs, then adjusted the plunging sweetheart neckline embellished with a tiny rosette made of Swarovski crystals—elegant yet simple.

Sam gave a soft whistle when he saw her. "I was right. You look amazing."

"Right down to my feet." The gown was meant to be floor-length and worn with heels. She lifted the hem, revealing her black lace-up hiking boots.

"Like I said, no one will be looking at your feet. Walk in like you own the place."

"Wish me luck." She leaned over, kissed him, checked to make sure no one was watching before she made her way to the motorized cart the guards were using to shuttle the guests from the parking lot to the villa's front gate. Sam was right. No one noticed her feet. Even so, she was careful to keep her boots tucked beneath her gown on the ride over. The shuttle stopped at a wide path paved with terra-cotta tiles, potted cypresses spaced evenly on either side. It led to the first flight of stairs cut into the hillside, and a landing where stone benches lined the travertine balustrade, perhaps to give the guests a place to rest before they tackled the longer second flight up to the massive front doors, which were standing open to allow the guests entry.

Remi walked up the path and stood at the bottom of the stairs, eyeing a few guests on the first landing, dismayed to see Luca, sitting on a bench at the landing of the first flight, smoking a cigarette, waiting for her and Sam. Bluffing her way into the party was one thing. Getting past him, something else altogether.

"You look lost."

She turned to see a man standing where no one had been a moment before. He wasn't a guard, since he was clearly dressed for the party, the cut of his jacket impeccable, the sheen of the cloth saying money was no object. She put him in his late thirties, though his brown hair was peppered with gray. He regarded her with a mix of curiosity and wariness, almost mirroring what she felt at the moment.

Her instincts told her that being an American at this event might make her far too noticeable. *"Parla italiano?"*

"Sorry, no. English only."

She looked up the stairs, saw Luca looking at her. Not sure if he'd sound the alarm or demand his fee, she stepped into the shadows of one of the cypresses.

Apparently, the man standing next to her noticed. "You might consider using the lift." He waved to his left, where she saw the narrow door to the elevator cut into the rock, a few potted cypresses positioned to make it look less noticeable. "Quicker," he said, reaching over, pressing the button. The door slid open with a quiet whoosh, and he reached out, holding it so it wouldn't close on her.

"Grazie," Remi said, smiling. In her best Italian-accented English, she added, "You are very kind."

She stepped on, expecting him to let go of the door. But he stood there a moment, looking out toward the path. A younger man, wearing a gray suit, no tie, his shirt open at the collar, carrying a slim briefcase in his right hand, ran up.

"You're late," the man standing next to her said.

"Sorry. Took a wrong turn." He handed over the briefcase and, without another word, turned and left.

Out of the three levels on the control panel, the top one could only be accessed with a key. He pressed the first button and, a moment later, the elevator rose. When the door slid open, he held it for her.

Remi, grateful that he seemed to be in a hurry, moved to the side, allowing him to pass her as he exited. He gave a polite nod to her quiet *"Grazie,"* then strode off toward the front doors, clutching the briefcase in his hand.

Sadly, Luca, the man she'd hoped to avoid, had definitely noticed her presence, taking the steps up two at a time. He blocked her way, his back to the house. "Where do you think you're going?"

"Looking for my husband," she said, keeping her

voice low. "He came up with the briefcase maybe ten minutes ago. I broke the heel of my shoe and had to go back to the car to change," she said, lifting her gown so that he could see the toes of her boots.

"You're expecting me to believe that he let you walk back to the car alone?"

"Since we were late, we worried we'd miss you. He was right here by the elevator when I left him. Surely you must have seen him if you were waiting?"

Luca studied her face, as though trying to gauge her truthfulness. "I wasn't watching the elevator," he finally said.

"Is it possible he somehow got in without you?"

He looked back toward the door, past the man checking invitations, then down toward the parking area, spying the few late stragglers walking from their cars to the shuttle. Remi followed his gaze, grateful that Sam was well hidden behind the oleanders. "Possibly," he said.

"I say we go in and look. He has to be here somewhere."

She started toward the door. Luca hesitated, then followed her, handing his invitation to the guard, who looked it over, waved them in.

What had appeared to be the entrance to the house was actually a wide veranda, with a view of the rolling hills and the lights of Rome in the distance. On their left was an open kitchen where the caterers worked. On their right, a wide travertine staircase led up to what was most likely the main living quarters, which formed a U shape around the veranda. Numerous doors on that level opened out to the wide balcony overlooking the lower veranda. That, unfortunately, left a lot of real estate when trying to figure out the best place to enter.

She and Luca moved away from the entry, Luca searching for Sam, Remi pretending to. The conversations she heard sounded like every other fund-raiser she'd been to. The value of a certain stock, who was wearing what designer, who was divorcing whom. The one thing she didn't hear was anyone talking about cars, classic or otherwise.

Odd, she thought, until it occurred to her that the party was probably a convenient cover for an auction that was dealing in stolen cars.

She was about to ask Luca if that was the case when she noticed the man she'd ridden the elevator with walking toward the stairs with the assurance of one who knew where he was going. He stopped as two men, looking like linebackers in expensive suits, blocked his entrance. Whatever he said, or showed to them, they immediately stood to the side, allowing him to pass.

"Who's that walking up the stairs?" Remi asked.

Luca looked that direction. "Probably one of the buyers. They're the only ones allowed up there. It's all prearranged."

She watched the door at the top open, and the man step in. The door started to close, but not before she caught a glimpse of another guard, this one blond with a goatee, inside the door, patting the man's jacket and pockets, searching for weapons. "Prearranged? How?"

He looked away so quickly, Remi became suspicious.

She moved so that he'd have no choice but to face her. "How were you going to get Sam in if it was prearranged?"

"I wasn't. The truth is, I don't even have access. This is as far as I've ever gotten."

"Did you really think you were going to get away with taking our money?"

The look of guilt on his face told her everything she needed to know.

"I think our business here is done," she said.

"You still owe me the entrance fee."

Several seconds ticked by while Remi contained her fury. Taking a calming breath, she leaned in close, whispering, "I'd like to see you try to collect it."

His jaw dropped. Remi plucked a flute of champagne from the tray of a passing waiter, tempted to toss it on him, instead walked to the balustrade that overlooked the sweeping stretch of manicured lawn surrounded by a high stucco wall, the moonlight gleaming off the deadly glass shards topping it.

Sam, hidden behind the oleanders, kept his binoculars focused on the palatial building while he examined the six floor-to-ceiling windows, each with two potted cypresses set on a Juliet balcony barely wide enough to fit them. The only security on this side of the grounds happened to be the two young men shuttling the guests and the guards at the door. He swept his eyes along the ten-foot wall surrounding the estate, not seeing any security outside the perimeter. There were a couple of cameras, however, mounted high on the corners of the house, one pointed toward the front entrance, the other toward the back. He looked for a camera aimed along the south face of the wall but didn't see one. It was either hidden behind the line of trees growing near the wall or someone felt it wasn't needed due to the wall's height and glass topping it.

The crunch of footsteps nearby alerted him to Remi's return. She crossed the graveled lot, circumventing the parked cars, until she reached the far side, where he was hiding behind the oleanders.

One look at her face told him something had gone wrong. "What happened?" he asked, as she crouched down beside him.

"I think Georgia needs to cross her friend of a friend off her Christmas card list." She told him what happened.

He laughed softly.

"How do you find that funny?"

"You've got to love the irony. If we hadn't been hacked, he'd be up there stealing our money."

Remi cracked a smile.

"What'd you find?" he asked.

"The party's definitely a cover. To let the high-priced buyers in without attracting notice."

"Any idea where they go once they're in?"

"They entered a door on the South Wing. That's all I could tell. No one's getting in without passing through heavy security. All the other guests are one level down, on the veranda."

That would explain why, with the exception of a few windows on the South Wing, most of the house was dark. Sam surveyed the second floor. A faint light was coming from the fourth window over, making him think it was a very small lamp or the door to the room was open and the light was from beyond it.

He handed Remi the binoculars. "Take a look. You see the light coming from the one window? Second floor. Could that be it?"

Remi adjusted the focus. "I can't be sure. It looks like the general location of the door where I saw the guy from the elevator go in. But there's a lot of windows on that floor, Sam. And I was looking in from the opposite side."

"One way to find out. Get a closer look myself."

"And what good is that going to do?"

"It may not do any good. Then again, I might get lucky. I won't know until I get up there."

"Not without me."

"Sorry, Remi. You're not dressed for the part."

She lowered the binoculars, giving Sam a look of mild annoyance. "Give me two minutes and I will be."

The truth was, he had a bad feeling about this place, and not just because of Luca's attempt to swindle them. Maybe it was just the fact there was a lot of cash being brought in, but this broker was going to a lot of trouble to guard this auction, which would lend credence to the cars having less than stellar certificates of ownership. "Someone has to stay and keep watch."

"Flip a coin. Winner stays here."

Odds he could live with—as long as Remi lost. He took a coin from his pocket, tossed it, the dull brass gleaming in the moonlight as it spun. He caught it. "Your call," he said.

"Heads."

He opened his palm, dismayed to see that she'd won. Even so, in the time it took Remi to change her clothes, he changed his mind. She reached for the backpack and its coil of rope, but he picked it up before she could. They'd learned long ago to trust each other's instincts, and clearly this was one of those times. "I have a bad feeling about this. I'm going instead."

"Which is why I'm going with you," she countered. "If something's going to happen to you, I plan on being there."

"Fine," he said, slipping the straps of the backpack over his shoulders. "But if anything goes wrong, you're heading back to the car and out of here."

"Scout's honor."

52

Sam held tight to one end of the rope, tossing the coil up and over the branch of a sycamore, catching it before it hit the ground on the other side. He tugged on the length, the limb feeling solid supporting his weight, then looked over at Remi. "This is your chance to back out."

"You're wasting time, Fargo."

He climbed up, using the other branches to balance himself as he edged his way along the limb, careful of the long, thick, pointed glass glittering below him like a deadly mosaic of colorful daggers.

Remi followed, retrieving the rope, and coiling it. When she reached him, he slung the coil over his shoulder and maneuvered through the tree until he was on the limb that ran parallel to the balcony. He judged the distance. There was at least five feet between the balustrade and the thickest part of the branch.

As long as he kept his balance, he could easily make it. That wasn't the question. What worried him was if the stone balustrade was securely anchored to the balcony and would hold his weight. The thrust of his jump, followed by Remi's, would not mix well if there was any dry rot or other degradation.

"Maybe I should go first," Remi whispered.

They were at least twenty feet from the ground. If that balcony was going down, it wasn't going to be with Remi. "It'll be fine." He hoped.

Remi reached out, grabbing his arm, as he was about to jump. "Company," she whispered.

From the corner of his eye he saw two security guards in black uniforms rounding the corner, walking directly toward their tree. Had it not been for Remi, Sam might have been mid-jump before he saw them. Too late to step back out of sight, he waited where he was, hoping they wouldn't look up. Unfortunately, the two men decided to stop beneath the tree, the taller of the guards pulling out a cigarette pack, offering one to the shorter man.

"Grazie," the man said, accepting a cigarette and a light. He took a deep drag, while the other man held the lighter to his cigarette, his face glowing, as he puffed. But instead of moving on, the two stood there, talking softly, their smoke drifting upward, while Sam balanced on the branch, trying to look as treelike as was humanly possible, while gripping the branches above him. Remi, at least, was partially hidden behind him in the crook of the tree.

A gust of wind rustled the leaves, sending tree pollen and smoke swirling around him. Sam felt a sneeze coming on and tried to alleviate the tickle by scrunching his face and wiggling his nose. When that failed to work, he let go of one of the branches, slowly bringing his hand toward his face, pinching his nostrils. The tickle disappeared.

The two men did not. They took their time smoking and laughing. At long last, the first guard dropped his cigarette in the grass and ground it out with his foot. The second guard took one last drag, then did the same, the two finally moving off to continue their patrol.

Sam waited a few seconds after they rounded the opposite corner to be sure he'd given them enough time before making the jump. He caught the travertine balustrade, pulling himself up and over onto the balcony. Remi followed with her usual catlike grace, and he caught her hands, helping her over.

The balcony was just wide enough for the potted cypresses on either side of the window, but not much more. He looked for any obvious signs of an alarm but didn't see anything. Of course, there was only one way to find out and that was to open the window. Perhaps with the party in full swing, and whatever was going on with this secret auction, the alarm—if there was one on this level—wasn't set. He peered in the window, the curtain inside parted enough to see into the darkened room.

"Bedroom," he whispered.

"It'll be faster if we split up."

She was right, but that feeling of foreboding wouldn't leave him. Going against his instincts wasn't worth the risk to save time. "We stay together," he said.

Fortunately, there was only a space of a couple of feet from one balcony to the next, and he held Remi's hand while she stepped across. She'd just swung her leg over the stone balustrade, sitting on the edge, when a light went on inside, illuminating the entire balcony. Before she had a chance to move, an audible click sounded as someone unlocked and opened the window.

Remi froze, as the floor-to-ceiling window opened out onto the balcony. She glanced over at Sam, who quickly moved behind the cypress on the other balcony, pressing himself against the wall. When she motioned that she should return to his balcony, he shook his head.

There was little she could do but wait and hope that whoever had just opened the window wasn't planning on stepping out for a better view. Trapped between the potted cypress and the balustrade, she moved back against the wall, feeling the sharp stucco at her back, her pulse pounding in her ears almost too loudly to make out the voices inside. "My apologies," a man's voice said. "The room should quickly cool off, though."

Once she realized they weren't coming out, she inched closer to the cypress and the open window, peering through the spiny branches, now able to see inside the room. Two men, both wearing dark suits, their backs to the window, stood near a massive mahogany desk. "You were saying that you've already made arrangements for the car?" he asked. No doubt this was the broker who'd arranged the auction.

"I plan to have it shipped back to the UK," the other man said. "One question I did have . . . Since I've no idea how you acquired the car for the auction—"

"We value the anonymity of our sellers as well as our buyers."

"Which I more than appreciate. And not where I was going."

"My apologies, Signore Wrent. What was your question?"

"While I appreciate your guarantee that this is the forty-fifty I was inquiring about, was there anything about who was the original owner? Photos, documents found in the car. Anything that will help prove the provenance?"

"It's the same car. I question what good the documents, if there are any, will do. Surely you must realize that the car can't be sold on the open market?"

"Very aware. I have no intention of selling it."

"If you don't mind my asking, what's so special about this particular vehicle?"

"I value history, which is why I'd like anything that seems of significance when it comes to the car's past."

"We'll include everything we have on it."

"I appreciate it."

A barn owl swooped down from the rooftop, past the window, the wide expanse of its wings drawing the notice of both men. Remi ducked back, catching a glimpse of the buyer's face as they turned to look.

The man from the elevator.

"If there's nothing else?" Remi heard the broker ask.

"Where is the car? Rather than make an extra trip, I was hoping to see it in person before I fly home."

"A warehouse outside of Paris, I'm afraid. Once the bank transfer is made, and the funds are placed in our account, we'll contact you with the location."

"Not before?"

"Surely you appreciate the position I'm in, Signore Wrent. While I believe you to be a man of your word, my commodity is not one that attracts the best of clientele. I find it safer for everyone involved to make sure all funds clear the bank before disclosing the location."

"And surely you appreciate my position? I don't intend to give up the funds until the car is in my possession."

"I suggest a compromise." The broker opened a desk drawer, took out a pen, wrote something on a pad of paper. "Since there's very little either of us can do until Monday, here's the address and phone number of my Paris office. We'll meet there. You transfer the money, I'll personally take you to the car. Understand, though, that this arrangement may add a few hours to your trip. The car is kept at a secure warehouse at the shipping yard."

"What time on Monday?"

"Shall we say eleven in the morning?"

"A rather tight schedule, but I think I can work around it."

"I'll see you then." She heard the squeak of his chair as he rose, followed by the sound of their footsteps on the tiled floor. "I hope you'll forgive me, but I do need to make an appearance with my guests."

"Of course."

Remi inched toward the cypress, peering through, as the broker ushered the other man toward the door. "By Monday, you'll be able to see for yourself. As I do with all my clients, I'll personally guarantee that this is the vehicle you purchased. I promise you that I have yet to know anyone who's not had complete satisfaction."

"Then I'll await your call."

"Signore Wrent. A pleasure doing business with you."

"And you, Mr. Rossi."

Lorenzo Rossi left the door open, returned to his desk, pulled something from his pocket. A key, she realized, ducking back as he took a seat, the chair again squeaking under his weight.

A few seconds later, the burly guard with the goatee entered, saying, in Italian, "You should be pleased with the price he paid. Your profit from that car far exceeds the total of the other cars tonight."

"Very pleased," Lorenzo said. "And curious. The only reason someone makes a bid that high is to ensure no one else will even bother."

"Did he say why?"

"History," Lorenzo replied. "He was asking about supporting documents and anxious to see the car before the money cleared. Between that and the price he paid, I find my curiosity aroused."

"Maybe we should take another look at the car before we turn it over to him?"

"Not a bad idea." He gave a tired sigh. "Time to play host."

The other man stopped suddenly, turned, and walked to the balcony, reaching out to close the window, his arm so close Remi could see the faint gray pinstriping on the sleeve of his suit coat. She held her breath. One look in her direction, he'd be able to see her on the other side of the cypress.

Sam raised his Smith & Wesson, aiming toward the adjoining balcony as someone reached out the window, the man's arm coming perilously close to his wife's head. Finger on the trigger, he pressed lightly, ready, should the unthinkable happen.

"Leave it open," a voice called out. "I'll be coming back up to put away the buy-in once I make the rounds downstairs. It gets stuffy up here otherwise."

The arm disappeared inside, and Sam lifted his finger from the trigger, breathing evenly now that the immediate danger had passed. A moment later, Remi looked over at him. "They're gone," she said quietly.

He stepped out, checking to make sure the grounds below were clear, before crossing over to her.

"*Reader's Digest* version," she said. "Definitely the right auction. The broker sold the car to someone, but I didn't quite get the name. The car's being held somewhere in Paris until the money clears. They never mentioned Gray Ghost, but they did say 'forty-fifty.'"

"They give any indication they'd be back up here?"

"After he makes the rounds of the party downstairs."

Sam peered into the darkened office. "Let's take a quick look before they get back."

He went first, gun drawn, just to make sure it was clear, Remi following. The first thing he checked was the door, listening for any sign of movement outside. Nothing.

"I think he locked it," Remi whispered. "At least it sounded like it."

He tried turning the knob. It held tight. Advantage: theirs. They'd hear a key in the lock. He returned to the window, looking out, the moonlight angling onto the balcony. The security they'd seen earlier hadn't reappeared. Last thing he and Remi needed was for some guard to suddenly become astute and notice the dim lights of burglars in their employer's office. He pulled the curtains, returned to Remi's side, slipping his backpack from his shoulder and taking out a very slim LED flashlight, which he handed to Remi. She at least saw and heard what went on, which meant if anyone should be conducting the search, it was Remi. "I'll keep watch."

She started going through the desk drawers, finding one of them locked. It took her a minute to pick it, and she pulled out papers, looking them over, trying to replace them as she found them.

Sam heard footsteps outside in the hallway. He held up his hand, aiming his gun at the door. Remi stopped her searching, watching him. He kept his focus on the bottom of the door, the thin line of light unbroken, until a shadow filled the gap—then moved past. He signaled to Remi, who moved from the desk to look over the shelves behind it. "Nothing," she whispered. "If he has anything in here about where this place is . . ."

They'd already stayed longer than was comfortable. Anything more, and they were pushing their luck. "Wrap it up. We need to get out of here."

She nodded. While he returned his attention to the door, she gave the room a slow perusal, picking up the pad of paper and ripping off several sheets, which she put in her pocket. Her attention landed on the phone. Suddenly she picked it up, punched in a number on the keypad.

"What're you doing?"

"Trying to call Selma." She listened for a moment, hung up. "Busy."

"Again?" That bothered him.

"There has to be some way to reach her," she said.

If they were hacked, all Selma's information, including her cell phone and their house phone, was compromised. Selma appeared on all of their credit reports as an authorized user. Time to figure that out later. Hearing voices in the hallway, he pointed toward the window. She nodded, starting that direction. Suddenly she stopped, looking on a shelf, eyeing the books behind the desk. Clearly something about them bothered her, because she started touching and pressing them. A soft click and a secret panel opened. "Sam . . . I think I found the buy-in he needed to take care of."

His gun trained on the door, he backed toward her, looking at the hidden cupboard—and on the shelf within, Remi's little blue light shining on the stacks of banded euros in denominations of twenty.

A little negligent, leaving money out where anyone could get it.

And a quandary. He and Remi prided themselves on their honesty. Stealing something that didn't belong to them was not an option.

But having been hacked and suddenly cut off from even the smallest source of income made the find extremely tempting.

They looked at each other, both ready to back off, until Remi said, "We could really use that right now . . ."

"Maybe so, but it's a good way to make someone really mad."

"He's a broker selling stolen cars. Who's he going to call? The police?"

"Good point." He handed her his backpack.

She unzipped it, picked up several stacks, stuffed them into the bag.

It was risky. Someone was bound to notice the missing money.

He heard footsteps in the hallway. The thin bead of light beneath the door was broken by the shadow of someone stepping in front of it. Unlike last time, this shadow didn't move on.

Sam aimed toward the door and backed toward the window. Reaching behind him, he pulled open the curtain. "Remi," he whispered, as someone inserted a key into the door lock.

She closed the panel, zipped the backpack shut, tossing it to Sam as she moved to the window. She'd no sooner stepped out onto the balcony than the door opened and the broker walked in.

The man stared at Sam, almost as though he couldn't believe that someone was standing in his office. His gaze flicked to the now-closed hidden panel, then Sam's gun. "Guards!"

55

Guards!" the broker cried again, his voice carrying out the window.

Sam clambered over to the next balcony. When he reached Remi's side, he eyed the limb five feet away, then the ground twenty feet below. "After you," he said, taking her hand, helping her up onto the stone balustrade. She made the leap as easily as a gymnast, her foot landing on the thick branch, balancing lightly, as she caught the branches overhead to steady herself. She quickly edged toward the tree's trunk.

The broker shouted that he'd been robbed. Sam holstered his weapon, hopped up onto the balustrade, and jumped just as two guards burst out onto the balcony. Remi already had her gun out. She fired. The left cypress's pot exploded, the evergreen tilting across the balcony as the two guards ducked back inside. One of the guards inched out again.

Crack!

Remi killed the other pot. She fired at the balustrade, keeping the guards pinned inside, as Sam maneuvered his way through the tree branches. When he reached her, he took her gun, gave her the rope. She slung the coil over her shoulder, balancing in the crook of the tree, as a shout came from below. The two perimeter guards exploded from around the corner, one of them aiming his gun upward, searching the row of trees. Sam wrapped his left arm around the trunk, leaned out, and fired at the grass in front of them. Grass and dirt blasted up, the men jumped back. Sam, shifting his weight, fired at the balcony. He used the momentum to pivot around, landing on the other side of the trunk.

Remi looped the rope around the branch and was already halfway down. Sam ducked when the guards from the balcony fired, shots hitting the thick tree limbs, splinters and sap flying out. Remi jumped to the ground. Sam tossed the gun to her, grabbed the rope, then jumped, too, as a second volley of shots hit the tree.

At the bottom he took her hand, and the two raced to the oleanders. When they reached the car, they crouched behind it, Sam rising high enough to peer through the window. Guests on the top terrace near the front doors were leaning over the balcony, trying to see what was happening. The guard up there was drawing them away, trying to usher them toward the doors.

The two young men working the shuttle were surveying the parking lot. A few cars were rolling slowly toward them. One of the men pointed at the first car, saying something Sam couldn't hear. The other nodded, walked up to the car, his hand reaching for his hip, probably for a gun hidden beneath his jacket, as he looked in the window. He waved the first car through but stopped the second car.

"How fast do you think you can change back into that gown?" Sam asked.

Remi looked at the men checking the cars. "Fast enough."

Staying low, she opened the back door, slid in, while Sam got behind the wheel. He started the car, hoping the two young guards were so busy searching the interior of the departing vehicles in front of them that they wouldn't notice him driving out from behind the oleanders.

He checked the mirror, saw Remi shrug out of her shirt, then slip the dress over her head, pulling it down over her hips. "Ready."

"Your hair."

She pulled out the elastic, fluffed it up. "Drive on, James."

Sam idled forward. One of the two men walked toward their car, looking in the window at Sam, then over to the empty passenger seat. *"Signorina,"* Sam said.

She rolled down her window and leaned out, immediately drawing the young man's attention away from Sam. *"Scusi,"* she said, her Italian and accent flawless. "Were those gunshots? I'm not in any danger, am I?"

"No, no," the man said. "Warning shots to scare off the wolves. They come down from the hills occasionally."

"How frightening," she said, her hand going to her throat. "You're very brave to stand out here."

"It's nothing," he said, taking a step back, his stance relaxing. He waved them through the wrought iron gates.

Sam, keeping his focus ahead, pulled out, then watched in the rearview mirror as the second man put his hand to his ear, obviously listening to a radioed transmission. He shouted something to his partner, and both men ran out the gates toward them.

"What's wrong?" Remi asked, as he hit the gas.

"I think they just figured out who we are." He saw the two men run into the road, drawing their guns. "Get down!"

He yanked the wheel to the left as they aimed and fired, twin muzzle blasts flashing in the dark, followed by the dull ping as one of the shots hit the car.

Gas pedal floored, engine roaring, Sam sped up the hill, cresting it, blinded by the headlights of a car coming straight at them.

56

Unable to see past the glare of the oncoming car, Sam slammed on the brakes, whipping the wheel to the right, the back end fishtailing. The acrid smell of burnt rubber filled the car, then dissipated as they sped down the hill. In the mirror he saw the red glow of the other car's taillights fading as it descended on the other side. No sign of approaching headlights—for now.

"Remi?"

Nothing but the sound of the wind rushing in her open window.

"Remi!"

Her hand came up between the seats, soon followed by the rest of her. "Sorry. Took me a moment to shove my heart back into my chest."

"That little bit of driving?"

"The longest ten seconds of my life."

"Less than five." He shot a look at the backpack on the front floorboard, at Remi in the rearview mirror. "Any idea how much you took from that broker?"

"I only had time to grab three stacks. Bands of a thousand."

"Three thousand more euros than we had a few hours ago."

"Get the plane out of hock?"

"With the price of fuel? We wouldn't get far. I vote we start with a cheap hotel for the night and regroup in the morning."

FINDING A CHEAP HOTEL without a valid credit card turned out to be harder than they thought.

Remi gave a sigh of frustration. "We need to call Georgia. She did say she had friends in the B and B business."

"It's just after midnight. A little late to try to find a working phone."

Remi smiled. "This is Italy. Pick any tourist attraction, and someone will have a cell phone."

Sam checked the map on the dash, made a left turn. About six minutes later, the lit arches of the Colosseum appeared in the distance against the black sky. He parked just up the road, and the two walked down the hill. Even this late, the street in front of the amphitheater was crowded with tourists, most using their cell phones as cameras.

The first few attempts to borrow a phone were met with suspicious stares, even more so when Sam offered money.

Remi surveyed the crowd. "Wait here a sec." She crossed the cobblestone street to a group of young men in their twenties clowning around while taking selfies with the Colosseum in the background.

The second she approached, the four men stopped what they were doing, their attention on Remi and whatever she was telling them. Suddenly there were four cells being handed to her. Five minutes later, she returned with an address on a scrap of paper. "We're in luck! One of Georgia's B and B friends has an apartment near the Trevi Fountain. He'll gladly take cash, and it's open for the next two days."

The location wasn't near the fountain, it was directly adjacent to it, as well as the Trevi Plaza, which was still filled with dozens upon dozens of tourists enjoying the temperate late-night air.

Marco Verzino met them at the door, led them up four flights of stairs to the topmost corner apartment, where he unlocked the door for them. "It's warm," he said, immediately opening the floor-to-ceiling windows, one of which overlooked the Trevi Fountain, bringing in the cooler air, the rush of the water below, and the drone of voices from the people milling in the square. A cheer erupted in the crowd. When Sam and Remi looked down, a man and woman were hugging in front of the fountain's pool as those surrounding them clapped.

Remi watched for a moment, asking, "Is it always this crowded?"

Marco laughed. "*Roma* doesn't sleep in the summer. The visitors thin out in the early-morning hours. But never completely." He held up a remote from the coffee table. "If it becomes too loud, close the windows. Air-conditioning in each room."

In truth, the sounds of the fountain masked the voices, and Sam and Remi slept very well. Late the next morning, they bought prepaid cell phones and a very soft pencil, then returned to the apartment, where Remi took the tip of the pencil, held it sideways, and lightly rubbed it across the pad of paper she stole from the broker's office. Soon, an address started to appear.

Sam tried calling home. No luck. "Selma and Lazlo are still off-line," he said.

"At least now we know where we're going in Paris." Remi looked up from the paper to the phone Sam held. "We have to assume that Selma and Lazlo are aware of the hacking by now."

"I'd think they'd call Georgia, knowing that was the last place we were headed."

They placed a call to Georgia, but she hadn't heard from Selma yet. "Selma's smart," Georgia said. "I'm sure she'll get in touch with me."

"When she does," Sam said, "give her our new cell numbers. Have her call the moment she can."

"I will. What about Chad and Oliver? Do you want me to text them your new numbers?"

"No!" Sam replied in a hurry.

"Why?" Georgia asked. "What's wrong?"

The last thing Remi wanted to do was worry her friend unnecessarily. "Where are they?"

"Waiting for their train. I gave them Marco's address

and dropped them off at the station about an hour ago. Why?"

"The phones," Sam replied. "If these people hacked ours, it's possible they hacked Oliver's and Chad's, to track them. They could be leading our enemies straight to us."

57

Selma opened her eyes, trying to clear the fog from her brain, as Lazlo strode into her office carrying a bag from their wireless provider.

"We have technology," he said, holding the bag aloft.

It took a moment for her to realize she'd fallen asleep in the recliner, the journal in her lap. She'd finished it once, and was on the second reading, hoping to discover what, if anything, was so important about any of the entries written in it. "Please tell me you've heard from the Fargos."

"Not yet. But I did get two working mobile phones that aren't connected to any Fargo accounts. We can use them as hot spots for the laptops for the internet."

"No regular internet?"

"That account was closed, and the poor girl trying to help me was far too confused." He handed her the bag. "A new account and mobile phones were faster than trying to deal with corporate. I don't suppose you had better luck with the banks?"

"The good news is, what wasn't frozen as a result of

the tampering I was able to freeze while the banks try to straighten everything out." She pulled out one of the phones, then walked over to her desk to look up Georgia's number. "The bad news is, it also keeps the Fargos from accessing any money."

"Surely someone's doing something to move things along?"

"The personal banker for their account talked to the FBI's cybersecurity division. They're opening a case. Which still isn't putting money in the Fargos' pockets."

"I wouldn't worry too much. They're resourceful."

Selma sat at her desk, putting the phone on speaker as she made the call. "Let's hope Georgia has some idea of where they are."

"Selma," Georgia said when she answered. "Perfect timing. I just got off the phone with Remi. Everyone's fine."

"Thank goodness," Selma said, as Lazlo pulled over a chair and sat next to her. Still, she wasn't about to relax until she spoke with the Fargos personally. "We were hacked. Big-time."

"They figured as much. They bought a couple of cell phones this morning. If you have a pen, I'll give you the numbers, and the address where they'll be staying temporarily."

"Do you know how long they'll be in Rome?" Selma asked, after writing down the information.

"Honestly, I don't. They're waiting for Chad and Oliver to meet up with them. But do call right away. I know they're anxious to speak with you."

Selma called the first number. Sam answered.

"Mr. Fargo . . ." she said, her sense of relief on hearing his voice almost overwhelming.

"We're fine, Selma. How are you and Lazlo?"

"Keeping busy. Trying to sort everything out. How'd the auction go?"

"Definitely the right place," Sam said. "Hold on. Let me get Remi. She has some names for you."

"The broker was Lorenzo Rossi," Remi said. "I didn't quite catch the buyer's name. It sounded like Warren. Or maybe Borden."

Selma looked over at Lazlo, who immediately reached for the yellow legal pad with her notes scrawled all over it. "Last name?" she asked.

"I couldn't tell," Remi said. "The broker had a thick accent, and I was listening outside, so I didn't have the best advantage."

"There was a Reginald Oren in the journal," Selma said. "Cousin to Jonathon Payton, the Viscount's son."

"Oren," Sam said. "Didn't Oliver say something about some relative making an offer on Payton Manor?"

"Definitely. And Allegra sort of brushed it off."

Selma circled the name on her notes. "This gives us a whole new angle to research," she said. "Reginald Oren stole the Gray Ghost. He's mentioned prominently throughout the entire journal."

"Interesting," Remi said. "I haven't finished reading it."

"Did you find out anything more?" Sam asked Selma.

"Lazlo and I are going through it a second time to see if we've missed anything."

"Sam and I can give it a closer read later," Remi said.

"As soon as we meet up with Chad and Oliver, we'll be heading to Paris. We think the Ghost might be there."

"Paris?" Selma said. "Let me get this straight. The car was stolen from London, shipped to Paris, sold in Italy, and now this long-lost relative, Oren, is buying it?"

"From a high-end broker," Remi replied.

"Was this a custom order?" Selma asked. "Maybe Oren wanted the car and paid someone to steal it?"

"The possibility exists," Sam said. "But whoever stole the Ghost from the London Motor Show would have to have had some inside knowledge about the Ghost and the Payton family. The setup was far too elaborate for a spur-of-the-moment theft."

"An inside job?"

"At the very least. Figure out who has that sort of connection to the family—"

"Allegra's ex-husband," Remi said. "The solicitor's investigator thought she was hiding something, and Oliver suspected he might be there."

Sam added, "Not sure of his name, but he's certainly a good possibility."

"I'll touch base with the investigator," Selma said. "Back to Paris. How are you two doing on cash?"

"We're fine. Remi managed to pick up a few thousand euros from the broker."

Lazlo smiled. "I daresay, he wasn't too pleased about that."

"Unfortunately, his guards may have taken it out on our car."

"Are you returning it to the rental agency in Italy?" Selma asked Sam.

"Considering our lack of finances, I think it'll be cheaper, and safer, to drive to Paris. I just need to figure out how to patch those bullet holes so they're not so obvious. I'd hate to get pulled over and have to explain how they got there."

"Duct tape," Lazlo said. "Just make sure it's the same color as the car."

"Let me know where you end up dropping it off," Selma told Sam. "Once we get the credit cards back on track, I'll notify the rental agency. And the insurance company. What about the jet?"

"In hock at Ciampino. The crew took the petty cash and are probably waiting to hear from you."

"We'll put that on our list," Selma said. "Any idea where in Paris you're headed?"

Remi read the address off the pad of paper. "See if there's anything on Lorenzo Rossi at that location. I gathered he wasn't going to release the Ghost until Oren's transfer cleared."

"Also," Sam said, "check for connections near the coast. If he's fencing stolen property from other countries, especially the UK, he's going to have something near major shipping areas. Quick in, quick out."

"We'll get on it," Selma said.

"Thanks. And if I didn't mention it, Remi and I are glad to hear from the both of you. We were worried when we couldn't get in touch."

"You were worried?" Selma sank back in her chair and looked over at Lazlo. "You should have seen us."

Lazlo gave a dry laugh, reached over, and grasped Selma's hand, giving it a reassuring squeeze. "The worst thing that happened was," he said, "we couldn't call for takeout. We did, however, raid the safe for petty cash."

"Glad you're both okay," Remi said. "We'll talk to you soon."

They disconnected, and Selma gave a deep sigh, noting Lazlo's expression mirrored hers—overwhelming relief that the Fargos were fine. A few seconds passed before either of them realized they were still holding hands.

Letting go, they looked at each other, both feeling a sense of embarrassment as they scooted closer to their own desks.

"Well, then," Lazlo said, "I'll give the banker a call and see if he has made any further progress."

Selma picked up the slim volume. "Guess I better get back to the journal to see if Jonathon Payton ever rescued Miss Atwater."

58

JOURNAL OF JONATHON PAYTON, 5TH VISCOUNT WELLSWICK

1906

Twas the longest fifteen minutes of my life, hoping that Miss Atwater had not been injured, certain she must be frightened beyond all belief. As I rounded the corner and saw the darkened building of my father's warehouse, I wondered if I'd misunderstood everything. Surely if anyone had been there, there'd be lights coming from within?

Wary, I crouched down behind a short brick wall and worked my way in that direction. Something moved in the shadows ahead. Two men were standing at the garage door, one acting as lookout while the other worked at the lock.

I heard the scrape of wood as they slid open the large door, wherein I saw the moonlight gleaming off the grey bodywork of the missing Rolls-Royce.

Gripping the brass handle of my cane, I watched for a few more seconds. Only two thieves. Thank heavens.

I started forward.

"I WOULDN'T DO THAT."

I turned, surprised to see my cousin. "Reggie. Why—" Only then did I notice the gun pointed at me. Until that moment, even with the incriminating evidence of seeing that car in our warehouse, I realized I'd been holding on to the belief that Reginald was innocent.

I could think of no reason as to why he'd stolen the car. Surely he knew that with the theft of the Ghost, and the imminent harm to the company as a result, we'd lose everything we'd invested. It wasn't so much the loss of my own fortune. It was the families on our estate who'd lose their homes. And the children at the orphanage . . . So many who'd be displaced . . .

"I— I don't understand," I said.

"You never did." Reggie stepped forward, his nose wrinkling in distaste as he smelled the scent of garbage clinging to my clothes. He nodded toward the warehouse. "Inside. I know how much you hate for anyone to cause a scene."

The confirmation that my cousin was behind this theft hit me hard. "I trusted you . . ."

Reggie gave an unsympathetic smile. "Your misfortune, it seems. Had you been smart, you'd have stayed in the garbage heap and slept it off. You would've awakened merely a poor man, not a dead man. No matter." He motioned with the pistol, pointing toward the garage. "Move. I'd rather not be the one to shoot you, but I will if need be."

"Where's Miss Atwater?"

"Safe enough. For now. I promise you, though, if you fail to cooperate, she'll be the first to go."

He raised the gun, and I started walking toward the building.

As I neared the warehouse, Reggie's two men, both armed with knives, stood just inside the door.

I gripped my father's cane, fearing not only what they'd do to me but also what might befall Miss Atwater. "Why?" I asked again, as Reggie pointed for me to enter.

"Why do you think? You've always had everything. I? Nothing. I thought you should know what it felt like."

"But we've always provided for you."

"Your father hated me. Hated my father to his dying day."

"You're wrong."

"Eddie!" Reggie called out, pushing me into the doorway.

My head still muddled from the coshing, I stumbled forward. A heavyset man with a jagged scar on his cheek grabbed me and threw me to the ground. My father's cane flew from my hand. Before I could reach for it, the scar-faced man dropped down, digging his knee into my back. "Mac," he called out.

The other man—Mac, I presumed—tossed a heavy rope toward us, dust kicking up as it landed near my face. Eddie tied my hands behind my back, then wrapped a length of the same rope around my feet, drawing them back. When he finished, he stood over me, his face filled with disgust, as he kicked me in the gut.

"Enough," Reggie said. The clip-clop of horse hooves caught his attention, and he peered out the door. "The lorry's here."

Mac and Eddie left me and rolled the carriage door wide open. Reggie picked up the lantern from the floor, the light flickering on the cobblestones as he stepped outside. He called back to the two of them. "Get the chest out. And careful with it."

"Where do you want us to stow it?" Eddie asked.

"Put it in the Grey Ghost. Should be safe enough in there."

The two men dragged a small chest from beneath a tarp. Whatever was in it was heavy, and the two had difficulty lifting it.

Recognition hit me when Reggie's lamplight flickered on the gold-leafed royal crest on the outside of the chest. "The train robbery, Reggie? You?"

My cousin looked surprised. "You think I'm not capable of something that daring? That always was your problem." He walked over to the Grey Ghost, standing aside as Eddie and Mac brought the chest over. "By tomorrow night, once I deliver the forty-fifty to my buyer, your father's investment in Rolls-Royce Limited will be for naught. And with my profits from the robbery, I'll have enough cash to buy back Payton Manor and all the lands your father stole from mine. What I won't be doing is wasting my money on those charities you support."

"The children—"

"That orphanage your father started will be the first to go."

"Finlay!" Reggie called out to the man in the driver's seat of the lorry. "A hand!"

The man secured the horses' reins, jumped down to pull out the ramps from beneath the lorry's bed, before climbing up to work the winch. He drew the length out, tossing the end to Eddie as my cousin walked around the vehicle, the lamp's light reflecting on the polished grey paint.

Eddie secured the winch to the Ghost and Finlay started pulling it up.

"Does this car really work?" Finlay asked, as Eddie and Mac started pushing the car toward the lorry. "Why don't we just drive it out of here."

"And get caught?" Reggie said. "Don't be an idiot. If a night watchman hears that engine starting, he might come 'round to investigate. Load it up, put the chest inside, and get the tarpaulin over it, before someone sees it."

Once the car was safely on the lorry, Reggie stood aside as Eddie and Mac hefted the chest, carrying it up the ramp. Whatever was in it was heavy, and Eddie nearly lost his grip, the chest slamming into the bed of the lorry.

I heard the ring of metal hitting metal, imagining what sort of treasures would be in a royal chest. Gold and jewels, perhaps.

"What about your cousin?" Eddie asked, when they were finished loading the chest. "What're we going to do with him?"

"Kill him, of course." My cousin's emotionless voice sent a chill down my spine. "Quietly, though."

Eddie looked over at me as though contemplating how best to carry out my demise. When he turned away to help the others cover the car with the tarpaulin, I shifted, trying to get to my cane, which had landed somewhere behind me. I felt it with my fingertips, managing to hit the release for the dagger hidden in the shaft. But then I heard the soft scrape of footsteps.

As I twisted around, I saw a flash of white from the corner of my eye. Whoever it was grabbed the cane from my fingers, drew the hidden dagger from the handle, and clamped a hand over my mouth.

Arthur Oren passed through airport security and walked to the executive lounge to wait for his plane back to the UK. If he'd had his way, he'd be in Paris to personally take possession of the car today, not Monday.

The video he'd seen before bidding on the car had erased all doubts that he was looking at the Gray Ghost. Still, it galled him that he'd had to pay such an exorbitant price to recover the very car that he'd stolen himself. And it angered him even further that he had to wait for his bank transfer to clear before he could view the car in person.

Still, it was now a matter of a day or two before he'd have the Ghost safely back in the UK. Only then would he learn the secrets she held.

Assuming the Fargos didn't interfere . . .

The phone buzzed in his pocket: Colton.

At last.

"You got my message?"

"I did," Colton said.

"It was the Fargos who broke into Rossi's office, wasn't it?"

"From the description they gave me, there's no doubt. I'm sending you a photo from their security cameras."

Oren's phone beeped with the incoming message. He opened it, saw a grainy photograph of a man and a woman climbing on the balconies of the Rossi villa. "So we know the Fargos were there," he said. "The bigger question is, what're you doing to make sure neither of them interfere in our plans again?"

"To start, we've tapped into the phones of Oliver and the mechanic."

"Weren't they in Milan?"

"They're heading south again, probably to meet up with the Fargos. When they do, we'll deal with them."

"Had you dealt with the Fargos back when I asked you to, we wouldn't be having this conversation, would we?"

Colton cleared his throat. "As I said, Payton and the mechanic are heading south. The path of their travel indicates they're on a train to Rome. Bruno and one of Rossi's men will follow them to wherever the Fargos are holed up."

"In Rome?" Two women walked into the lounge, both rolling small luggage bags alongside them. "You really think you're going to be able to do anything with that many people around?"

"I assure you that the location makes no difference whatsoever."

"I want them—" Oren, seeing both women watching

him, stopped just short of saying the word *dead.* He forced a slight smile, lowering his voice as the women took a seat a few feet away. "Just see that the job's done. I'm tired of waiting."

He disconnected, then took a better look at the digital photo that Colton had sent of the security camera from Rossi's villa. Though grainy and dark, the sight of the woman's face shot a feeling of dread through him.

It couldn't be . . .

The woman from the elevator? But she spoke no English. Her accent was impeccable. She— She what? Pretended to be Italian?

The knowledge of how close she'd been to him sent his thoughts racing. He wasn't used to this sense of panic or the feeling that he was losing control. He wanted to throw his phone across the room, to smash something, anything.

The sight of the two women watching him forced him to take a calming breath. What he needed to do was reevaluate. He hadn't gotten this far in life by letting his emotions rule him.

He had only himself to blame. Recalling the photos that Colton sent in the original dossier on the Fargos, he opened that file, took a second look. The truth was, he hadn't given the photos more than a cursory glance. Who cared what the spoiled rich wife of a multimillionaire looked like? How was he to know that this Remi Fargo was anything more than just a pretty face who could shoot straight?

He stared at her photo a few seconds more, angry that

he hadn't recognized her when she'd stood next to him outside of Rossi's villa. Of course, he'd had other things on his mind, like securing the Ghost before someone else bid on it.

A small consolation—and little he could do about it for now. As infuriating as it was that Colton, once again, had let the Fargos slip past him, Oren knew better than to voice his displeasure too much. Like it or not, he needed Colton. That didn't mean he intended to let Colton do as he pleased. Oren had Bruno to keep an eye on Colton's men, which meant there was little they could do without him knowing.

Distrust, unfortunately, came with the territory. Someone had stolen the Ghost from right beneath his nose, and when he found out who was responsible, he fully intended to exact his revenge.

For now, though, the Fargos were his main concern. The photo of Remi on the balcony bothered him more than he wanted to admit. He didn't like the fact that they'd gotten that close without him knowing it.

He'd like it a lot better when they were dead.

60

Remi joined Sam at the open window, where the early-morning sun turned the fountain's shimmering mist a pale silver as it rose from beneath the two horses pulling Neptune on his shell-shaped chariot. The soothing sound of rushing water almost muted the voices of the dozens of tourists packed around the base, watched over by the two carabinieri officers whose patrol cars were parked nearby. They were, apparently, permanent fixtures during the daytime.

"I wonder how many reports those officers take each day. Pickpockets, lost kids . . ."

When he didn't respond, she checked the direction of his gaze and noticed he appeared lost in thought. "Sam?"

"Sorry. I was trying to figure out how we can get out of here if Oliver and Chad are being followed."

"You don't think they'd come in from the direction of the fountain square, do you?"

"I doubt it. The standard route for the taxis is to drop everyone near the front of our building." He walked to the window on their left, this one facing north. Remi followed him. The fourth floor gave them a clear view down the narrow cobbled street that led out to the main road. Within the few seconds they stood there, two taxis pulled up, dropping off passengers who came to see the fountain. "What we need is a quick getaway. We don't want to be trapped up here if Oliver and Chad are spotted ringing the doorbell downstairs."

"Maybe we'll get lucky and they won't be followed."

"Not likely. It's the only way Bruno and company can find us."

"Too bad we couldn't slip Chad and Oliver's phones in someone else's pocket, like we did at Castle Rising in King's Lynn."

"Except we were the ones doing the following . . ." Sam's voice drifted off. He watched the taxi taking off with a new fare. "Actually, you might be onto something there, Remi."

"Whose pocket are we slipping their phones in?"

"Ours."

"You mean you want them to follow us?"

"That's the plan. At least to start off with. Paris is a fifteen-hour drive from here. We get them to follow the phones for a few hours, I'm hoping we'll be halfway to France before they realize we're gone."

Less than an hour after Sam outlined his plan, Chad and Oliver arrived in a taxi that let them off in the square of the small church across the street. Unfortunately, Bruno and his new partner, a blond man neither of them had seen before, pulled up about a half block behind the church, on the opposite side than Sam had predicted, cutting them off from the car he'd parked around the corner. Sam surveyed the crowded square, a look of concern on his face. "We're going to need a distraction to get to the car."

"On it," Remi said, pulling out her phone. She called the emergency number, reporting two armed men standing in front of the building across from Santa Maria à Trevi Church. "I heard them talking about shooting up the fountain. I saw guns beneath their suit coats."

Two minutes later, the officers from the fountain rounded the corner, both looking in the direction of Bruno and his partner. Bruno suddenly stopped, as though realizing they were the focus of the officers' attention.

"That's them," she said to the woman on the phone. One of the officers touched his ear, adjusting his earpiece, to hear the dispatcher. When Bruno's partner turned to run, the two officers tackled him. Bruno, however, took off in the opposite direction.

"One down, one to go," Sam said, as Remi ended the call. "Nice work. You get the car, I'll get Oliver and Chad before Bruno catches up to them."

Remi pulled up a few minutes after that, glad to see Bruno was nowhere in sight.

"Good timing," Sam said, as he slid into the front passenger seat and Oliver and Chad got in the back. She drove to Rome Termini. At the train station, Sam took Oliver and Chad's phones, walked inside, and returned a few minutes later. "One is on its way to Austria, the other to Germany."

"That should keep Bruno busy for a while."

He opened the glove box and pulled out the tracking device Oren's men had hidden in their rental car. "Might be a good time to reactivate this little thing before we take off."

Remi looked over at him. "You don't think he'll suspect that it's suddenly starting up?"

"He might. But these things are designed to sleep if there's no movement, to preserve battery power. And what better place to wake it than where the phones were last seen?"

"But where?" Remi asked. Sam nodded toward the bus, and Remi smiled. "Pick you up on the other side?"

"See you there."

Sam jogged over, pretended to drop something next to a bus scheduled for Naples, then planted the device.

"Why go to the trouble?" Oliver asked when he got back in the car.

"Confusion," Sam said. "Your phones are here. If Bruno's still tracking them, he'll end up at the train station, trying to find the both of you. And if we're really lucky, the device I stuck under the bumper of that bus will cloud things even more. Naples is a long way from Paris."

"So is Rome," Remi said. "We better get started."

61

Sam took the first shift at the wheel, and, minus a few breaks for food and fuel, they drove straight through, arriving in Paris a little after two in the morning. Once again, limited to cash only, Remi's friend Georgia was able to find them a Paris apartment in the 20th arrondissement. Situated in a working-class neighborhood, the second-story apartment offered a partial view of the Eiffel Tower from the kitchen window—provided they leaned to the left.

Late the next morning, as Oliver and Chad returned from a trip to buy groceries for a late breakfast, Sam sat in the kitchen, looking over a map of Europe.

Remi brought two mugs of coffee to the table, taking a seat next to him. "What if he was lying about the location?"

"In case he can't trust Oren?" Sam replied.

"Exactly. How certain are we that the Ghost's not in Paris?"

"We can't be sure," Sam said. "Still, the Gray Ghost isn't something you can hide in plain sight. A bit of a risky move to bring it this far inland. We need to think logically."

He studied the map for possible routes. "If we knew how he got it out of the UK, that might narrow down where he has it stored."

"So where would he keep his less than legitimate goods?"

"Somewhere easy to get to, and easy to ship out after a sale, I'd think. We can safely assume they got the Ghost out of London in a truck. From there, it's anyone's guess."

"They transport trucks through the Channel Tunnel," Remi said. "That's the closest and fastest route from the London Motor Show."

Oliver looked up from the cutting board, where he was slicing fresh bread. "Except," he said, "the police were notified right away. The investigator told me that the first thing they were checking was transport trucks and containers headed to France. I'd think the tunnel would've been the first thing they checked. And the easiest."

Sam drew an X through the London Eurostar route, then circled Dover. "Good point. Less risky to send it to a major shipping port, where no one would notice one more container."

"Calais's busy enough to escape notice," Chad suggested, as he brought over the cut apples and the grapes. "I've taken the ferry over quite a few times."

"That'd be my first pick," Sam said. "But we still have to find the specific facility Rossi's using or it'll be like—"

"A needle in a haystack?" Remi suggested.

"Exactly. I doubt Rossi's got a website announcing which warehouse he's using for his stolen goods."

"Of course, we're assuming he's using one of his own," Remi said.

"High-value and high-risk. There's no way he's going to entrust it to anyone else."

"So how do we find it?" Chad asked.

"It's Sunday," Remi said. "What better time to visit?"

"Might be a night operation?" Sam asked. "What do you think, Remi?"

"After a quick recon trip during daylight hours to see what we're up against, we can make that decision."

Late that afternoon, they drove out to Rossi's business office. As they stood across the street, it didn't take long for Sam to discover that getting in after dark wasn't going to be as easy as they thought. The office was housed in a business district with high-level security, including a bank on the first floor of Rossi's building.

"So much for that idea," Sam said. "That bank adds a layer of protection Rossi couldn't get anywhere else."

Remi gave a facetious smile. "I suppose pretending to be from Oren's shipping company for a pre-inspection of the car would be too obvious?"

"Just a bit."

Oliver looked relieved that they seemed to be backing out of the idea of breaking in. "So we're not coming back tonight?"

"No." Sam examined the windows of the four-story structure. Rossi's export management company was on the third floor. "Breaking and entering into a building containing a national bank is likely to buy us a few years in prison. All we can do now is come back in the morning when the place is open for business."

"Cutting it short," Remi said. "They're meeting at eleven."

"If we want access, that's our only choice."

They returned the next morning at eight. The bank had its own entrance in the lobby. Those who were not bank customers had to check in with the security guard before being allowed to access the elevator.

After watching the people going in and out of the lobby's front doors, Sam and Remi looked at each other, Sam saying, "You know what this place reminds me of?"

"That time in Madrid . . . ?"

Sam smiled. "I think we have our plan."

62

Allegra and Trevor spent most of their time on the couch, side by side, staring at the television. Though she tried to concentrate on the plot of the movie playing, she couldn't. Trevor, she was glad to see, laughed in all the right places. Somehow, he was able to relax. The resiliency of teenagers. She prayed that when this was over—when she somehow found a way out of this—he'd have no lasting damage to his psyche.

A knock at the door sent her heart leaping in her chest. Dex immediately reached for the gun in his waistband as he rose from his seat to see who was there. She grasped Trevor's hand, silently reminding him to remain still, to stay quiet.

Not that he needed any warning.

The bruise on his cheek from where Dex had struck him with the journal was fading, yellowing at the edges. Trying not to let her attention catch on it, she watched as Dex crossed the room, looked out the peephole, opened the door. After Frank walked in, Dex checked the street in both directions. Satisfied no one was out there watching, he closed and locked the door. "About time."

The broad-shouldered man's right arm still bandaged and in a sling. Apparently, he'd been shot in a gun battle with the Fargos. A shame they'd missed, she thought as he scrutinized them. "Still here?" he said to her.

She ignored him, kept staring at the television. Trevor did the same.

"You want a beer?" Dex asked him.

"And something to eat."

Dex looked over at Allegra, then cocked his head in the direction of the kitchen.

She immediately rose. "I'll make us lunch. Come help me, Trev." When Dex looked as though he was about to object, she said, "Where's he going to go?"

"Go on," Dex said.

Trevor followed her. While he got the bread, jam, and butter out, she opened a bottle of beer for Frank and an ale for Dex. "If he let's down his guard," she whispered, "you get out."

"I'm not leaving you, Mum."

"You are—"

"What're you two talking about in there?" Dex yelled.

Allegra mouthed, "Quiet," then took the bottles out to Dex and Frank. "Trying to find something to eat. Is bread and jam and butter okay?"

Frank, who'd sprawled himself on the couch, put his feet up on her coffee table. "If that's all you have . . ."

Dex grabbed the ale from her hand. "Make cheese sandwiches."

"We're out of cheese."

"Jam's fine," Frank said.

"Not for me," Dex said. He wasn't a fan of sweets. "What else do we have?"

"Nothing. Nothing for dinner. Or breakfast. I wasn't expecting Frank back so soon."

"Blimey, Dex. You starving them on purpose? Send one of them to the store."

"I don't trust them."

"I'd offer to go for you, but the arm . . ." He pulled at the white sling.

Dex took a long swig of his beer. "Looks like we'll starve."

"You could always go," Allegra said to Dex.

He narrowed his eyes at her.

"Frank's here," she pointed out. "He can stay with us."

"I don't mind," Frank said.

Dex seemed to think about it, lowering his bottle to the table. "Yeah, okay. They try anything . . ."

Frank slashed his finger across his neck, making her glad Trevor wasn't in there to see it.

"I'll make a list," she said.

Ten minutes later, Dex was gone. She breathed her first sigh of relief since this nightmare began—until she saw Frank resting his hand on the butt of his holstered gun. "Another sandwich?" she asked.

"I'll wait."

"Beer?"

"Sure."

She signaled for Trevor to stay at the kitchen table, as

she opened another beer and brought it out to Frank. "How long do we have to stay here?" she asked.

He took the bottle, gazing at the television. "Until we get the car back and find what's hidden in it. I mean, who knew?"

"Knew what?"

"There was a treasure somewhere."

"In the car?"

"That'd be rich. Someone would've found it by now, don't you think?"

"How'd it get stolen?"

"Some train robbery back in the 1900s."

"The car, I meant. The Gray Ghost."

Frank looked at her, his brows raising. "You're kidding, right?"

As much as she wanted to tell him that she found none of this laughable, she dared not do anything to arouse his anger. Keeping her expression as calm as possible, she picked up Dex's half-empty ale and carried it to the kitchen, looking back at Frank. "I know how it was stolen from my uncle." After all, she played a small but major role in that crime. But what choice did she have? "I was wondering how it was stolen from your boss."

"You mean, you really don't know?" He stared at her, shook his head. "That's rich."

A slow realization burned in her gut. "You and . . . Dex?"

"Who else?"

"Are you insane? What happens when your boss finds out?"

"How would he do that?"

"I— I don't know." She couldn't believe what an idiot she was. Clamping her mouth shut, she pretended to do a bit of cleaning, working her way to the coffee table, turning up the volume on the television as she slid the remote control next to a magazine, then picking up Frank's empty sandwich plate, returning it to the kitchen. "Trevor, come help me do the dishes."

Trevor pushed back his chair from the table and trailed after her.

She turned on the water full blast, letting it run. "Do you think you can climb out the window upstairs?" It could open only a few inches, the crank having been removed, but she was certain he could force it open wider. The window frame was old, made of aluminum. "You can tie a couple of sheets together from the linen closet."

"I'm not leaving you here."

"You have to," she whispered, looking back toward the living room. Frank's attention was on the television. "Your father helped steal Uncle Albert's car from the man who stole it to begin with. When that person figures it out, he'll send someone here to kill him. And us. Assuming—" She was about to say "your father" again but stopped when she realized how horrible it sounded. As though this was Trevor's fault more than hers.

The fault was hers, and hers alone.

"Dex isn't right in the head. When this is over and he gets what he wants, he'll kill us. I just—" She wiped away a few tears. "Please go. Tie a couple of sheets together. I could bear anything except the thought of you getting hurt. Please."

"What if something happens to you?" he whispered back. "How am I supposed to go on?"

"Because I love you. I will always love you. And you think about that every single day."

"Mum . . ." Tears pooled in his eyes.

"Please . . . Please, Trev."

He nodded, and she hugged him, amazed at how much he'd grown, feeling his warmth, his heartbeat against her ear, as she pressed her head against his chest. She wanted to remember this moment, everything about him, in case it was the last time. Finally, she pushed away. "Hurry."

Frank walked in just as she turned toward the sink. "What's going on?" he asked.

"Trevor doesn't feel well. I told him to go take a nap."

"Any more beer?"

"Sorry. I put it on the list for Dex."

He grunted some response, then went back to the living room, this time taking a seat in Dex's armchair to watch the show.

Allegra, grateful the curtains and blinds were closed, returned to the kitchen, rearranging the dishes in the cupboards, trying to make enough racket that it would cover any noise that Trevor might make climbing out the window.

Twenty minutes later, as she finished scrubbing the sink, she heard what sounded like a snore. She froze. When she heard it again, she turned off the water and stood there for several seconds. There it was again . . .

The third time she heard it, she looked to the back door. It opened to a small patio area and a square of grass, where Trevor used to play when he was little. She'd have to jump the fence to the neighbor's yard and get out that way. Once she found Trevor, they could go for help.

She didn't even know if she could actually get over the fence. Still, she had to try, and she started to edge her way toward the kitchen table. All she needed to do was get on the other side of it, open the door . . .

If Frank opened his eyes, he'd be able to see the back door from the armchair.

What if he was setting her up?

Grabbing a dish towel, she dried her hands, casually walking toward the living room to take a look.

Frank's head was tilted back, eyes closed, mouth open.

Seconds ticked by.

Slowly she started to back toward the kitchen table. She could do this. Three more steps.

Two.

One.

As Allegra reached for the handle, the front door burst open. She dropped her hand, looked over, saw Dex, carrying two bags of groceries. A look of suspicion clouded his face when he noticed her proximity to the back door.

"Where is he?" Dex demanded.

Frank woke with a start. "What the—?"

Allegra's heart was thumping. Dex's eyes bored into hers, and he stalked over to the table, dumped both bags down, one of them spilling onto its side. A yellow onion rolled out, across the dark wood tabletop and to the floor.

"Trevor!" Dex called.

Her heart beat with every second of silence.

He was gone.

She wanted to cry with relief—even when Dex pulled out his gun and pointed it at her. She wondered if it would hurt. It didn't matter.

Trevor would be safe.

"I'll kill you for this." Dex raised the barrel toward her.

"I'm here!" Trevor stood at the top of the stairs. He glared at Dex. "You want to shoot someone? Go ahead. The neighbors will hear. They'll call for help. Try it."

"Shut up and get down here," Dex ordered. "Help your mother with the groceries."

Allegra's knees started shaking. She grabbed a chair at the table, leaning against it. The tears came, not because Dex would've killed her but because Trevor never left. How could he do this to her? Why?

Why wouldn't he listen?

Her son started down the stairs, his expression one of pure anger, and she wondered for a moment if it was directed at her. But when he passed Dex, his back to the man, he looked right at her and mouthed, "I'm sorry."

She reached out, grasped his hand, trying to smile at him. He put his arm around her. Once out of sight of both men, he whispered, "I am not leaving you. Ever."

Her heart broke a little that night. After dinner, she and Trevor remained at the table while Frank and Dex watched TV, the two men drinking, unfortunately not near enough to inebriate them beyond loose conversation. At one point, Frank lifted his beer, asking, "Whatever this thing is, it can't be hidden in that car."

"Probably not," Dex said. "Or someone would've found it by now, right?"

"Exactly what I was thinking. Bigger question is, how do we find it?"

"It's got to be in that diary."

"The one you don't have?"

"Like I said, we don't need it. My kid's got one of those memories like a computer. I swear, he remembers everything. Trev," he shouted. "Get out here."

Trevor looked at her, worried. "I don't know anything about where it's hidden," he called out.

As much as she'd wished that Trevor had left that afternoon, she realized that he'd grown up, taken responsibility for something he believed in. Her. She smiled, trying to will what little strength she had to him so that he could also fight this battle. "Tell them what you read. It keeps them happy."

He reluctantly rose and walked into the front room. "Where do you want me to start?"

"Where'd we leave off?" Dex asked.

Frank drained the last of his beer, then set the empty bottle on the table. "I think that Payton fellow was captured. He was trying to use that hidden dagger to get away, but someone took it from him."

64

JOURNAL OF JONATHON PAYTON, 5TH VISCOUNT WELLSWICK

1906

All hope seemed lost as I waited to feel the dagger thrust into my back. Imagining death had never been this frightening. It was mere seconds, but so many thoughts flitted through my head. The atrocities my cousin had committed and that he was behind the robbery . . . I thought of the poor engineers, as well as the hired detective, who'd lost their lives at my cousin's hand. I thought of Miss Atwater and prayed she would somehow escape to safety.

All this while I braced myself for the dagger to come down toward me. But instead of pain, I felt it sawing the rope.

"DON'T MOVE," someone whispered in my ear, though I barely heard it over the pounding of my heart. Whoever it

was draped the rope over my wrists, then disappeared into the shadows.

Reggie returned inside, eyeing me, squinting as he examined the rope at my feet and hands. "How'd you loosen that?"

I forced myself not to look behind me. "What? Reggie—"

My cousin held the lantern aloft, his expression scathing. "Reginald—I've always hated the name Reggie."

"Please. You're not like this. Think of your wife. Your son."

"That's exactly who I'm thinking of." He straightened, looked behind him, the Grey Ghost now on the bed of the lorry. "Eddie, Mac, leave the car and get rid of my cousin. Make it look like an accident. Finlay, take the reins. Time to go."

"Reg— Reginald! Don't do this. Please!"

Reggie ignored me as Eddie jumped down from the back of the lorry, drawing a knife from his waistband as he stalked in my direction. Mac joined him, while Reggie held the lantern aloft. Eddie lifted the blade, the flickering lantern flame reflecting on the cold steel.

"Two against one?" came a voice from behind me. "That's hardly fair."

Mac and Eddie stopped in their tracks, both men looking around, trying to find the source of the voice.

"Who's there?" Reggie asked, holding the lantern higher as he searched the warehouse.

"The name's Isaac Bell." Mr. Bell stepped out into the light, walking toward us, until he stood between me and my would-be murderers. Dressed all in white, he held my fa-

ther's brass-handled cane, the hidden blade returned to its sheath. He looked at Reggie, then turned his attention toward Mac and Eddie. "And the lot of you are under arrest for train robbery."

The shock on Eddie and Mac's faces lasted a few seconds before both burst out laughing.

Eddie pointed his dagger toward Mr. Bell. "Followed us all the way from New York, did you? By yourself? Aren't you the funny bloke." He took a step forward.

Isaac Bell blocked his path with my father's cane. "Sorry. I can't let you do that."

Eddie, knife in one hand, grabbed the cane with the other, using it to pull Isaac toward him. His leer twisted the scar on his cheek as he glared at Mr. Bell. "I'll slit your throat and shove your fancy stick in after it."

"Will you, now?" Isaac said, taking a half step back.

Eddie held tight to the cane.

As Isaac ran his left hand down the cane's shaft, gripping the handle with his right, I thought he'd pull out the blade. But, no. He leaned in, drove the cane forward, rammed the man with his shoulder. Eddie's dagger flew from his hand, sliding across the wood-plank floor. As Eddie staggered back, Isaac swung the cane around, striking Mac in the chest with the heavy handle, bringing him to his knees.

Reggie aimed his gun at the detective. Isaac pivoted, swinging the cane again, knocking the pistol from his hand.

Reggie started to reach for it, but Isaac kicked the pistol away, swung the cane against Eddie's spine, knocking him into Mac.

Even then the three men sought to attack. But Isaac

pressed the cane's catch, drawing the hidden dagger from the handle. "Perhaps I wasn't clear enough," Isaac said, as he shoved the point toward Mac's throat, stopping just as it drew blood. "You're under arrest." The sound of an approaching horseman caught their attention. Isaac was the only one who didn't look, his attention on the three men. "Get the gun, Payton!"

The moment I grabbed the pistol and pointed it at them, my cousin ran out the door.

"I say . . . Reggie?" I recognized my friend Byron's voice. He'd gotten my message. "Where's Payton?"

Reggie raced past, climbing up onto the lorry. "Go! Go!"

Finlay shook the reins.

The lorry lurched forward, the wheels squeaking beneath the weight of its load.

"They're getting away," I called out, as Byron dismounted, clearly not understanding.

Isaac quickly assessed the situation. "Watch these two, Payton. Shoot if you have to." Isaac ran out, grabbed the reins of Byron's horse, mounted, and raced off after the lorry.

I held the gun pointed at the two, my fears of being left in charge turning my stomach. This was not me. I was the last person meant to be a hero. Even so, I realized that if either of these two men tried to escape, I would have to shoot them or let them go. Not wanting anyone's death on my conscience, I saw the rope. "Byron. We need to tie these two. Quick. Now!"

"I—"

"Now!" I ordered, before I lost all nerve.

Byron nodded, grabbing the rope that had been used to

hog-tie me, securing it around their wrists. Certain that wouldn't be enough, I told him to wrap it around their waists, so that they were back-to-back.

"What, in heaven's name, did they do?" Byron asked.

"Robbed a train."

Byron looked over at me, his astonishment evident. "The robbery where the engineers—" His face paled. "They were murdered!"

"Go get a night watchman," I said. "And tell him to bring help."

Byron stood, eyed the two men, who were struggling against their bonds. "Do you think it wise I should leave you?"

In truth, the last thing I wanted was to be left alone. With no other choice, I pretended a bravado that I did not possess. "I really don't want to kill these two, but I will if they try to escape."

Both men stilled, eyeing me in turn, the pistol in my trembling hand.

Byron nodded. "I'll be back shortly."

When he left, the quiet of the place terrified me. I thought of Miss Atwater. If I felt like this, what must she feel? "What have you done with Miss Atwater?" I demanded.

Both men refused to answer.

"Where?"

The man called Mac gave a cynical laugh. "You're alone. Your cousin tells us you're a coward. Afraid of your own shadow. Let us go now and we'll be gentle on you."

I felt a bit hot under the collar at his words, not just because Reggie had talked about me to these cutthroats but because they were true. I was a coward.

I glanced at the dagger from my father's cane, recalling how Mr. Bell had used it on Mac, immediately gaining his compliance. Of course, it had a lot to do with how he'd wielded the cane prior, but I was fairly certain I could at least put the point to someone's throat.

Keeping a wide berth, I circled the two men, picked up the cane's dagger, then approached, pointing it and the pistol at them. Both my hands were shaking. "Where is Miss Atwater?" I demanded.

The two men stared straight ahead.

Overcoming my cowardice, I looked at Eddie's scar, placed the tip of my blade against his other cheek. "Lest you want this side of your face to match the other," I said, trying to sound as threatening as Mr. Bell, "you'll tell me what I want to know."

"You're as mad as your cousin."

"Where is she?" I shouted. My hand shook so much the blade pierced his skin, bringing forth a drop of blood. A mere two days ago, I might have drawn back in horror, but I pictured Miss Atwater, frightened and alone, and I pressed harder. "Where?"

"We don't know," Mac said.

I kept the blade at Eddie's cheek, applying more pressure.

Eddie's eyes widened in surprise, and perhaps with a bit of fear. "He said he was taking her to the Dowager Cottage."

I lowered the blade, shocked. 'Twas my grandmother's cottage, empty until Reggie had moved in with his wife and child. Before I had a chance to question him further,

Byron and two night watchmen arrived. They took both men away, leaving Byron and me to wait for Mr. Bell. And just when I was about to give up hope, I heard the clip-clop of horses' hooves and the squeak of the lorry's wheels.

Mr. Bell was driving the lorry, Byron's horse in tow. Bell tossed the reins to Byron, dragged Reggie from the floorboard and deposited him at my feet. His hands tied at the back, Reggie started to rouse, apparently having been knocked unconscious.

"Where's the other man?" I asked.

"The driver? I'm afraid he didn't make it. Not too bright, that one. What about your two?"

"Night watchmen took them." I told him what I'd learned about Miss Atwater.

"Good," he said, as Reggie started to look around.

"What now?" I asked.

Isaac pulled Reggie up by his shoulder, dragging him so that he was seated, his back to a workbench. "We find out who hired your cousin."

"I don't understand."

"I suspect your cousin was a pawn to whomever set out to ruin Rolls-Royce. He took advantage of his connection to you and the company to steal the forty-fifty."

His words stunned me, since it meant that I was also a pawn.

Mr. Bell must have noticed my expression. "All is not lost, Payton. Chess happens to be one of my specialties."

Reggie glared. "I'll never cooperate."

Isaac Bell spared him a look and gave him a dismissive

smile. He walked me to the door, his voice low. "I intend to question him further. I'd like to know what happened to the rest of the money stolen during that train robbery."

"It wasn't in the chest?" I asked. "I saw them load it onto the lorry."

"At least half of the money's missing. I'd say half a million. No doubt hidden away."

"Then what was in the chest?" I asked.

"Engine parts, to get the Silver Ghost up and running."

It didn't occur to me until that moment how devious Reginald's plan had been. With the Grey Ghost missing, and no parts to spare, Rolls-Royce would never get the Silver Ghost finished in time for the Olympia Motor Show. Yet one more blow to the company we'd invested everything in. If not for Mr. Bell, Reggie's attempt to ruin Rolls-Royce would have succeeded.

About to leave, I gave my cousin a parting glance, recognizing his smug look. "You know where that money is, don't you?" I asked.

His expression darkened, his smile cruel. "Since you helped me hide it, that makes you complicit."

"I did no such thing."

"You're a fool if you think otherwise."

Horrified at the thought, I wracked my brain, trying to determine if there was any possibility that I might have taken part in his dastardly plans. I could think of nothing and looked to Mr. Bell for guidance.

"Perhaps," Bell said, "you should determine if Miss Atwater is safe."

"And what of him?" I asked, nodding toward Reggie.

"As I said, your cousin is only part of the equation. I intend to use him to find out who was really behind the theft of the Grey Ghost."

Reggie's face twisted with triumph and hate. "Perhaps you didn't hear me. I don't plan on cooperating."

"Fortunately, I don't require your cooperation." Bell's smile had a rather devious edge to it. "In fact, I don't even require you to be conscious."

The plan was simple. Once inside the office, Remi would come up with a way to find out the location of the warehouse holding the Gray Ghost while Sam acted as lookout. Oliver and Chad would wait in the car, ready to pick the Fargos up for a quick getaway.

At the moment, Chad was finding a suitable place to park that wasn't too far. Remi, Oliver, and Sam were seated on a bench in the shade of a chestnut tree, Remi reading up on the import/export business on her phone. A row of motorbikes parked in front of them offered some cover, just in case anyone in Rossi's building across the street happened to look their direction.

Oliver eyed the windows across the street. "Are you sure this is a good idea?" he asked. "Those are armed guards in that lobby."

"They're for the bank," Sam said. "After what happened at the villa, I'm more worried about what Remi might find upstairs in Rossi's offices."

Oliver shifted nervously. "All the more reason not to go."

"We'll be fine. Remi's got quite the knack for pretending to be something she's not."

She looked up from her phone. "If that's supposed to be a compliment, Fargo, you've missed the mark."

He leaned toward Oliver and in a stage whisper said, "She's very good at subterfuge. Sneaky operations," he quickly added.

"Better," she said, returning her attention to the phone.

"What if something goes wrong?" Oliver asked. "Bad enough my uncle's in jail for something he didn't do. I couldn't bear it if something happened to either of you."

"We'll be fine," Sam assured him. "Just make sure you and Chad are ready with the car. We might have to leave in a hurry."

Chad walked up a few minutes later. "I finally found a place to park." He pointed down the tree-lined street. "The patisserie on the corner. It was the closest available."

"It'll do," Sam said.

Remi dropped her phone in her purse, then stood. "I think I have all I need to know."

If anything, Oliver looked even more worried. "You couldn't have read through it but once."

"Good memory," Sam said. He looked at her. "Ready?"

She leaned over and kissed him. "See you soon."

REMI SMILED at the security guard before announcing her appointment at the Rossi Export Management Company. The guard looked her over, then buzzed her into the lobby. "Third floor," he said.

She took the elevator up, walked into the shipping company, her expression somber, her head tilted at just the right angle to imply a certain haughtiness that demanded immediate attention. "Mr. Rossi, please," she said to the receptionist, a woman in her twenties, her blond hair pulled back in a ponytail.

"And you are . . . ?"

"Rebecca Longstreet. My U.S. attorney should have called to arrange a meeting. Short notice, but I'm only in the country until this evening."

"Regarding?"

"SRF Import/Export." Remi strode into the middle of the office, giving the place a thorough perusal. "Who's in charge?"

"Monsieur Marchand."

Remi gave her a blank stare.

A look of confusion crossed the young woman's face. "Did you need to speak to him?"

"If he's not expecting me," Remi said, "he should be."

"Of course. One moment, please." The woman rose from her seat, knocked on the door behind her, opened it, then disappeared inside. A moment later, she returned, holding the door open for Remi. "Monsieur Marchand can spare you five minutes."

As Remi walked in, a portly man in his fifties pushed his chair back and stood, his smile wide, as he held out his hand. "Mademoiselle Longstreet. Please. Come in, sit. May I get you a drink?"

"No, thank you."

He walked around his desk, holding the chair for Remi. "To what do I owe the pleasure?"

"A slight falling-out with my former logistics company manager. And a need for an immediate replacement."

"What sort of volume does your company handle, mademoiselle?"

"About twenty or so fewer full containers a month than last year. But I'm hoping that once we speed up the freight process, we'll double that load." She cleared her throat, started to speak, smiled. "Actually, I will take that offer of a drink."

"Of course. One moment."

When he walked out the door, Remi saw a stack of papers on a low file cabinet in the corner next to the window. She quickly walked over, looked out the open curtains, saw a glimpse of the Seine between the buildings across the street. She looked down, moving the papers with her fingers, quickly reading the addresses. Just from this short stack, she saw that Rossi had two warehouses in Calais and one in Brussels. Somehow she needed to narrow down which warehouse or they'd never arrive in time to get the Ghost before Oren took possession. Before she had a chance to search further, Marchand returned with her water. He stopped short when he saw her standing by the file cabinet.

She nodded out the window. "I was admiring the view of the river."

"Most of our visitors do," he said, barely sparing a glance himself. "Your Perrier. My apologies, as we have no glasses."

"*Merci.* The bottle is fine," she said, taking it from him. "You were saying? About your business?"

"Yes. About our recent downturn," she replied, twisting the top of her bottle to break the seal. The water fizzed slightly. "Something I hope to turn around."

"You'll forgive me if I seem too inquisitive, but in order to know if your company will be a good fit with ours, I need to have some idea of what volume—"

"Assuming your warehouse can handle loading thirty or forty containers a month," she said, citing what she'd read that morning about the company she was modeling hers after. Marchand leaned forward with interest on hearing the number of containers she'd mentioned, and she took a sip of her water, letting her words sink in, before asking, "Are there certain ports you use more frequently than others? If they line up with ours, it might be easier to seamlessly move our shipping to your facilities."

"It all depends on the origin and destination of the load," Marchand replied.

"Calais?"

"One of our busier ports. Do you mind my asking why you're searching for a new logistics company?"

"As I said, a slight falling-out with the former company, combined with a desire to move my business to Paris—not that I'd consider it without thoroughly investigating the logistics company."

"We're very well respected. Your business would be in good hands. Of course, I should let Monsieur Rossi welcome you personally. We're fortunate that he's making a rare appearance here today. He usually works out of our offices in Rome, but he's scheduled to meet with a client later this morning. I expect him any minute, in fact."

Definitely not what Remi was hoping to hear. Rossi was arriving far earlier than she'd expected. Realizing that she needed an alternative plan—and quick—she took her phone and accessed the calendar. "I may have a conflict . . . Let me call and see if I can cancel my appointment." She turned toward the window, pretending interest in the view again, as she called Sam. "It's Rebecca. About that appointment I have this morning . . . Is there any way I can change it? The man I hope to meet, Monsieur Rossi, is on his way as we speak."

"If he's in that black BMW," Sam said, "then no. It just pulled up."

Remi scanned the street, noticing a dark sedan double-parked directly below, its emergency flashers blinking. The driver opened the back passenger door, and two men in business suits got out. Granted, identifying the tops of their heads from the third floor wasn't the same as seeing them face-to-face, but with one being dark-haired and the other blond, reminding her of the shooter on Rossi's balcony, she suspected Rossi and his bodyguard had just arrived.

With only one elevator, Rossi's arrival meant Remi was going to have one heck of a time trying to get out without being seen. Sam, still on the other end of the line, said, "You have about three minutes. Just saw him walk into the building."

"How unfortunate," Remi said into her phone, thinking what a waste to have come all this way and be so close to having the information they needed. She looked back at Marchand, who was eagerly watching her, and gave him an apologetic smile, before turning back to the window. When she saw the curtains falling to the sill behind the chair, she knew exactly what to do. "Since I can't cancel the appointment, please inform them that I'm on my way. And regarding that personnel matter we hoped to resolve, they should keep the line of communication open. I just don't want to hear anything on my end."

There was a moment of silence. Remi wondered if she'd been too subtle, until Sam responded, "Will do."

She looked at Marchand, as she lowered her phone. "I am so sorry. My appointment can't be changed. Will

Monsieur Rossi be here later this afternoon? Perhaps I can return then?"

"I would have to ask him," Marchand said. "It would be a shame if you were to miss this opportunity."

She turned back to the window, leaning against the sill. "I do hope I can work things out. Such a lovely view," she said, sliding her phone out of sight, into the right-hand corner of the sill, beneath the curtain, before turning back to Marchand and smiling. "My apologies for rushing out."

"Mademoiselle, I look forward to meeting you again."

"Soon, I hope."

He gave her his card, and she left. The long hallway was deserted, as she approached the elevator, noticing it was heading up. If Rossi was on it, she'd never make the stairs without being seen. Wondering if there was a doorway she could duck into, she spied the fire alarm on the wall nearby. She pulled it, walked quickly toward the staircase, as a high-pitched electronic chirp sounded, followed by the metallic clang of a bell overhead. As the alarm blared, several office doors opened, and the hall filled with people, creating a barrier of bodies between Remi and the elevator, as its door opened. When she reached the stairwell, she caught a glimpse of Rossi striding toward Marchand's office, a look of annoyance on his face at the disturbance. Remi hurried down the stairs, until she reached the ground floor, and emerged into the alley.

Sam was waiting at the corner of the building. "Love your Plan B," he said, handing her his phone.

"Did it work?"

"If you mean, did I hear the alarm going off? Then yes. After that? Anyone's guess," he said, as a car pulled up beside them in the alley. Chad was behind the wheel, Oliver in the front passenger seat.

Sam and Remi got into the back. As Chad pulled out into traffic, taking a left turn, away from the bank, Remi, checking to make sure the mute button was on, put Sam's phone to her ear. The alarm sounded for a few seconds longer, then finally stopped.

"Circle around," Sam told Chad. "We'll follow Rossi's car when it leaves."

Remi tapped Sam, put her finger to her lips, as a man started speaking Italian. "Rossi," she said. "Talking to his bodyguard." And, sure enough, when they stopped down the street from the bank, they saw the bodyguard out front, on his mobile phone. "Rossi's saying he'll be down soon . . . Now he's cursing because Marchand still isn't in his office because of the alarm. Never mind, he just walked in."

The two men started speaking French, at a slower pace, and she switched the phone to speaker so that everyone could hear.

"Where were you?" Rossi asked Marchand.

"Making sure the employees obeyed the fire drill."

"Suzette said something about a visitor?"

Remi turned up the volume, curious if Marchand might tell Rossi about her visit. "An inquiry about shipping services."

"We have no time for that. You've made the arrangements for the container to ship?"

"Of course. Just as you requested." There was a moment of silence, then Marchand saying, "You're leaving so soon? What of Monsieur Oren? I believe he's expecting for you to personally—"

"A change of plans. Call me when he's on his way."

After the secretary's faint voice bid Rossi good-bye, they heard a loud sigh.

Remi regarded the phone. "Marchand's awful quiet, now that Rossi's left."

"Probably crying over the loss of your shipping business."

"I might have made it too enticing." About three minutes later, Rossi walked out of the building, but instead of getting into the car, he nodded to his driver and walked off with his bodyguard down the street.

Remi looked over at Sam. "Maybe the Ghost really is here in Paris."

"I would've bet our last euro that car was in Calais," Sam said, unbuckling his seat belt. He leaned toward the center, speaking to Oliver and Chad in front. "Pop the trunk, Chad. Remi and I will follow them. You two take the car and wait at the apartment. We'll meet back there tonight. The moment we figure out where we're going, we'll text."

"And if something happens to you?" Oliver asked.

Sam opened his wallet to see how much cash they had. A little more than a thousand euros left. He handed half to Oliver. "We're at the tail end of the money. If you don't hear from us by morning, get in touch with Selma, and head back to Manchester."

"Wouldn't it be easier if we all stuck together?" Oliver

said, his face etched with worry. "Look what happened in Rome."

"You'll be fine." Remi reached over the seat, grasping his shoulder. "You're a pro at this by now."

He gave a timid smile. "Do me a favor? Don't let anything happen to you."

"Not a problem," Remi said, with a big smile, slipping her purse straps over her shoulder before getting out of the car.

Sam took his backpack from the trunk, then he and Remi followed Rossi and his bodyguard.

The two men, about a block ahead, made a right turn. Sam looked at Remi, as they quickened their pace to keep up. "Quick thinking with that phone. Did I ever tell you how brilliant you are?" he said, as they rounded the corner, emerging into a busy square filled with hundreds of tourists.

"Apparently, not that brilliant. They're gone."

Remi looked around at the myriad shops and restaurants. Rossi and his guard could have disappeared into any one of them.

"The Metro," Sam said.

"They don't seem like the public transportation type."

"But they don't seem like the tourist type, either."

He had a point.

They took the stairs down, bought two tickets, then looked at the two tunnels leading to the different platforms and the various trains on each.

Sam eyed the choices on the sign, checking the listing of transfers. "This way," he said, leading Remi to the left.

"I hope you picked right, Fargo," Remi said, as she and Sam took the escalator down into the depths of the Paris Metro.

"Have I ever guessed wrong?"

"There was that time in—"

Sam suddenly pulled her to the side, as they stepped off the escalator. "They're about fifteen feet ahead of us."

She saw Rossi and his guard turn left into an archway

that led to the train station's platform. Sam took her hand, guiding her past a first and second archway, taking the third that the men just took. They stopped short of the platform when a loudspeaker announced the Metro's arrival. As the two men stepped on board, Sam and Remi crossed the platform and entered the last car.

Remi found an empty seat. "How'd you figure this out? The Metro—"

"Is the fastest way to the train station from Rossi's office. Send Oren by car while he takes the train. That gives him at least an hour-and-a-half head start. The time he would need to search the car before Oren got there."

"Color me impressed, Fargo."

When they reached Gare du Nord, Sam and Remi followed as the pair weaved their way through the crowd, not to the ticket booths but toward the Calais platform, which meant they bought their tickets online.

Sam gave her his wallet. "I'll keep an eye on them."

Although she picked the shortest queue for tickets, it moved slowly. By the time she reached the front, the train to Calais was set to leave in less than five minutes. The woman in front of her was at the window, busy asking questions about what to do with her luggage once she was on the train.

Remi watched the clock ticking. Worried, she leaned forward and said, "About how much longer will you be? I'm about to miss my train."

The woman looked back at her, an annoyed expression on her face. "If you don't mind, it's my turn."

"I apologize," Remi said, clasping her hands together.

"I just found out my father's been taken to the hospital. He might not make it."

The woman appeared unmoved.

"And his dog is locked in the house with no one to take care of him."

"Why didn't you say so?" The woman moved aside, allowing Remi to pass.

At the window, Remi laid out the exact amount in cash, bought the tickets, then hurried toward the platform, the woman yelling after her, "I hope your dog is okay!"

The platform was nearly empty when she arrived, everyone having already boarded. Sam was nowhere in sight. A soft beep indicated the doors were about to close. After one last look around, she stepped aboard the train just as the doors slid shut. Sam walked toward her from the next car as she worked her way past the passengers stacking their luggage on the racks.

"Wasn't sure you were going to make it," Sam said.

"Not sure I was, either." She and Sam found their seats in the very last second-class car. Remi used Sam's phone to text Oliver and Chad to let them know where they were headed and that they'd be in touch if they found the Ghost. When she called to check in with Selma, it immediately went to voice mail. Remi left a message.

Selma called back about a minute later. "Sorry, Mrs. Fargo, I was using the phone for a hot spot to get on the internet. We still don't have everything up and running yet, but we should have a working bank account in the next day or so."

"Good to hear," Remi said. "We're on our way to Calais."

"You have a lead on the Ghost?"

"We hope so. We'll find out soon."

Sam leaned toward her, whispering, "The investigator?"

"Sam wants to know if you've heard from Bill Snyder on Albert's case."

"I called him to pass on our new phone numbers," Selma said. "He thinks this hacking business bolsters the case that Albert was set up."

"That's good news, at least. What about Oliver's sister? Anything on her?" Remi heard what sounded like a sigh of frustration from the other end. "She is okay, isn't she?"

"He saw her at the door, so he's sure she's fine. But there's not a lot of movement in the house, other than her ex, and another man who's visited a few times. He fits the description of the man Sam shot when you were using the Faux Ghost to rescue Chad's mother."

"Frank."

"Possibly. His worry, right now, is triggering a hostage situation if he attempts to make contact. He's fairly certain both men are armed."

Remi repeated the information to Sam.

"There's not a lot we can do about it," Sam said. "We're going to have to trust that Snyder can handle things."

Allegra turned on the water, filling up the sink, while Trevor cleared the dinner dishes from the table. He set them on the counter beside her, his fingers lingering near the black-handled butcher knife on the cutting board.

"No," she whispered, pushing his hand away.

"Why not? I sleep three feet from him."

She wasn't about to let Trevor take this half-baked plan to kill his father, then live with the guilt of that for the rest of his life. "Because I said so."

"We have to do something."

"We will."

He turned away, but not before she saw that stubborn tilt to his chin.

"You have to trust me, Trev."

He refused to look at her as he walked out.

"Trev?" Allegra turned off the water and started to follow him, until she saw Dex watching her. Not wanting to alert him that they'd been talking about anything other than dirty dishes, she picked up his empty bottles from the table, taking them into the kitchen, as though that had been her intent.

Long ago, when Dex first raised a hand to her, she was certain she could change him. It never occurred to her that the person she needed to change was herself.

Looking back, she knew the only reason she'd found the strength to leave Dex at all was her fear that he'd turn his violence toward her son instead of her. And ever since, she'd harbored a sense of guilt for not providing the perfect life for Trevor—that, somehow, refusing to let him see his father was depriving him of some necessity. That guilt was at the foremost of her mind when Dex showed up at her door after all that time. She'd thought that if she let Trevor see him, just for a short while, it would be enough. Dex would leave, and they could get on with their lives.

That Dex would've involved them in something so horrible never occurred to her. How could she have been such a fool?

She dropped the bottles in the trash, started the water again, eyeing the knife, the dried bits of onion stuck to the blade. It didn't matter what happened to her. She was going to make sure that her son walked out that door uninjured.

Somehow, she had to convince him that she was on his side or he'd never let down his guard.

With sudden insight, she knew how to do it, and by the time she finished the dishes, her plan was fully formed. She grabbed the dish towel, drying her hands on its once-cheery blue and white checks that now looked stained and dingy from too much use. "We need laundry detergent," she said, walking into the front room, where Dex sat, watching TV.

"It can wait," he said, not looking at her.

"How long? We—"

He glared at her. "Seriously? That's what you're worried about?"

"Actually, no," she said. "I— I heard something."

"Heard what?"

"The other morning," she said, lowering her voice. Dex's attention was on the television, his expression telling her he was only half listening to her. "When I thought it was you down here, talking on the phone. Whoever Frank was talking to, it was about you."

His focus shifted from the television to her, the annoyance on his face replaced by suspicion and wariness. "Out with it, then."

"I—" Her resolve started to falter, and she was grateful she still held the dish towel, using it to hide her trembling hands. She checked the stairwell, making sure that Trevor wasn't hiding there. "I heard him telling this person that once he made you take care of us, he'd take care of you."

He gave a slight shake of his head and turned back to the television. "Go back to the kitchen."

Sow distrust. She had to make him think she was on his side. "Did you hear me? He wants you to take care of us. And then, he's going to turn around and take care of you. You know what that means . . ."

Dex clutched the arms of his chair, his eyes boring

into her. "He is going to take care of me. By giving me my share of the Ghost money."

"He's twisted you against your own family. Trevor's your son."

"Is he? Because you changed that when you divorced me and got custody. Wouldn't even let me see the boy. Look at him now. Coddled so much, he'd rather spend his time upstairs than watch the telly with me. Anything happens to him, it's your fault, not mine."

The knot in her gut tightened, almost paralyzing her. Dex didn't love anyone or anything beyond himself. Not even his son. Trevor was merely collateral damage in Dex's revenge on her. But with crystal clarity she realized that she'd forgotten the one thing she needed to do to focus Dex's anger elsewhere: make it about him. Giving a casual shrug, she started back toward the kitchen. "Well, I just thought you should know what else he said about you."

"What?"

"He told whoever he was talking to that he was only using you to get the journal." The lie came so easily, it surprised her. Still afraid to even look at him, she stared down at the dish towel as she let the words sink in.

"What else?" Dex asked.

"Something about you being a loose end, but that he'd take care of it." She finally dared a look. "After that, I don't know. I— I didn't hear the rest."

Dex's expression hardened as he stared at her, his breathing sharp and shallow. "Loose end, eh?"

"That's what he said." An apologetic smile. "I just thought you should know because, well, I have an idea."

"Why should I trust you?"

"Because I'd never do anything that might harm my son."

The television droned on in the background, the laugh track sounding desperate and hollow, while Dex pinned her with his stare, his fingers drumming a beat on the arm of the chair. Finally, after what seemed the longest seconds of her life, he nodded. "Let's hear it."

"We have Trevor write the journal—what he remembers of it."

"Why bother? The couple times he's sat down with me, it's not like I learned anything that's going to help. Wasn't any mention of any treasure hidden anywhere, was there?"

"Not any obvious mention," she said. "But you know best. I was only trying to help." She shook out the dish towel, returned to the kitchen.

A few seconds later, he walked in after her. "What do you mean by obvious mention?"

She picked up a plate from the dish rack, drying it, as she talked, not wanting to seem too eager or too interested. "My brother and I read that journal quite often when we were young." She looked over at Dex, saw him hanging on every word. "We even acted out the parts. Trust me. If that treasure had been mentioned anywhere that was noticeable, we'd have found it."

"Then why's everyone looking for it?"

"Simple. The treasure from the train robbery was never found, my ancestor wrote about it, and his cousin was responsible for stealing it. Arthur Oren is a direct descendant of that cousin and he's looking for it. Who knows what stories his family passed down. It's quite obvious, don't you think? If Arthur Oren believes the answer's in that journal, it must be."

"The journal we don't have. I doubt those Fargos are going to drop by and give it to us."

"I'm quite sure you're right," she said, placing the dried plate in the cupboard, picking up another. "But we have the next best thing. Trevor." She glanced at him, offering a slight smile, pleased to see that he was hanging on her every word. "So instead of having him sit down and tell us what's in it, we have him write it down."

"What good's that going to do?"

"Even if they somehow get the journal from the Fargos, we—you'll—have a head start. And with Trevor's insight, if there's anything to discover—"

"He'll figure it out."

"Exactly," she said, running the dish towel over another plate.

"Except he already told Frank what he'd read."

She nodded toward the trash, overflowing with empty bottles. "Between all the beer Frank drank and his pain pills, you think he's going to remember even a tenth of what Trevor told him?"

Dex said nothing for several seconds, probably because he'd also been drinking. "How long do you think it'll take him?"

"If he uses the computer, maybe a day or so."

"Trev!" he yelled. "Get down here."

Trevor took his time coming down the stairs, refusing to look at Dex, his eyes on her the whole time. "I'm tired."

"I know," she said. "But we need your help . . . I need your help," she added, willing him to cooperate, hoping he'd read between the lines. "Do you think you could type up what you remember of the journal so that we could read it?"

His eyes flicked to his father, then back to her. "If I got some sleep. My brain's too fuzzy. I'm tired."

"It doesn't have to be the whole thing," she said, knowing that she needed something to show Dex or he'd change his mind come morning. She guided Trevor toward the office and into the desk chair, not giving him a chance to refuse. "Just a chapter."

Turning the computer on, she hovered as only a mother could, moving the bills out of the way, tapping her finger on the business card, tucked in the corner of the blotter, left by the investigator when he'd shown up at her door to take the journal. "You can do this," she said softly. "I know you can."

Trevor poised his fingers over the keyboard, opening the word processing program. A blank document appeared, and he started typing.

Dex moved in beside her, and she rested her hand over the card, watching Trevor type. When she realized he was starting with the first chapter, she suggested he start later in the journal.

"I thought we wanted the whole thing," Dex said.

"We do," she said. "Eventually. But if we start where

you fell asleep that afternoon, you'll be able to finish it faster. Jonathon Payton was going to find Miss Atwater after she'd been kidnapped, and the detective was going to force Reginald Oren to help them capture the person who was behind the theft."

"Start there," Dex said.

Trevor lifted his hands from the keyboard. "I can't concentrate with the two of you standing over me."

Allegra glanced at Dex, relieved when he backed away. She followed him from the room, grateful when she heard Trevor typing, yet worried she might've been too subtle about what she wanted him to do.

69

JOURNAL OF JONATHON PAYTON, 5TH VISCOUNT WELLSWICK

1906

I raced home on Byron's horse, not willing to believe that Miss Atwater was there until I saw her with my own eyes. Once I reached Payton Manor, I turned over the horse to our caretaker, ran into the house, through to the back and across the garden to the Dowager Cottage, throwing open the door. Reggie's wife and child had gone to visit her mother, so I was surprised—and hopeful—to see a light on and Miss Atwater sitting at the pianoforte, plunking at the keys.

"Are you hurt?" I asked, once I'd caught my breath.

She stood, her expression one of confusion and surprise. "No, of course not. Merely worried about you. Your cousin happened by in his carriage, telling me that you sent him to pick me up, as you were worried about my safety. He said you went to fetch a night watchman."

"My cousin?"

"Indeed. He was very apologetic, insisting that I wait here until you or he came back."

"And you're not hurt?"

"What could possibly befall me here, other than trying to amuse myself while I wait? The pianoforte is in terrible need of tuning. Several of the bass keys don't even work."

I wanted to laugh at the absurdity of such a statement.

And I might have, except she seemed to realize something was amiss. "Tell me, what troubles you so?"

"Nothing."

"'Tis something," she said. "I can see it in your eyes."

I considered shielding her from the truth, not because she was a woman too delicate to hear, more because I wanted to see her again and worried she might recoil after hearing the sordid truth. Still, I wanted no lies between us. "My cousin was the mastermind behind the train robbery. He killed the engineers and the detective."

As my words rushed out, telling her everything, a look of horror clouded her eyes. She shook her head. "No . . ."

Fearing that my revelations had forever turned her against me, I apologized.

She said nothing for several seconds, then, "He was lying to me? About men following you?"

"No. His men were following me. They knocked me out. When I came to, I— I managed to call for help. When I couldn't find you—" The very memory caused me pain. I ignored it, drawing her to the pianoforte bench so that she might sit.

"I was in the same carriage as that madman?"

"I'm so sorry," I said again. "If I could change things, I would."

Her hand went to her mouth, covering her trembling lips. Suddenly she reached for my hand, encouraging me to sit beside her. "You came looking for me?"

"I was worried about you."

"At great risk to yourself."

"I cared nothing for that. Only to find you."

"Mr. Payton—"

"Jonathon."

"Jonathon . . ." Her voice softened to barely a whisper, as though trying out my name for the first time, to see how it felt.

"Miss Atwater?" I said when nothing more was forthcoming.

"Surely you're not going to leave Mr. Bell to face your cousin all on his own?"

"I— I hadn't really thought about it. I— I needed to see you safe."

"And I am. But Mr. Bell . . ."

Miss Atwater's concern made me realize the truth. Isaac Bell was out there because of my cousin. "I owe him my assistance." I said, standing. "I'll see you safely home, then go to him straightaway."

She stood as well. "I think you should go to him first. And I shall go with you."

"You couldn't possibly. What if something happens to you?"

Her dark brows arched, a look of determination on her face. "Please, don't think me too forward, but you've stolen my heart. I'd never forgive myself if something happened to you when we've only just found each other."

In that one moment, I realized that if this were my last day on earth, I wanted it to be with her. "Miss Atwater," I said, holding my hand out to her.

She clasped it tightly in hers. "Mr. Payton."

When we arrived at the warehouse in my father's carriage, Isaac Bell seemed to accept her presence without question. He was, after all, a man of extraordinary intelligence. Byron was a bit shocked, but he quickly came 'round, and the three of us listened while Mr. Bell outlined his plan. Miss Atwater glanced at my cousin, bound, gagged, and seated against the wall of the warehouse. "And what of him?" she asked Bell.

"He will be in the carriage, where you and Payton will be in charge of watching him. The two of you need to remain out of sight. Byron will pose as your driver."

Concerned about Miss Atwater's proximity to a murderer, I hoped to change Mr. Bell's mind. "Is there some reason we aren't turning him over to the authorities?"

"We may still need him," Bell said. "You never know when something might go wrong."

Arthur Oren's dark mood lifted considerably as he arrived at Lorenzo Rossi's Paris office. By the time he took the elevator to the third floor and the receptionist announced him, nothing could detract from the feeling of triumph now that all his meticulous planning was finally paying off.

The receptionist returned, saying, "Monsieur Marchand will see you now."

"I was told Lorenzo Rossi would be meeting me personally."

Before she could answer, a heavy middle-aged man stepped from the doorway behind her, extending his hand in greeting. "Monsieur Oren. A pleasure."

Oren shook his hand, looking past him into the empty office. "Where's Rossi?"

"He's on his way to Calais to make sure that your order is ready for shipping. I'll order a car to be brought 'round." Marchand waved a hand toward his office. "Please, come in, sit. Would you care for a cup of coffee, or something else to drink, while we wait?"

"No, thank you," Oren said, as Marchand took a seat behind his large mahogany desk. Oren eased into the leather armchair near the window. "I was under the impression that Rossi was going to meet me here, and we'd drive out together."

"For which he sends his apologies. He felt it necessary to make sure everything was prepared for shipping. Of course, I shall accompany you to the warehouse personally, once the transfer is made."

"That wasn't our agreement," Oren said, forcing himself to remain calm. He'd already been duped before, which resulted in the car being stolen from his own warehouse. That theft he'd deal with, once he found out who was behind it. This time he wasn't about to let the car out of his sight. "The transfer will be made when I see the car and verify that it's the vehicle as described. Until then, the money remains in my account."

Marchand looked through the open door at his receptionist, who was sitting at her desk, then looked back at Oren. "Monsieur Rossi's reputation is without question," he said, his voice sounding strained and on edge. "If he says the car is there, it's there. To suggest otherwise—"

"Is prudent, and good business," Oren replied. "Perhaps, though, I need to point out why I'm taking such precautions. This car was stolen from my warehouse less than a week ago. As such, I am paying good money for the return of property that is rightfully mine to begin with."

"Understand that Monsieur Rossi is merely brokering the deal. He does not involve himself in such matters."

"While I respect his position, I take offense that he's not respecting the terms of our agreement."

"What terms?"

"That my purchase was conditional. I see the car in person, he gets the money. In that order. If he can't honor those terms, I'm prepared to walk away," he said, though he had no intention of doing so.

Marchand stared at him for several seconds, then sputtered, "You're expecting me to call him with your demands?"

"In fact, yes. I'll wait." When Marchand failed to pick up the phone, Oren stood. "Or explain to him why I left."

"Monsieur, there is no need to be hasty. It's just that I've never yet run across anyone who's doubted the word of Lorenzo Rossi. It's simply not done."

"And yet, I'm doing it."

"Please, have a seat," he said, picking up the phone, pressing a button. "I'm calling now."

Oren returned to the chair, his eye catching on a compact dark rectangular object on the windowsill just visible beneath the right curtain panel. He pulled the curtain aside, picked up a mobile phone, pressing the home button. The screen lit up. But when he tried to get beyond the home screen, he found it was locked. "Yours?" he asked Marchand.

"No."

"A rather odd place for a phone, don't you agree?"

"Perhaps it was left by the lady who was— Ah, Monsieur Rossi." He held up a finger and started speaking

French, a language Oren did not understand. He did, however, recognize his own name in that conversation, and assumed Marchand was informing him of his demand to see the car. That, he wasn't worried about. This phone, however . . . left by a woman . . . "What woman?" he demanded.

Marchand hesitated in his conversation with Rossi. "Pardon?"

"You said a woman left the phone. Who was she?"

"The lady was here to inquire about shipping services. She must have left the phone there when she was admiring the view."

Oren looked out the window, saw what, in his mind, was only a pedestrian view of the river between the buildings. Not something worthy enough to forget a phone. He gripped the device, suspicion fueling his already mounting anger over the delay in getting back the Gray Ghost. That Fargo woman had infiltrated Rossi's villa the night of the auction. No doubt she was here, trying to learn the location of the Ghost. "Let me talk to Rossi."

"Monsieur Oren would like to speak with you," Marchand said into the phone. He pressed a button on the receiver. "You're on speaker."

Oren approached the desk. "When you were here in the office earlier today, did you mention the location of the warehouse?"

"Why do you ask?" Rossi said.

"I believe Remi Fargo was here. She left behind a mobile phone. If I had to guess, in order to listen to the conversation in your manager's office."

"Marchand," Rossi's sharp voice cut in. "Please explain what he's talking about?"

"A lady was here earlier, looking for shipping management. Monsieur Oren seemed concerned with her presence."

"And you didn't think to mention this to me?"

"If you recall, I did. I was not, however, aware I should be suspicious of anyone inquiring services. We do run a legitimate business here."

There was a stretch of silence on the other end of the line. Oren pictured Rossi seething at the thought that he'd been victimized by the Fargos yet again. Finally, Rossi spoke. "The very idea that they managed to get the location from me or my manager is absurd."

"Not absurd," Oren said. "So I ask once again. Did you mention the location of the warehouse?"

"The most they would've heard is that we were en route to the warehouse. No address given. And since I've just arrived at the warehouse and have seen the car with my own eyes, I'm quite certain your fears are unmerited."

As much as Oren wanted to believe him, he'd already had enough experience to know the Fargos could easily slip past the most secure barriers. "Do not underestimate them. Or are you forgetting who it was who robbed you at the villa?"

"Not likely. I particularly remember the video of you riding the elevator with the woman."

Tempted to point out that it was Rossi's lack of proper security that had allowed the Fargos to breach his walls in the first place, Oren brushed aside the barb. Trading insults was not in either of their best interests right now. Recovering the car was his first priority. "Keep an eye out for the Fargos. Make sure that you haven't been followed. I'm on my way there now."

Sam and Remi ducked behind a row of parked cars in a lot down the street from a busy warehouse, Sam watching through his binoculars as Rossi stood on one of the loading docks, talking on his phone. After several minutes, he ended the call and returned inside, pushing open a glass door of the warehouse's office. Sam had a clear view and he quickly scanned the grounds. A forklift on the dock backed up with a full pallet of cartons, beeping as it maneuvered toward one of the trucks. Beyond the open bay doors were row upon row of boxed goods, on pallets and on shelves. To the right, adjacent to the property and secured behind a razor-topped chain-link fence, was a yard filled with metal shipping containers stacked two high.

"You think it's in one of those containers?" Remi asked.

"I doubt it's out there. Something that valuable, they're keeping inside under lock and key."

"I knew this was too easy."

In truth, it had been. There were enough taxis leaving the station that Sam and Remi wouldn't stand out, and they easily followed Rossi's cab, until it turned into the industrial area. Sam directed his driver to continue past, then double back. "One thing in our favor," Sam said, lowering his binoculars. "We still have time before they ship it out. Oren's not here, yet."

"What are you two doing?"

An unarmed security guard in a light blue shirt with patches on the sleeve stepped out of the building behind them. Tall, slim, white hair and beard. The expression in his green eyes was wary as he approached.

"I've got this," Remi whispered. She stood, smiled sweetly at the man. In French, her accent impeccable, she said, "We're private detectives. Hired by the wife of the warehouse owner across the street. Messy divorce, and he's refusing to pay child support because he insists he's losing money. She's certain he's hiding profits."

The man's look of wariness suddenly changed to one of understanding, as he regarded her and Sam. "That might explain some of the unusual activities we've seen. One of my guards reported a truck being unloaded there late one night. I remember thinking it odd, when I read his report."

"What night was that?" Remi asked.

"Wednesday, I believe. I'd have to check the report. Whichever night it was, they were in and out pretty quick."

Sam met Remi's eyes. That would fit the time line of when the Ghost was stolen from Oren. Sam's French was too stilted. Last thing they wanted was to arouse the guard's suspicions, so he gave Remi a slight nod.

"Did your officer include in his report anything unusual about the truck?" Remi asked.

"Besides the late hour? Just that they drove the truck in, dropped off a shipping container, then left. If he's hiding something from his wife, it's probably there."

Remi and Sam both turned toward the warehouse, seeing two trucks backed up to the docks, the doors open, the forklift drivers moving in and out as they loaded them with full pallets.

The security guard nodded toward the right side of the warehouse. "That third door is where they unloaded the container."

"It's still there?"

"The container? That I can't say. It's been closed up tight ever since." He pulled his phone from his pocket, reading a message on the screen. "As much as I sympathize with your plight, my employers are on their way here. They're acquainted with Monsieur Rossi, the owner. Friends, even. I don't believe they'll be so understanding if they discover you here."

"Thank you," Remi said. "We've seen enough to file our report."

He returned to the building, opened the door, stopped, looked back, his green eyes alight as he regarded them. "Not that I'm the expert, but if I wanted a better view, I'd walk around the corner and approach from the west."

They thanked him again, but he'd already disappeared inside.

Sam lifted his binoculars and took one last look inside the warehouse. A wall separated the main area from the third bay. A closed door near the loading dock led into it, but they'd never be able to get inside that way. Not without being seen. There was a fenced yard on the west side, filled with shipping containers. That meant there should be an exterior door leading into the building. "Let's take a walk."

He and Remi headed down the street toward the corner, crossing once they were out of sight of anyone inside Rossi's warehouse. Other than the dozens of shipping containers stacked in the yard, the west side of the building appeared deserted. A door toward the back of the structure gave them hope they might actually have a way in. He and Remi followed the chain-link fence topped with razor wire until they reached a gate secured with a padlock. Sam picked it, and they slipped in. Pea gravel crunched beneath their feet as they walked between the containers, almost covering the soft beep of a forklift coming from behind the building. They reached the end of the row. Sam looked out, then ducked back, as the forklift shot around the corner, driving straight toward them.

As Sam and Remi sank back between two containers, the forklift driver stopped at the end of their row, maneuvering toward the stack of containers, the metal clanging as he slid the forks under the topmost one. A steady beep sounded as he backed away with it, disappearing behind the warehouse.

When he was gone, Sam looked at the fresh marks in the gravel, which exposed the dirt beneath, in the empty row next to them. "We need to hurry. He may be back."

They crossed the open space toward the building, Remi taking the corner, to watch for the forklift driver, Sam going up to the door, the sign posted on it, in both French and English, announcing that it was an area restricted to authorized personnel only.

He picked the dead bolt, signaled Remi over. Once inside, he closed and locked the door behind them. The sounds of the busy warehouse next door filtered through the walls. Skylights lit the space, a lonc shipping container in the center of the floor. Thankfully, the doors of the container faced away from the front of the warchouse and the office doors and toward the overhead door. Sam lifted the hasp, metal scraping against metal as he pulled open the container.

The entire front end was filled with boxes, stacked side by side, on two pallets. "Not what I expected to see," Remi said.

Sam saw a pallet jack against the wall and rolled it toward the container, the wheels squeaking. "If you were going to hide a thirty-two-million-dollar car in a shipping container, would you risk boxes tumbling down and possibly damaging it?"

"Definitely not." Remi, hearing muted voices on the other side of the door, looked that direction. "But we don't even know if the car's in there."

"I'd stake our last two hundred euros on it. With Rossi's sideline as a broker of stolen goods, he's getting that stuff in and out of the country somehow."

"Shipping containers filled with fake fronts of real boxes?" Remi said.

"Exactly." He guided the jack by its tiller, pushing the forks beneath one of the pallets and raising it. As he pulled back, he felt how light the load was as it rolled, and it confirmed what he'd suspected. The entire pallet was stacked with empty boxes secured together.

Light filtered into the dark space behind it, and he could just make out a canvas-covered shape inside about the size and shape of the Gray Ghost. "That is a beautiful sight. Let's get this other pallet out."

She looked back at him. "We can't just roll the car out."

"It might be our only option," he said, testing the weight of the other pallet, also too light to have anything in the boxes. "If we can get that overhead door open, once the car is in public view, Rossi can't exactly say he didn't know it was there. If he's smart, he'll back off and claim he had no idea it was *the* Gray Ghost. The police will come, do an investigation, and the Ghost goes home."

"But Albert's still in jail."

"One thing at a time, Remi." He pulled his flashlight out of his backpack, shining it into the container and under the car to see how it was secured for shipping. Nylon straps and wheel blocks. For an hour-and-a-half ferry ride, probably good enough.

And to their advantage. All they needed to do was call the police and—

The motor connected to the overhead door started to whir. "Sam," Remi whispered, looking into the container, then back toward the door as voices drifted toward them.

Sam returned the jack to the wall and followed Remi into the container. "Help me move the pallet back in place."

They grabbed the wooden frame, dragging it back so it was even with the other pallet, hoping the scrape of wood against metal would be covered by the sound of the overhead steel door rising. Once the pallet was in place, he and Remi felt their way in the dark to the back of the Ghost, crouching beneath the canvas covering it.

Remi took his hand. "What happens when they discover the container door open?" she whispered.

"We're about to find out." He drew his gun, resting it on his knee.

At first, they heard nothing but their own breathing. A moment later, footsteps, followed by someone saying, "Who left the container open?"

"I thought I closed it. Was the door locked?"

"Of course it was locked. You saw me put the key in."

"Open it. Make sure the car's still there."

Sam heard footsteps, the squeak of the pallet jack as someone rolled it over, shoving the forks under the pallet, then rolling it out. Light filtered in beneath the canvas along the sides of the container. As Sam gripped his gun, he felt Remi tense beside him.

One of the men pulled the canvas up from the front, revealing the Gray Ghost. "Still here. Why? What's wrong?"

"The buyer found a phone in Marchand's office. He thought someone might be following Rossi."

"If they were, they didn't find anything."

"Let's cover it up. This thing's shipping out."

"I thought the buyer wanted to examine it first."

"He called back. He wants it out of here on the very next shipment. Worried that someone will get to it before he does."

The other man laughed. "And what? He thinks somebody's going to spirit it out of here? They'd be dead before they ever made it past the door."

They dropped the canvas over the front of the car and moved the false front back in place. The darkness returned.

"Crisis averted," Sam whispered. But then they heard

the clang of metal, followed by the unmistakable sound of a lock clicking shut as someone secured the container's door closed.

"You're sure about that?"

"Of course," Sam said, as he holstered his gun and lifted the canvas. He felt his way to the front of the container.

A moment later, Remi joined him. "I hope you have a plan."

Sam took out his cell phone to see if there was any chance of a signal. None. "I'd say we're going to ride this thing to the UK."

"And then what?"

He shined his flashlight on the Gray Ghost.

"That, Remi, is a darn good question."

Sam and Remi climbed into the front seat of the Gray Ghost. At least they would have a comfortable ride. To Remi, being trapped inside the box of metal was unnerving. But that was nothing compared to the helpless feeling when the container was actually being moved onto the back of the truck, which rumbled down the street a few minutes later.

"We'll be fine," he whispered to her in the dark, as she slipped her hand in his.

Eventually the truck stopped, and they heard a voice coming from near the front as someone spoke to the driver. One word stood out to Sam: *Radiographie.*

"They're going to scan us?" Remi whispered. "How much radiation are we talking?"

"If they were, with accelerator-driven, high-energy X-rays—"

"I already don't like the sound of that."

"It's not going to happen. Trust me."

"And when the two of us start glowing? What then?"

Sam laughed, as he put his arm around her shoulders.

"We're not going to glow. We're sitting in a car that's on every wanted poster in every law enforcement agency in the entirety of Europe and the UK. Rossi's already paid off someone to make sure this container bypasses the normal security routes. That includes being x-rayed."

Sure enough, they heard someone shouting that the container had already cleared, was sealed, and didn't need to be scanned.

Remi elbowed him. "I hope you're not gloating, Fargo."

"In the dark? Is that even possible?"

The truck started moving. Once they were on board the ferry, the sway of the ocean and the lack of windows made her think of a submarine. She tried to drown out the creaks and groans of metal around them. A giant swell lifted the ferry, then dropped it. Nothing she wasn't used to, except for the part that they were locked inside a metal box and couldn't get out. "How do we get out of here if the boat goes down?"

"Think positive, Remi. Ever imagine that you and I would be crossing the channel in an '06 Rolls-Royce?"

"Pretty sure that never entered my mind."

"And yet, here we are. That's one for the books."

She moved closer to Sam, taking comfort in his calm presence. "I'm still worried," she said.

"Better to worry when there's something to worry about."

"Being trapped in a shipping container isn't worrisome?"

"We have each other, don't we?"

They were quiet a few moments. The larger swells turned shorter, choppier.

"The wind's picking up," she said. "And now I keep thinking about that cargo ship with all the cars that sank in the channel back in the early 2000s."

"Remember when we first met?" Sam asked.

Remi pictured the little jazz bistro in Hermosa Beach, the Lighthouse Cafe, where they'd spent hours talking the night away. "Are you trying to distract me?"

"You know what stands out when I think of that place?"

"Besides me?"

He laughed, rubbing his hand up and down her arm. "The lighthouse on the neon sign inside the bar."

"So, it's not me?"

"Best night of my life."

Remi looked over at him, unable to see anything in the dark. "Better than the day we married?"

"Think about it. A chance meeting that brought us together. Lighthouse. Beacon in the dark. It's—"

"Symbolic." That made her smile.

"If we hadn't struck up a conversation, we would've missed each other. Like two ships in the night."

Remi laughed. "Hope you weren't planning to put that on our anniversary plaque."

"Too sappy?"

"And clichéd."

"How about . . . the tower, with the light emanating from it, and you. That's what I think about"—he cleared his throat—"whenever I want to get my mind off something."

Remi leaned her head on his shoulder. "Who thought being locked in a box could be so romantic?"

"Who knew?"

Remi closed her eyes, doing her best to let the feel of the ocean soothe her. Finally relaxing in the crook of his arm, she actually dozed for a while, then woke with a start, having completely lost track of time. "Where are we?"

"Almost to Dover," Sam said.

"We need a plan," she said.

"Bonnie and Clyde."

His comment surprised her, and she sat up. "They died in a hail of gunfire after being ambushed."

"Epic blaze of glory."

"In the movies, Sam. This is real life?"

"Okay. Forget the blaze of glory part. Concentrate on the epic portion of the plan."

"I'm listening."

A sudden jar alerted them that they'd arrived in Dover. Sam slipped his flashlight from his backpack and turned it on. "First thing we're going to need to do is figure out if this car runs."

"Chad said it did."

"Let's hope nothing's happened to it since then."

"I doubt they've had the time or inclination to worry about batteries or draining fuel."

"Well, let's find the battery and make sure it's charged."

"I think you need to bang on the fuel tank to be sure it's not empty," Remi said. "You know, just planning for the blaze of glory."

Sam and Remi found the battery and were rewarded when Remi tried the horn. The battery had juice. Sam determined there was enough fuel for their escape.

"We'll have to time it perfectly. Move the blocks and get the straps off, then start it the moment they open up the container. I'm hoping the shock value will work in our favor. We can drive right on out."

"The pallets, Sam. You forgot the pallets."

"This baby can blast right through them."

"What if they move the container inside a warehouse first? Nowhere to drive, at that point."

"We go to Plan B, Remi."

"The Plan B, where we have an actual backup plan? Or Plan B where we're making it up as we go along?"

"I'm shocked that you have so little confidence in me."

"Not you, Fargo, Bonnie and Clyde. This whole blaze of glory thing—"

"Forget that. Once they get the Ghost off the ferry, we've got to be ready. We might not have a lot of time to make our move."

IT TOOK ABOUT AN HOUR for the truck and cargo to clear customs.

What Sam didn't expect was that the truck and container would be moved onto a train. Fifteen minutes later, they were rolling down the tracks.

"Do we have a signal yet?" Remi asked. "Selma's bound to be worried."

Sam took out his phone to check. With the container now in the open, Sam found one and called, putting it on speaker.

"Mr. Fargo? Is that you? Your voice is cutting out. Where are you?"

"In a container on a train. With the Ghost. Just leaving Dover."

"Container? Dover? To where?"

"We were hoping you'd know," Sam said. "Long story

short, we got locked in the shipping container with the Ghost, which is supposed to be on its way to Oren via ferry from Calais."

"Hold on . . ." The silence lasted for several seconds until she came back on the line. "Oren has industrial property in Manchester, but Lazlo thinks he might have something outside of London. We'll see if we can't narrow it down."

"Let's hope it's London," Remi said. "We haven't eaten since breakfast. I don't think I can do four more hours locked in here."

"Hate to say it, Remi. It's possible we'll be shuttled into some warehouse where we'll be stored until Oren's crew comes."

"Cheery thought, Fargo," she replied. "We still need to figure out how we're getting out of here when we do land somewhere."

"Blaze of glory, Remi. Blaze of glory."

"Pardon?" Selma said.

"We're planning on driving the Ghost out of the container and making our getaway," Sam said.

"A bit hasty, aren't you, Sam?" Lazlo chimed in. "I'm afraid the Ghost isn't as easy to start as the Ahrens-Fox. Eleven years of technology between the two."

"While Lazlo was researching the events of '06, he learned a little about the workings of automobiles back then," Selma added.

"Yes, you see, there are thirteen steps to starting the Ghost. The automobile was not designed for your fast getaway. I think this will take more than a little planning on your part," Lazlo continued. "I'll have Selma send you a list that will take you through the steps so that you can get the car running."

"And you'd better be sure that there's a battery, it's charged, and there's fuel in the tank," Selma added.

"Done, done, and done," Remi answered.

"We'd better get going. Sounds like we have a lot to organize before we're on firm ground."

Sam ended the call, the dim light from the screen fading to black.

Shortly, Sam's phone signaled Selma's text had arrived. Reading through the complicated procedure, Remi said, "Right now I wish the '06 Ghost came with a phone charger."

Sam and Remi divided up the thirteen steps, trying to streamline their jobs, to make the process move as quickly as possible.

The next thing they knew, the train came to a stop.

Outside, they heard shouting, metal clanking, and the rumbling of the container as the truck drove off the train bed and onto the road. Sam and Remi gripped the door and seat back, grateful that the Ghost offered a measure of safety. Twenty minutes later, the truck stopped, started backing up. When it came to a rest, something heavy hit the top of the container, metal grinding against metal. The box shifted, and was suddenly lifted.

"We'll be fine," Sam said, with bravado.

"You seem awful sure of yourself."

"We're sitting in a car worth thirty-two million dollars. You really think they're going to let anything happen to it?"

The sensation was similar to being in an elevator, quickly rising, then lowering to the ground. "Careful!" came a shout, and their descent slowed, the landing so gentle that they barely noticed. "Leave it there, boys!"

"I believe," Sam whispered, "we've arrived."

Silence surrounded them once more. "How's this blaze of glory going to work?" Remi whispered. "The moment they open this container and move the pallets, they're going to pull the canvas off and see us."

Sam was already rethinking the plan. The only reason they hadn't been discovered the first time was that the Ghost had already been strapped down for shipping, and they didn't need to check it carefully. "We need somewhere to hide . . ."

"There's nothing in here. Only the car and the false front—"

"That, Remi, is brilliant."

"I love being brilliant. But how is that going to help?"

"They're hollow," he said, shining his flashlight on the boxes. "Come on." He gave the light to Remi, shoved his knife in at the top right corner of a box about waist height, carefully slicing down at the edge, around the bottom, up to the top left corner, turning that side of the box into one large flap, revealing the empty space within. "You're hiding in here."

"That box isn't big enough."

"Not yet, but it will be . . ." he said, leaning into the now-open carton and slicing open the bottom of it as well as the top of the box beneath it. "In you go." He pushed the large flap aside and helped Remi climb in. She squatted down, pulling the flap closed. He'd kept his cuts to the very corners and edges. Satisfied that as long as anyone didn't look too close, they wouldn't see. He repeated the process with the second pallet. Grabbing his backpack, he dropped the knife inside, climbed in, carefully pulling his flap closed. And it was none too soon, judging by the voices he heard coming from outside. Sam drew his gun when he heard the container being opened. This was the moment. If the cut boxes were noticed, he and Remi wouldn't survive, once they were discovered . . .

"Get that forklift over here," someone shouted.

An engine revved, Sam shifted suddenly as the prongs were inserted under the pallet at the base of the false front. As the pallet was pulled from the container, he could just make out the empty warehouse through the cut he'd made in the corner of the box. The vibration from the forklift as it drove the stack of boxes across the floor caused his carton flap to open. He grabbed it, pulling it closed, hoping his fingers weren't visible as he held it shut. A moment later, his limited view suddenly darkened, and he realized the entire unit had been shoved up against the wall, blocking his and Remi's flaps from opening.

"How's the car?"

"Looks fine."

"Let's get that other pallet out of there. We'd better have that car out of there before Mr. Oren arrives."

Sam and Remi could do nothing but sit and wait as the two men freed the Ghost from the container.

A cell phone rang. "Mr. Oren. It's here . . . But it's already out of the container . . . Right." Sharp footsteps echoed across the warehouse, then, "Let's close up the warehouse. Oren wants it to stay put until he gets here."

"When?"

"Shouldn't be too long. He took the train under the Channel. Now, hurry it up. I'd like a bite before we leave."

Sam heard heavy footsteps receding as the men walked out. A door slammed shut, silence.

He pushed on the cardboard flap, but it hit the wall. It was too close. Holstering his gun, he pulled out his knife and sliced a new opening through the sides of the boxes until he was free. Sam saw that Remi couldn't get out of her hiding place, either, and quickly sliced an opening for her.

The warehouse was empty except for the pallets, the shipping container, and the Gray Ghost. The car was a thing of beauty, unmatched by any vehicle save the more famous Silver Ghost. The two side-by-side overhead doors were operated by wall switches. To the right was the entrance door, with small window, and, beside it, an alarm panel on the wall, blinking red.

He turned on the phone and saw Selma had texted the address of Oren's London area warehouse. He called the police, giving them the address that Selma had provided.

"That's a large complex, sir. Can you narrow it down?"

The GPS on his Italian cell phone wasn't registering. Wondering where, exactly, they were, he looked out, saw a row of similar warehouses, the nearest one with a forklift driving out the open bay door with a pallet of goods. "The best I can do is, we're at the end of a road, next to a blue warehouse."

"Please stay in a safe location until help arrives, sir."

"They're on their way," Sam told Remi.

Remi looked at the alarm panel. "What if we set it off? That should tell them where."

"If the crooks are setting that alarm, the only ones getting notified are the crooks. I doubt they'd have a system that connects to the police."

"I think it's time to see if the Ghost really does run."

Sam looked out the window again, then looked to Remi. "Ready?"

"Blaze of glory."

Sam and Remi smoothly went through each step. Sam had just flooded the carburetor, and was putting down the hood.

"Sam, a car just drove up. I'm not sure, but I think it's parking between the buildings."

"We're good to go. I can finish starting the Ghost. Open the overhead door."

"The alarm—"

"No choice," Sam said. "We've got to go."

Sam hopped into the driver's seat, and Remi hit the button. The overhead door started to roll up. The alarm panel on the wall started beeping as she ran back to the car, jumping from the left running board into the passenger seat.

The engine started easily. He pulled the ignition lever on the left side of the steering wheel down to its stop when the engine began to fire. He eased the throttle, to build up the revolutions per minute, as the engine smoothed out.

"Chad is a man of his word. A consummate musician. Just listen to her purr."

"Sam, I'm not sure we have time for accolades right now."

"Remi, you're ruining a magic moment."

"A bullet will ruin your magic moment."

"Ah, Bonnie and Clyde."

"Right. Blaze of glory."

Sam put the car in first gear and eased off the clutch. The car's response was immediate, and Sam drove toward the door.

The side door suddenly opened. The two men walking in stopped short when they saw Sam at the wheel.

"Hey!" one shouted.

The Ghost surged forward.

One of the men ran after them, drawing his gun.

"Put that away, you idiot! You might hit the Ghost!"

"They're getting away!"

"Get the car!" the other shouted, running after them.

The Gray Ghost increased speed, Sam popped the clutch into second and cruised into the street, gaining speed, putting distance between them and the warehouse. A silver sedan pulled up, the men jumped in, the sedan's tires burning rubber as they sped after the Ghost. Sam pressed the Rolls as fast as he dared, hitting the horn as a forklift came whipping down a truck ramp. It stopped, the driver stunned to see the antique car zipping past.

"They're on our tail!" Remi said.

Sam glanced back. "I get the feeling they're under orders to preserve the car."

"No wonder. That's definitely Oren with them."

Sam shifted into third and stepped on the gas.

"Slight problem . . ."

The Ghost didn't respond. It gave one last cough, then died.

Remi gripped her pistol, looking around for help, as Sam tried to restart the Ghost as it rolled to a stop in front of one of the many warehouses on the street. It was closed.

She aimed at Oren's car, pulling up behind them. "Let's hope he was serious about not shooting at the Ghost."

"That won't keep them from dragging us out of it," Sam said.

"They're going to have to get close enough to do it," she replied, finger on the trigger.

Oren's car suddenly slowed, tires screeching as the vehicle came to a stop, shifted into reverse, then started forward again, making a sudden left turn, engine roaring as it raced off.

"Police," Sam said, as the smell of burnt rubber drifted toward them. He put his hand on her gun, pulling it down, out of sight.

Remi turned, saw a patrol car speeding toward them. "Just when things were starting to get fun," she said, holstering her gun and pulling her jacket closed.

* * *

THE FIRST THING they did was call Selma with the news that they'd recovered the Gray Ghost. As soon as they finished giving their statements to the investigators at the police station, they called again with an update.

"Any word from Oliver and Chad?" Sam asked.

"About an hour ago, Mr. Fargo," Selma replied. "Oliver was ecstatic to hear the news. They should reach Manchester this evening."

"Good to hear. How's the financial end of things looking?"

"We're making progress. The FBI's actually taking the case on, with their cybersecurity division helping to coordinate with the UK agencies."

"I meant short-term," Sam clarified, as he and Remi walked outside the station. "As in we'll be lucky to have train fare to Payton Manor."

"There should be a car waiting for you. A black Mercedes."

He looked around the lot and saw the vehicle, which had been idling, was now headed toward them. "Love the efficiency, but how do we know he's not one of Oren's men?"

"Unless Oren managed to get to your personal banker, you should be in the clear. His nephew works in their London office. I think you met him at one of your fund-raisers last year."

The Mercedes stopped a few feet away, and a short man, early forties, got out of the front seat, looking at them over the roof of the car. "Mr. and Mrs. Fargo. Good to see you again."

Sam recognized Geoffrey Russell. "Efficient as ever, Selma. We'll be in touch, once we hear from Oliver and Chad."

Geoffrey smiled as he opened the car door for them. "I hope you'll forgive my delay in getting here, but Miss Wondrash wanted to make sure that your crew was taken care of and the jet released. It's still a tangled mess. A few last-minute details with the Italian government, but nothing to worry about. The only issue is, we'll need to sit down, look over some legal documents, sign them, and—"

Sam's cell phone buzzed. "Excuse me," he said. "Oliver. You heard the news?"

"How soon can you get here?"

"Why? What's wrong?"

"The private detective called. Something about Dex and the Ghost."

"The Ghost? It's safe. In police lockup."

"Can you just get here? I don't know how much time we have. I'm very worried. Trevor's there, and—"

"Say no more. We're on our way." He disconnected, looking at Remi. "We need to go."

"What's wrong?"

"That issue with Allegra and her ex. It's coming to a head." He turned to Geoffrey. "I don't suppose you could give us a lift to the train station?"

"But the papers. They're at the office. Surely you can spare an hour to—"

"The papers have to wait."

The man looked horrified. “You realize you’ll be losing tens of thousands of dollars? The interest alone is frightening.”

“Can’t be helped,” Sam said, patting his pockets. “Any chance you can loan us train fare?”

SAM AND REMI settled into their seats, as the train pulled away from the station. “I should’ve asked him for snack money,” Sam said.

“He bought us first-class tickets. It comes with a meal.”

“How long has it been since we’ve eaten? I doubt it’s going to be enough.” His phone rang. Chad was on the other end.

“Oliver wanted to make sure you’re on your way,” Chad said.

“Barring some unforeseen problem, we should be there in about two hours.” Sam moved closer to Remi, putting the phone between them so that she could hear. “Do you know what’s wrong?”

“Just that he’s beside himself after talking on the phone to the private detective,” Chad said, lowering his voice as though Oliver was nearby, “who’s confirmed the ex-husband is at the house. Poor chap. Worried about his sister and nephew, of course. We’re there now.”

“At Allegra’s?”

“At the solicitor’s. Waiting for Bill Snyder to come in and tell him exactly what’s going on. I thought I’d check in and let you know where we are, and that I’ll be ’round to pick you up when you arrive. I don't think he's in any condition to drive."

"We'll see you then," Sam said.

"Should we call the police?" Remi asked, after he'd disconnected.

"Bill Snyder knows what he's doing. If he thinks the police should be called, I doubt he'll hesitate. Let's wait to see what's going on."

"I hope we're not too late."

By the time Arthur Oren returned to his Manchester estate that evening, his temper had cooled significantly. It flared again when Colton walked into his office.

"I take it you weren't successful in recovering the Ghost?" Colton asked.

"Are you trying to be funny?"

Colton took a seat, crossing his long legs, as he looked around the room. "Where's the child?"

"With his mother."

The man pulled out his cigarettes, tapping one from the pack. "What happened?" he asked, between puffs, as he lit it.

"The Fargos happened. Somehow they got into the warehouse. By the time I arrived, they were driving off in the Ghost."

"And they're still alive?"

"The police arrived or they wouldn't be."

Colton blew a stream of smoke to one side, his dark gaze holding Oren's. "How'd they even know where it was?"

"I have no idea. But somehow they've managed to be a step ahead of me the entire time."

"Is it possible someone's been feeding them information?"

"I don't know how." But the idea bore merit. They'd managed to infiltrate Rossi's villa and his office. "Unless, of course, Rossi lied about having mentioned the location of the warehouse."

"What would that have to do with anything?"

Oren handed him the phone he'd found in Rossi's office. "Can you have one of your men break into this thing?"

"It's a prepaid phone. You won't get anything off this." He tossed the phone into the trash basket next to Oren's desk. "Where's the Ghost?"

"I have no idea. Would the police hold on to it?"

"I expect they'll process it for prints and such."

Oren wasn't worried. His wouldn't be found. He never had the chance to touch it.

"The bigger question is," Colton said, "will they search it and find whatever it is you're looking for? I don't suppose you have any idea what it is yet, do you?"

"If I knew that, we wouldn't be having this conversation."

"What makes you think they haven't found it?"

"We would've heard something."

"You're sure?" Colton asked. "Isn't there something in this journal you've been trying to get from Payton Manor?"

Colton's comment stirred the anger that had been festering in Oren's gut ever since the Gray Ghost had been stolen from his warehouse. He'd been so close to having both the journal and the Ghost in his possession, only to have both taken from him in a matter of days. "Payton's sister."

"Allegra?"

"Yes. How is it she suddenly turned against us?"

"I'm not sure she was ever with us. And from what I understand, the solicitor the Fargos hired is now in possession of that book. His investigator confiscated it from her."

"How do we get it back?"

"Carefully. Having the journal is one thing, interfering with a murder investigation quite another."

"That's the best you can do?" Oren said. Colton's icy smile made him glad they were on the same side. The man wouldn't hesitate to plunge a dagger in the heart of his own mother, if she stood in his way. Oren rose from his chair, walking to the window, looking out into the garden where a groundskeeper was clipping the hedge. "Considering that your men committed that murder, being worried about obstruction of justice seems the least of your problems."

"Our problems," Colton said, whispering in his ear.

How had Colton gotten so close without him noticing? Oren took a breath, keeping his focus out the window, acting as though Colton's sudden proximity hadn't disturbed him in the least. "Meaning what?"

"Meaning that they're conducting a murder investigation, and any attention directed toward us is dangerous. I've heard that Scotland Yard's involved."

"Why would—"

"The dead security guard from the London Motor Show. They did an autopsy and know the cause of death wasn't due to the fire, as they'd originally thought."

"What does that have to do with who investigates?"

"Since they don't know where he died, they've decided that a mutual investigation is in order. Scotland Yard has more resources."

It took a few seconds for Oren to process that information. "What do you think they'll find?"

"If we're careful, nothing." Colton peered out the window, as though searching for whatever it was Oren had found so interesting. Eventually he turned back, but instead of taking his seat, he walked to the door.

"Where do you think you're going?" Oren asked.

"You said you wanted the journal. Albert Payton's solicitor had it. Seems to me that if his client is being tried for murder, the Crown would want that as evidence. I intend to make that happen."

"And what good will that do?"

Colton stopped by the door. "Two things. One, give us a chance to see it. Two, and more importantly, expose the Fargos."

"How?"

"You know as well as I that they have that journal."

"And you think they're simply going to turn it over to you?"

Colton's smile chilled him to the bone. "Allegra's been the weak link in this. Time to pay her a visit. We pressure her. The rest falls into place."

78

Remi was glad to see Chad waiting for them at the train station. "How is Oliver doing?" she asked him.

"A nervous wreck, pacing the floor when I left. He wasn't happy about waiting at the detective's office alone. Snyder said he'd come straightaway the moment his replacement arrives. In light of Dex's call, he's hesitant to leave Allegra's house without someone watching it."

Bill Snyder's office, on the second floor of a brick building near the city center, was across the hall from the solicitor's. When Oliver saw Sam and Remi walk in, he looked as if a weight had lifted from his shoulders. "Thank heavens," he said.

Remi drew him to one of the chairs, taking a seat next to him.

"You're here now."

"What happened?" Sam asked him, as Bill walked in.

"Dex left a voice mail at Payton Manor. Somehow he heard we'd recovered the Ghost and wants to trade the car for the goods," Bill said.

"Right. The goods on who framed my uncle for murder. And now I need to figure out what to do."

"Well, you'd better make the call," Sam said.

Bill nodded. "If it's something we can use, the sooner we discover what it is, the better. We can set up in the conference room and put it on the speakerphone." He led them across the hall, where they all took seats around the large table.

"What should I say?" Oliver asked, as Bill placed the phone in front of him.

"First thing is find out if Allegra and Trevor are okay. We need to hear their voices, not just take his word for it."

"Remember," Sam added. "Be firm. Keep the pressure on him. Don't let Dex order you around."

"I won't," he said, his expression wary, as he made the call.

After it rang several times, a man picked up, saying, "Who's this?"

"Is Allegra there? This is her brother."

"Where are you calling from?"

Bill slipped his boss's business card in front of him, tapping on it.

"The solicitor's office," Oliver said. "To find out the legalities of signing the car over, since it's part of the estate. May I talk to Allegra?"

"She's busy. You can talk to me."

Sam mouthed, "Pressure."

Oliver nodded. "Busy or not, put her on or our conversation is over."

"Allegra!" Dex called. "Get over here and tell your brother you're fine."

A few seconds of silence, then Allegra saying, "I'm fine."

"And Trevor?" Oliver asked.

"Trevor!" Dex shouted.

"What?" This voice came from farther away.

"It's your uncle," they heard Allegra say. "Talk to him."

"What for?"

"Satisfied?" Dex said.

"Quite," Oliver replied. "What's this information you're willing to trade for?"

"What you need to get Albert out of jail."

When Bill made a rolling motion with his hand, Oliver nodded. "I need something a little more concrete or we don't have a deal."

"Your uncle didn't kill the security guard found in the warehouse, a man named Colton did. It was ordered by Arthur Oren, to frame him."

"What about the video evidence?" Oliver asked, reading Remi's note.

"That was Bruno, dressed up like the old man."

"Then where was my uncle at the time?"

"You'll get that information, and all the other evidence, when I get the Gray Ghost. Bring the Ghost, paperwork signed, tonight. You get what you want—evidence. And I get what I want—the car. And I mean the real car, not some trumped-up fake like you tried to pass off on Frank and Bruno."

"I'm waiting to meet with the solicitor," Oliver said.

"There are legal papers from the estate that limit what I can sign over. I—I'll ring you as soon as I get the papers drawn up."

"Tell you what," Dex said. "I'll ring you. Is this a good number?"

Bill nodded.

"Yes."

"Tell them to hurry with the paperwork, before I change my mind."

The line went dead.

"When can we get the car?" Oliver asked.

"We can't," Sam said. "The Ghost is in police lockup near London. It's evidence in a murder case."

Oliver's face paled. "I just promised it to him. If he finds out it's not—"

Bill stood, walked over to the watercooler and filled a cup, bringing it over to Oliver. "It's not like we can just walk in and they'll release the car. It could be tied up for weeks. Months, even."

Chad sat up, clapping his hand on the table. "What about the Faux Ghost? Do what we did with my mum?"

Sam shook his head. "Doubtful we could pull that off a second time. You heard what he said."

"Quite right," Oliver said. "Angering Dex isn't a good idea. He's prone to violence. I don't know what he'll do if he discovers we can't get him the Ghost."

"Actually," Remi said, "if we can get a document that sounds legal, we won't need the Ghost at all." She looked at Sam and smiled. "Remember that time in Belize . . . ?"

What happened in Belize?" Bill asked Sam, after requesting the transfer of ownership document from his secretary.

"Remi went in the front door, distracted our target, while I went in the back and helped our friends escape." Of course, that was an oversimplified version that ignored some of the more dangerous aspects of the event—something they didn't need to go into right now.

Not that an investigator like Bill needed further explanation. He knew the inherent dangers and looked aghast as Sam's words sank in. "You're actually considering sending your wife into that house? You realize Dex is armed."

"It worked before. And, to be fair, Remi's armed, too."

Bill turned to Oliver, perhaps hoping to find an ally. "You can't be okay with this?"

"I'd rather no one had to go in," Oliver said. "But after everything we've been through the last couple of weeks, I pity the poor man who gets in Remi's way."

When Bill looked at Chad, he immediately raised his hands. "Sorry, mate. I don't think my vote counts."

"Mine, either," Bill said. "I'll get the files." He returned several minutes later with photographs of Allegra's house and the neighborhood, as well as printed copies of a satellite map. As they were looking them over, his secretary returned, handed him a folder. "The amendment. In triplicate, as requested."

"That was fast."

"We had a copy of the Viscount's will, due to the investigation. I scanned it, changed the names, then added a signature page. Easy-peasy."

"Thank you, Chelsea," he said. "I'll see you tomorrow." He slid the file across the table toward Remi. "Your prop."

Remi opened the folder, looking over the papers, while Sam studied a photo of Allegra's neighborhood. Victorian, brick-faced terraced houses lined both sides of the street, each three-story unit sharing a common wall with the next, while the high-peaked slate roof on each was decorated with wrought iron crests running the length. "Which unit is hers?" he asked Bill.

"Second house from the far end."

"No access from the backyard?"

"No," Bill said. "Unless you hop a fence from a neighboring unit. Which sort of makes your Belize plan a moot point."

"You're assuming we were talking about the back door. I see a lot of windows here. What's in this room?" Sam asked Oliver, pointing to the uppermost window located beneath the front-facing gable.

"Mostly, trunks and boxes. As far as I know, the room

facing the back is still empty. Allegra had thought about turning it into a guest bedroom but never got around to it. The stairs are frightfully narrow. Her bedroom and Trevor's are on the first level, with the loo."

"What's on the ground level?"

"Front parlor, kitchen, a dining area, and a windowless room, at the back of the stairs, she uses for an office—not much bigger than a closet, I'm afraid."

Sam examined that upper-level window, an idea forming. "Can you map out the floor plan of the attic?"

"Of course." Oliver drew a rectangle, divided it into two rooms, one facing the front, an identical room facing the back—the doors to both opening to what he described as a dark, narrow stairwell, in the middle.

"This should do nicely," Sam said. "If we can stall Dex until tomorrow night, that might be our best option."

"The attic?" Oliver said. "How?"

"Rooftop entry, after dark," he said, as the phone rang.

Bill glanced at the caller ID. "It's Dex's mobile."

"Should I answer it?" Oliver asked.

"Typically," Bill said, "Chelsea would answer."

"I can be Chelsea," Remi said.

"He might suspect you if you sound American."

"I'll make sure to sound like a proper Brit," she said, in her best upper-crust accent. "David Cooke's office . . ."

"Well done. Let's give it a try, shall we?" Bill hit the speaker button.

There was a few seconds delay after Remi answered. And just when they wondered if Dex was going to answer at all, he said, "Oliver Payton told me you had some paperwork for me."

"Who's calling, please?"

"Dex Northcott."

"One moment, Mr. Northcott. Let me see if it's finished." She put the call on hold and looked to Bill for further direction.

"Tell him the copies are ready for delivery tomorrow, midmorning, as promised."

Remi hit the speaker button and repeated the information.

A long stretch of silence followed. Finally, Dex said, "Oliver told me he'd have the papers tonight."

Sam drew his finger across his neck, telling her to cut that line of thinking. She nodded, saying, "I'm terribly sorry, but Mr. Cooke's left the office for the evening, and he has to sign off on them."

"Call him," he ordered. "I'll hold."

"One moment, please." Remi pressed the button.

Oliver stared at the blinking light, his expression troubled. "I don't like that he's rushing this."

"I can tell him no," Remi said.

Oliver shook his head. "The man has the temperament of a firecracker with a short fuse. He's likely to take it out on Allegra or Trevor."

Sam looked at the photographs, then at Bill. "Any objections to moving it up to tonight?"

"Not sure I'd be able to bring in anyone to help on such short notice."

"There's five of us," Remi said.

Bill turned to Oliver and Chad, a dubious expression on his face. "Nor do we have the proper equipment. Radios and earpieces, gear to get from the roof to the window—"

"If we can come up with enough cell phones and a long enough rope," Sam said, "we can hit from the top and the bottom. Assuming you're all in." When each of them nodded, he looked at his wife. "Reel him in, Remi."

She pressed the blinking light. "Mr. Northcott? It just occurred to me that my tram stop isn't too far away from your address. Since I'm working late tonight, I can bring the papers by on my way home."

"How long? I have to leave in an hour."

Sam brought his hands together, pulled them apart, indicating she needed to stretch the time. They needed to wait for dark.

Remi gave him a thumbs-up. "Unfortunately, I'll need to fax a copy to Mr. Cooke to have him sign off on it. He's in a dinner meeting with a client and can't be disturbed. But if you're willing to delay a few hours, I should be able to reach him after. Say, around ten or half past?"

"I'm the paranoid type, so don't be surprised if I search you for weapons when you come in."

She disconnected, and Sam outlined the plan. At half past ten, they drove to Allegra's to drop off Remi for the short walk to her house. She must have sensed Sam's anticipation as she slipped out. "Don't worry, Fargo, I've got this."

The knock at the door startled Allegra, even though she'd heard Dex talking on the phone and knew someone from the solicitor's office was dropping by. She'd been pinning her hopes on that email Trevor had sent to the private detective, but he'd never received a response. Realizing that they were truly on their own, she'd urged Trevor to continue typing the journal, but at a slower pace.

He was in there now.

She spent her time in the kitchen, pretending to be busy. Allegra stepped out, saw Dex walking to the front window, resting his hand on the butt of his gun as he parted the curtain to look out. Satisfied, he moved to the door and opened it a few inches.

"Mr. Northcott?" came a woman's voice. "Chelsea Roberts, from the solicitor's."

Dex opened the door wider. "You have the papers?"

"In my satchel. Might I come in?"

He stepped aside, let her in, and, as usual, threw the dead bolt on the door.

"My card," she said, handing it to him. "I've jotted down Mr. Cooke's mobile, should you need it later. Is Allegra here?" she asked, looking around expectantly. "I'll need her signature as well."

"Allegra!" Dex called.

She stepped out, staring at the slender red-haired woman standing in the dim light of the front room. "Just tidying up. Who's this?"

The woman moved into the light, her smile somewhat familiar, as she held a card toward Allegra. "Chelsea Roberts. From your uncle's solicitor."

Allegra took the card, doing a double take when she saw the handwritten message scrawled across the back of the card:

TREVOR TO ATTIC. THEN FOLLOW.

She stood there, frozen, realizing at once who the woman was.

"Something wrong?" Dex asked.

Before she had a chance to respond, Remi stepped in, looked at the card, plucked it from her. "How terribly embarrassing. My grocery list." Remi handed her a second card, saying, "This one has Mr. Cooke's mobile. Emergencies always arise in these odd cases. Shall I set up on the table?"

Allegra looked at the new card, saw a mobile number jotted on it, then back at Remi, amazed at how calm she appeared as she opened her briefcase on the table, carefully setting her mobile phone next to it. "Yes, of course. Would you like a cuppa?" replied Allegra.

"Thank you, no. We really do need to get moving. Is your son about?"

"Trevor!" Dex called. "Get out here!"

Trevor emerged from the office, his expression guarded.

Remi offered a bland smile. "So sorry. Didn't mean for you to call him just yet. Perhaps you might want him to wait upstairs while we discuss the particulars?"

"Why?" Dex asked.

Remi pulled a folder from her briefcase. "Matters pertaining to what happens if an heir dies. The sort of thing I'm not sure is entirely appropriate for children to hear."

Dex appeared unmoved.

Allegra, seeing her chance, realized she needed to be careful—firm enough that her son listened but not too concerned that Dex would take notice. "Do be a dear, Trev, and run up to the attic. There's some headache powder by my pillow."

When he hesitated, she looked at Dex, saying, "He listens to you."

The backhanded compliment worked. Dex gave him a curt nod. "Off with you, then."

Allegra kept her eyes on the papers Remi held, worry turning to relief when Trevor did as he was told.

Remi smiled as she handed them each a packet of papers, saying, "Because your son's not of age, it's important that you both understand the clause concerning the rules of inheritance regarding the viscountcy."

"What's there to understand?" Dex said. "His uncle's giving him the car."

"All this does is temporarily allow the Viscount's

grandnephew to take early possession of what will eventually be his, should Oliver Payton die without issue."

"What do you mean, early possession? Won't the car be Trevor's once this is signed?"

"Technically, no," she said, removing two pens from her briefcase, holding one out to each of them. "The vehicle is part of the Payton estate and can only be passed down to an heir. Should anything happen to that heir, it goes to the next heir."

"Me. His father."

"Blood heir of the viscountcy. In other words, if something happens to the remaining Payton men, should the current viscount die, the title and estates and everything attached to it, including the car and any money, will pass to the closest blood relative."

"Who'd that be?" Dex asked.

"I expect the Payton family would know better than I . . ." She looked at Allegra. "Madam?"

"As far as I know," Allegra said, "Arthur Oren is our closest blood relative."

"Over my dead body," Dex replied, taking the pen. "Where do I sign?"

"The last page," Remi said. He quickly turned to it, and she added, "Might I suggest you read the entire document first?"

"Isn't that what you're supposed to have done before you got here?" He signed it, then looked up at her, his expression one of annoyance. "There's a space here for Trevor's signature."

Remi gave him a neutral smile. "We will need the boy's signature, before it's legal. I assumed the two of you might want to discuss things prior."

"Trevor!" he called, as Remi's cell phone buzzed on the tabletop.

She picked it up, looking at the screen. "My husband. Probably wondering when I'll be home," she said, putting it to her ear. "Hello?" She smiled politely at them while she listened to the caller. "Oh, I thought they weren't coming until tomorrow. No worry, I'm almost done here. See you soon." She ended the call, her expression apologetic. "I hate to be a pest, but I'm quite late, and it seems we have unexpected visitors dropping by. My husband's worried he's going to have to entertain them himself. If it's more convenient, I can drop by in the morning . . . ?"

"No," Dex said, as he stalked toward the stairs. "Trevor! Get down here!"

His back to them, Remi gave a slight tilt of her head.

Allegra nodded. She knew Dex would never dare leave her alone down here with anyone he didn't know and trust. "I'll just pop up there and see what's keeping him so long," she said, resisting the urge to move any faster for fear of putting Dex on guard.

Mustering every bit of calm and strength she possessed, she looked right at Dex as she passed him. "Probably in the loo," she said quietly, casually walking up the stairs. "Trevor!" she called, glancing back to see Dex watching her. When she reached the first-floor landing, she made a show of looking in the bathroom, then down the stairwell, noticing Dex had moved up two steps. "Not there. I'll check in the attic."

He moved up another step.

Worried, Allegra rounded the corner, picked up her pace, taking the stairs quickly. When she reached the attic, she pushed open the door, looked around the dark room, unable to see a thing. "Trevor?" Her panicked whisper cut through the silence, as someone stepped from behind the door. Sam, she realized, her hand going to her heart as it raced out of control. She saw the pried-open casement window, the rope harness hanging in it. "Is he—"

"Safe? Yes," he said. "Let's get you out of here."

He drew her to the window, helping her into the harness, though she tried to stop him. "Arthur and Colton are coming. They'll recognize her. She'll be trapped."

"We know. They're parked out front. We think they're waiting for someone. She knows to go out the back door. We're sending the rope down for her." He tugged on the harness, and someone up above started lifting her.

"You don't understand," she said, grasping his hand, trying to make him listen, before it was too late. It was her fault. Dex had suspected her when she'd tried to get Trevor to leave that first time when he'd gone off to the store. "She can't get out the back. Dex nailed the door shut."

Sam stared at Allegra, seconds slipping away, hoping he'd heard wrong. So much for Plan B, he thought as someone knocked at the front door.

Sam leaned out the window, telling Chad, "Hold up."

He looked at Allegra, trapped in the harness, hanging in the window, probably scared to death about her son. Right now, he needed her help in evening out the odds. "Any way you can get Dex up here?"

"Promise you won't kill him?"

A promise he couldn't make. "I'll try not to."

Her gaze flicked to the doorway and then nodded. Sam helped her out of the harness. She looked back at him and stepped out into the stairwell. "Dex!" she shouted. "Trevor's gone!"

Dex swore, his heavy footsteps echoing in the stairwell as he ran up. Once again, Sam helped Allegra onto the sill and into the harness, giving the rope a firm tug.

She reached out, her eyes pleading. "He wasn't always this way."

The moment Chad started lifting her out, Sam hid behind the door, listening for Dex.

By the time Dex reached the attic, the knocking at the front door growing more insistent, he'd slowed considerably, his breathing labored. "Allegra!" He saw her feet disappearing out the open window, and he rushed toward her, his gun drawn.

Sam crossed the room, jamming the nose of his Smith & Wesson into Dex's ribs. "Nice of you to join us," he said, grabbing Dex's shoulder, forcing him back and off-balance. "Drop the gun."

Dex held tight. "You know who's at the door? They'll kill you."

Sam slammed him to the floor. "Make a sound, and I'll use you as my shield. Let go of the gun," he said, this time jabbing the barrel of his .38 into the base of Dex's skull. When Dex loosened his grip on the weapon, Sam grabbed it, dropping it into his pocket, as they heard the sound of shattering glass downstairs, then someone trying to shoulder open the front door. "Move, or make any noise, you'll regret it. Understand?"

Dex nodded.

Sam moved toward the stairwell, hearing wood splintering as the door was kicked in, a man shouting, "Dex! Where are you?"

Sam looked over at him, putting his finger to his lips.

"The attic!" Dex shouted, giving Sam a triumphant look at the sound of someone running up the stairs. "They know you're h—"

Sam pointed his gun at Dex. "I was trying to be nice."

Dex's mouth clamped shut, his eyes going wide.

The sharp crack echoed off the walls. Dex screamed, as he rolled onto his side, gripping his thigh.

Now that he didn't have to worry about an attack from that direction, Sam turned back to the stairwell as Frank reached the landing.

Sam fired.

Frank ducked back. "Fargo's here!"

"Kill him!"

What Sam didn't hear was anyone mentioning Remi's name. He took that as a good sign, his eye on the landing below. Frank peered around the corner.

Sam fired again, keeping him contained. Time to even the odds. "Is Arthur with you?"

For a few seconds, the only thing he heard was Dex moaning in the dark behind him. Finally, a new voice, saying, "What do you want, Fargo?"

"Just thought you'd like to know who sold the Ghost to Rossi."

The following silence lasted for several seconds. Even Dex's whimpering stopped. "Who?" the man called.

"Might want to ask Frank. Or Dex, assuming he lives long enough."

Another stretch of silence, then the sound of heavy footsteps coming up the stairs.

"He's lying!" Frank said. "I swear!"

The muted gunshot echoed up the stairwell. Someone was equipped with a silencer. That meant only one thing.

He'd gotten Trevor and Allegra out just in time. These men weren't here to negotiate with Dex—or anyone else, for that matter. They'd come to kill.

Sam backed into the room, seeing Dex, his eyes wide with fright. He leaned down, whispering, "I'd play dead, if I were you."

As dark as it was, he couldn't be sure, but it looked like Dex's face paled. Sam grabbed the rope Chad dropped for him, slipped on the harness, holstered his gun, and climbed up onto the sill. Dex, he saw, decided to take his advice, slapping one bloody hand on his chest, closing his eyes, doing his best to feign a mortal wound.

Sam tugged on the rope.

Just in time, Chad pulled him up and out of the window. Sam braced his arms on the roof's edge as Chad held him by the harness. "Hold up," he whispered, worried about the noise if he climbed up. Allegra and Trevor, arms around each other, were huddled near the chimney, their eyes locked on Sam.

He craned his neck, trying to see below, just as Bruno stuck his head out the window.

"Where's Fargo?" came a voice, deeper than Oren's. Colton's, possibly.

"Not here." Bruno never looked up. "Must have hid in that other room after he shot Dex."

"Search the house. Make sure he's not here."

Sam heard their retreating footsteps. He signaled for Chad to lower him to the ground, catching sight of Dex on the attic floor as still as death. The man didn't deserve to live, as far as Sam was concerned, but he'd promised

Allegra, and halfway understood why she'd asked to spare his life. Killing the boy's father while he was perched on the roof, waiting for this to be over, was bound to leave a deep scar. And there was little they could do except try not to make any noise until help arrived or Sam cleared Allegra's house.

But, right now, his wife was down there—where, he didn't know—and he was going to make sure she walked out unharmed if it was the last thing he did. He touched down, saw the shattered window glass glittering in the moonlight on the pavement in the tiny patch that was the backyard. Someone had smashed that window from the inside. And since it happened at the same time that Arthur and company had arrived at the door, he knew it was Remi. One thing was clear. She didn't go out through the window. There were too many glass shards remaining at the base of the sill for anyone to have climbed through. And there were no broken branches in the hedges growing against the fence.

Remi was still inside the house.

Gun out, he made his approach. Time to go in and get her.

The odds weren't in Sam's favor. Three against one—and that was assuming Dex continued to play dead and Frank really was dead—with no idea where Remi was. If she was hiding anywhere, it was in that windowless space at the back of the stairs that Allegra used for an office, the only place she could get to once she realized she wasn't making it out that back door.

He had three rounds left in his Smith & Wesson, but he also had Dex's semiauto, and drew it from his pocket. A Browning 1911-380 with an eight-capacity magazine. He checked, saw it was full, with a round in the chamber. Preferring his more familiar firearm, he was about to tuck the Browning into his waistband but changed his mind. There would be an inquest, and using Dex's gun to kill anyone would cut down on any questioning about why the permits they'd wrangled the last time they were here had expired.

Both weapons were .38 calibers—a lot harder to match when you were digging bullets out of the floor. The less shots with his gun, the better, and he holstered it, gripped the Browning, flicking the safety off with his thumb.

The backyard was relatively dark—the two floodlights mounted above the small covered porch were off. He was going to have to kick open the back door. He made a wide berth around the broken glass, ducking as he passed the window. Unexpectedly, the floodlights clicked on, blinding him.

A shot rang out, as Sam dove toward the porch, a lance-like pain in his right shoulder catching him by surprise as he hit the ground, diving beneath the porch for cover, out of sight.

Someone had gotten a lucky shot.

Time to switch things around. Not sure where the shot came from, he pressed himself against the bricks near the door, waiting, listening, figuring someone had to be in the kitchen to have turned on those lights. This was going to complicate things.

He heard an audible click above him, and the lights shut off. Motion detector. The graze on his shoulder pulsed with pain, and he reached up, feeling the blood seeping from the shallow wound. Had to be someone at one of the upper windows.

Careful not to trigger the motion detector again, he peered out, just as Bruno's head emerged from the second-floor window. Sam fired, driving him back, buying time. He kicked the door. It budged about an inch, the nails holding tight. He kicked it again. It flew open, hitting the wall.

A burst of suppressed shots peppered the door, splinters flying.

From the corner of his eye, Sam saw the muzzle blasts coming from the front room. Just a few feet from where Remi had to be hiding.

"Give it up, Fargo!" Colton called out. "You're only making it worse."

"For who?" He pressed up against the bricks between the open door and the window, moving the Browning to his left hand. Reaching inside the doorway with his other, he felt the wall, searching for the light switch. There were two. He switched off the motion lights, was about to withdraw, then froze. Finger still on the switch, he moved back as far as he could without losing contact, pointing the Browning with his left hand toward the window. He pressed the switch. A brass light fixture over the dining table lit up, casting light into the front room. Sam sidestepped across the porch, looked in the window, saw two men. Oren near the foot of the stairs, a gun held down, and his hired help, Colton, aiming his gun at the back door.

When Colton realized his mistake, it was too late. Sam fired, grazing his left side. Colton whirled around, ran for the stairs, as Sam fired twice more, driving both men back up the stairs. He fired off a fourth round into the grass as he slipped into the kitchen, to make them think he was at the window. Once inside, he saw Remi's open briefcase on the table. The kitchen was empty, no cupboards large enough for her to hide in. "You're surrounded!" Sam called out, though, in this case, who was surrounded was Chad, on the rooftop, with Bill and Oliver listening in the van to direct the police—when they finally got there. "There's nowhere for you to go."

Unless they wanted to try to get out the upstairs windows, they were momentarily trapped. His weapon aimed at the stairwell, he quickly looked around, saw what looked like a closet door at the back of the stairs, and crossed the room.

"Remi?" he whispered.

She opened the door, a sight for sore eyes. "Took you long enough."

He grinned. "Where's your gun?"

"Briefcase. Barely made it here in time."

He glanced back toward the table. Getting to it meant risking exposure to the stairwell. Instead, he pulled his Smith & Wesson from his holster and handed it to her, as the faint sound of sirens drifted in from the open door. "Hear that, Oren?" he yelled. "You're going to lose. The police are on their way."

It was Colton who responded, shouting from inside the stairwell. "If you want any witnesses alive to testify that Albert's innocent, you'll let me walk out of here. The case is ironclad. You need them."

Before Sam had a chance to respond, they heard Oren's voice, tense. "Are you insane? You're just as guilty."

"Only if they catch me. Drop the guns, both of you, or I'll blow your heads off . . ." It was a moment before Sam realized Colton wasn't talking to him. Two handguns landed on the floor at the foot of the stairs. "We're coming down," Colton shouted. "If you want your witnesses, you won't shoot."

Two hands popped out past the wall, fingers splayed. Bruno said, "Don't shoot . . ."

Sam and Remi, guns at the ready, watched as Bruno emerged, hands raised. "Stop!" Sam said. "Kick the guns toward me and get down on the ground."

Bruno shoved one, then the other, toward them across the bare wood landing.

"Facedown," Sam ordered.

Bruno complied. Oren stepped out next, hands up, with Colton using him as a shield, gun to his head. "Nice and slow," Colton said, blood running down his shirt. "They're yours, once I'm out the door."

"Can't let that happen," Sam said.

Remi, finger on the trigger, took aim.

Colton looked right at her as he jammed the gun against Oren's jaw. "Risk losing your star witness?"

She squeezed.

The shot grazed Colton's skull. He stumbled back, momentarily stunned, as Oren pulled away, diving for the floor. Exposed, Colton looked at Remi, raising his gun.

Sam fired twice. One to the gut, one to the head.

Colton crumpled to the ground. While Remi covered him, her gun aimed at the other two men, Sam moved in, checking to see if he was dead.

"Show-off," Remi said, as he picked up Oren's gun, handing it to her, then picked up the other two weapons from the floor, placing them on the table out of reach, as sirens blared out front.

He nodded at his Smith & Wesson. "We might want

to tuck that away for now. In case any of those police are armed."

She returned the gun to him. "Bad time to mention we need to smooth out that trigger pull? I missed a perfectly good head shot."

"Or," Sam said, holstering his .38 before the police walked in, "you knew we wanted to avoid an inquest over bringing firearms into the country?"

She looked at him and laughed.

Several days later . . .

Remi read the text from Selma. "Bad news," she said, as she and Sam sat in the garden at Payton Manor. "Selma and Lazlo have declared the journal a dead end. If there's some secret treasure, they can't figure it out." She looked around the peaceful garden and sighed. "It'd be nice to know what happened to it before we leave. If only to keep anyone else from bothering the Paytons."

"Since Oliver intends to move the car to a museum, I don't think it'll be an issue." He looked at his watch. "Nearly six. We better get ready for dinner."

Oliver had decided that a celebratory dinner was in order, now that Uncle Albert was finally released from custody, and all the financial accounts were slowly being released, and life at Payton Manor was returning to normal. Since the Dowager Cottage where Albert usually dined in the evening was far too small to accommodate everyone, they all gathered in the south dining hall of the manor house.

Uncle Albert, Remi noticed, looked the picture of

health, considering where he'd been ever since his arrest. He was talking animatedly to Oliver about the roses in the garden. Remi reached over, grasped Sam's hand under the table. "Oliver seems much happier."

"With the weight lifted from his shoulders? It has to be a relief to have his uncle back."

"And to know that he won't have to sell the Ghost after all." She smiled happily, watching everyone interact with ease, the stress of the last couple of weeks having faded. Trevor was the one that impressed her the most. For the first few days, after his return to Payton Manor, he'd been quiet, jumping at every little sound. Now, looking at him as he and Chad talked and laughed together, he seemed like any other sixteen-year-old. Chad was definitely having a positive influence on the boy, she thought. Trevor was telling Chad how his mum was always after him about being on the computer and not meeting any nice girls.

Chad laughed, then leaned toward him conspiratorially. "You think that's bad, Trev? My mum and aunt both go at me. 'Do you have to work on cars all day?'" he said in falsetto. "'Comb your hair! How are you going to get a girl looking like that?'" Suddenly aware he was being watched, he looked around the table, saw Allegra, and turned a shade of red when their eyes met. Clearing his throat, he looked back at Trevor. "But you should always listen to your mum, right?"

Trevor looked down at his near-empty plate, his eyes sparkling. "Right."

"A toast," Oliver said, lifting his wineglass, looking at

Sam and Remi. "I meant to do this at the start of dinner. A toast to the both of you, since we wouldn't all be gathered here without your help. I don't know how to thank you except to say, welcome to the family."

"That," Sam said, "might be the best thank-you ever."

Oliver looked around the table. "And, of course, the reason we're all gathered—to celebrate Uncle Albert's return."

Albert lifted his water glass. "Not sure what all the fuss is about. Nice chaps at that place, but they wouldn't let me come home. I don't think I want to stay there again."

Mrs. Beckett smiled at Albert, as she cleared off his empty plate. "I expect you'll be glad to sleep in your own bed tonight, now that this Ghost business is finally settled."

"Settled? How?" he asked her.

"It was stolen and now it's back."

"The Ghost? Stolen? That car was cursed from the get-go." His gaze landed on Sam. "Did I tell you that you look like Cousin Eunice?"

"You did," Sam said.

Albert gave a firm nod. "She and my brother found that old car in the barn when they were about Trevor's age. One of the Paytons hid it there during the war. Cursed. Didn't want anyone else to get hurt."

Trevor sat up with interest. "How do you know it was cursed, Uncle Albert?"

"Things started happening. Don't remember what they were now . . ." He seemed drawn to Sam, lingering on his face. "Cousin Eunice and my brother found that sheet music after they read the journal. No stopping them after that."

"Stopping them from what?" Sam asked.

"Searching for the stolen treasure from the train." Albert looked at Oliver this time, his rare lucidity holding. "Your father used to pretend he was that American detective from the journal."

"Isaac Bell?" Trevor asked.

"The same. And Cousin Eunice was always miffed because she wanted to be the detective."

Remi turned with an amused expression toward Sam, whispering, "See? That is where you get your sense of adventure from."

Trevor's eyes were glued on Uncle Albert. "Did they ever find it?"

"Find what?"

"The treasure. From the train robbery."

"No one has, though we all looked. Wasn't in the Ghost. Wasn't anywhere. I expect Reginald buried it, expecting he'd be able to come back one day. That's what I would've done." He looked around the table, his expression one of confusion. "Is it somebody's birthday?"

Oliver smiled. "We're celebrating your return home."

"Are we? I daresay, it'll be a long time before I decide to stay in a hostel again. Ghastly place. Not sure it's worth celebrating."

Mrs. Beckett, hovering nearby, walked over, putting her hand on his shoulder. "It's getting late. How about we pop over to the cottage for some lemon ice?"

"Jolly good idea," Albert said, standing. He cocked

his head toward the table. "They're not all coming, are they?"

"No, M'lord," she said.

"We've talked about this 'M'lord' thing, haven't we?" he asked, as she led him from the room.

"Yes, M'lord."

"Thought so."

Oliver watched them until they disappeared through the doors. "Well, at least we know he didn't seem to suffer any lasting damage from his incarceration."

Allegra stared down at her plate, clearly weighed down by her guilt.

Trevor, however, didn't seem to notice. "I think Uncle Albert's wrong about Reginald burying that treasure."

Everyone turned toward him at once, Oliver asking, "Why do you say that?"

"Because of the journal." Trevor seemed hesitant to continue. "What I remember of the last entry and what Reginald said about Payton."

"The lad has a remarkable memory," Oliver explained. "Like Remi's. Look at something once and it's imprinted in his brain."

Sam glanced at Remi. "You read it. What do you think?"

"Sorry, Fargo. The furthest I read was when Payton, Miss Atwater, and Isaac Bell were coming up with a plan to find out who hired Reginald Oren to steal the Gray Ghost."

Almost at once, they turned toward Trevor. Allegra nodded at him. "Go ahead, Trev. Tell them what happened."

84

JOURNAL OF JONATHON PAYTON, 5TH VISCOUNT WELLSWICK

1906

I noted the time on my gold pocket watch, precisely eleven p.m., before settling back in my seat, ignoring my cousin, who was slumped on the floorboards of the coach, hands tied, mouth gagged, barely stirring the entire time, perhaps because of the laudanum we'd dosed him with. Byron drove the coach, while Mr. Bell stood on the footman's platform, and Miss Atwater sat across from me, a determined expression on her face. I looked down at my cousin, half tempted to cosh him on the head over the trouble he'd caused. But Mr. Bell said we might find use for him before the night was through, and so I resisted.

When the coach slowed, and I felt Isaac Bell jump off the back, I pulled the curtain far enough to see out, watching, as he walked off, stirring the tendrils of fog that snaked out across the cobblestones.

The vehicle lurched forward, the steady clip-clop of the horses' hooves picking up speed. We neared the tavern where I'd found myself earlier that night, but then continued on, stopping farther up the road in the shadows to watch and wait. I looked down at Reggie, whom eventually we'd be turning over to the police. Our goal this night, however, was to find the buyer, the one who set out to ruin Rolls-Royce and bankrupt the investors. The only bit of information Mr. Bell had managed to wrest from my cousin was the name of a man who was acting as a liaison between him and the buyer. That, Bell said, was all that he needed.

When the carriage came to a stop, I again pulled the curtain to peer out, seeing that the fog had thickened considerably in the few minutes it had taken us to circle around. I searched for Mr. Bell and saw him lingering beneath a gas streetlamp, the flickering light reflecting off the grey mist around him. A moment later, he stepped inside the tavern, looking for the man that Reggie had said was waiting there to buy the Grey Ghost.

MY COUSIN BEGAN TO STIR *as the laudanum wore off, and I reached down, lifted his head so that I could see his face. "You're awake," I said.*

Reggie's eyes opened, then widened as he saw me watching him. He tried screaming through the gag tied around his mouth, as he struggled to free himself from the ropes around his wrists and feet. When that failed, he kicked at the coach door. As Miss Atwater scooted to the other side, I brought the heel of my boot down on his shins. "Do that again and you'll regret it."

He tried speaking through the gag. I dug my heel in harder. "Do not test my patience." I leveled my sternest look on him. "A word of warning, cousin. You make a noise loud enough to be heard by anyone other than me, I'll kick your teeth out. Do you understand?" I asked, enunciating each word clearly.

For the first time ever, I saw fright in Reggie's eyes.

I hated resorting to violence, but Mr. Bell's life depended on my cousin's silence. Bell told us that if the man in the tavern suspected anything was amiss, if he suspected Isaac at all, he'd likely try to kill him.

I refused to have anyone's death on my conscience, especially Mr. Bell's. Not that I was worried the man couldn't handle himself—after all, he'd single-handedly taken down both Reggie and his accomplices and recovered the stolen Grey Ghost in the process. What we hadn't recovered was the stolen treasure, but Mr. Bell assured us that it was only a matter of time.

I looked out the window, saw Isaac Bell stepping out of the tavern, looking very much like the dandy he was trying to portray. A swarthy dark-haired man followed him out, and the pair walked in our direction.

When they reached the coach, Isaac rapped on the door, calling out, "Apparently, this man is under orders that he's only to deal with Mr. Reginald Oren. They're insisting on seeing him. Now."

Miss Atwater and I exchanged glances. She lifted her hand as though holding a glass to her lips.

She was as brilliant as she was beautiful. I realized, though, that to allay suspicion, such news of Reginald's intoxication would sound better coming from a woman. I leaned toward her, whispering that she should respond.

She hesitated but a second before leaning toward the window and pulling the curtain open just enough for the pair outside to see only her. "He's . . . had a bit much to drink, but I'll see if I can't rouse him."

"Thank you," Mr. Bell said. He stepped back from the coach, giving a bland smile.

The other man looked in the window, trying to see, but she closed the curtain. "This better not be some trick," he said.

"I assure you, it's not," Isaac said.

Using my father's dagger, I leaned in close to Reggie, whispering a reminder about the loss of his teeth if he so much as uttered something I didn't like. I pulled down his gag and dragged him up, hoping the man outside didn't notice the odd rocking of the coach as I forced my cousin to the window, whispering, "Be careful."

Miss Atwater pulled the curtain for him to look out.

"What?" Reggie barked.

The man shifted on his feet as he peered into the window. "Mr. Keene said you were the only one we were to talk to. No one else."

When Reggie said nothing, I pressed the point of my father's dagger into his spine. "So here I am," Reggie said. "Now, make the sale."

"You're sure?"

"You heard me. I'm here now. You want the forty-fifty? Tell Keene to bring the money."

"This wasn't how you said it—"

I pressed harder. Reggie's shoulder jerked toward the window. "Tell Mr. Keene to bring the money to my uncle's warehouse," he said through gritted teeth. I poked him again. "And to hurry. Before I change my mind."

The man narrowed his eyes as though not quite trusting what he was hearing. After a moment, he shrugged, looking at Isaac. "I'll be off, then."

After he left, I wanted to follow, but Isaac bade me wait. "Why?" I asked. "He'll lead us right to this Mr. Keene."

"Barclay Keene?" Miss Atwater said.

"And who would that be?" Bell asked.

"The man who owns the Barclay Keene Electric Motor Works," she replied. "He's married to the sister of the headmaster at the orphanage. I've heard tell the business is struggling financially."

"Interesting," Bell said. "Perhaps where some of that money embezzled from the orphanage is ending up?"

It made perfect sense to me. What I didn't understand was, why weren't we immediately going after Keene to make an arrest? And so I asked Mr. Bell.

"Because we only have the word of your cousin, an admitted thief and murderer. Not much good against that of a prominent businessman, wouldn't you say? My feeling is, the more evidence against Keene, the better."

"But there's our good word," I said. "And that of Miss Atwater."

Miss Atwater reached out, placing her gloved hand on my arm. "What is it you suggest, Mr. Bell?" she asked.

"We wait at the warehouse for this Barclay Keene to bring the money. He can hardly deny his involvement, then, can he?"

Though it was a tense hour waiting in the cold warehouse, Miss Atwater and I hid in the shadows, along with two constables, whom Mr. Bell had called in. Finally, Mr. Keene and his man arrived. Byron, still playing Reggie's coach driver, met them at the warehouse door, and the two men walked in, Keene's eye on the Grey Ghost, which we'd parked inside.

"Nicely done," Keene said, trying to hand his satchel of money to Reggie, who was seated in a chair, with Mr. Bell standing right behind him. Keene, apparently, failed to realize that something was amiss until he noticed Reggie wasn't reaching out to take it.

He couldn't. His hands were tied behind his back, though that detail was concealed by the cloak Mr. Bell had put over my cousin's shoulders.

"What on earth?" Keene said.

Reggie gave him a cynical smile. "I have some bad news, Keene."

The older man frowned, not understanding until the two constables stepped into the light, surrounding him. The man from the tavern drew a dagger, lunging at one of the constables, but Isaac Bell was quicker. He tackled the younger man, and the blade clattered to the floor. I stepped forward to help, but Keene drew a pistol. I stopped as he fired, the bullet so close that I felt my cloak move as it passed. Had he not hesi-

tated before taking a second shot, distracted by Bell calling my name, I'd be dead. I knew instinctively what Bell wanted. I tossed my father's cane. It barely hit Bell's hand, the shaft almost a blur as he swung it toward Keene, knocking the pistol from his grasp, then bringing it upward in one fluid motion, striking Keene's jaw with the brass handle. As Keene stumbled, Bell recovered the man's gun, aiming it at him. "I believe our work is done here," he said, when Miss Atwater cried out.

We all turned to see Reggie slumping to the floor, shot by Keene's pistol.

I rushed to his side, kneeling. "Reggie . . ."

His face ashen, he looked at me, asking for his wife.

"Of course," I said, looking around for help. "Let's get help first."

But Mr. Bell, seeing the growing stain on Reggie's torso, shook his head. "Bring her here," he said quietly, as he folded Reggie's cloak and pressed it to the wound.

"Byron," I said. "Would you . . . ?"

My friend nodded, ran from the building. Mr. Bell and I laid Reggie on the floor, while Miss Atwater took her own cloak, fashioning a pillow for Reggie. I was at once amazed by her fortitude, as well as by her forgiveness of the man who'd kidnapped her.

After several minutes, his breathing grew shallow, and we knew his time with us was nearing an end.

"The treasure, man," Mr. Bell said, patting him on the cheek to rouse him. "Where is it?"

"My wife . . . Where . . . ?"

"On her way," I said.

"Tell her . . . The music . . . Give it to her, would you, cousin?"

"What music?"

Bell said, "I saw sheets of music in the chest with the car parts."

"Miss Atwater," I said. "Would you mind?"

She stood, her gaze lingering on Bell's bloody hand as he pressed the cloak to Reggie's stomach. Looking away, she hurried to the chest on the floor beside the Grey Ghost, lifted the lid, and pulled out several sheets of music. She carried them over to us. "This?" she asked him.

He opened his eyes. "She wanted . . . to learn . . ."

"Save your strength," I said, seeing what an effort it was for him to speak. "She'll be here."

"The treasure!" Bell asked again. "Tell us!"

And just when I thought he'd left us, he looked right at me. "You . . . helped . . ."

"Helped what?" I asked.

But it was too late. He was gone.

Keene denied knowing anything of the treasure or the train robbery. He was in it only to ruin Rolls-Royce. The saddest part that night was having to tell Reggie's wife, Elizabeth, of all that had transpired, once she'd arrived.

Her stoic expression, as she listened, nearly broke me. A tear slipped down her cheek. "Where is he?"

We stood aside. Her breath caught. She walked over, looked down at him, sank to her knees and called him a fool. "Why?"

Her ragged whisper tore through me. I put my hand on her shoulder, but she pushed me away, then started out.

Miss Atwater held out the sheets of music to her. "Your husband wanted you to have these," she said.

Elizabeth took the music, looked over each page in disgust, tossed it all into the Grey Ghost. "Music won't feed my child," she said.

"Mrs. Oren," Isaac Bell called out as she started to walk off. "I'm very sorry for your loss. But if you know where the stolen money is . . ."

"If my husband took any money, he failed to tell me about it. So, please. Allow me to take my leave. I need to return to my son."

And though I insisted she was welcome to stay at Payton Manor, she refused. I fear she blamed me for her husband's death. Perhaps she was right. The next day, she took her son and left, with naught but the clothes they wore. For weeks after, we searched the Grey Ghost, the warehouse, and Payton Manor, thinking that a half million dollars would be difficult to hide, but we never located any sign of the missing money. And this despite Mr. Bell's assurances, his last words to us being "You'll find it."

The five of them listened, transfixed, as Trevor related what he recalled from the last journal entry.

"No doubt about it," Sam said, "the sheet music is the clue. Maybe the notes are a code. Has anyone ever really looked at it since it was found?"

"The music?" Oliver asked. "I wouldn't even know the first place to look. We could try to ask Uncle Albert, I'm just not sure it would do any— I say, Fargo. Didn't Uncle Albert say something about your mother and my father finding the music back when?"

"He did at that." Sam checked the time, took out his phone, and called his mother. He turned it on speaker so that everyone could hear.

"Sam? Is everything okay? How's Albert?"

"He's fine. Everyone's fine," he said. His mother had been upset with him for waiting so long to tell her about everything that had happened—until he'd explained about the hacking. He'd insisted that he would've called her earlier, except he was worried that she'd end up getting hacked, too. He wasn't sure if she believed him and started right in with the question, hoping she wouldn't think to belabor the point. "Albert was telling us about how you and his brother found the sheet music in the Gray Ghost that was mentioned in the journal."

"Sheet music?" Several seconds ticked by, then she laughed. "That was so long ago, I'd almost forgotten. We used to play detectives. Something about a treasure we were going to find, and the music was a clue."

"Do you know where it is?"

"The treasure?"

"The music."

She laughed again. "It was falling apart when we found it all those years ago. I expect it ended up in the trash, at some point."

"Did you get a good look at it?"

"Decades ago. Hold on . . ." She must have muted the call, as it went silent. A few seconds later, she was back on the line. "Just saying good-bye to my afternoon charter. Now, what is it you're hoping I saw?"

"Anything. Something written on it. Notes circled."

"If there was, it had faded by the time we found it." She started humming a somewhat off-key but familiar tune. "'Come away with me, Lucille . . .'"

"'In My Merry Oldsmobile'?" Sam and Remi asked together.

"That's the song!" she said. They heard a muffled noise, as though she were covering over the receiver. A moment later, she was back. "Hate to cut it short, but I need to return to my guests."

"Thanks, Mom." Sam smiled at Remi. "Reggie's version of a message in a bottle to his wife?"

"Except the car's been searched," she said.

"Many times," Oliver added. "Maybe someone knew about the music. After all, there were several people in and out of the warehouse that night. Byron, the night watchmen. Maybe one of them went back."

"I don't buy it," Sam said. "As good a detective as this Isaac Bell was, I'd have to think searching the Ghost for the missing treasure was the first thing he did."

Oliver tried for a cheerful smile. "Doesn't really matter now, does it? We're all safe, and that's what counts."

Trevor looked crestfallen, as he turned toward Remi. "You read the journal. Reggie told Jonathon twice. You know what I'm talking about, don't you?"

Remi locked eyes with the boy. Sam knew how her brain worked. She was mentally ticking off the facts she'd read with a speed that always amazed him. Suddenly she smiled, then looked at Sam. "That music was a message to his wife. After all, Reggie specifically requested that it be given to her. And if you recall, when Payton told him to think about his wife and child before he did something he'd regret, Reggie specifically said that's exactly whom he was thinking of. He—"

"Knew the risks," Sam said. "Maybe preparing for the eventuality he might not come back and sending her a message in case something happened to him?"

"Maybe," Remi said, looking up something on her phone. "Another possibility is that Reggie was trying to make things right at the end."

"How?" Oliver asked her.

"With his dying declaration. Trevor's correct," she said, earning a smile from the boy. "He'd told Payton not once, but twice, that Payton had helped him move the treasure. Admittedly, the first time it was more of a taunt, right after he'd been captured by Bell. But the second time was after he'd been shot, and he specifically told them to give the music to his wife . . ." Remi's attention was suddenly drawn to something on her phone's screen.

"It makes sense," Oliver said. "We know Isaac Bell was desperately trying to get him to say where he'd hidden the treasure before he died. And we know Reggie's last words to Payton were 'You helped.' Still, was the answer in the journal or not?"

"I think it is," Remi said. Sam recognized that look in her eyes. There was no "think" about it. She knew what the answer was and held up her phone, showing them a photo of the sheet music from the internet. "That song was very popular in 1905 and early '06." She glanced at Sam. "Maybe a bit of that British irony, when you think about it."

"You mean he picked the song for the car reference, but not because he hid the treasure in the car?"

Her catlike smile was all the answer Sam needed.

Remi knew exactly where that treasure was.

86

Sam sat back and watched as Remi and Trevor discussed what was in the journal, the others looking on. As their discussion progressed, he could see the boy's confidence growing, as she subtly guided him, allowing him to see what she saw, without ever giving away that she even knew the answer. After a few more minutes of back-and-forth between the two, Remi nodded thoughtfully. "I wonder if any of this has something to do with Miss Atwater?"

"Maybe," Trevor said, his gaze fixed on his water glass, lost in thought. Suddenly his eyes widened, and he shot out of his seat, looking over at his mother, then Remi. "It was all about the music!" He ran toward the door, his demeanor one of pure excitement.

The others hesitated, not quite sure what to think, but, just as quickly, they hurried after him, through the garden, to the Dowager Cottage, Sam and Remi bringing up the rear.

Trevor banged on the door. Finally, Mrs. Beckett

opened it. "We need to see Uncle Albert," he said, darting past her. "It's important."

Albert stepped into the parlor a moment later, as they all filed in after Trevor. "What's all this? Didn't know we were having guests, Mrs. Beckett."

"Neither did I."

Trevor walked over to the pianoforte, pulling out the bench, taking a seat, lifting the cover from the keys. "Miss Atwater sat right here, next to Payton." He hit one of the bass keys, then another, and another, each making a plunking noise. "She told him it needed tuning."

Sam and Remi stood back as Oliver and Chad lifted off the top of the piano so that they could see inside. Oliver told Trevor to do the honor of looking in, handing him his cell phone to use as a flashlight.

Trevor hesitated, glancing shyly at Remi. She smiled at him, and he turned on the light, shining it into the depths of the piano. He looked back at her, then his mother, his face filled with wonder. "There's something down there. Mum . . . You have to see this." He handed her the phone. When she and Oliver moved in, Trevor looked over at Remi. "You were right, Mrs. Fargo!"

"Me? You're the one who found it. I was thinking of the piano bench. That's where you keep music, isn't it?"

Sam put his arm around Remi's shoulders. "Sure it is," he whispered, as Oliver and Chad searched for the clips to remove the front of the piano. The antique bench didn't have storage for music, and he doubted his wife would've forgotten that fact from their visit that first night at Payton Manor.

"Here, now," Albert said, marching over to the piano as Oliver and Chad removed the front cover. "What are you doing there?"

"Have a look, Uncle Albert," Oliver said.

He peered in, saw something, harrumphed, shaking his head as he returned to the dining room to finish his lemon ice. "No wonder that thing never sounded right."

They fished out a single leather satchel from the depths, and Oliver carried it to the table.

"Open it," Trevor said, excited.

Oliver opened it. There were a handful of gold sovereigns shimmering in the lamplight—along with a much larger rectangular flat item wrapped in oilcloth.

Sam read the date on one of the sovereigns: 1905. "Talk about mint condition. Considering the price of gold, I'll bet they're worth close to three hundred times their face value."

"Hardly the half million in gold still missing," Oliver said.

Trevor moved in for a closer look. "Do we get to keep any of it?"

"Sorry, lad," Oliver said. "Stolen. Which means it all goes back to the Crown." He lifted a corner of the oilcloth, his brows going up. He looked at Remi. "What was it you were saying about British irony earlier in the evening?" He removed the cloth entirely, showing them stacks upon stacks of white one-hundred-pound notes from the Bank of England, as well as the engraving plates. "I daresay, this might be the King of Irony."

"Why?" Trevor asked. "That's the missing money, isn't it? Half a million?"

"Worthless," Oliver said, nodding at the stacks of money. "Since 1945." He gave a deep sigh. "This might've all been avoided, had the journal specified the money stolen was banknotes instead of gold sovereigns."

IT WAS LATE by the time Sam and Remi made it to bed.

Remi snuggled in close next to Sam. "Not quite the haul we thought."

"Still, quite the find. Just thinking about what might've happened if those plates made it into Reggie Oren's hands, had Isaac Bell not stopped him. Boggles the mind."

"I'll bet those stolen engraving plates are why they decided to hire someone with Isaac Bell's expertise." She scooted up onto her elbows and kissed him. "Job well done, Fargo."

"I do have one question, Remi . . . How'd you figure out the money was hidden in the piano?"

"The piano was the only thing that Payton had helped Reggie move."

"Brilliant and beautiful."

87

A year after Sam and Remi returned to their home on the cliffs above the restless surf, they were enjoying a late breakfast when a semitruck and trailer pulled up and stopped in front of their driveway. A few minutes later, Selma and the driver came out on the balcony.

Selma did not look happy. “Mr. and Mrs. Fargo, this fellow claims he has a large shipment that is scheduled to be delivered to this address. I told him he was crazy, but he has a bill of lading with your name on it.”

Remi laughed and said, “Obviously, a mistake.”

Sam quickly interrupted, “Oh, I think I might have failed to mention . . .”

“Sam, you failed to mention what?”

“It’s your birthday present,” Sam said, with a big smile on his face.

Remi began to smell a rat. “You know very well my birthday is in April, not July.”

The driver shrugged and said, “Sorry, folks, I have no choice but to unload the shipment here.”

"Yes, let's take a look at it," said Remi. "I can't wait to see what it is."

The driver entered the trailer, banging and clanging around. He lowered a ramp and stepped out with a small electronic transmitter. A motor tautened the cable as the shipment began to move from the darkened interior of the trailer. When something big and red made its appearance, Remi broke into unrestrained laughter.

"It took a year to give it a first-rate restoration, but she's a beauty," Sam said.

Selma and Lazlo stood in awe, seeing the 1917 Ahrens-Fox fire engine gleaming under a bright sun. The front repair of the sterling valves and silver pump were touched up with chrome and nickel plating, creating a blinding reflection. The original red paint and beautiful gold-leafed decorations were buffed to a shiny patina.

Sam lightly rubbed his hand over a fender, as if it was a shrine. "They were able to save the ladders, hoses, and the wooden wheels. It's still all original. Just think, one hundred years old," said Sam, "and ready to put out a fire."

"It looks like new," said Remi, as she admired the golden trim. "I can't believe it's the same vehicle we crashed through those iron doors with. How did you get it looking so new?"

"I hired a company in London who are experts at restoring vehicles," answered Sam. "I think you'll agree, they did a flawless job."

After writing a check to satisfy the truck driver, Sam

and Lazlo disappeared and returned with a battery and a jerry jug of fuel. “Everyone ready!” Sam called out as he helped Remi and Selma on board. Even Zoltán jumped onto the floorboard, next to Remi.

“He’s not a Dalmatian, but he’ll have to do,” said Remi.

Then with Sam at the wheel, Lazlo ringing the bell, Remi leaning on the siren, and Zoltán howling, the Ahrens-Fox flew through the streets of La Jolla like a dragon from the past.

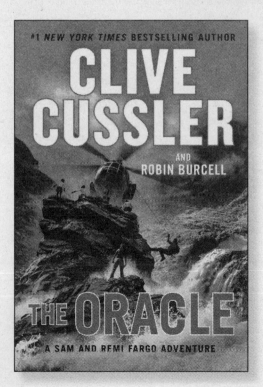

Sam Fargo took one last look in the binoculars, then handed them back to his wife. "Remember that time in Mozambique?" he asked her.

"You, Fargo, are brilliant." Remi grabbed Nasha's hand, pulling her away from the truck.

Sam jumped into the driver's seat, starting the engine, while Hank climbed into the passenger seat. "What's going on?" he asked Sam.

"We're creating a diversion for the women."

The color drained from Hank's face. "Us?"

"You should probably get out and wait with them."

"No. I'll wait here."

Sam glanced at Remi through the open window, waiting for her to move the car. The moment she was clear, Sam hit the gas, made a three-point turn, then spun the tires, kicking up enough dust to cover for the women as they ran to the side of the road toward the brush.

Hank glanced their direction, but the dust obscured his view. "Where're they going?"

"Trying not to be targets," Sam said, moving his foot from the brake to the gas pedal. The truck lurched forward.

"But—" Hank gripped the dash as the front of the truck tapped the rear bumper of the Land Rover, pushing it forward. "Are you insane?"

"There's a tack strip up ahead. And if that growing cloud of dust just beyond the bend in the road belongs to whoever placed it there, we're about to encounter some very nasty people."

"But that kid—"

"Thinks there are two men in that yellow car who plan to hit us from behind. In other words, we're about to be ambushed."

Sam stopped the truck, allowing the rental car to drift forward on its own, hopefully far enough that their attackers wouldn't realize that the women were hiding much farther back. With one foot on the brake, he hit the gas again, spinning the tires and raising a dust cloud so thick, he hoped no one from either direction would know if anyone was hiding in the truck or had abandoned it. Which was the point.

Sam drew his gun then looked over at Hank. "Follow me."

Hank shook his head.

"Suit yourself." Foot on the brake, he stepped on the gas, raising even more dust before shutting off the truck and opening the door. "If I were you, I'd get down on the floorboard. If you're lucky, the engine block will stop any stray bullets."

* * *

REMI, TAKING ADVANTAGE OF THE dust cloud, led Amal and Nasha toward the side of the road. "Stay low," Remi said. Amal started to part the long grass, but Remi grabbed her arm. "Not there. They'll see the broken stalks." She pointed to a natural break in the vegetation. "That way. Hurry."

Amal scrambled into the space. Remi turned to guide Nasha in after her, surprised when the girl pulled a thick but loose clump of grass from the dry ground, using the root ball to erase their tracks from the side of the road. A moment later, she scurried into the field after Amal, grabbing a handful of dirt, rubbing it into her short, dark hair, attempting to blend into her surroundings.

Remi, both fascinated and horrified that a child that young was proficient in camouflage techniques, belly-crawled next to them, drew her gun, then double-checked her phone to make sure the ringer was off. Just in time. She peered through the tall grass to her left, watching the yellow vehicle's tires bouncing across the ruts in the road, jarring its occupants.

The car drove past. It skidded to a stop about fifteen feet behind the Fargo's supply truck. Dust rose, then drifted in the wind as two men got out, their backs to the women. They stood behind their open doors, each holding a handgun, aiming toward the truck.

"That's them," Nasha whispered. "Two of the Kalu brothers. Bako is the one closest to us."

"Whatever happens," Remi said. "Keep your head down and don't make a sound."

She nodded.

Remi set her cell phone on the ground in front of her, calling Sam's number. "We're in place. I take it you and Hank made it to the sidelines?"

"He wouldn't leave."

Her gaze flew to the supply truck. A complication they hadn't expected or needed. She had little time to worry about it. Another dust cloud in the distance—this one from the opposite direction—grew rapidly. Within seconds, the square front end of a white pickup came into view, the vehicle slowing as it veered around the suspicious layer of leaves and grass stretched across the road. It skidded to a stop in front of the now empty Land Rover and beyond it, the Fargos' supply truck. Both doors of the white pickup opened, but no one got out. Their tinted windows blocked Remi's view.

Crack! Crack!

Two shots hit the dirt in front of the white pickup. The shooter—the driver of the yellow car—draped his arm over his open door, his handgun haphazardly pointed toward the new visitors. "This cargo belongs to us! Leave!"

"Didn't see that coming," Remi whispered. "Different groups?"

"Looks like it," Sam said. Ears ringing from the gunshots, she barely heard his low voice coming from her phone. "This is not going to end well."

Though she couldn't see Sam, she knew he was positioned on the same side of the road to her right—which meant he had a far better view of the pickup's occupants. The driver stuck both hands out his open door to prove he wasn't armed. "Don't shoot!" he shouted. Tall and slim, he had a scar running down the left side of his face. He stood next to his truck, staring at the Kalu brothers. "I'm sure we can work this out in a friendly manner."

"Scarface," Nasha whispered.

"Makao?" Bako seemed shocked to see him. "I—I didn't know it was you."

"So I see. Turn around and we'll just forget this happened." Makao gave a semi-smile at his would-be attackers.

Bako's brother motioned with his gun. "This is ours."

"Keep it." Makao rubbed at the scar on his cheek, then slid behind the wheel. He backed the pickup, made a three-point turn, but instead of driving off, he stopped the vehicle. Two men pointing assault rifles jumped up from the pickup bed. A deafening *rat-a-tat-tat* followed as they peppered the Kalu brothers, their bodies jerking from the force of the bullets. Nasha stifled a sob as they slumped to the ground. Though Remi wanted to comfort the child, she didn't dare let up her guard. Thankfully, Amal reached over, placing her shaking hand on the child's shoulder, whispering something into her ear.

"Remi?" Sam's low voice from her phone brought a sense of relief. They were in this together. They'd get out of it the same way.

"We're fine," she said as the two shooters hopped out of the pickup bed. They circled around the far side of the Fargos' Land Rover, aiming their rifles at it. One glanced in, then pointed toward the supply truck. They walked past it, their lower legs visible beneath the truck's frame. When they reached the cargo area, one stopped behind the rear wheel. The other continued on, eying the Kalu brothers sprawled on either side of the yellow car. Deciding they no longer posed a threat, he turned back toward the truck, pulling up the canvas to look inside. "Empty!" he shouted.

Makao, who remained at the driver's door of the white pickup, said something to his passenger. The man got out, walked toward the supply truck, his weapon aimed at the door where Hank hid.

Remi followed him with her gunsight. "Sam . . ."

"Do *not* take that shot, Remi. They'll know where you are."

She kept her finger on the trigger. "We can't just—"

"*Yes.* We can. There are two more gunmen on the other side of the truck. Without a way to draw them out, we're trapped."

He was right. Both men had taken cover, one behind the rear wheel, the other behind the front, no doubt aiming toward the truck's door, in case someone came charging out on that side. "This worked so much better in Mozambique," she said.

"Yeah, well, there were about five less gunmen."

A sharp intake of breath from Nasha caught her attention. "Look, Mrs. Fargo. Bako's moving."

She followed the direction of the girl's gaze, seeing Bako on the ground, slowly reaching for his gun. "Sam. By the yellow car. He could be our distraction."

"They'll kill him before he ever gets a second shot. We need something else."

Once again, her husband was right. Unless they found a way to draw those other two onto this side of the supply truck, they'd still be outgunned and outmanned. Her gaze hit on the Land Rover. "Amal, where's your phone?"

"In the car."

"Get ready, Fargo." Remi slid her phone toward Amal, then raised her gunsight, taking aim. "Time to even those odds."

Sam's soft laugh sounded in Remi's phone just before Amal called the number. A moment later the faint but shrill ring of her phone sounded from the open car window.

Scarface held up one hand. "Wait," he said, then walked toward the Land Rover.

Remi smiled to herself when she saw one of the two men on the far side of the supply truck move toward the engine block, his head and shoulders visible over the hood. "Come on . . ." she whispered, hoping the remaining gunman would step into view.

To her right, Scarface reached into the window and pulled out Amal's purse, fishing out her phone. When it stopped ringing, Amal ended the call. He narrowed his gaze, tossed the phone and purse into the car, then looked over at the man standing next to the supply truck. He nodded.

The gunman yanked open the truck door, pointing his weapon inside.

Hank cowered on the floorboards, covering his face with his arms. "Don't shoot!" he cried.

SAM, HIS FINGER ON THE trigger of his Smith & Wesson .38, watched with clinical detachment as the gunman pulled Hank from the truck's cab. Like Remi, Sam was belly down in the grass, his phone set out in front of him. He gave a quick glance toward the lone survivor sprawled in the dirt near the yellow car, saw the man slowly lifting his gun in a vain attempt to take down his four attackers. He was bleeding out fast and Sam didn't know if he'd even have the strength to get off a shot.

"Hold . . ." Sam said softly into his phone. Remi, an expert sharpshooter, could easily drop the man holding the gun to Hank, and was no doubt worried about his safety. At the moment, Sam didn't care if Hank lived or died. He wasn't about to risk his wife's life, or that of Amal and Nasha, because the man was too stupid to follow instructions.

The gunman pointed his weapon at the archeologist. "Where are the others?"

Hank scooted back, hitting the side of the truck, looking around in desperation, whether for them or an escape, Sam couldn't tell.

"Tell. Me. Where. They. Are." With each word, he shoved the barrel of his gun against Hank's chest.

"They just ran."

"Which direction?"

"I—I didn't see!" Hank cried, his gaze flicking to the side of the road. "Too much dust."

Crack!

Bako's shot went wild.

The two gunmen on the other side of the truck spun around, spraying bullets at the yellow car in a deafening barrage. At the same time, the gunman closest to Hank grabbed him, using him for a shield, blocking any chance of Sam taking him out. "Remi!" Sam shouted into the phone.

She fired before he finished saying her name.

The gunmen fell to the ground, taking Hank with him. The man near the front of the truck stepped out into the road, belatedly realizing the shot came from the grass. He swung his rifle in Remi's direction. Sam fired twice. He fell back against the truck.

Makao, seeing his men fall, ducked behind the Land Rover, then raced to the pickup, jumping in. The remaining gunman raced after him, grabbing onto the tailgate as the vehicle sped off.

Sam kept his sights on the truck, waiting until the dust settled to make sure it wasn't circling back. Finally, he glanced in Remi's direction, not yet seeing her in the tall grass. He grabbed his phone. "Remi . . ."

"Here."

"Keep the others down. Let's make sure it's clear."

They rose at the same time, guns at the ready as they walked toward the three vehicles.

The only thing moving was Hank, his breathing shallow, his face pale as he struggled to his feet, trying to push the dead man off of him.

"Stay there," Sam ordered, then moved to the right as Remi moved to her left, checking the downed men, kicking any weapons from their reach in case anyone had miraculously survived.

They were all dead.

"Clear," he called out.

"Same," Remi said as they met on the other side of the supply truck. They circled back. "It's safe," she shouted. "You can come out."

Amal and Nasha slowly rose, the young girl reaching for Amal's hand as they made their way through the tall grass.

Sam eyed the dusty pair. "Nice job blending in."

"The child's a natural," Remi said, then, in a lower voice, added "I hate to think how she knows what she knows."

That sort of knowledge didn't come from living in the city—or a peaceful village. "Definitely makes you wonder," Sam replied, leaning down to pick up one of the fallen assault rifles. He turned on the safety, then slung the gun across his back.

Hank rose to his feet, leaning against the truck, his gaze landing on Nasha. "You stole my keys. Those men were after you."

Amal pulled the girl to her side. "If not for her, we'd be dead."

"Pointing fingers gets us nowhere," Sam said, not wanting to spend any more time there than necessary. The longer they remained, the greater the risk those robbers would return with reinforcements. "Remi, make sure we haven't missed any stray guns. Hank, why don't you have a seat in the car, turn on the AC. Amal—" He was about to order her to join Hank. Seeing her ashen tone, he tempered his voice. "Are you going to be okay?"

She gave a shaky smile. "I—I think what I need is fresh air."

He nodded. "Nasha," he said, "come with me." He started walking toward the Kalus' bullet-ridden car, stopping when he realized the kid hadn't moved from Amal's side, instead watching him with a healthy dose of suspicion and wariness.

Remi cleared her throat, and he looked at her blankly, finally raising his brows in hopes she'd clue him in to whatever she was thinking.

"Nasha," Remi said. "I think my husband wants to ask you a few questions in private. You can trust him."

She shook her head. "I don't trust any man."

Of that, Sam had no doubt, especially coming from a child who knew the skills she knew. "Remi?"

She held her hand toward the girl. Nasha took it, and Remi guided her toward Sam, who was standing near the dead men by the supply truck. The girl refused to look at the bodies.

As much as Sam hated what he was about to do, he didn't have much choice. "I need you to look at them. Do you know them?"

She hesitated, slowly turned, her gaze skimming across their faces before turning back, pressing her face into Remi's side. "No," she whispered.

He led her past the supply truck toward the yellow car. "You know them?"

She glanced at them then quickly looked away. "Yes."

"Who are they and why are they here?"

"I told you. The Kalu brothers. They came to rob you."

She shook her head but refused to look at him.

"Nasha . . ." He saw her shoulders tensing and kneeled down in front of her. "Why did you come?"

She stole a glance at the dead man on the passenger side, then looked at Sam, her dark eyes welling with tears. "Bako wanted to smash my fingers, because I—I tried to hide the money that Mrs. Fargo gave me."

Had the man not already been dead, Sam would have killed him right then and there. He stood, trying to reconcile what had happened to what little he'd learned from her. "You think they called some friends to help them?"

"No," she whispered.

"The men in the white truck. You're sure you've never seen them before?"

She shook her head. "I've only ever heard of Scarface. The Kalus work alone. They have no friends."

Sam gave her shoulder a gentle pat. "No more questions. Why don't you wait in the car. You'll be much cooler in there."

Nasha shook her head. "I don't like that man."

"Hank?" Remi asked. "Why?"

"Because he doesn't like me."

"To be fair, you *did* steal his keys."

"He was easy." Nasha glanced toward Amal. "What's wrong with your friend?"

Remi saw Amal's distant gaze. She was either in the middle of one of her seizures, or about to have one. "She'll be okay. Do you think you can hold her hand and get her to the car?"

Nasha nodded then hurried toward her.

Remi joined Sam by the Kalus' vehicle. "Amal had another seizure."

"All things considered, it's not surprising. If she's not better by tomorrow, we'll bring her back."

"What about Nasha?"

"There is no way in hell that I'm taking her back to Jalingo. You heard what she said he was planning to do to her?"

Remi looked at the dead man. "I suppose it would be a total waste of ammunition to put another bullet in him."

"Definitely. More importantly, Nasha said the Kalu brothers worked alone. So who is this Makao that the Kalu brothers seemed to know?"

"You have to admit that the two groups meeting here in the middle of nowhere is an interesting twist of fate."

Sam was a firm believer that twists of fate were a very rare occurrence. "Whoever this other group was, it had nothing to do with the street thieves from Jalingo."

"Agreed." Remi nodded toward the guns she'd collected in the back of the supply truck. "We've got enough firepower. I say we go find these guys."

CLIVE CUSSLER

"Clive Cussler is just about the best storyteller in the business."
—*New York Post*